Praise for the "World of Change" Series

"...from this point I couldn't put the book down until the last page. It is engaging, terrifying, suspenseful, and surprising."

— Books and Pals Reviews

"The author's imagination has created a great universe and left me wanting to know what happens to Aleria in the next book in the series.

Highly recommended."

— Amazon Reviewer

"Out of Mischief is definitely a fun read, and I would recommend it for young adults and grown-ups alike"

— Amazon Reviewer

"The book's strength is the depth of character of its protagonists and antagonists."

— Amazon Reviewer

"I always find myself easily drawn into the complex worlds Mr. Long creates...I would happily recommend this novel to readers of fantasy, adventure, and romance."

— Cas Peace, author of the "Artisans of Albia" Saga

Mountains

of

Mischief

Gordon A. Long

AIRBORN PRESS
Delta, 2015

MOUNTAINS OF MISCHIEF

Published by
Airborn Press
4958 10A Ave, Delta, B. C.
V4M 1X8
Canada

Copyright Gordon A. Long
2015

ISBN - 978-0-9921243-7-3

Cover
Design and Photography by Gordon A. Long
Model: Josie Buter

Other Books by Gordon A. Long

Other Books in The "World of Change" Series:

Book 1: Out of Mischief
Book 2: Into Trouble

Storm Over Savournon
(A Novel of the French Revolution)

Sword Called Kitten Series:

Book 1: A Sword Called...Kitten?
Book 2: The Cat with Many Claws

Non-Fiction

Why Are People So Stupid?
Expressive Poetry Performance

Thanks

To Elizabeth Hull for her ideas and her editing
To Dusty Hagerud for his design assistance

CONTENTS

1. Guns!...1
2. Bearding the Lion.. 12
3. The Firing Range 17
4. Dust and Disarray 23
5. Briefing by the Expert................................. 33
6. Misgivings 38
7. Plots and Plans... 49
8. Lavan 60
9. As if It Isn't Obvious................................... 72
10. Followed... 81
11. Tracking the Trackers 89
12. A Loyal Man 96
13. Beyond Hungry Hill 106
14. Oudonsford Ale 113
15. Jameta... 126
16. Troublesome Lords 133
17. Interrupted Bath.. 144
18. Standoff on the Moor 152
19. Tyn Terfyn... 161
20. The Lore of the Old Ones.......................... 170
21. The Ghost Beast 184
22. Tyn Dyfnant.. 193
23. A Dusty Search.. 216
24. The Secret of the Mountains..................... 223
25. A Long Night.. 236
26. The Final Defense of Tyn Dyfnant............. 246
27. No Promises... 259
28. Outside the Door... 271
29. Alone in the Dark.. 282
30. An Old Song.. 288
31. Inferno 297
32. Meeting the Monster................................... 303
33. Double-S Assistance.................................... 315
34. An Arm to Swing On.................................... 323
35. A Promise at Last... 330

1. Guns!

"Something is not quite right here." Aleria frowned and ran her hand across the pommel of her sword.

Erlon glanced over at her. "Fifteen armed men pounding their chests on the road in front of us and no time to circle the wagons? Not quite right, you call it?"

"You know what I mean."

"Aye." The big soldier rolled his shoulders, flexing his sword arm. "Look at the leader. He's no bandit."

"He's not. Too young, too handsome, too...I don't know." She glanced back at her wagons, drawn up in pairs, guards on the ground with swords, teamsters on the wagon seats with spears. The best they could do in the time they had. *I sure hope Erlon knows what he's doing. I certainly don't.*

"And look at the site." The guard Captain shook his head. "Lousy spot for an ambush, flat and open. More like a battlefield. Somebody is really stupid."

"Or has a sense of honour."

"I think I just said that."

She raised her eyebrows. "Well, at least if he's young there'll be a lot of ballyhoo, and we can get an idea..."

The dark-haired youth down the road jammed on his helmet and drew his sword. "These are the ones, men. Take them!"

As the bandits charged, Erlon slipped out his big hand-and-a-half sword, stepped forward and raised his voice enough to carry to his men. "Dalmyns, hold your positions. When they see we're serious, they'll stop, just like usual." He glanced back at Aleria and lowered his voice. "I hope."

"This battle isn't going according to plan and it hasn't even started yet. Keep your eyes open, Erlon." Aleria looked around, a frisson of fear weakening her legs. *This wasn't supposed to happen. Not here, this close to Kingsport. Not on my first trip as Wagonmaster.*

The guards and teamsters stood firm, swords and spears ready. Aleria's heart warmed at the show of discipline. *Good men to have at your back.*

She drew her own weapon. She felt better with its solid weight in her hand. "Did you hear what the leader said? 'These are the ones.' We've been targeted. Why? We're not carrying anything unusual. I don't like this at all." She glanced at Erlon, but he just looked back. *He's waiting for my orders.* She straightened her shoulders. *This is your duty, girl. Learn it or lose it.*

The attackers neared. "They're showing no sign of breaking off, Erlon. What would you usually do?"

"If I thought they really meant it, I'd move out where there's room for my sword. They often find that discouraging..."

But I have to make the decision. Not much choice. The charging bandits were almost upon them. "They mean it, Erlon. Go out there and discourage them."

He glanced over his shoulder at her, winced and shook his head, once. "Waste." Then he strode forward, and she admired the ease with which he spun the huge sword, splitting the charging line with a left and right sweep. *Don't get killed, Erlon. I'd really be down the river with no way back upstream.* Then she had no more time to watch because the attackers were on them. As she had been trained, she stayed out of the main crush, moving around, lending help where needed, trying to keep a picture of the whole battle, which was breaking down into a series of individual matches. *Not good for us. We're outnumbered. What do I do now?* She was confronted by a young bravo whose face, under the brow of his helmet, was somehow familiar. He slammed his blade against hers and pressed his attack.

He was a passable fighter. Not up to her own level, but she was hard put to occupy his sword, monitor the progress of the battle and think at the same time. Their assailants were better armed and far better trained than the usual bandits, and her men were being forced into a tighter and tighter position. She had seen this swordsman before. *Somewhere recently, but not in the context of...*

She was so preoccupied that she failed to notice his backward step and dropping sword, and she almost ran him through. "...Geran!"

He spoke at the same time. "Aleria! What are you doing here?"

"I could ask you the same. I didn't figure you for a bandit, Geran."

"I'm not!" He turned towards his leader, who was engaging one of the other guards in a fierce individual match. "My Lord. Stop! There's been a mistake!"

The leader broke off, glanced their way, his sword still threatening the guard. "No mistake. These are the ones, and we've got them outnumbered. Fight on!"

"No, my Lord." The lad raised his voice. "Break off! Break off in the name of Newsom."

The call seemed to work. Aleria, too, raised her voice. "Dalmyns, hold."

Erlon's command rolled over the dwindling sounds of battle. "Dalmyns, secure positions."

She checked her men. They straightened their line in front of the wagons, all on their feet. Two bandits down, but not much blood. One standing aside holding his upper arm.

"You were told not to use that name!" The young leader strode towards them, his sword at a business-like angle, and she wondered if she would have to protect a bandit from his own commander.

"My Lord, this is Aleria Dalmyn!"

"I don't care if she's the king's aunt! Who the hell's Aleria Dalmyn?"

Geran gulped. "My Lady, may I present Lord Ferrel anNewsom? My Lord, Lady Aleria anDalmyn."

The appellation set the young noble back. "How in the names of the gods do you know someone of Elite rank?"

3

"He knows me because we happen to drink in the same tavern." She stepped forward. "But you're asking the wrong question."

"Aye." The lad sneered. "The real question is why someone of your rank is involved in a gun-running business."

"Gun-running? Whatever are you talking about?"

"I'm talking about the cargo of rifles you are carrying through my land, to take to my enemies."

"You're a little out of line, young man. Dalmyn wagons do not carry guns. We are taking a load of household goods and tools to the anLexing demesne. Last I heard, they were your neighbours, not your enemies."

"Household goods? Hah!" He spat on the ground, but off to the side.

"Yes. And tools." She considered. "Dalmyns don't usually allow this, but we are passing through your land, so I'll stretch the point. Do you wish to inspect my cargo?"

Geran was making frantic signals, and the young lord glanced at him. "No, Lady Dalmyn, I must take your word for it."

"Thank you, my Lord." She presented her iciest smile. "Now what's this about gun-running? I don't like the Dalmyn name mixed up in anything illegal."

Once he had cooled down the young noble began to realize his position. "I don't really know, my Lady. My father had reliable information that anLexing was receiving a load of guns soon. Your train fitted the description perfectly, so..."

"...so someone has made a large mistake. You had better go back to your father and tell him to question his informers with a little more diligence next time. Dalmyn Cartage does not carry contraband. Period."

"I'm sorry my Lady. I'm sure I don't understand what happened."

"Neither do I, but you can be sure we will be looking into it. Now, do I and my wagons have your permission to cross the anNewsom demesne, as is provided for in your hereditary agreement for right of passage with family anLexing?"

"Of course, my Lady. I must apologize..."

She favoured him with a more reassuring smile. "Don't worry, Lord Ferrel. We will both look into this, find the error and correct it. The cartage of illegal weapons is a serious matter."

"We can agree on that."

"Farewell, then, my Lord."

"And you, my Lady."

As the young noble turned away, Aleria caught Geran's eye. "If I need to get hold of you in Kingsport?"

"The Falcon. Jems' daughter, Juli..."

"Geran." She grinned, punching his arm. "Are you messing around with the innkeeper's daughter?"

"No, my Lady. Not messing around. She takes my messages, finds me jobs..."

"...and a lot of other things. Sounds cosy." She nodded to where his party was disappearing into the brush. All of them seemed mobile, so no serious damage done. "If I get any information on this problem, I'll let you know."

"Thank you, my Lady. I'll see you at the Falcon."

"Where I'll be Aleria, as usual."

"Right you are, my Lady." He grinned and sauntered off.

She turned to Erlon. "Well, someone's happy with the results of the battle. Everybody in one piece?"

"No injuries."

"So let's line 'em up and move 'em out."

"Yes, boss!" He strode away calling orders, and his guards bounded onto their appointed wagons. She swung up into her usual position beside Maddoes, the driver of the lead wagon, and nodded to him. He cracked his whip over the horses' backs, and soon they were rolling again.

They did not travel for long. Down in a wide river meadow with plenty of view in all directions she called a halt and strode back along the wagon train. When Erlon reached her she was untying the tarp from the fourth wagon.

"That last load of crates doesn't suit your fancy?"

"It does not. They came in late, they came on the wagons without papers or labels. We have only the word of the Lexing agent that they are...what did he say they were?"

"I don't remember."

"Which means he was sly enough to slip them in without telling anyone what they were. We'll be watching that one in future."

As she spoke she hoisted the bales of cloth off the top of the load, and Erlon passed them down to the circle of curious teamsters. Underneath lay three long, flat crates and two smaller square ones. The driver handed her a box hammer; she used the claws to pry up a slat and tugged away the straw packing.

An unladylike oath escaped her lips as the shine of well-oiled metal rewarded her search. She glanced up at Erlon, leaning over the edge of the wagon bed. "Levis Double-S rifles."

He scratched his chin. "Only the Royal Army is supposed to carry Sustained Shot weapons."

"You can see why. What kind of trouble would there be if one of these trumped-up outland lords had a dozen Double-S rifles to use in their constant border skirmishes?"

He shook his head. "Where do you think they got them?"

She shrugged. "From a crooked quartermaster or a wrecked wagon. Or out the back door of the Levis factory in Domaland. All that matters is what we're going to do with them."

"What are we going to do with them?"

She looked down at the anxious faces surrounding the wagon. "We aren't delivering them, that's for sure."

"Are we going home, then?" Maddoes threw up his hands.

Aleria squashed the urge to agree with him, to give up and take this mess back to the Capital and dump in at someone else's feet. *I can do better than that. I must.* "I think not. Dalmyn wagons fulfill their contracts. We have a load of legitimate goods, so we deliver it."

"But what if Lexing takes the guns? Shouldn't we hide them somewhere?"

"I'm not letting these weapons out of my sight until I hand them over somewhere safe."

Erlon nodded. "That would be the Royal Army Training Camp at Decker?"

"As safe a spot as any." She tapped the slat back in place and motioned to the bales of cloth. "Let's get loaded and rolling. Erlon, ride with me."

Maddoes shifted over and the two leaders crowded onto the lead wagon seat. They jounced along in silence, eyes on the surrounding country.

It's time to come clean.

She turned to the big soldier. "Erlon, do you know why I'm here?"

He glanced over at her, then looked ahead. "You mean, besides as Wagonmaster for one of your father's trains."

"That's what I mean."

"Probably information gathering."

"Why did you assume that?"

"Well, first I thought they might have just sent you out for the experience." He shrugged. "But I know you're involved in...other things. Politics, that sort of stuff."

"Exactly. And that's why I'm here. There are political ripples coming from somewhere in the Northeast, and I'm here to get information. Nothing overt. I'm supposed to be pleasant and sympathetic with the customers. Find out what their beefs are. I'm not spying, or anything." She tossed a hand toward the fourth wagon. "And we certainly didn't expect something like this to happen."

"So, what do we do now?"

Aleria shrugged. "We could be in trouble. This trip wasn't set up to pack a load that valuable."

"For certain. Not enough guards, no helmets for the drivers..."

"...and no outriders."

They both scanned the surrounding hilltops. Erlon shook his head. "This is like carrying blasting powder with a lit fuse. Who knows where this shipment was really headed?"

"We assume it's for anLexing, but we can't be sure. That's another reason not to turn around. The tarps have been pulled back on a nasty secret, and I don't want to run for five more days with this cargo. If we can navigate the Lexing demesne those guns will be safe at Decker the day after tomorrow."

"But we can't just pull through his land and not make his delivery. He'll be suspicious. He might decide to come out and get them, and if he does, he'll be prepared."

"So our best plan is not to look guilty. We bring him his goods, then we leave before he realizes we're not giving him the guns. Assuming they were destined for him and not somebody else who planned to take them from us like the Newsoms might have."

"We carry them right into his manor and out again? That's risky."

She glanced at his frown. "With a cargo like this, everything is risky."

He shrugged. "You're the Wagonmaster."

"I'm very sensitive of that, right now. I could get a lot of people killed in the next few days."

"Maybe that's a good thing." He grinned.

"I fail to see how."

"Lexing will be well aware that if he attacks a Dalmyn wagon train to get his guns, between your father and the king, there won't be enough of him left to use them."

"Thanks. That means whatever I do, I can't lose. Except for a few loyal men." She turned to the Lead Driver, quiet as usual. "What do you think, Maddoes?"

"I think you'll do what's best, Aleria." The man shot a stream of tobacco juice past the offside wheel.

"I know. My decision, and it's not fair to try to spread it around." She turned to look back at her train, jolting along

8

behind her. *You're supposed to be good at action, Aleria. Use those brains!*

"How does this sound? We put the guns in this wagon, down in the bottom. We tarp them well. Once we get into the Lexing courtyard, we line up for a quick departure before we unload."

"Guards stay with their wagons." He glanced at the lead driver. "Maddoes stays with his team?"

"Right. And you stay close to anLexing. Don't threaten him, but...well, you're tall, he's short." She looked up at him. "Just...loom. If he tries anything he's the first to die. Make sure he knows it."

Erlon grinned, a quick slash of white, even teeth. "I find looming very effective. What about the ammunition?"

She considered. "If we split the guns and ammunition up it's twice as easy for them to get one or the other."

"But neither set is any good without the other."

"If they have the guns, they'll be able to get more shells."

"Not before the Royal Army and the Dalmyn mercenaries feed them to the crows."

She nodded. "We'll put the ammunition in the last wagon under the driver's duffle." She glanced around again. "Let's find a safe place to pull over for the night. It's going to be a long one."

"I'll sashay ahead and enjoy the woodland scene." Erlon jumped down off the wagon and trotted alongside. "I'm more worried about trouble in front than trouble behind."

"Do you want a horse?"

"That'll slow the wagons. I'm used to running."

She nodded again, and he jogged forward, leaving her up on the wagon seat to think of all the things that could go wrong.

* * *

It did turn into a long night, and when Aleria finally got to sleep she tossed and turned in a continuing series of dreams about impossible defences against overwhelming odds. Safety was at her fingertips, but she could never seem to reach it. In the morning she woke slowly, sweating in the heat of the early spring sun on her tent. She dragged herself out of her cot and braided her hair extra tight in the Mercenary's Crown in case she needed helmet padding today. The pain of the pulled hairs cleared her mind.

After breakfast, she circled the whole crew around her for a council of war.

"We are going into a tight spot, but there are no better options. Those guns must be protected. If one of these fractious border lords gets his hands on them, there'll be hell to pay. Are we agreed?"

The expected number of nodding heads. *They're with me so far.*

"Our plan: the rifles are with me, the ammunition is in the tail wagon. If we are attacked, we circle up as usual. That puts the weapons and the ammunition next to each other. We hand out a new gun to anyone who can use it." She looked at her crew's faces. She didn't expect many of them had ever held a gun, let alone fired one like this. "If that doesn't work, another option is to split the train and try to get at least half of the load to the Royal Army Training Camp at Decker. Those two wagons are all that count. If you have to, you leave the rest of the stock and equipment behind. If you must, take the loads horseback. That's fine, too. Whoever ends up with either load takes responsibility for it and keeps it moving towards Decker. Do you follow?"

Again the nods, although she noted glances around the circle. *Assessing allies, working out the odds. Fair enough.*

"Inside the Lexing manor yard, stay with your wagons, but keep aware of Erlon and me. If we are forced to break for it, remember that the two important loads must not be left inside together. Help each other with the unloading, but make sure those two wagons always have extra men nearby. Don't make it obvious."

One of the men met her eyes, and she nodded for him to speak. "We can unload those two slower, so that by the end we're all grouped near them."

"Good idea, but don't leave the others unattended. We'd like to get them all out if we can." She thought a moment, then shrugged. "We can't plan this down to the last detail. You've been in tight spots before. I trust you to watch each other's backs and do what's right at the time."

The nods were firmer this time.

And that's all I can do. "Let's roll." She found a smile. "Makes up for the boredom on the trip so far." They grinned as well, and several slapped others on the back as they separated to their positions.

She glanced at Erlon, and he strode forward.

I've done my best. The next few hours will see whether I'm up to the job. Of course, I might be dead, which would solve my problems. She thought about facing her father and Raif if she bungled this. *I might be happier, dead.*

She stood up and waved the wagons to start. Maddoes cracked the whip, and she sat with unladylike speed. Ignoring his glance, she stayed in her position, staring forward.

11

2.   Bearding the Lion

Early that afternoon the wagon train pulled out of the pass and paused looking down into the valley that led to anLexing's manor. The Trench was a deep fold in the north-south mountain range bordering Galesia to the east. It was a fertile rift in the headwaters of the great Chanaan River, protected by the mountains from the cold winds of winter and by its altitude from the heat of summer. The river ran a gigantic "s" shape, north-west from the mouth of the Trench, curving around until it ran south from Oudonsford to Kingsport, then south and west to the Chanaan Canyon through the costal range to the seaports of Domaland.

The Lexing manor sat on a bench overlooking the lush bottomlands. It wasn't quite a castle, but the sturdy wall with corner turrets looked functional, and the gatehouse, complete with portcullis, would be hard to take without a serious ram. High above – an impressive but impractical perch atop a crag – the ruins of an ancient fortress scowled over the sunny valley. Aleria hoped that the warlike nature of the Old Ones did not still prevail in this modern age. *Some chance. If I recall my history lessons, this area was populated centuries ago by misfits who couldn't get along with anyone else. I wonder how they'll get along with me.* She gathered her courage and nodded; Maddoes clucked to his team and they started the descent.

AnLexing was an effusive personality who could have been considered bluff and hearty, but his lack of stature and rotund figure gave his expansive gestures an edge that bordered on pushy. Aleria had to force herself not to stare at the little goatee that he affected, bobbing up and down as he spoke.

"So, my Lady," he favoured her with a full courtly bow, "the Dalmyns grace our goods with their best protection. Welcome to my humble demesne."

She sketched a curtsey, grinning in self-deprecation at her inappropriate garb. "Just keeping an eye on the countryside, my Lord."

"Everything here? Any trouble?"

She slanted the manifest so he could watch her ticking off items. "Down to the last brass nail, checked and double checked. No problems to speak of on the road. We met young anNewsom the other side of the pass, but that was all."

All the heartiness left his face. "That young rake. Scuttling around with a bunch of hired swords, trying to look important."

"Keeping watch over his family's prerogatives, I gathered. We parted amicably."

"Hmph. Glad for you. We don't always get our own rights that easily."

"Sorry to hear that." She waved the papers. "Once you open the crates, if there's any problem, well, your agent in the Capital seems very...thorough."

He turned his hearty smile on her, waving expansively at the angle of the sun. "Surely you'll be gracing us with your presence this evening."

She matched his expression. "I'd like to, but we're carrying an important delivery expected at the Royal Army Training Centre. Some sort of rush, so I promised they would be there tomorrow night." *He doesn't need to know my promise was to my own crew.*

Again his smile disappeared as if a door had closed. "What delivery is that?"

She tossed her head towards the lead wagon, now almost empty. "No idea. Only a few crates, but the Army thinks they're important enough to pay top rates, so Dalmyns will get them there."

He glanced at the goods scattered around castle bailey, scuttled to her wagon and frowned at the rectangular shapes under the tarps. "But...but those are..."

Erlon sauntered closer.

"Aye, that's them." She followed at her own pace. "Most definitely for the Army." She looked at the manifest with concern. "Is there something missing from your order?"

His mouth worked and his eyes seemed glued to the canvas-covered mound. "No...no, that's fine. I thought..." He frowned up at the soldier towering over him.

"As I said, if there's any problem, Dalmyns will make good. You know that." She glanced around. "And now, since we're unloaded, I suppose we'd better chase that last bit of sunlight."

She smiled at him, nodded a graceful acknowledgement of his rank and swung up on the lead wagon. Her teamsters, whose eyes had not left her during the final conversation, were in their places and had the wagons moving before she was settled. With a cheerful wave she faced the front, determined not to turn her head until the last rig was out from under the portcullis.

When she did look back, the ammunition wagon was clear and the manor gates were swinging ponderously shut. She grinned at Maddoes. "They seem to be closing up at a timely hour."

He spat his usual stream of tobacco. "Mebbe they got a belly ache, 'n' goin' ta bed early."

"I don't imagine anLexing will sleep well tonight."

The teamster shook his head. "Nor does he deserve to." He spat again. "Double-S rifles." He turned to her. "Do you realize that this is gonna keep happenin'? Sooner or later, there's gonna be bandits out there with Double-S rifles. What'r' we gonna do about that?"

She shrugged. "I guess we'll get one of those Rapidfires."

He frowned. "What's that?"

"It's a bunch of gun barrels welded together side-by-side in a circle. You spin them around, and as each one comes to the top, it fires. Then it goes to the bottom and another cartridge gets fed in."

"You mean it keeps shooting, without stopping to reload?"

"I've seen a demonstration. It was fantastic. You hold down the trigger and crank the handle and it keeps firing. Scary. The test model I saw kept breaking down, but I'm sure they'll fix the problems."

He slapped his knee. "Can you imagine a wagon with one of those mounted on the back?"

"Can you imagine one of those mounted behind that jack pine over there as we drove past?"

He stared at her in shock, then shook his head. "Where's it all gonna end, Aleria?"

"It won't end." She slapped his shoulder. "Whatever they invent, we'll figure out ways to do our work and life will go on. Change happens, Maddoes."

"I dunno. My family's been in cartage for generations, and I bet if my great-grandad was to sit on this bench he could handle wagon, harness and team without a thought."

He glanced at her sideways. "But I doubt he'd understand an Elite lady sittin' on the bench beside him in swordsman's breeks."

She laughed. "I'm not the first woman to take up a sword, Maddoes."

"No, but you're the first one I ever met." Then he laughed. "You shoulda seen Lord anLexing's face when you told him those boxes were for the Army. Like a kid gettin' throwed out of the candy store empty handed."

Her light mood vanished. "He doesn't know what a favour we did him. The king will not be happy."

"No, I imagine he isn't." The old teamster turned a sly look on her. "Lord Raif Canah gonna tell his Majesty all about it?"

She wrenched around to face him. "What do you know about what young Lord anCanah does or doesn't do?"

He laughed. "Miss Aleria, how long've I bin workin' for the Dalmyns?"

"Ever since I can remember...and as you just reminded me, your family for generations."

"That's right. We ain't em-ploy-ees, like the drivers for the other companies. We're family retainers. Do you think you can get up on the wrong side of the bed, and it won't be all over the office and out to the yard before your foot even hits the floor?"

"But that's...that's..."

"That's the way life's always bin in the Dalmyn demesne, my Lady. And all the other demesnes, I'd guess. Don't know why it'd be such a surprise to you."

"So you think you know all about my dealings with Raif anCanah."

"Not all of them." He shrugged. "But we sure know about those little packets of paper we used to hand you, but now we give to Koren."

She put all the threat she could into her voice. "And what happens to them?"

"I'm just an old teamster, M'Lady." He stared forward, flipped the reins across the horses' rumps. "I wouldn't have no idea."

"Right. And you stick to that story if you know what's good for you."

"Yessirree, M'Lady. I get the message clear."

That was a conversation stopper, and she used the pause to scan the wagons and the surrounding area. As she looked forward, she caught him, out of the corner of her eye, glancing at her several times. Finally he spoke.

"You don't need to worry, M'Lady. You got a loyal crew. None of us would ever tell."

She snorted. "Kind words, Maddoes, but since we pay spies in most of the other Elite and Exalted households, I assume that they have spies in ours."

"What?" He was truly shocked. "Not one of us!"

"No, Maddoes, I hope not one of you. But one of the kitchen flunkies, or one of the new chambermaids...it's a large group of people, and they can't all resist temptation. Loyalty is a precious commodity."

He spat again, slapped the reins, and slouched further down on the seat and said nothing. For a long time.

3.   The Firing Range

Captain Teille, the commandant of the training camp at Decker, was pleased to see company at his lonely outpost, but Aleria's announcement spoiled his day. "You have what?"

Aleria shrugged. "I have about a dozen Levis Double-S rifles in my wagon. May I assume you weren't expecting a delivery?"

"Levis Sustained Shots?"

"That's right. And a couple of smaller boxes. Wonder what's in them?"

The officer drew himself up and frowned. "Lady anDalmyn, what exactly are you getting at?"

"I don't know, Sir. It came as a shock to me when I discovered them. They were slipped at the last moment into a shipment for the Lexing manor. When I crossed Newsom land they tried to take them from me. Could have been a ploy, but Lord anLexing was very upset when I said I was bringing them here."

"Now, that doesn't surprise me." Captain Teille shook his head. "Lord anLexing is getting a whole lot too concerned with his rights and his prerogatives. You think he was the intended destination, my Lady?"

"I believe so."

"The question is what to do now."

"I don't think you have to worry about that, sir."

"What do you mean? I've got nobles in my area receiving forbidden Mechanical weapons!"

"All you need to do is keep those guns until your superiors decide what to do with them. The rest will be taken care of."

"How can you be so sure of that, my Lady?"

"Captain Teille, you know how the politics go in the Capital. I imagine you know who my father is. These people made a large error, using Dalmyn wagons for their little plots. Perhaps it occurred to you that it's unusual for some-one of my status to be guarding a simple delivery?"

"It did."

"But you were too polite to mention it."

He smiled. "Something like that."

"Enough said. This problem will be solved at its source, not out here. You can be sure of that."

"Thank you, my Lady."

"By the way," she grinned at him. "I never did count those guns."

She could see the temptation tugging at him, but his honour won out. "I wish you would, my Lady. If you report to your people and I report to my superiors, it would be best if the numbers tally."

"A good point, Sir." She slapped him on the shoulder. "Let's go open those boxes." She glanced at him sideways. "I don't suppose anyone would care if those guns got...worked in a bit?"

He returned the look. "I am allowed a certain latitude out here at the Training Centre that officers in more traditional positions do not enjoy. It would be a great loss for my recruits if they were to miss out on such an important opportunity."

"Let's get those crates opened, then."

Soon they were on the firing range. Aleria's men and the base officers clustered around, trying for a look at the powerful new weapons.

One of her guards reached out and caressed the barrel of the gun she was holding. It was a business-like weapon: no special carving or etching, just terrible killing power. "So, how do these things work, Aleria?"

She glanced to the Captain, but he shrugged, so she took the initiative. "I've never shot a Levis, but I watched a demonstration at the factory in Domaland last year. You see this little cylinder full of shells? You slip it into this gap in the breech, see?" She demonstrated. "Now a cartridge is lined up with the firing chamber. You push this lever, and the bullet

18

slides up and forward. Ready to fire. It also cocks the spring on the firing pin, so the one motion does it all. Now you fire..." she put the gun to her shoulder, aimed at the target and squeezed off a shot. There was a burst of applause when she hit just left of the centre cross.

"The recoil shoves the empty cartridge back into the cylinder. You push the lever again, and it moves the cylinder around one notch and slides the next cartridge into the chamber, and you're ready for another shot." She grinned ruefully and rubbed her shoulder. "The recoil is also much stronger than a muzzle-loader."

Maddoes hesitantly raised a hand. "But..."

"Yes, Maddoes?"

"On a single-shot rifle there's a hammer. You can ease it back down if you don't want to shoot again. That there gun ain't got one. It's primed to fire, right now. What if you decide not to fire it? That's a dangerous weapon you're waving around there, cocked and ready to kill."

"Which is why I'm not waving it around. However, there is a safety lever, here, which you shove forward, and it stops the trigger from moving." She demonstrated.

"The only way to unload the spring on the firing pin is to take the cylinder out. Then you can remove the cartridge from the chamber and release the spring. That's a design flaw, and I hope someone in the Levis factory in Domaland is as smart as you are, Maddoes."

The old teamster went red at the respectful laughter and shuffled behind Erlon, who reached for the gun. "May I?"

Again looking to the Captain for permission, she handed it over. Erlon stood at the firing line, examining the weapon. Suddenly he dropped to a prone position, his elbows braced wide, the rifle propped in front of him. Before anyone could register what he was doing, he had fired three quick shots into the centre of the target. He stood again, staring down the range.

"This weapon is sighted a bit to the left, but that speed does my heart good."

19

Aleria noted that the first shot was an inch to the left of the centre cross and the two subsequent shots were side-by-side in the middle.

Erlon handed the gun back. "Fine weapon, though. I wouldn't use it for firewood."

Wordlessly, Aleria held the rifle out to the officer, but he refused it with a grin. "I'm finding this very interesting. Perhaps some of your other men...?"

"I don't expect any more surprises." Aleria smiled as well. "You go ahead."

The Captain took the gun with a great deal of respect. He levered a cartridge in, took a precise stance and fired. Methodically, he loaded another cartridge and fired again. A little more quickly, he sent a third bullet down the range. Then he straightened, glancing from the target to the gun and back again. His shots had grouped in the centre. "Impressive. I did have to aim right a bit. Very complicated Mechanicals. I wonder how they stand up in field conditions."

"That will be up to you to find out, sir."

"Only if my superiors allow it, I'm afraid. Latitude is not to be confused with freedom."

He handed the gun back to her for a demonstration of changing over the cylinders, and they continued to admire the Mechanics of the weapon and speculate on its source and possible uses.

Soon Aleria felt she had gleaned any information she could and got the wagons moving again. The grateful Captain had scared up a single wagonload of equipment that needed to be returned to Kingsport, so they weren't deadheading completely. They would drop in at a few manors on the way west, hoping to pick up more trade.

That night, camped in a lonely dell, Aleria leaned back from the campfire, handed her dirty plate to the teamster on kitchen duty and focused her eyes on Erlon, who was lounging on the mossy bank beside her.

"You know I have to ask. Nobody in this realm should be able to shoot like that. There's no legal way to practise. Outside the army..."

He grinned. "I'm from Shaeldit, remember?"

"And? Nobody is allowed to bring guns into the realm. Anywhere."

"We made our own guns." He shrugged. "It's not magic."

"To make a gun from scratch? By hand?"

His smile widened. "Maybe if they're made by hand that makes them legal. There are fine gunsmiths up in the hills. They heat up a sheet of good steel, roll it around a rod and forge-weld it, then drill it out to the exact size. If you use a flint to set the powder off, you don't need much machining at the breech. Muzzle-loaders, of course. You make your powder last with a gun like that."

"Did you ever make one?"

"Heavenly days, no. Takes a lifetime to learn that kind of skill. I bought my gun from over the mountain."

"Over which mountain?"

He laughed. "Sorry. It's an old expression. Through Monteligna Pass in Ferboden."

"Are you telling me you can buy guns in Ferboden?"

He became serious. "You can buy almost anything you want in Ferboden. You only have to know who to ask."

"What does that mean? I thought their 'People's Government' or whatever they call it controlled the whole economy."

"They wouldn't be the first rulers to discover that you can't control everything. The government tries to manage all the markets but they do a rotten job of it. Somebody's always short on something. So people find ways to get what they need from other people. I think they call it the 'People's Market' to be funny."

"I'm beginning to see. So when Roeble takes his caravans into Ferboden, he's not dealing with the government market. He's dealing with these other people."

He paused for thought. "You'd have to ask him."

"No, I'm asking you. He may be a valued ally, but you were with him on our payroll. I'm sure you're not going to tell me anything he wants to hide from us, but even if it was, your duty is to Dalmyn."

"Since you put it like that, yes, I got the impression he was trading with unauthorized, even illegal merchants. There were several rendezvous in out-of-the-way places with people who looked far from official. He took me along because it's dangerous, especially for a foreigner."

"I knew it was dangerous. I'm beginning to figure out why."

He shrugged, and the muscles bulged under his thin shirt. "That would be your responsibility, I guess."

"I'm counting on you to help me." She couldn't resist reaching out and laying a hand on his shoulder. "You did a great job in the battle, and the men look to you for leadership."

"Don't worry. We'll be fine." He glanced across at her, then into the fire. "If we can't beat them or outsmart them, we'll turn you loose to impress them with your beauty."

She slapped the side of his head. "Don't you talk to me about looks, Mister Haven't-Had-a-Shave-All-Week. You're not impressing anyone."

He didn't even flinch. "I was thinking I'd wait till we hit the Dalmyn yard at Kasnel. There's a bathtub and a mirror in the bunkhouse there. It's only three more days."

"Well, make sure you do. I will not offend the good citizens of that village by wandering around with a ruffian."

"We're going to wander around, are we now?"

"It's been a tough trip. The men need a break."

His face grew serious. "Can't argue with that."

4.   Dust and Disarray

The ensuing journey brought home to Aleria forcibly how little she knew of her crew. She had plenty of time to watch them on the route back to Kingsport, and she discovered how much she had to learn about her duties. As far as she could tell, they were a competent, loyal bunch, but as the boring days rolled on, she could feel a sense of laxness creep over them. They were still doing their jobs, but she thought they moved with reduced enthusiasm and there was less laughter.

It was a dry day on a soft stretch of road, and the tailwind was blowing a huge cloud of dust over them. For once, the lead wagon was the worst place to be. Erlon strode past her, and she jumped down to follow him, breathing easier as the dust plume thinned farther ahead of the train.

"Let me guess. You can't see a thing in this mess, so you're going out front to clear air so you can assess our route."

He grinned down at her, a drop of sweat leaving a dirty line down the side of his face. She resisted the temptation to reach up and wipe it away.

"Aye. The wages don't exist to make me sit on a wagon seat in that dust."

"And is that a subtle plea for more pay?" She flicked her fingertips at his arm.

He flinched back, still smiling. "Would there be any use in it?"

"I suppose I'll have something to say about the size of your bonus." She shrugged. "That's if we get home in one piece."

His face straightened, and his eyes scanned the surrounding hillsides. "So far, luck has not smiled in that respect."

"Nonsense." She dropped her joking tone. "Our luck hasn't been good, but your handling of every situation has been exemplary."

"And I fully intend to keep it that way." His grin returned. "Especially if it gets me out of that dust."

"In that case, I should help you in any way I can." She pointed forward, and the two stepped out faster.

"Can I ask you a question?"

He looked down at her. "You're the boss."

"Your guards are doing a good job."

"I hope so...?"

"And the question is, are my teamsters doing the same?"

"Couldn't say for sure." He frowned and gave it some thought. "The horses are pulling well. The equipment is holding up. I don't know that much about driving."

"That's not exactly what I mean. You've guarded a lot of trains. You can tell how it should look. It seems to me the men are getting loose. Nothing particular, but do you notice an edge to their voices sometimes? No, I don't suppose so. Maybe I'm borrowing trouble where there isn't any. Maddoes keeps on them about the stock, but in general..."

"He's been pushing them a bit, lately."

"You noticed, too? I thought he might be."

"You could always ask him."

"I could."

"But you won't, because you think you're supposed to know the answer without asking."

She turned to him. "Well, a good Wagonmaster would know the answer, wouldn't he?"

He shrugged. "If you want to be a good Wagonmaster, I guess you'd better ask him."

"You're not much help."

"What do you want, Aleria?" He tossed up his hand. "It's not something I know that much about."

She wiped a forearm across her face. "Sorry. I don't need to dump my problems on you. That only makes your duties harder, and the way this trip has been going, we need you at the top of your game."

"Don't worry. There's not a problem."

There was a shout from behind them, and the whinny of a horse. Then a string of curses blasted through the dust.

Their eyes met and they sprinted back along the halted wagon train. By the time they reached the tail end the cloud was blowing away, and they could see the cause of the trouble. Two wagons were jammed side-by-side, their wheels locked. The drivers were standing at their benches, shouting at each other in colourful language. A couple of guards stood on the ground gawking: one with a smirk on his face, the other looking embarrassed.

As Aleria took in the scene, Erlon dropped his big hand on the shoulder of the smiling man. "You're not at a circus, you two. Eyes outward."

They obeyed at once, moving out to either side of the train, hands on swords.

I guess I'm supposed to do something, too. She strode up beside the wagons, aware of her height disadvantage. "All right, what's going on?"

They ignored her, continuing their harangue. She felt a moment of dismay. *What do I do now?* She looked around. The other drivers were gathering. *What if they won't stop?* She began to call out again, then realized how ridiculous that was. *Come on, Aleria. You must take control.* Her frustration boiled. Instead of speaking, she vaulted up onto the driver's seat beside the nearest man. She reached down and grabbed the back of his neck, jamming her thumb in a spot that would get his attention. She forced her voice to be low and calm. "I believe I was talking to you."

The man froze, a squawk of pain cutting off as she pressed harder. "Now you be quiet, and you," she glared at his opponent, "tell me what is going on."

"The idiot tried to pass me."

"I did not!"

"Yes, you did. How can anyone think you were trying to do anything else?"

"Well, you pulled over, and I thought…"

"I didn't pull over to let you by. I was…"

"GIVE IT UP!" Aleria glanced down at the wheels of the wagons. "It's obvious this wagon ran into that one from behind. Now, don't tell me what was going on, because I'm sure you know how this sort of thing is supposed to be handled. But I will now allow you both the chance to pass the whole rest of the train."

They stared at her, puzzled frowns forming.

"Because you get to ride at the front in the worst of the dust for the rest of the afternoon. Now get those wagons untangled and get out on the road. You're holding us up!"

She jumped down off the wagon and strode away, passing Maddoes as she threaded through the other teamsters.

He nodded to her and stepped forward. "I heard a horse. Is one of them hurt?"

She paused to listen to the answer and was pleased at the driver's subdued tone. "No injury, Maddoes. That was part of the problem. Ol' Buck, he don't like to be passed, and when Jerd tried to go by, he broke into a trot. Took me by surprise, and then..."

"Aye. Buck don't like to be passed, and you don't either. I doubt you was holdin' him back any."

The man mumbled a response, the wind gone out of him.

Aleria nodded to herself. Then she turned to the ring of watching men. "Listen, now. The circus is over. Get your rigs straightened out and as soon as these two hit their new positions of honour, let's get moving. It's been a bitch of a day and everybody's on edge. Settle down and we'll ride it out."

There were several affirmative murmurs, and the men trudged back to their wagons. She went over to stand beside Erlon. "All clear?"

"Everything calm, boss."

She glanced around to be sure that no one was within earshot. "See what I mean? That was a completely stupid trick. They never would have tried it if I was on top of them like I should be. And they ignored me when I spoke to them. What if the crew gets out of hand? What do I do?"

26

He grinned. "From the stories the men tell, your great-grandfather would have horsewhipped both of them on the spot."

"Thanks. I'm sure that's a great way to create a tight crew. Do you see anyone abusing the horses like that?"

"No, come to think of it. Dalmyns are good to their stock."

"That's right. The best driver lets the sound of his whip do the talking. And we're good to our men, too. How can I do that and maintain discipline at the same time? What do you do?"

"Easy for me." He shrugged. "I'm a better fighter than any of them."

"So they have to do what you say."

"No, so I know their duties better than they do. That gives me an advantage."

"And it doesn't help me, because I don't know their duties better than they do."

Their wagons straightened out, the two teamsters moved up to the front and the whole train started rolling again, dust rising as they gathered speed. The leaders turned to walk alongside.

"I know how to organize a trip. It's the rest of it I'm not so sure of."

"What rest of what?" He scratched his head.

"The bigger scene. How they get along. Morale and all that. If they get snarly and start sniping at each other, all I can think of is to bash a few heads together."

"The idea has its appeal."

"It would make me feel better, but it wouldn't solve the problem."

"Right. So you have to find out what the problem is."

"Yes. Then maybe I can solve it."

"So what's our problem here?"

"That's the problem. I don't know."

He shrugged. "The problem is likely the heat, the dust and the boredom. I suppose I could organize a nice little bandit attack."

"Thank you for the kind thought, but I prefer the boredom." She gazed around at the dry terrain. "There aren't even enough trees for the birds to sit on. They haven't had a bird bet for days."

"That is a completely inane pastime."

"It's harmless. It doesn't hurt the birds, and it gives the men something to talk about."

"Huh. They might as well flip a coin: king or country. Who cares which bird will fly away first?"

She grinned. "The guy who bet on it."

"I'd have to be pretty bored."

"They are."

He nodded. "Which brings us back to where we started."

"Well, I suppose when we hit Kasnel tomorrow they can find something to do."

"Maybe start a fight in a bar or steal some farmer's spring vegetables."

"Great. Something else to worry about."

He slapped her shoulder. "At least it will keep you from getting bored."

That evening they camped out again, and once supper was over and the stock was settled for the night she called the men together. She looked them over in the firelight. *A rough lot, but highly competent. All I have to do is weld them into a good fighting unit. Which I have no experience at, either. Who trusted me with this duty, anyway? Oh, yes, my father. Wonderful.*

"Listen, now. We had a little kerfuffle back there." She eyed the two culprits. "A whole lot of stupidity, but no harm done. However, I did see something that bothers me. Jerd, what was the real problem today?"

He looked at her, then glanced at his partner in crime. Finally he shrugged. "I don't know, Ma'am."

She noted the honorific. *Good.* "What was wrong was that you two were haranguing each other and when I asked you to stop, you didn't."

"Oh."

"That's right. Oh."

"Sorry, Ma'am."

"I don't need an apology. My feelings don't get hurt that easy." She fixed him with a glare, then raised her eyes to include the whole group. "But I don't care what's going on, I don't care how noisy it is. Even in the middle of a battle, you HAVE to hear my voice. A woman's voice carries over a bunch of men. Even when you're screaming and yelling, you can hear my orders. IF YOU'RE LISTENING! The guards know Erlon's voice. No, it's not because it's so loud. He doesn't even need to shout. They're listening for it, because if he says, 'Pull back,' the man that ignores him might end up feeling very, very lonely."

She could see the realization dawn. "So keep that in mind for the future." She grinned. "I might even test you in Kasnel tomorrow night. If I walk into a bar and see a bunch of you, I might whisper, 'Drinks on me,' and see who notices."

Jerd laughed with the rest. "Right you are, Aleria. We'll be lissenin' for sure."

"See that you do. Like I said this afternoon, the last couple of days have been a bitch, but it's nothing you haven't been through before. Don't take it out on each other." She spun and pointed at one of the habitual offenders, a guard who took offence too easily when he was drinking. "And don't take it out on the good citizens of Kasnel tomorrow, either. Otherwise I might be whispering, 'Everyone back to the bunkhouse,' instead."

The guard nodded, glancing at Erlon, who stared at him.

The next day's run went smoothly, as did their evening in Kasnel. Aleria played her game in several bars and had to pay out most times, including once for a couple of local miners with good hearing. Her men were prepared to defend her, but she laughed. "I deserved that. Come along and join us, gentlemen. Dalmyn Cartage comes through on our promises."

Finally she and Erlon settled in a little cafe where they ordered coffee and a slice of home-baked pie.

"Aleria, we're still four days out and I don't think it will get me fired, so I'm going to say this."

"What? You sound very serious."

"I am. You have to stop touching me."

"What?" She glanced around to see if anyone had heard her exclamation, then lowered her voice. "Touching you?"

"Do you touch any of the other men?"

"Sometimes."

"If you need to, if they're in the way, that sort of thing. This isn't that sort of thing."

"It isn't?"

He sighed. "I hoped we could talk this through."

"We are."

"No, you're giving the pat responses that don't mean anything."

"I am? Oh. Yes, I am, aren't I?" She looked into his face, and pulled back her hand that, of its own accord, had been dropping onto his arm. "So now what?"

"You stop talking, and I start. You listen and think. All right?"

"I'm not sure it is. I'm the boss. Isn't it supposed to be the other way around?"

His lips stretched, but it wasn't a smile. "It's not that easy when it comes to people. Especially people that you...get along with. When we're talking about the job, certainly, you're the boss and I listen. When it comes to you and me..."

She raised a hand to stop him. "Anybody speaks who needs to. And now it's your turn."

"Good enough. Except I have nothing to say any more."

"I suppose not. It's not as if anybody is disagreeing with you."

He grinned. "At least we're not going to argue."

"Hmph." She turned and looked up at him. "What now?"

"I don't know. Am I fired?"

"Shouldn't I wait until I see whether I can work my wiles on you first?"

Something went out of his face. The image of Kalmein adWoling flashed across her vision, and her disastrous attempt at romance at the Spring Ball. *Not that. Never again.*

"...joking, joking, Erlon. No wiles. I promise."

He frowned down at her, then turned his attention down to his pie, chewing with force.

Damn and double damn. I've done it again. She stared at the top of his head. *What's wrong with me?* "I mean it, Erlon. I promise I will not flirt with you. It would be demeaning to both of us and put our positions at risk. I understand. Is that what you want to hear?"

He glanced at her, dropped his eyes and took a few more bites. Then he looked up again and the old spark was back. "Is that a wile?"

Relief gushed through her. "Probably." She grinned. "Let's wait and see if it works."

She held out her hand, but pulled it back before she touched him. "Erlon, I thought I lost you for a moment there."

"So did I, Aleria."

"I begin to see the problem. No, I saw the problem all along. It just smacked me in the face. Getting mixed up with the crew would be a big mistake."

It was his turn to appear stricken. "It's not that I..." He scrubbed his hands over his face, then dropped them. "I don't know what to say."

"Is that because you're afraid of losing your position, or because you're afraid of losing my friendship?"

"Both, I suppose. No, I'm not worried about my position. Your father isn't like that. Dalmyn's is a big outfit. If there are problems between us, you'll find a place for me."

"But it won't be as much fun as the trips I take."

He glanced at her. "We've only been out sixteen days, and this one's already fun enough for me."

"All right. We don't rush this. We go back to work as usual. I keep my hands to myself..."

"I'm not saying you even have to do that, Aleria. I'm just saying we must be very conscious what we're doing. You don't drift into a liaison by force of habit. Our problem out on the road today. How much different would it be if you and I were..." he leaned forward and lowered his voice, "sleeping together? What if something serious went wrong, and your father found out?"

"I see what you mean." She shuddered. "Even if it didn't directly affect what happened..."

"Exactly. We have to be very careful. With our positions and with each other. That's what I wanted to say in the first place."

"So why didn't you say that in the first place?"

He rolled his eyes. "Because then we would've missed all the fun we just had."

"I'm glad we enjoyed it."

"Umm..." He toyed with his fork a moment, then looked straight at her. "And I hadn't really figured it out yet, either."

"That much is apparent." She grinned to take any sting out of the comment. "And now?"

"Now we go on like before." He pushed his empty plate away. "You do what you want. Just be aware of it."

"Fine."

"And you can touch me if you want. We're friends."

"But I'm also the boss, and I won't forget it."

"And if you touch my butt, I'll break your arm."

She grinned. "I can live with that."

"You can?"

"Without touching your butt? Yes. A broken arm, I'm not so sure. We're still in rough country."

Loud laughter seeped in from the street. Boot heels stumbled on the boardwalk outside, and a slurred voice shouted. Erlon's eyes slid to the door. "Good point. We both better get back to our duties."

They did another sweep of the main street and returned to the Dalmyn wagonyard at a decent time. The last of the crew trickled in soon after. The weather hadn't changed; it would be a hot and dusty day again tomorrow, and they knew it.

5.   Briefing by the Expert

It was good to get back to the city. To luxuriate in a scented bath and then relax in the garden while a servant brought her a glass of chilled wine.

Her mother sat down on the next lounger. "You're looking ladylike today."

Aleria grinned. "Never thought I'd say it, but a light cotton dress has something to recommend it. Especially over swordsman's leather breeks and that damned vest."

"I gather 'that damned vest' is a necessity?"

"Aye. It serves two purposes. It's heavy leather, so it provides some protection in a fight, and it also downplays my shape. I don't want to be a queen bee leader, with a bunch of drones circlin' around on the promise of honey."

Her mother shivered delicately. "That sounds perfectly horrible, but it's a great image for several people I can think of." She glanced at her daughter. "And your grammar seems to be slipping."

"I suppose. I do tend to talk more like the men when I'm out on the road. There are enough differences between us; there's no point in exaggerating them."

"Hmm. But at home...?"

"Oh. I see. Once I'm home, there are enough differences between me and the rest of my set..."

"Something of that sort. You always were quick to pick up on things."

"That's what makes me such an easy daughter." She laughed at her mother's expression. "Now, before you get out the hairbrush to beat me, what's been going on since I left?"

Her mother leaned back, staring for a moment at the deep blue of the early summer sky. "I'm sure your other sources will put you in touch with the political situation."

"Luncheon with young Lord anCanah tomorrow. And his lady wife, of course."

"Give Mito my love. I am not familiar enough with Raif to know whether he's lovable."

Aleria laughed. "Sometimes. More often lately, I'd have to say. Marriage seems to agree with him."

"Hmm. Time to move to more serious matters. Don't be surprised if there's something in the wind. There are a lot of nervous people in the city, and his Majesty knows it. Too much unrest at all levels, including the Ranked ones."

"Does any of that unrest affect Dalmyn Cartage directly?"

"That mess you stumbled across in the Northeast where we have our coal hauling contracts does. I note that the people causing the trouble out there are Ranked. Might be a fit for you, since you're already in the middle of it."

"That I am. Anything else I should know?"

"General closing of ranks, I'd say. If you consider who is inviting whom for tea, you might find it informative."

"Sticking to the close friends, taking no chances?"

"I'm afraid so."

She shot a glance at her mother. "And you?"

"Oh, young Lady anCanah and I have been spreading ourselves around. It reassures the lower Ranks to see our good example."

"Take your nose out of the sky and tell me about Mito. How is she doing?"

"Doing well, I'd have to say. Especially at the reassuring part. She is so pleasant and concerned. The wilting ones blossom when she talks to them."

"And you don't do so well at the concerned and reassuring part."

"I do not. So we tend to gang up on them. She reassures the timid ones and I whip the troublemakers into shape. We do what we can in our small way."

"Which I'm sure is considerable. I'm glad. I didn't toss my friend up to Exalted Rank just to waste her on tea and frilly fashions. I expect results."

Her mother sat up and looked at her. "And I suppose you'll be expecting results from yourself as well?"

"I haven't done so badly, I suppose." Aleria shrugged. "The results with a certain misdirected delivery were quite good, come to think of it."

"So I gather. Oh, I remember something. If you get sent farther down the Trench there's a family you'll run across. AnLlannon. Ever heard of them?"

"Can't say as I have. Why should I look for them?"

"An interesting lot. I have a small acquaintance with Lady anLlannon from years ago. A formidable sort."

"Sort of like you?"

"In a less relaxed way. You might pass along my greetings. I liked her husband. Not the typical backwoods lord. Rather bookish, as I recall. He was one of that group campaigning for a Chair in Agriculture over at the University. It didn't garner much support, but that gives an idea what the man is like. Serious about his husbandry."

"Loyal?"

"Hard to say. Lady Llannon would be loyal to her class, if anything. He will probably be loyal to anyone who will leave him alone with his books and his farming."

"Offspring?"

"None that made names for themselves, either good or bad."

"Thanks, in any case. Every bit of information counts. Do you have anything about the other lords in the area?"

Liniema went on, discussing the backwoods Ranked classes, regaling her daughter with tales of their intractable nature and their strange customs. Finally Aleria stopped laughing long enough to interject.

"Where do they get such ideas?"

Her mother shrugged. "Word has it that the Old Ones retreated to the mountains when we Galesians moved into the central plateau. Perhaps a few of these are descendants."

"Yes, a name like 'Yannon' has a strange ring. How do you spell it?"

Her mother grinned. "With two 'l's."

"I remember now." Aleria snapped her fingers. "The names from History class. All double letters and weird pronunciations. Yes, if I go up there, I'm must do some research on the Old Ones." She regarded her mother. "Have you heard a whisper that I might be going there?"

"For that you must ask your political and commercial masters, of which I am neither."

Aleria stood. "And your grammar is getting exceptionally sticky."

"Setting a good example, my dear." She rose as well. "I hear your father's delicate footsteps." She swooped up Aleria's empty glass and made her way to the door, greeting her husband with a kiss as she passed him. "Your turn, my Lord. She is now aware of the social background."

Kensel's bemused smile stretched into a grin as he approached his daughter. "Do you get the feeling you're being set up?"

She kissed his cheek and motioned for him to sit across from her while an alert servant brought his drink. "I've been home less than a day, and already you're thinking of sending me away again. Should I be reading something into this?"

"Yes, you should." He sat and looked at her.

"That smile is definitely smug. What's going on?"

"Certain people are very happy with you."

"What a pleasant change."

"We take our pleasures when we find them. Highly placed people, as it happens."

"Hmm. As long as one of them is the son of a certain duke, my luncheon tomorrow will be more pleasant. Especially for him."

"Oh, he is pleased. His father too."

"Fine. You know, there was a lot of luck involved."

"I'm sure there was. And bad luck as well. And shoddy procedures we have already dealt with."

"We know how those rifles got into the cargo, because I stood with my manifest in hand and watched it happen and

36

didn't notice I'd been fooled. I doubt if that trick will work again. But I also wonder how Newsom got his information."

Her father nodded. "We must consider the possibility that it came from our demesne, but I don't think so. I imagine someone was following the shipment."

"That's the easiest explanation. However..."

"Yes, yes, we have been keeping a closer eye on our people. Questioned everyone up and down the line. It's not good for morale, but it was unavoidable."

"I'm sure."

"There's the bell for supper." Her father rose. "Why don't you come down to the yard after you're through with Raif tomorrow and we can discuss this further. You may have more information than I do by that time."

She remained seated for a moment. "As long as you still want me to take the responsibility after you've heard about all my mistakes."

He reached out a hand to help her rise. "I'm sure they weren't serious. You came through where it mattered."

"This isn't false modesty, Father." She gripped his hand and would not let it go. "I learned a lot on this trip. The first thing being how much I have to learn."

"Sounds like you're making good progress. Come on. Let's go to supper. I hear the new spring wine is in."

She smiled at him as he ushered her gracefully into the house. *Father knows when to set business aside and relax. I wish it was that easy for me.*

6. Misgivings

Aleria gazed around the private dining room, taking in the delicate service, the silver, the company. "Rather fancy for a business meeting, don't you think? Do you always bring your wife to this sort of event?"

Mito refused to rise to the bait, pouring tea and looking serene.

Raif grinned and leaned forward to whisper. "It's a trick to fool our enemies."

"Hmm. Well, gives me a hint of confidence, anyway."

"It does?"

"Yes. The fact that you're smart enough to keep Mito up to date. There may be hope for you yet."

He laid his hand over his wife's and smiled at her. Then he turned to Aleria. "Fine. We have revealed that this is a business meeting, so tell me about your little trip."

Dropping the levity, she gave him a precise and detailed account. Both her friends stopped her from time to time with questions, and when she finished everyone sat back, Raif nodding as if to a thought of his own.

"That makes a great deal of difference. Thank you, Aleria. You have clarified the scene for me. I'm getting a good picture of what is going on out there and who is doing it." He thought a moment. "Did you hear anything about Greyson anLlannon while you were there?"

Hmm, anLlannon again. "No, we turned north to Decker to deliver the rifles. His land is on the south side of Lexing."

"Of course. The reason I ask is that anLlannon is the biggest player in this game whose position is unclear. The man never comes out of his demesne."

"I hear his wife does."

"You know his wife?"

"My mother does. Nothing to help us, though."

Raif nodded. "Well done in any case, Aleria. We're on the right track."

"In what way?"

He glanced at her.

I know that look. He's about to drop a rock on my toe.

"In quite a few ways." He took a sip of tea, staring out the window.

She reached over, took the teacup away and forced his hands flat on the table, making him face her directly. She slapped the backs of his hands with both of hers. "Now, Raif anCanah, you stop the game and tell me exactly what you think you're doing."

His eyes met hers with the usual frustrating innocence.

"Don't give me that look. You know what's going on."

He smiled a bit. "I like to think I do. But you always want to know why."

Aleria turned to Mito. "How can you put up with him?"

"I married him." Her friend shrugged. "It makes a difference."

"Whatever suits you." Aleria shook her head and turned back to Raif. "I'm obviously involved, and I need to know a whole lot more than I have figured out for myself."

He nodded, serious now. "You do. There is a problem in the Trench, and you fell into it. There's a lot of pushing and shoving out there. Are you familiar with the history?"

"Nothing particular."

"The usual. A small political mistake festering until it creates a major outbreak. It happened a hundred years ago. No heirs, deeds lost in a fire that killed the lord. Forbach, I believe his name was. But then King Buhl III decided that there were too many small demesnes out in that area, and divided the land among the neighbors. Unfortunately, Buhl was good on the decision-making part, but less thorough on the thinking-ahead part, and he drew very arbitrary boundaries. The lords out there have argued over the borders ever since."

"Waiting their chance to 'right the wrongs,' I suppose."

"Exactly. And anLexing is more edgy than most. He got his fingers into two extra holdings, one through inheritance and one through marriage. Now he's getting ideas. His immediate neighbors aren't enthused."

Aleria slapped her hands on the table, making crockery jump. "What's wrong with these people? Don't they realize that they would do much better if they cooperated, instead of fighting all the time? Take anLexing. The only reason he can get his goods delivered at a reasonable rate is by routing them through the Newsom demesne. So, does he take his hereditary leave of passage as a benefit of cooperation? No, he takes it as a right that he is owed."

Raif grinned. "Spoken like a tradesman, not a landowner. To be fair, that leave of passage is worth fighting for. If he lost it, he'd have to ship up through Oudonsford and all the way around the north end of the Trench."

"Don't talk to me about the two-way nature of cooperation. It frustrates me so much!"

"Especially when you're trying to do business in the area."

"Precisely. That stupid attack. If Geran hadn't recognized me and called a halt, there would have been someone killed. My men were outnumbered and I was about to get serious."

Mito's head cocked to the side. "When someone attacks you, at first you don't take it seriously?"

Aleria shrugged. "First you assess their resolve. Sometimes it's only a probe. They push you, see how hard you're willing to defend yourselves. If they get stiff resistance they pull back. Just because they're criminals doesn't mean they're stupid. This bunch was deadly serious from the start. There was no talk, no posturing, just a straight-out attack. If Geran hadn't stopped us…"

"…we'd have had a grave diplomatic situation on our hands. The king isn't interested in any more internal squabbles right now. He's got more pressing problems to handle."

"More pressing than internal warfare?"

"In case you hadn't noticed, Galesia is a small, backward nation with a failing economy."

"What?"

"That's right. Our lack of iron means we bring a lot of expensive imports into the country. As the rules against Mechanicals are relaxed, the imports are increasing. Our only exports are timber, grain, wool and a small amount of finished goods. Where do we get the money to pay for the imports?"

"I never thought of it that way. What can we do?"

"We don't worry about it. King Otta is putting his energy into correcting that situation. We have been assigned to put our resources into solving the problem in the Trench."

"So what are you planning?"

"I have two possibilities. One, I go out there in full panoply with twenty lancers, throw my weight around."

"And give them all sorts of attention they don't deserve."

"And probably accomplish nothing, because that sort of attitude caused the problem in the first place. The other choice is to slip out, maybe with one of your wagon trains, and look around quietly."

"And probably have nothing happen, because nothing usually does, and it would be a waste of your time." She lowered her head, looked at him from under a frown. "Which leaves us with a familiar argument."

He laughed. "No argument here. Things have changed a whole lot since the last time you wanted to go chasing off on your own."

"Well, I'm glad you recognize that." She flexed her sword hand. "I'm a bit more able to handle myself now."

"Granted. Will you do it?"

"Just like that?"

"Just like that."

"On your authority. You have that kind of authority?"

"I do."

"Things really have changed."

He smiled.

"Don't look so smug. You've earned it as well."

His smile disappeared. "A chance to keep up our well-deserved reputations."

"How do you want to handle this? Do you expect me to take any action, or only gather information?"

"Information, of course. I can't think of a situation where you might take action."

"I can. A dozen well-armed and loyal men constitute a large enough force to tip the balance in many a backcountry squabble. With some kind of official position, I could be more effective."

"Of course. I can get you a letter of marque from the king if you want."

"A letter of marque? I read the Romances. That's for a pirate ship."

"It is, but being landlocked, Galesia is marvelously short of privateers. The principal is the same. It gives you the right to act for the king independently, up to and including open hostility."

"King Otta will sign over that kind of power to me?"

"I told you this was serious. His Majesty was impressed by your handling of the situation with the rifles, and he appreciates our support. He will sign it."

"Wait, wait." She stared at him in horror. "Let's look at this a moment. The king is going to send me into the worst hotspot in the realm, with the power to use his name to make decisions that could stop or start a rebellion? I'm not sure I'm ready for that yet."

"Do you want me to go with you?"

"Definitely not!" She glared at him. "You did that on purpose."

"I did."

"And you're the only other choice?"

He wavered a hand left, then right. "It isn't all a matter of maturity and ability. Disloyalty rears its shaggy and talon-studded paw."

"The usual court intrigue. What is it this time?"

"It's not so much whether the problem gets solved as who solves the problem. His Majesty thinks that if those of us who work the northern part of the kingdom solve the problems

42

up there, the peace will be longer lasting. He doesn't want to repeat Buhl's mistake of imposing an unworkable solution from the Capital."

"So there's no onus on me to do it right. Only the loss of the king's support for my father's enterprises over the whole North if I botch it up."

"Something like that."

"Then get me the damned letter from the king. I don't want to fail through lack of clout. Don't worry, I won't overuse it."

"I never thought you would. Once word gets out you're working for the king, it changes the type of information you get."

She laughed. "Yes. After that, you can never believe a word they tell you."

"Unfortunately true. The main reason I can't implement my first plan...what? Why are you looking at me like that?"

"There wasn't a 'first plan.' You never meant to go out there. Don't answer. You can see it on his face, can't you, Mito? How did anyone with a face like that ever think he could be a spy?"

"I sort of like his face."

"You're biased. A husband whose face shows everything is an asset if you happen to be his wife."

Raif chuckled. "I thought I did pretty well as a spy."

"Well, don't even think of trying it again!"

Aleria turned in surprise at the vehemence in Mito's voice. Then she laughed. "I couldn't agree more."

His hands came up in surrender. "So we are agreed that you'll do it?"

"Of course." She snorted. "All you had to do is ask me. Why do you insist on this whole rigamarole?"

He shrugged. "It was entertaining."

Mito's face became serious. "And if anything goes wrong, you can say that you offered to go yourself. That sounds far too ingenuous for belief."

"Mito! That's a bit harsh. He would have gone if I couldn't." She regarded her friend. "You're very serious about this."

"It's not a great choice, is it? I don't want my husband in a dangerous situation, so my best friend goes instead. That makes me feel really happy."

"And I'm happy that you're happy. Don't worry. This shouldn't be any more dangerous than my usual duties. I'm only collecting information. If all goes as planned."

"Carrying a letter of marque." Mito sighed. "I know I shouldn't worry so much. But I do. I can't help it."

Aleria leaned over and gave her friend a one-armed hug. "Always nice when somebody cares."

"So." She straightened. "Some time soon, Dalmyn will start a new route out east of Oudonsford, down into the northern end of the Trench. I take charge of the wagons. I keep my head down and my ears open."

"Doesn't sound like you."

"Well, I might ask a few questions. Innocent ones. If anyone mentions the topic."

"I trust your judgement. Usually."

"Don't worry, I'll be careful."

"Of course."

"I will! I have nothing to prove, Raif. I'm doing my job as I always do. Merchants don't hunt trouble."

"But agents for the king do. I know you, Aleria. I wouldn't send you if I you couldn't take care of yourself. Come and pick up your letter of marque before you leave."

"And be careful."

She grinned at both of them. "Of course I will."

She left the AnCanah mansion with a lift to her step. This sounded interesting. It would make her parents happy, too. They had known she was looking around for a longer journey, perhaps with Roeble's caravans. Only a late snow in the passes was keeping him back from his spring foray through the mountains to Ferboden, down in the Southeast. Well, that was out of the question, now. She had an assignment from the king. *All I have to do is deal with a problem nobody has solved in a century.* As she thought of it, her pace slowed. *What am I letting myself in for?*

* * *

Her father had no qualms: at least none that he would reveal to her. "There are several good reasons for sending you out as the company representative, Aleria."

"I assumed there would be."

"We know you, we know your reactions, and we can be confident we understand your reports."

"Which is not the same as believing everything I tell you."

"No, it isn't." Her father's face became serious. "I never believe everything anyone tells me. Not even you."

"Not even Mother?"

He grinned. "Especially her. Whatever she tells me has already been filtered through a very opinionated mind. Sort of like you."

"But you understand the filters. That's fine."

"The last and best reason is that for all the reasons I can think of, you have the best chance of success."

Her warm glow of pride was washed out by a rush of doubt. "I wish I felt so confident."

"What do you mean?"

"There are a lot of bets riding on this expedition. Sending your trusted daughter may be a good idea from everybody's point of view. But I'm young, I'm inexperienced and I don't have the most balanced approach to life. In the past, I have put myself in circumstances where I was threatened, beaten, and raped. Circumstances that required me to kill several men. Not the best of recommendations, don't you think?"

He shrugged. "I prefer consider those incidents as experiences that will make you more careful."

"Careful is not a problem. I'm more worried about competent. This last trip was my first time leading a wagon train, and I made a lot of mistakes."

He flicked that objection away with a toss of his hand. "You have been in a responsible position with several trains that went into foreign realms with far more danger. This is only a delivery on what will become a regular route, inside the realm."

"With a letter of marque."

"If you look at your letter, you will find that its main intent is to allow you to ask for help. A reasonable precaution."

"The Trench is as far as you can get from 'inside the realm' without climbing a mountain and falling down the other side. But I take your point." She sat back. "There's a new one for your list of concerns regarding my character. Maybe I'll be too cautious."

He grinned. "Not likely to happen, but I'll keep it in mind."

"So what am I supposed to do if anLexing and anNewsom are in full scale battle when I get there?"

"No idea."

"None?"

"No, that kind of decision is for your political master to discuss with you."

"Come on, Father. You must be able to give me some advice."

"Not my place. You get your commercial orders from me, and your political instructions from the proper person."

She snorted. "If I didn't have it figured out already, now I'm sure. You've been talking to Raif. That's exactly the kind of thing he would say."

"Your young friend isn't the first to run a spying business."

She stared at her father. "You mean...you...?"

He held his hands out, palms towards her. "Not something a wagonmaster needs to know."

"No wonder you and I have been having arguments lately." She jumped to her feet. "You're starting to sound like him!"

Her father's answering grin did not last. "Raif and I have been working together to set up this operation, and I find myself in a mentoring position. I also remember what it was like, running the political side of this type of organization. If

Raif and I are taking the same approach, that's good from your point of view."

"If I must serve two masters, it's better if they agree."

"Very much better."

She frowned. "But if you start ganging up on me…"

* * *

On her return to the city she had resumed her training with Master Ogima, and it was easy to drop into the Falcon one day on her way home from practice.

When she entered, Juli was behind the bar: a pretty girl with a stocky figure and curly black hair that spilled down her back. She also had a fine, pale complexion, which reddened when Geran's name came up.

"Oh, yes, Miss. Geran comes in sometimes…he told me what happened…"

Aleria grinned. "Good. So you have an idea what's going on. When is he likely to drop in next?"

The girl nibbled a finger. "Let's see…they were only in the city overnight, and went right back out to the Newsom demesne," she leaned closer, "with a wagonload of weapons."

Aleria straightened. "Weapons?"

Juli's lip twitched. "Regular ones, Miss. Not a Mechanical one in the bunch."

Geran has told her a lot. Either the lad has a loose tongue or he's in deeper with Juli than I suspected. "That's fine."

"And he was hoping to be back within six or seven days. At least that's what he told me."

"But he would give you an optimistic estimate, considering who he was talking to."

The girl reddened again. "He's got no worry on my account, Miss."

"I'm happy to hear that. He tells you a lot, then? About what's going on?"

47

Juli glanced around and leaned closer. "It's important that I know what his plans are, so I can recommend him when work is offered."

"And that's all?"

"Well...sometimes it's helpful for him to know what's going on. That way he doesn't get into difficult situations by mistake."

A couple of men entered the bar, and Aleria straightened. "You go tend your paying customers. Tell Geran I'm looking for him and I'll drop in once in a while to check with you. Is that all right?"

"Oh, certainly, Miss Aleria. He'll be glad to help."

"Right. And Geran calls me Aleria."

"Yes, but my father wants me to be polite to the customers, Miss Aleria."

"Whatever keeps the boss happy. See you in a couple of days." She strolled out while Juli moved over to serve her clients. *So we have a little information gathering service operating right under our noses. Very interesting. Perhaps very useful.*

7.   Plots and Plans

There was a message waiting when Aleria and her father returned home from the yard three days later. It was brief and to the point. Raif anCanah requested a meeting with "Representatives of Dalmyn Cartage," to discuss "a project of mutual interest."

Aleria glanced at the paper – plain newsprint, no heading, no seal – then looked back to her father. "You gentlemen move fast when it suits you."

"There is no use letting this problem fester. Any day with no one out there might be the day it blows open on us."

"So, when am I leaving?"

"How should I know?" He grinned. "I'm not the wagonmaster."

"Huh. And I'm supposed to think that means I'm really in charge."

He put a hand on her shoulder, spun her to face him. "Never doubt you're in charge, Aleria. You'll be far enough out that any help will be several days away. Nobody expects you to follow detailed orders in circumstances we can't predict."

"I wouldn't have it any other way. When shall we invite our partner in crime to come and plan this caper?"

"As it happens, he is available late tomorrow morning. Why doesn't he meet us here?"

She narrowed her eyes. "I can't be in charge if I don't know what's going on behind the scenes."

He held up his hands in defence. "There's nothing going on. He mentioned it when we spoke yesterday. Now I know why. A thorough man, your Raif."

"I never complained about that. Other things, yes."

"Less lately, I notice."

"That's true. Marriage has mellowed him. I only need to hone him up once a month, now."

"Since this is officially for Dalmyn Cartage, I will answer." He picked up a plain note pad, scribbled, "Here, at the time we discussed, would be convenient," and signed it.

She slipped it from the table, folded it twice and strode through the passageway to the kitchen area. Two of the lads were polishing silver. She chose Milt, the fastest and most reliable, and handed him the message. "Deliver personally to Raif anCanah or Lady Mito."

He gave a sharp bow, and the paper disappeared into his sash. "Right away, M'Lady."

"Quick as usual," she held up a cautioning hand, "but no need to attract attention."

He grinned, nodded and darted away.

* * *

Raif showed up the next morning on a fine hunter that needed several more miles of run before he settled for the day. The young lord reined in until the horse stood still, then he dismounted and passed the lines to the stable boy. "He's a bit frisky. No harm in him." He watched the horse's feet dance. "Unless he steps on you."

The boy checked the quick-moving hooves, keeping his sandaled feet well out of the way. "He'll be fine, M'Lord." The boy shot a quick grin to Raif. "I hope I will be."

Raif chuckled and laid a hand on the horse's neck, stroking until it settled once more. "There you go, lad. The rest is up to you."

"Whose horse?"Aleria took his arm as they strolled into the house.

He shrugged. "He was supposed to be for Mito, but he's pretty frisky."

"He calms quickly. I'm sure she can handle him."

"Yes...well, we'll have to see."

She glanced at him, but he stared straight ahead. *Hmm. I wonder...*

"Father's waiting in his office. Anyone else needed?"

"Not at the moment. We'll want the other leaders once they're chosen."

Once again it didn't seem the time for questions, so she let that one ride, too.

Her father rose to greet Raif, and they sat around the low coffee table at the opposite end of the office from his desk. A servant brought in tea and a selection of cakes. Aleria sipped but ignored the dainties.

Finally, she looked around. "Shall we call this meeting to order?"

Raif glanced at her father, then nodded. "Your mission in general is already set. The path? It should follow an accepted cartage route, so I defer to you."

Aleria realized that her father wasn't going to answer. "We are discussing a new line out of Oudonsford, making a northern circle along the curve of the river, down the Trench and through our little battleground. Or the reverse, first through Newsom to the Trench, then back north along the river again."

Her father nodded. "It could be a profitable route if those border skirmishers would stop their squabbling for long enough to make a decent business of their demesnes. I suggest you take the southern route and get to the trouble spot quicker. There's nobody important on the river back to Oudonsford."

Raif nodded. "A sound plan. I agree with hitting those two first."

Aleria frowned. "I don't want to jump ahead, but it already seems to me that Lexing is the problem."

"I don't like the man much, but we can't let personal animosity affect our diplomatic efforts." Raif shrugged. "Newsom has not been easy to get along with, either. You might almost forgive Lexing looking for an edge."

Kensel raised a finger. "And farther south, up the Trench? I only met anLlannon once. Seemed a reasonable sort, though a bit strange. I've heard they keep the lore of the Old Ones alive, up there. Not a peaceable legacy."

"I've been checking." Raif shook his head. "Nothing. They 'keep themselves to themselves,' as folks put it."

"So Llannon is still an unknown quantity?" Aleria got nods from both. "Mother gave me some background on Lady Llannon. Apparently Lord Llannon is of the bookish sort. We have anything else about him?"

Her father's face brightened. "Yes, that sounds familiar. He managed to marry into an old family from the Capital. Before my time, but I seem to recall that she was quite the lady in her day. Gave a lilt to the gossip when she married and went off to the mountains."

"That jibes with what Mother said. So my route is chosen?"

Kensel nodded. "Your crew can do the next run upriver to Oudonsford. At least that's profitable. Once we move into the hinterland it's a more iffy financial proposition, but you often take a loss to get started in a new enterprise."

Raif grinned. "If you're angling for an advantage, His Majesty would look favourably on any supply route that passed through the training base at Decker."

"Any goods for the Royal Army would be handled with the utmost discretion and care."

"As they would need to be."

The older lord raised a warning hand. "Any dangerous goods must be properly labeled and crated. And there's a surcharge."

Raif laughed aloud. "You'll have to deal with the Royal Quartermasters on that. I'm sure they will be very thorough."

"Enough merchantery." Aleria sat back and regarded them. "What's next?

"Details can be worked out later." Raif nodded. "Now. Crew?"

Aleria glanced at her father, then spoke. "Any reason for change to the usual components? Wagonmaster, guard Captain, lead teamster, drivers, a few extra guards."

Both men nodded, and she thought some more. "If we're going into wilder country farther from help, let's borrow from the caravans. I want my guard Captain ahorse. Another mounted scout would be helpful." When no one interjected, she continued.

"We need be sure of our crew for this trip. The teamsters must be solid, experienced, and good fighters. The guards the same. But if it came to a choice, in this situation loyalty might be more important than fighting ability."

Her father nodded. "Couldn't agree more. Who do you want?"

"I get to choose?"

He grinned. "Most wagonmasters take that for granted."

"Yes, but these are special circumstances. I'm new at this, and I don't want the added trouble of breaking in a new crew. Erlon?"

"Don't know the man." Raif raised his eyebrows. "Is he one of your regulars?"

"He was with me on my last little junket and did excellent work. He's rather large and quite frightening when he swings that big sword of his. Often scares off the bandits before they get near the wagons."

"Loyalty?"

She deferred to her father.

"He has only been with us a few years, but he did well with Roeble on our first venture across the mountains. I took Erlon's report after this last trip, and he has a high opinion of Aleria's handling of the situation. I think he's our man."

"Good. Lead driver – Maddoes?"

"He's brighter than he lets on. I suppose you noticed."

She grinned. "He doesn't even try to fool me. And his family has been in our service for generations."

Raif nodded. "It sounds like the makings of a close-knit crew. The others?"

"We can discuss the drivers with Maddoes later, but we'll need Erlon to help choose the guards. He should also be part of the rest of the planning."

"How convenient." Her father waved a hand to the servant who stood at the door, and the man disappeared.

"Let me guess." She frowned. "You already knew I would choose him, and he just happens to be waiting outside."

She could see the guilt on their faces, so she favoured each with his portion of her glare. "Don't worry. I have decided there is no use getting angry. Until I find more worthy partners, I have to put up with you two. However, if one day I decide to throw over the traces and become a bandit queen, defying all authority, remember that you share the responsibility!"

Their grins were cut short by the appearance of Erlon at the door. Kensel waved him in.

It was the first time Aleria had ever seen him in anything but swordsman's leathers. The shape of the business jacket slimmed him down and sharpened his figure. *Hmm. He cleans up nicely. Too bad...*

"Glad you could be here, Erlon. You don't know Raif Dalmyn, do you?"

Erlon strode in and sat on the indicated chair with a formal nod to Raif. "Your reputation precedes you, my Lord."

Raif raised his eyebrows. "If my reputation came through Aleria, I'm not sure that's a good thing."

"My hat may sit at a slant, my Lord. I shall try to keep an open mind."

"I appreciate the effort."

Aleria leaned forward. "It's somewhat complicated, Erlon. As you can tell from this meeting, we are not on a simple hauling job. We are acting as emissaries for his Majesty. As such, our guards are in one respect under military command. Raif is our senior officer and our contact with the Royal Army. Since the training camp at Decker is our closest source of aid, it might be smart to keep on the good side of those with epaulettes on their shirts."

"An intelligent course of action. But in another respect?"

"Once we are on the road we are Dalmyn Cartage under our own command and we act as we deem necessary."

Erlon leaned back, gave both Kensel and Raif a calculating look. "I can live with that. I have every confidence in Dalmyn leadership. If they trust the Royal Army, how can I bet on the other bird?"

Raif snorted. "Never been a regular soldier, have you?"

"Can't say as the need ever arose."

"If you get along well with Aleria, that's as it should be. I've dealt with irregulars before. The Royal Army can benefit from working with independent thinkers. Hence this expedition."

"Good enough." Aleria thought a moment. "We can choose the guards later, because we need the rosters to find out who is available at short notice. Raif, I'd like Erlon to hear your opinion on the type of intervention that would be appropriate from the military's point of view. And his Majesty's."

"I brought the rosters from the yard."

"We'll do that after Raif is finished." She looked at the young lord. He gave a private grin at something and began to outline the criteria for the expedition, its goals and the problems he had discussed with Aleria earlier. Soon both her father and Erlon were interjecting comments, and the conversation rolled between the four of them for some time.

Once Raif seemed satisfied, she brought the meeting to a close. "That is enough for me. I want time to think. Erlon and I will check the rosters and we'll talk to the guards tomorrow. They need a small amount of information about the nature of our assignment, Raif, but you can't brief them. It would be very unusual procedure for anyone but Erlon or me to discuss details of the run. You'll have to trust us not to give them too much information."

He smiled and said nothing.

"Oh, one more detail I should clear with you. We should tell anNewsom about the guns. We owe him the truth. He's sitting out there thinking they're still on the way somewhere, and he's getting more and more nervous. Nervous people cause trouble."

Raif nodded. "I won't argue with that."

"So if he finds out in a subtle way that the contraband was dealt with and that I'm on my way to give him more information, he'll be less likely to start any preventative action."

Raif glanced at her father, who nodded, then back to her.

"And you have a way to get him that information? It can't be anything official."

"I think so."

"Ah. Your soldier friend."

"Right. He has a contact the city."

"It could help calm things down. I trust you not to tell anybody anything they shouldn't know."

"Thank you, Raif. I'll take that as a compliment. Anything else?"

"Yes, one more thing. In the king's opinion, the letter of marque changes your role slightly. He has requested that you take a message from him, to be delivered to whom ever you think needs it."

"The king requests, does he? What is the message?"

"Nothing specific. Simply the observation that his attention has been drawn to the troubles in the area, and that you are only his first response."

"That's it?"

"It is. You are to spread that message as you see fit."

She glanced at her father. *This is going to change things.*

The elder Dalmyn met her eyes and nodded slowly. "And Aleria may choose the recipients of this message?"

"As she sees fit. It isn't an unusual point of view, and not much of a threat. It could be useful."

"But it might reduce my information gathering role."

"It might, so I assume you will use it sparingly." Raif dusted his hands together. "So that's it? Any further discussion?"

He and her father shook their heads, and they all rose. After a few more pleasantries Raif left, and the remaining three looked at each other.

"Will you stay and give your opinion on the men, Father?"

"You want me to?"

"You haven't taken them on the road, but you know most of them and their families. I'm not stupid enough to miss out on a source like that, just to exert my independence."

"Fair enough. Roll out that roster, Erlon."

Their heads came together over the chart, and Aleria started a list. It didn't take long, since they all agreed on the crew. After a while, they sat back, satisfied.

"So the only one we haven't chosen is the outrider."

Her father nodded. "That's a problem. There are no mounted guards on staff. We don't need them inside Galesia. Many of our guards are competent enough ahorse, but that's not their primary skill. Because of the loyalty factor, I don't want to bring in one of the mercenary cavalry we hire when we go outside the realm. I wish there was someone we could trust. A family member or one of our allies."

Aleria shrugged. "We're not leaving for a few days. Let's keep our eyes open and see what comes up. Any ideas, Father?"

"I'll send out a few feelers. Someone we trust will have someone he trusts sitting around."

"That's our best bet. Erlon, leave that roster with me. We'll meet at the yard tomorrow and talk to any of these," she waved the list, "who are around."

"Right, boss." He grinned and rose, stretching his arms over his head. His hands almost touched the ceiling. "See you at the yard tomorrow." He nodded to Kensel as he left. "My Lord."

After he had gone, she glanced over at her father. "What do you think?"

"It seems the basis for a good crew."

"It has to be." Her lips tightened. "I need all the help I can get."

"You do, and that's no reflection on your ability. One reason we are involved in this operation is that Dalmyn can field a competent crew for any enterprise."

Gordon A. Long

Aleria shook her head. "The crew isn't a problem. It's the leadership that worries me."

Her father looked at her a moment. Then he stepped forward and grasped her upper arms. "As it should."

She raised her eyebrows.

"That's right. Every leader going out on every expedition worries." He turned her and walked alongside, one arm over her shoulders. "But you're not talking about that kind of worry. The best balance is when you are sure of your abilities and only worry about the unpredictable. However, someone just starting out cannot be that sure, and I am happy that you are not. I don't want the old Aleria, roaring in full of confidence. I want a thoughtful, concerned wagonmaster who is clear on the responsibilities of her job."

She looked up at him. "But there are plenty of wagonmasters on the payroll with far more experience than me. Why not one of them?"

"All the political reasons. There are many men who could take on this duty, Aleria, but while they have more experience, there are few who could be given the inside political knowledge you have. Of those, none has your reliability."

"Reliability!" As they entered the family sitting room she pulled away from him and threw herself into her lounger. "That's not a word that is often paired with my name."

Her father grinned as he took his chair. "Not that kind of reliability. Loyalty."

"Oh, that."

"Yes, that. Don't underestimate it."

"I realize that it is far the best for Dalmyn if we solve this problem. The king will be happy. Your customers in the North will be happy. You have already been as good as promised a lucrative Royal Army contract." She sat up. "But Father, those are all your good reasons for sending me. They don't mean I'm any more able to do the job."

He shrugged. "I have made my living by knowing who to trust and by my skill at assigning the right person to the right task. I should think I'm getting good at it by now. In my opinion you are the right person. Perhaps you should trust me to know what I am doing."

"Oh, I trust you. I'm not sure I trust me."

"Are you working up to telling me that you aren't going?"

"No. No, I'm not going to quit on you. I just don't want to disappoint you. I don't think I could bear that."

He got up and came over to sit on the lounger beside her, taking her hand. "I'm not worried you will disappoint me. I don't want you to disappoint yourself. No one expects one hundred percent success on this trip. It's far too complex a problem for one person, any person, to solve. I want you go out and study the area for further expansion of our routes. The king wants you to investigate the political trouble and refine our knowledge of the situation. You don't have to solve the problem. Nobody has been able to do that for a hundred years or more. Don't even think about going that far."

"Hmm. Maybe I had too high an opinion of myself. So my assignment is to complete the route, get what information I can and come back with my crew intact and my horses still pulling. I can do that."

"Yes, you can. Anything more would be extra. Don't try too hard for extra..."

"...because that's where failure lies. Got it. Thanks, Father. I guess you really do know how to run a business."

"And you're only finding that out now? Thanks."

"I'm experiencing it now. It's different."

8. Lavan

Aleria was intrigued to receive a note from Roeble Cloete, asking her to meet him at the tea-shop before training the following day. Now that he was an important ally of her family, she dressed more appropriately than her usual pre-training garb, in a mid-calf skirt with matching blouse. When she entered the room, he raised his eyebrows, nodded in appreciation and held her chair for her. Then he sat, took a deep breath and came straight to business. "Aleria, I have a large favour which I'm not sure I should ask of you."

She thought of a quick retort to this strangely worded request, but he was serious, so she answered in the same vein. "We have been over the mountain together, Roeble. You can ask."

"Well..." He shrugged. "Here goes. It's my wife's nephew."

He seemed so uncomfortable that she had to grin. "What? You want me to marry him? Is he handsome?"

He smiled in chagrin. "I'm not handling this very well. I stay away from actions that don't feel right, but this is family pressure, and..." He spread his hands.

"Family pressure." She nodded. "Fair enough. You have to ask me. Ask me. If I don't like it, I'll say, 'No,' and you can go home and tell them with a clear conscience that you tried. We needn't chase around the coffee table like bashful lovers."

He burst into laughter. "Aleria, your way of expressing yourself..." Then he sobered. "It's my nephew, Lavan. He thinks he's a swordsman. He wants to be a caravan guard."

"Ah. But you can't take him out on one of your long trips, because...?"

His shoulders rolled uncomfortably. "Well...I don't know about him."

"Hmmm. Not trustworthy?"

"No, it's not that. I've known him all his life, and I don't have enough distance to make a decision."

"Well, you're not exactly persuading me to take him, are you?"

"No, I'm not." He shrugged. "In this business you need to trust every man you carry. I don't want to saddle you with a problem. But your father says you need someone..."

"If he's that bad, why are you even asking?"

"Because he may not be."

She grinned again. "This young fellow really has you twisted around. I just have to meet someone who could mess up the incisive mind of Roeble the Merchant Prince."

He did not respond to her levity. "Would you? You don't want to reject him out of hand?"

"Roeble, you wouldn't be asking if he didn't have some worth, would you?"

"No, no, that's right. He is a very decent sword. Kensel's note mentioned a rider. He won quite a bit of silver in the King's Trophy last year. He's polite, he's easy to get along with, he's enthusiastic, he's unquestionably loyal, he's..."

"So maybe you really do want me to marry him."

"Huh. That would be the end of my problem, but the start of yours."

"I'll talk to him. Send him around. Oh. And you can do me a favour in return."

"Good. I like to even things out."

"Erlon. He's hired to Captain the guards on my next run. He went out with you that first caravan to Aesmark. The one I didn't go on."

"That he did."

"Anything to note? What is he? Who is he?"

The merchant shrugged. "An experienced caravan guard."

"And...?"

"A good soldier and a ferocious fighter. I recommended that your father promote him the moment we got back."

"What else? Come on, Roeble. Merchants are supposed to be able to read people."

He grinned. "What do you know already?"

"He's Galesian, I suppose. He has no accent when he speaks. But...no, his voice has a singsong quality, and he uses a lot of strange expressions. I thought it was just his way, but maybe it's from his heritage somewhere. If that matters any. What do you think of him as a person?"

"He gets along well with everyone. I don't see him as any kind of disturbing element in the crew. Don't know how it will translate into giving orders, but he's competent."

"Weapons? Fighting methods? I've only seen him in a real fight once."

"That hand-and-a-half sword of his is straight out of a museum, but the weapon looks new, so he had it made specially. Can't comment on his style, because the weapon creates it. Outside the realm he carries a bow."

"I've seen it." She thought back. "Seems small for a man his size."

"It has to be. You can't climb around the mountains and dive through the jungle with a longbow. Gets in the way."

"Mountains? I thought he came from Shaeldit."

He nodded. "Yes, but his mother was Loatan. When they married, the father's family disowned him, so he went to live with her people in the hill country out south of Shaeldit. That's where Erlon was born, brought up and trained. Hence the bow. And a lot of other things that you wouldn't notice until you went up against him, and then it would be too late."

"Like the fact that he's a crack shot with a rifle." She thought a moment. "I thought the Loatans were a short people. Short and broad."

"I suppose that's why he's so wide in the shoulders."

"I suppose." She glanced at him. "You went into some strange situations out in Aesmark. Loyalty?"

"Rock solid. Aesmark always means bribery, threats and inducements, but he never wavered. Mature behaviour for a young blade, I thought."

"Fair enough."

"Does that help?"

She grinned. "I guess I'll be finding out more."

"I hope the surprises are all good."

"So do I. You have to trust somebody."

"And your guard Captain would come first on a trip like this one."

"Precisely."

Roeble finished his drink and rose. "Well, back to training, I suppose. You and I must stop frequenting tea shops together. Word might get around."

"Bring your wife next time."

He didn't smile. "She'd enjoy that. She has little contact with the men, but she wants to understand what I do. Another woman..."

"Good enough. She can invite me around to tea when I get back."

"Fine." He pushed his chair back. "Let's go see what tortures our dear Master has invented for us today."

"I hope they're entertaining. Then I can inflict them on my guards for the next month."

* * *

The following afternoon Juli's head came around the moment Aleria entered The Falcon. She said nothing, but her glance slid to a table in the corner by the window, where two men were sitting. The girl made a drinking motion, but Aleria shook her head and strolled towards the men. "Any battles lately, Geran?"

The lad jumped to his feet, and his companion, after some hesitation, did likewise.

"Oh...hello, Aleria." He grinned. "No, I've been keeping out of trouble..." He glanced at the other man, who nodded and slipped away.

Aleria took the vacated chair. "Somebody I shouldn't meet?"

"Oh, no. Our business was finished, and I knew you'd want privacy."

"Speaking of privacy," she leaned her elbows on the table. ""It seems you have a willing ear." She motioned with her head towards the bar.

A red stain creept up the young soldier's neck. "Oh. Well, I gotta tell Juli what's going on..."

"She told me. So you trust her?"

"She's never let me down."

"Fine. Then she should hear this, too." She caught the barmaid's attention, waved her to join them. When they were seated together she looked into the eyes of each. "Now, this goes to no one else. I'm trusting you, Juli, because Geran was very helpful to me recently, and I'm hoping that both of you will continue to be."

Their eyes met, and both nodded. *They know what I'm asking.*

"Good. Geran, has there been any more trouble of the kind we had?"

"Not a whisper. We've been patrolling, but there's been nothing. I guess that shipment we were looking for was a false alarm."

"Not exactly. You don't need the details, but could you take a message to Lord Newsom? The old man himself, not that firebrand son of his."

"Of course."

"Tell him he can relax about that shipment, because it has been handled."

"He'll be glad to hear that."

"You think so?"

Geran grinned. "Well, if he can't get his hands on it, I suppose he'll be happy no one else gets it either."

She nodded. "Also tell him I'll be visiting soon, and I can give him more information. For the moment, if he could keep things calm in his neighbourhood, there are those who would be grateful."

The soldier frowned. "And who might 'those' be?"

"I'm sure you can figure that out for yourself, and so can he. Tell him."

His face cleared, and he nodded. "I'm to tell him that the shipment was taken care of and that you're coming out to talk to him about it. Till you get there, the higher-ups will look kindly on those who keep things under control."

"I couldn't have said it better. Juli, do you understand?"

"Nothin' unusual there." The barmaid shrugged. "You're gonna meet with Geran's boss. Nobody wants fightin'." She grinned. "Nobody told me nothin' important."

"True. I can see you have great discretion."

"But what do you want me to keep my ears open for?"

Aleria glanced at the girl. "Nothing at the moment. Of course, we're always interested in word of any unrest, any serious complaints. Would it be worth my while to drop in for a chat the odd time?"

"You never know. I might pick up something of interest."

Aleria nodded. "We'll leave it at that." *Hmm. I wonder what kind of payment...*

"And then you can do me...us a favour."

"If I can."

"Well, Geran isn't gonna make any advancement playin' hide and seek out there in the mountains. Sure, it's good experience, but we want him to get ahead. Get a position of responsibility."

"A position not so likely to get him killed?"

"That would help, but he's not gonna duck his duty because of that."

"Of course not. But I can't help you there. Not at the moment." She stared into Geran's disappointed eyes. "It wouldn't look good. You can't go jumping from one side to the other. You're in a delicate enough situation right now. AnNewsom knows that you're a friend of mine. If we run up against each other, he'll see you for a potential traitor. So I can't show you any preference at the moment."

"And he wouldn't be any use to you if you did."

She glanced at Juli. *She really does have the boy's interest in mind.* "That's true. I don't want him to turn down other work to stay there on my account. As I said, I can't be secretly putting him on the Dalmyn payroll while he's working for Newsom. That could lead to all sorts of unpleasantness."

"But I can tell you what will work." She turned back to the soldier. "Get a reputation as a reliable, loyal man. Everything you have done so far has been to your employer's benefit, so you're in the clear, there. Get a reputation for finishing what you start. You handled that situation out in Newsom very well. That means I'll back you if anyone asks. But I can't hire you at the moment. In the future...?"

"Thanks, Aleria, I guess that's the best I could expect."

"I wish I could do more."

"Maybe the time will come."

"I hope it does." She grinned. "There is one thing you can do for me." She turned to the girl. "I've got a political problem, Juli."

"A political problem? How can I help?"

"Well, I want to reward Geran for a service, but it wouldn't be a good idea for him to receive anything from me." She slid two coins across the table. "So what if you take a couple of crowns and buy yourself a nice present?"

"A present for me...? Oh. Right." She turned to the puzzled lad. "Geran, you are such a sweetheart! I've been just dying for one of those new silk kerchiefs down at the market." She jumped up and rewarded him with a smacking kiss. The coins disappeared from the table as she moved.

He was quick to respond to the caress, but he stared at Aleria, then the girl and his frown cleared. "Oh. Yes, you're welcome, Juli. I worked hard for that present, so I hope you enjoy it." He glanced at Aleria, and a twinkle appeared in his eye. "I did mention that she would look beautiful in one of those scarves."

"Watch out for him, Juli. He's a flatterer as well."

"It's only flattery if it ain't true." The barmaid bumped his shoulder with her hip. "So I'm assumin' it's true. Right Geran?"

"Oh, yes, my Lady. Would I say it, otherwise?"

Aleria laughed. "There. All my problems solved, yours just beginning." She rose, gave them a casual wave, and turned away. She had a few other errands to run.

* * *

Lavan turned up the following afternoon. He breezed into the wagonyard and charmed the clerk at the front desk into bringing him back to Aleria's office without asking her first.

She looked up from her work. He was slim, not much taller than she was. Olive skin stretched thin on a fine-boned face. *Yes, the girls would like this one.* She rose and checked him over, ignoring his big, friendly smile.

"And you would be Lavan Auswand."

"Aleria AnDalmyn. I finally get to meet you. This is just so wonderful!"

"Well, it's good to meet you, too, Lavan. Your uncle has told me a bit about you."

He grimaced. "Most of it bad, I suppose."

"Now, why would you think that?"

"Oh, let's say that he's known me all my life, but I've also known him for a similar length of time. What he doesn't realize is that his prejudices have played into my hands in this case."

"Have they." She sat and motioned him to do the same.

He leaned forward, his hands clasped together. "Most definitely! You see, I want to go out on the caravans. I want to earn my sword the right way. I have no problem with work, Lady Dalmyn. I can ride all day in the heat. I can fight on foot, on horseback, with sword or spear. I'm a good bowman, if we're going outside the realm.

"But have you any idea how hard it is to get a position, a real guard position on a caravan, not just babysitting the minor trains on the delivery runs? So the only way I could go out is with Uncle Roeble. What he doesn't realize is that I'd much rather go out with you!"

She looked for signs of a jest, but he seemed serious. "And why is that?"

"Because you're Aleria anDalmyn. You're the one that faced Lord Fauvée in his own manor and killed those five bandits who were terrorizing the countryside..."

"Well...that's not exactly..."

But he rode right over her objection. "...and you're the one who smashed the statues in the Temple grounds." He sat back and stared at her with satisfaction.

"I did what?"

He grinned. "Don't worry, I haven't told anyone. But it was obvious. Once things calmed down and the Artists Guild had a chance to look at those statues, everyone realized that they were Mechanical-made copies that someone had planted, then smashed up to make a protest. They thought it was the Artist apprentices or students at the University. I knew better. So I did some checking. People...chat with me."

"Well, that's an interesting theory." She turned her mouth down. "I'm glad you show an inventive mind. And you say you haven't taken advantage of your perspicacity to spread this little gem around?"

He shook his head so hard she thought he would injure his neck. "Oh, no, Lady Dalmyn. That would spoil the fun."

"And also you weren't too sure. It would be very difficult persuading anyone that a schoolgirl could pull off a stunt like that. Those were heavy statues."

"You and a few friends. The Dennal Twins? Mito anTrus?"

She had him by the throat, his chair tipped back against the wall before he could draw a triumphant breath. She shook him twice. "If you mention Lady Mito anCannah in the same breath as any touch of scandal, there will be a large line of people waiting for a chance to tear little pieces out of you. Her husband, Lord Raif anCannah, will be second behind me. Do I make myself clear?"

She shook him again and let his feet back to the floor.

He rubbed his throat ruefully, but seemed unabashed. "Well, that confirms several theories."

She took a threatening step forward. "Such as?"

"No, I'll keep my ideas to myself." He grinned. "Please believe me, I always have, and your reaction proves me right. And I will remove Lady anCannah from any speculation. I always liked her, anyway."

He glanced at her. "Not that I didn't always like you, as well. I mean your reputation. It's just that..."

She sighed. "Don't bother to explain. Everybody always likes her. I don't expect everyone to like me, so you're safe." She shot him another threatening look. "As long as you keep your wild theories to yourself. Not that I'm admitting anything. It seems a harebrained idea to me, and I doubt if anyone would believe you anyway. I just don't like gossip."

His face changed, one eyebrow rising. "In spite of what it has done for your reputation? I would think you'd be quite pleased with gossip."

She thought a moment. "Gossip can be a useful tool, I admit. In general, though, it's useless, and at the worst it can be downright destructive."

"I must agree with you, there. Like any good tool or weapon. In the right hands, essential. Wielded by fools..." He shrugged expressively.

Aleria considered this turn of conversation. *There seems to be more to this youth than at first appears.* "So, why should I take you on?"

His face took on a glow. "Why? Because I can handle it. I can take care of myself in any situation, and help my fellows at the same time. I am going to be a famous fighter, and I will bring nothing but glory to the Dalmyn name. I'm a good bowman, an experienced pikeman and I'm far above average with my sword." He slapped the fancy bronze hilt at his side.

"Far above average?"

He grinned, shrugged. "That's what all my instructors said."

"Hmm. I think you'll find that proficiency on the practice floor doesn't always translate into ability in battle."

"Oh, I know about that. I've prepared myself for the reality of battle."

"Have you?"

"Of course. You must develop the right mental attitude. You must practice how you're going to feel, so that when the real fear and horror hits you, you're ready for it."

"And you can do that?"

"Of course. It just takes concentrated practice."

"Hmm. Well, that's an interesting theory. I'll be intrigued to find out what happens when it comes face to face with reality."

His face brightened. "Does that mean you'll take me on?"

"I will. There's a specific position as outrider. The first part of this trip is routine, up the road to Oudonsford, and we can work you into the group without too much trouble. How are your riding skills...?" She sighed and waved off his enthusiastic response. "Top marks in your riding classes."

"Is there anything wrong with that?"

"No, no, Roeble did mention your riding."

"I have my own horses. Trained both of them myself. Very surefooted and fast."

"That's a bonus. We'll pay the usual stipend for them, with extra if they're as good as you say. You'll fit in with the lads with no problem. We do a lot of training on the road, so before we get into any real need, you'll have time to learn our methods."

He jumped up and grasped her hand. "That's wonderful, Lady Dalmyn. I'll make sure you aren't sorry, believe me."

She retrieved her hand, tingling from the pressure. "You realize that this is just a minor train on a delivery run?"

He grinned. "Oh, if you're going along, I'm thinking it might turn out to be more than that, my Lady."

"That's fine then, Lavan, and now that you're hired on, you can call me Aleria like the rest of the men do."

"Thank you again, Aleria." He drew himself up. "I swear I will perform my duties to the best of my ability, and beyond."

Once again she searched for any sign of irony, to no avail. "Well, that's it. Bring your duffle and your horses to the Dalmyn Yard tomorrow morning. We have a barracks there and a simple training ground. We leave in three days, so that will give you a chance to get to know everyone, find out what to carry, that sort of thing."

She stretched out her hand, ready this time for the crushing grip, but he restrained his enthusiasm and only grasped it firmly. "Thank you again, Aleria. I'll be there with bells on."

"Yes, well, forget the bells, and just bring your sword."

He thought about responding, but then he grinned, spun with a soldier's about-face and strode out, his scabbard bruising two desks on the way.

Aleria sat watching the door shiver into stillness. She nodded to herself. If he hadn't been family, Roeble wouldn't have thought twice about taking him. She'd seen the type before. *Nothing wrong that the lads and the road won't dust out of him in a month or so.*

It occurred to her that while Roeble was too careful to trust a favoured nephew as a guard, her father would trust her with the reputation of the Dalmyn family. She wondered which one was right.

9.   As if It Isn't Obvious

As Aleria was following the servant through the meandering halls of the anCannah city mansion the next day, she saw a familiar figure approaching. When the Duke reached her, she dropped in a full curtsey.

"Oh, get up, Aleria. You only play that game when you want something."

"Not this time, my Lord. Just trying not to be predictable."

The duke flicked his fingertips at the servant, who bowed and faded away. "So, since I find you roaming the halls of my family retreat, am I allowed to ask what brings you here?"

She shrugged. "Mito and Raif wanted to ask me something. I was rather surprised myself. Any idea what it's all about?" She glanced over at him. "You always know what's going on."

"Not this time, I'm afraid."

"I'm sure I'll find out soon enough. Whatever the two of them have cooked up, it's bound to be entertaining."

The hallway they were strolling along opened into a large reception room with pools of seating arrangements spaced along it. The Duke nodded to a pair of chairs, and they sat.

"This is your fault, you know."

She regarded him. "It is, my Lord?"

"Oh, yes. Part of it was involuntary, of course. Your meeting with Raif, and everything that followed. But when I think of the stupid things I might have done, trying to find Raif a lady of appropriate stature...well, you foiled all my plans. And look at the result."

"Like her, do you?"

He shook his head and grinned at her. *Yes, the Duke of anCannah is definitely grinning.* "I won't say this to anyone else, but it's a good thing he got to her first."

The comment was so unexpected that Aleria burst into laughter before she considered.

"And why is that so funny? Does the old man seem so inappropriate?"

She shook her head and held up her hand to forestall a response until she had control of herself. "No, my Lord. This is something I can't really say to anyone else either, but on their wedding day I expressed the thought that I might find an alliance with you to be interesting."

"You were interested in marrying me?"

"I was joking, my Lord."

"Again I fail to see the humour."

"Nothing to do with you, my Lord. It was the concept of Mito having me for a mother-in-law."

"Now that, I can laugh at."

He proceeded to do so. Aleria caught his mood and joined in.

There was one of those, "Why haven't you noticed me?" coughs in the doorway. They looked up to see Raif regarding them uncertainly.

"Do come in, dear boy. Don't stand there like a clumsy girl at a ball."

"Thank you, Father. I did not want to intrude."

"Not at all. The lady and myself were only discussing various marriage possibilities."

Raif frowned in puzzlement. "Who is she marrying?"

The Duke reached out his hand, and she laid her fingers in it delicately, simpering up at him. He gazed at her and raised her hand to his lips. Then they both looked at Raif.

His eyes were wide, his mouth gaping.

He glanced at her. She glanced at him. They could not contain themselves. They broke into laughter again.

Finally, they wound down. The Duke mopped his brow. "We have found a family joke that will never grow old."

"Mito and I are in the west drawing room when you're finished this stage rehearsal." Raif put his hand to his face and walked away, shaking his head.

His father sighed and rose. "Ah, the young have no sense of humour. Present company excepted."

She dropped him the usual proper curtsey. "Have I your leave to continue to my appointment?"

He clicked his heels. "If we're going to find out what's happening I suppose you must. It is always a pleasure to chat with you, my Lady. You know the route?"

"I should by now, my Lord." She waited until he turned away, then strode towards Raif and Mito's private sitting room.

As she entered, Aleria regarded the two of them. They looked posed for a portrait: Mito perched on an ornate teak chair, her husband standing behind her, his hands protectively on her shoulders. She grinned. *So that's it. About time.* "What's the big mystery?"

"Aleria, we'd like you to come for dinner on Feastday."

"Love to. I'm on the road the next morning, but can start the trip with a hangover. Anything special?"

"Well..." she glanced up at Raif. "It's an important affair with the family and I...need some moral support."

"So it's the big day, then."

"Pardon?"

"The day you tell them the happy news."

She chuckled as Raif's mouth dropped open. Mito sighed.

Raif frowned. "You already told her."

"Of course I didn't."

"But..."

Aleria got control of her voice. "Raif, when was the last time we had an argument, let alone a fight?"

"Let me see..."

"Don't bother. It's been two months. Even before I went on the last trip. Mito has been positively broody since I got back, and you haven't let her out of your sight. And then the horse she can't ride? She's pregnant."

"Yes, she is."

"Wonderful!" She pulled her friend up off the lounge for a hug.

"Careful!"

Aleria grinned at Raif and reached out to slap his shoulder. "Don't worry. She's tough as nails." She looked down at Mito.

74

"You are, aren't you? No problems or..." she waved an uncertain hand, "...I don't know."

"No, I'm fine. It's good to have someone who doesn't treat me like a piece of crystal." She reached up and ran a finger down her husband's cheek. "Not that I don't enjoy it, of course."

"What names have you chosen...? I caught that look. Well, let me give you a hint, my friend. Don't let him choose the name."

"Why not?"

"Take it from me. At least go for final veto. Did you check what his family's names are like?"

"Not really."

"Well, do your research. You'll see."

Raif took all this with aplomb. "My family's names are traditionally rather...traditional, I suppose. We'll discuss it."

"I'm sure you will. Now, I have a lot of things to do in the next two days, and you've just stolen my packing time. Have I your Lordship's permission to return to my work?"

"Of course, my Lady."

"Speaking of work, I solved the outrider problem."

"Who did you get?"

"A lad by the name of Lavan Auswand. Well trained and a good rider. Nephew of Roeble."

"Auswand. Didn't he compete in the King's Trophy Races last summer?"

"I gather he won a few."

"Young, isn't he?"

"He's a bright button, he has good sources of information and he has the discretion to keep what he learns to himself. He'll do fine."

"Good. The Cloetes are close allies, and if he messes up, Roeble will kill him."

"Why, Raif, I would never resort to threats."

Mito grinned. "You don't need to. There's always someone else who is willing."

Aleria made a turn around the room and glanced back over her shoulder. "Being young and pretty has its advantages. Men just keep wanting to protect me."

Raif laughed. "My observation has been that when you walk into the room, men start looking to protect themselves. But that's only one man's experience."

When their laughter died down, Raif stood. "You ladies will find things to discuss."

Aleria glanced up at him. "What makes you think we have anything to say that we don't want you to hear?"

He shrugged. "Maybe you have things to say that I don't want to hear?"

"Aha! So there are things you don't need to know!"

"Something like that." He took his wife's hand and gave it a kiss and a caress, winked at Aleria and strolled out.

The two women watched him go. A comfortable silence rolled over them. Aleria considered her friend, sitting so relaxed in the ornate chair, her clothing perfectly attuned to the style of the room and the time of day.

"It's a good thing you're my friend."

"I never thought otherwise," Mito raised her eyebrows, "but why is it so true at this specific moment?"

Aleria waved her hand around the room in general. "Because otherwise I might find myself drowning in jealousy."

"You? Jealous of me?"

"That's right. You have it all. Everything you and I talked about when we were in school. Rich, handsome, loving husband. Important duties – I talk to my mother. I know what you two are doing – now a family..."

"You could have had it."

"You mean I could have married Raif. Oh, certainly. Where would that have got me?" She leaned forward, her elbows on her knees. "I tell you what. You go through one day of your life. Everything you do, you ask yourself, 'Would Aleria enjoy doing this?' Not, 'Could Aleria do this?' Of course I could. But would I enjoy it? Would I get up in the morning looking forward to it?"

Mito grinned. "I don't have to waste a day to find the answer to that."

"Right. And it's not that you don't deserve it. You put up with a lot of hardship in order to become the person you are. That person happens to be the wife of a future duke, and you are the perfect gentlewoman."

"Which you are not."

"Which is the other reason I am not eaten up with jealousy at you." She stood and paced the room, swinging her hand towards the perfect décor. "I don't want or need what you have."

"But you want and need what I have in a different sense."

"That's right." She spun back to face her friend, sitting there so calmly. "What I need is your kind of satisfaction. Your kind of accomplishment."

"I doubt if that is what you need."

"You do?"

"That may be what you want. But how would you feel if the pattern of your life was set right now? Everything accomplished." Mito's hand described the same arc. "Your whole path settled, stretching out before you. How would you feel? Think about it."

Aleria thought about it. Her feet itched, and she strode the length of the room again. "I'd feel as if it was all over. I'd feel trapped, constrained. My existence would be a misery, and I'd make life a misery for everyone around me." She thought some more. "Which is what I've been doing with my life so far. Why change?"

Mito shook her head. "You're doing it again. You're letting on that it's so awful to be around you. As far as I can see, you've spent your life exploring and testing, and all it has done for your friends is make our lives more interesting by association. Aleria, you don't need the finished product. You need to want the finished product."

"You mean that what I need is the struggle to get somewhere. It doesn't matter where."

"It does matter where. It has to be somewhere important. But once you get there, you won't be happy for long. You'll run off to somewhere else important."

"Sounds like a formula for a life of unhappy, never-ending struggle."

"Sounds like a life of adventure and accomplishment."

Aleria put her face in her hands and sighed loudly through her fingers. Then she squared her shoulders and looked at Mito. "I suppose you're right, as usual." She turned and walked to the window."

"Aleria, sit down."

"What?"

"Sit down. Here." She motioned to the chair opposite her.

"But..."

"You're pacing around like a cat in a cage. What's going on?"

"Nothing." She plopped herself on the chair. "Tell me about your plans for the little one."

Mito smiled and shook her head. "My upcoming bliss is the last thing in the world you want to talk about. There will be plenty of time for that when we get closer to the date. Something is bothering you. Talk."

Aleria sighed. "It's this new mission into the Trench." She clenched her hands. "I'm absolutely terrified I'll do something stupid and bring my family into disrepute. With my luck, I'll start a war."

"Fine. So you'll be careful."

"Easy for you to talk."

"I'm not worried. You are one of the most dependable people I know."

Aleria half-rose. "What are you talking about?"

Her friend's gentle gesture pushed her back into the chair. "When you were younger, everybody expected you to get into mischief and stir everything up."

"And...?"

"And you never disappointed them. When you put your mind to something, it gets done. Not the way everyone expects, but it does get done."

Aleria slouched back in her chair. "Sounds like a great recommendation."

"But it is. I'm sure that's what your father and Raif and the king see in you. Someone who gets things done."

"I don't know. I suppose."

"I don't suppose. It's a given fact. But that's not what started this conversation. It was nothing to do with politics. Is something missing in your life?"

She shrugged. "Well, I watch you and Raif together, and I wish sometimes…."

"Nobody within bowshot at the moment?"

"No one at all. I was even tempted to get involved with Erlon during the last trip. It would have been a disaster."

Mito grinned. "But he has the most amazing muscles! Not bad looking either."

"Exactly. But it still would have been really stupid."

"So you did the right thing. Temptation is only a sin if you fall prey to it. You may be growing up."

"I'd better. This expedition is no place for childish pranks. I suppose I should take you as my example."

"Whatever for?"

"Well, you put up with trouble for years, never having what you wanted, and it paid off, didn't it? I've spent my girlhood having everything I wanted. Maybe I should put up with a bit of hardship for a change. It might pay off."

"It might. From personal experience, I don't recommend you go looking for it."

Aleria slapped her hands together and dusted them off. "And now that your husband has given me my orders, and you have straightened out my head, I'm ready for my mission." She stood to attention and saluted. "Thank you, Ma'am!"

Mito rose. "If it suits you to think that I was in any way assigned to do anything, you go right ahead. It should serve to remind you what a solid backing you have here in the Capital. Both personal and political. You go out there and do your best."

Aleria put an arm around her friend's shoulders. "And you can send Raif out to rescue me when everything falls apart."

Mito returned the hug. "Oh...I think maybe not this time."

Aleria felt a sense of determination flowing through her. "You're right. Not this time. My father thinks I can handle it and his Majesty thinks I can handle it. Hell, even Raif thinks I can handle it! Who am I to be the one holding back?"

Mito pushed her forward. "That's the old Aleria attitude. No weeping and wailing and being the victim. Go out there and lead your men to victory."

Aleria glanced back over her shoulder. "I think maybe I will." She turned and strode out of the beautiful room, down the elaborate hallway, and out into the real world.

10. Followed

Aleria swung up on the wagon seat beside the lead driver, stashing her pack beneath her legs. "Let's roll 'em out, Maddoes. And take it easy. It's going to be a long trip, and we want to keep the stock in good shape."

"Allus do, Aleria."

"Aye, that you do. I'm just making sure."

"As you allus do, Aleria."

"As I should. So roll 'em easy, and let's make a nice, smooth trip to Oudonsford. Eight days if the weather holds, and a tankard of the Angry Log's smooth ale at the end."

Maddoes cracked his whip above the backs of the horses. They leaned into the traces and the wagon rolled off smartly. The way they trotted made the load seem light, but after a week of steep hills and mud-holes the cargo would become a heavy drag on the stamina of the team.

But it was a sunny day and the caravan moved out well, threading through the outskirts of Kingsport and hitting the dusty road north. It was the biggest train she had ever been in charge of: twelve wagons and eight guards, with Erlon and Lavan on horseback as well. To make things interesting, a bulky wagonload of Mechanicals of some sort, heavily tarpaulined, requiring a four-horse team. Lavan's spare horse was tethered behind it in a nose-to-tail string with Erlon's spare and two extra dray horses.

Lavan was a newcomer dropped into a good position, so she had kept a close eye on him during the preparation days. His horsemanship was so superior to that of the other guards that she was soon reassured. None of the rest would complain for the same reason. Plus his stock. Lavan's two horses were long and lean, one a palomino, the other a pinto. While a bit showy for guard duty, they were both in top condition, and they could run faster than anything in the Dalmyn stables.

Erlon was riding his favourite horse, a bay mare that looked like she should be pulling logs out of the bush. His spare, a dark brown gelding, was almost as heavy though longer in the leg. These two would plug away all day, carry his weight without complaint and do excellent duty in harness if an extra team was needed.

As Aleria had expected, Lavan cantered past, heading out to "scout," as if they needed it this close to the city. She smiled and waved him on.

"Let 'im stretch 'is legs a bit, hey?"

"He'll calm down after a while. It's his first trip."

"Oh, we couldn't miss that."

"How's he been doing?"

The old teamster spat over the side. "He'll be fine. The boys bin razzin' him a bit, but he takes it in good sport. I was watchin' him train with the guards yesterday. He's doin' fine with them. Quick sword. Needs to strengthen his wrist."

She nodded and pulled a clipboard and pencil out of her pack. She had left a few pages of number-work for this time, and as long as the weather held dry and the road stayed smooth she could get it done. She liked working on the road. It filled the time, and she found that her mind moved well to the rhythm of the horses' hooves.

She didn't even glance at Lavan when he trotted past, headed for the back of the train. But soon he returned, pulling his horse alongside her. She looked up this time. "Having a nice ride?"

He did not smile in response. "Is there any reason that someone should be following us?"

"On this busy road? Who can tell?"

"I see your point." He waved a hand towards the road behind them. "But there's two horsemen back there, just far enough to stay out of sight, going exactly our pace. Now, why would a horseman go the speed of a freight wagon?"

She grinned at him. "I can think of several reasons."

"I suppose..."

"...and one of those reasons is that they are following us. Keep an eye on them, but don't get close enough that they realize what you're doing."

When they stopped for lunch Lavan was a while catching up. He ground-tied his horse and strolled over to where she was sitting on a log.

"Still there?"

He nodded. "They ought to pass us now, though."

"That they should."

They didn't. It might mean nothing, but Aleria spread word for all to keep their eyes open.

When lunch was over and they lined out on the road again, Aleria told Lavan to stay with the train. "Up here a ways where the trees get thick you're going to take a run up the mountain. Hide your horse and slip back down close to the road. Watch them go by, get any details you can. See that path to the right up ahead there? That's Enderbie Trail. It takes off here and loops back to the main road a few miles farther on. You can whip up that and get ahead of us. Erlon, I want an eye on anyone ahead. Maybe someone is following from in front as well. If that's the case, we might be in trouble."

Erlon frowned. "This close to the city?"

"Nobody's going to try a full attack. Something else is going on. You know what we're carrying."

He grinned. "Not in detail, but some of it's for the Royal Army, so I can guess."

"Exactly. For all we know, the Army sent its own minders. We'll see."

The two riders trotted away, and Aleria went back to her papers. There was nothing else she could do. After a while, though, she found she wasn't concentrating and put them away. It felt better to be scanning her surroundings, in spite of her confidence that an attack was out of the question.

She was beginning to get nervous when both her outriders came trotting down the road together. They split and turned back on either side of her wagon.

"Well?"

Erlon wiped sweat from his forehead. "Clear as fine silk ahead."

"Lavan?"

"I hid, they rode past. Two men, tough-looking but nothing out of the ordinary. Swords but no armour or helmets; nothing like that. They didn't say anything I could hear. Nice horses. Speedy, in top shape. Top quality gear, but not fancy." He tossed his free hand up in frustration. "They were walking their horses. Looked like travelers setting out for a long ride."

"Anything else?"

"Umm...they look sorta military, I guess. Can't say why. The way they sit a horse, maybe. Style of their gear. Sorry, Aleria."

"Don't be sorry. You got what you could. If you got nothing, maybe there's nothing to get." She looked at Erlon, but he had no comment.

"Then we let it ride. Unless anybody wants to ambush them and torture them until they tell us what they are doing?" She glanced at each of them. "Good for us. We're civilized people." She waved her hand, and the riders trotted away: Lavan to range ahead and Erlon towards the back of the train.

And so it went all afternoon. Lavan checked a few times, and Erlon went back once "to make sure the kid wasn't making swords out of sticks," but the report was always the same. Two horsemen walking their mounts up the road, minding their own business.

Aleria held an impromptu strategy meeting before they stopped for the night. Her outriders ranged on either side of the lead wagon again, looking to her for instructions.

"I figure it this way. Either they're shadowing us for an outside reason, in which case we can do nothing except be alert for an attack, day or night. If, on the other hand, they have a closer connection..."

"What do you mean, closer?"

She regarded Lavan a moment. "If they have a man in our train and are expecting to make contact with him."

Erlon slapped his hand on his saddle. "I like that option. It means they'll make a move, and we can take a shovel to that."

"Erlon, you will not remove heads."

"No?"

"You will not. You might enjoy it, but we are in the middle of a civilized realm with laws and rules and all sorts of things. No heads."

"But it worked so well last time…"

"That was different. That was out in the wilds of nowhere. Not here."

"Aleria, you are not fun." Erlon turned to Lavan. "She's just not fun when she gets like this."

"Isn't she?"

"No I am not. I start worrying about somebody attacking my caravan and I get all protective and broody."

"But then she remembers about the law and doing right, and all those responsible things."

"Oh. I see. And then she won't let you…?"

"She won't let me solve the problems my way. I have to do it her way."

"I see. No heads off?"

"No joking, kid. He did it oncet."

Lavan's eyes turned to Maddoes. "He did?"

"Yep. We was out with Roeble, headed over to Aesmark for the first time. This big mob of bandits attacked, runnin' every which-way, but one of them got too far out in front. Erlon broke the man's sword with the first swing, took off his head with the second. Took the heart right out of the rest of them."

Erlon slanted his head. "Aye. They never even pressed home. Split on either side and kept running."

Aleria sighed. "If we're through reliving old times, can we get back to the matter at hand? Which does not include heads rolling."

Erlon shrugged. "You're the boss."

"I am, but I'm clear out of ideas. What do you think?"

There was silence, except for the clop of hooves and the jingle of harness. And the squeak of an axle.

"Fix that tonight, will you, Maddoes? It's beginning to annoy me."

"Sure thing, Aleria. I was plannin' to."

"I'm sure you were, Maddoes."

The teamster spat over the side of the wagon. "How stupid do they think we are?"

"Maddoes?"

"Nobody messes with a Dalmyn train. Everybody knows that."

"I see what you mean."

Erlon nodded. "Right. What's going on?"

"What does he mean? What _is_ going on?" Lavan reined his horse closer, his face a rather comic picture of puzzlement.

Aleria looked at him. "There are two answers. Either whoever is running this affair thinks we're pretty stupid..."

"...or he doesn't care if we know. Or he actually wants us to know!"

"Very good, Lavan. All we have to do now is figure out which one and why."

The boy slammed his hand against the saddletree. "So we're no further ahead."

"No, we just jumped up one level in the game. Because this is a game. Whatever his reasons, the person in charge of our friends back there has laid down a challenge. We figure it out or something bad happens. Are we agreed?"

She looked around at three serious nods.

"Good. So let us proceed to ignore our tail and camp for the night. If they are legitimate travelers, they will pass us or camp nearby. It's the only spot for miles. If they don't camp here, that gives us more information. Plus they'll be spending the night in a dry camp in the rocks. Their bad luck. Pull over under those cottonwoods, Maddoes. I like this place. If we drop a line in the river we might get a salmon for supper."

The road had dipped down beside the Chanaan, and the campsite stretched out over a grassy spit of sand, shaded by huge trees. It was a popular spot, if the number of fire rings and horse droppings were any indication. It also had the advantage of being surrounded on three sides by the river.

Setting the wagons in a solid defensive line across the shoreward end, they turned the stock loose on the spit and settled in. It took them a while to set up camp, and during that time no party of horsemen dropped in to visit.

After they had eaten they all relaxed wherever there was a comfortable spot. Erlon stretched and pushed his mug firmly into the sand. "A nice place, but not overly social."

"Yes. Company would have been pleasant, don't you think?" Aleria leaned back against the log beside him.

"How's the kid doing?"

She grinned. "Oh, he'll be fishing until dark."

"Why do you say that?"

"Because he caught one. Addictive habit, fishing."

"I like fish for breakfast. More power to him."

* * *

Later in the evening she and Erlon stood looking out at the moon on the river. "I think I'll take a little walk."

Aleria regarded at the moccasins on his feet, the long knife slung at either hip. "Do I gather I'm not invited?"

"You're too noisy. You'd insist on talking."

"I can tell when I've been insulted. Do you want a more silent companion?"

"No, I'll stroll back down the road a ways. If I don't make curfew, wait for daylight."

She punched his shoulder. "We'll be looking for you at the first glimmer. Be careful."

"Always am." He faded away into the night. It was hard for her eyes to follow him, and she was sure the guards on duty didn't see him go.

He was back in similar fashion just as she was thinking of giving up and going to bed.

She started when he appeared at the fire. "Any luck?"

He shook his head.

"You want to talk to the guards?"

"No, they're doing fine."

"Not if the enemy has someone as good as you."

"We can tell them in the morning. I don't expect an attack tonight."

"I certainly hope not."

11. Tracking the Trackers

The morning meeting was instructive. Erlon called up the four guards who had been on duty the evening before: Domin and Jatto when he went out, Levan and Jerd for the trip back.

"Well, now. Any of you notice anything last night?"

They looked at each other. Domin, with his usual grin, held out empty hands. "What do you mean?"

"I mean anything unusual. When you were on guard duty."

Domin's face took on a crafty look. "You mean other than you goin' out and comin' back?"

"What?" Erlon's face began to redden.

Now Aleria saw the hidden glances.

"You mean you saw me and you didn't say anything?"

"Why would we? You didn't want a fuss."

"And you saw me. Both ways."

There were shared grins, but nobody spoke. Aleria felt it was time for her to intervene. "Listen, now, you lot. How did you spot him?"

"Well, Ma'am, we knew he was gonna go." Jatto shrugged. "So we kep' an eye on him."

"How did you know he would go?"

"Had to, din't he?"

"He did. But good for you for knowing."

"Ah, we bin out with Erlon before. We know he'll do what he's gotta."

"And coming back?"

The grins stretched. "Well, Ma'am, if he thought he put one over on us, we figured he'd come back into camp the same way. So we told Levan and Jerd when they relieved us, and they watched there extra careful."

Lavan grinned. "He came back just before you went to bed."

"So you watch when I go to bed, do you?" She walked over and stared into his eyes. "I thought you were supposed to be looking outwards."

"Have to know when the boss goes to sleep." Lavan chuckled. "Then the boys can relax a bit."

She cuffed him hard on the shoulder. "Enough sass. Well done on keeping your eyes open." She turned to include the whole troop. "We don't know anything about the two horsemen that were following us. It's possible somebody is playing a game. If so, we'll show them that the Dalmyn team is nobody to get onto the field with. Got it?"

There were several grunts of agreement.

"But let's not knock ourselves silly with this. Ordinary alert, that's all. Breakfast is on. Then we get hitched up and on the road." She clapped Erlon on the shoulder, turning him to walk beside her. "A good crew."

"Huh!"

"No, no, don't be upset. That was fine."

"It was?"

"Oh, yes. They know you're good. They only caught you because they cheated. They cheated because they're watching their leader, because they know what to expect from you. Which is exactly what they're supposed to do. And they're all cheerful as hell right now, because you gave them their joke and took it in stride. You lost nothing, and the morale of the crew is up."

"I suppose. The buggers!"

She glanced at him. "You'll be getting them back, will you?"

"I'll think of something, but it has to be very good. Something that will keep their points even sharper."

"You can make this work, but be sure it keeps their eyes outwards."

"Aye." He lost his grin. "You and I can keep our eyes open inside the camp."

Her cheerful mood dampened, she climbed up on the wagon seat and settled her sword beside her.

"First course, my Lady." Lavan handed her a plate of biscuits in gravy, and she felt better as she dug in.

They left their pleasant spot after a breakfast that included a filet of deep red salmon for everyone. Lavan's stock in the crew went up several notches.

Out on the road they set up their usual line of travel. Their shadows had disappeared.

"Not there?"

Both Lavan and Erlon shook their heads.

"Good. So they had nothing to do with us." She reached out and punched Lavan's knee, the only place she could reach as he rode beside her. "I know they were your own special problem. Don't pout. There will be more."

He grinned sheepishly, trotted ahead and was soon out of sight.

The sun shone down and the road began to turn dusty. By afternoon they all had light waterskins, and Maddoes insisted that they water the horses regularly in spite of the time it took. "This dust is hard on them, too. If they don't need it, they won't drink it."

Aleria did not comment. It was his decision to make, and she trusted his judgment. It was just another long, hot day on the wagon seat, and Aleria suffered through it as she had many days like it. At least the road was flat, following the course of the river most of the way, rising slowly but steadily. There was one tough pull up away from the river in the heat of mid-afternoon. The men got off and walked to ease the horses as much as they could. In spite of the heat, Aleria enjoyed stretching her legs.

Up on top the road leveled off, and it was an easy roll through the cooling afternoon to Aliandria. There was a Dalmyn way station there, and the teamsters replenished the oats for their horses and turned them loose in the pasture, where they rolled ecstatically in the long grass, then settled down for a serious feed.

Aleria stood beside Feneu, the stationmaster, sharing a grin at the antics. He stood watching, then glanced at her. "Someone askin' about you."

"I don't like the sound of that."

"That's why I'm telling you, Ma'am. Coupla guys pulled through at lunch. Got friendly with one of the hostlers who was over in the café. Nothin' obvious, but he knew to pass it on to me."

"Two riders, well armed, dark brown horses? Sort of nondescript otherwise?"

"That's the ones."

"Thanks, Feneu."

"Any idea who they are?"

"None. They followed us all yesterday and then disappeared. Didn't see them today. Could be they hustled ahead. We're keeping our eyes clear, don't worry."

"Thought you would."

That seemed to be the end of it. She informed her crew of the development, and they slept easy. Because of the heat, most of the men chose to pitch their tents instead of using the bunkhouses. Aleria did the same.

* * *

It was a long, dusty road the next day, but worth it, because they finished at Dragon Lake. After unhitching the horses the men turned them loose. They waded up to their bellies in the water. The men joined them, whooping and splashing and getting soaked. Aleria took a more genteel turn in the water and promised herself a better swim around dusk when the visibility wasn't so good. She had an arrangement with the men; they knew that sometimes they were required not to wander out of camp in the direction she had taken.

This time, however, Erlon balked. "I'm not sure it's such a good idea, going alone. Those riders are around somewhere."

"Well, I'm not taking one of these mutts along for a watchdog!"

"I guess it has to be me, then."

She looked at him. "You mean that, don't you?"

"I don't deny you deserve a swim like the rest of us, but I'm responsible for your safety as well. Oh, certainly you're the boss. But I'm not going back to tell Lord Dalmyn that I let his daughter wander off on her lonesome and get killed when we already knew there was a problem."

She sighed. "Can't argue with that. You keep watching the woods, and I'll take care of the water. I doubt if there's going to be an attack from that direction."

"Old folks talk of a dragon that lives in this lake. You be careful."

She looked closer to be sure that he was smiling before she laughed. "Wonderful. I'll get my soap and towel."

The water was cool and refreshing, and she swam out into the middle of the lake, which wasn't far. When she returned, he was still sitting there, his eyes scanning the forest. She dried and dressed. "You can turn around now."

When he did, she laid a hand on his shoulder. "Thanks. I really enjoyed that, and it was good not to worry."

"All part of my duties, Ma'am."

They walked in companionable silence back to camp.

It was not a calm night. Twice Aleria awakened and listened, hand on sword, but there was nothing. In each case, she had a hazy recollection of a sentry calling his challenge. In the morning she caught Erlon as he was washing his face.

"Busy night?"

He nodded as he scrubbed his neck with the towel. "Three times. Somebody scouting us. Didn't get too close. Could have been animals, but I don't think so."

"I trust these boys. If they say it was a scout..."

He nodded. "Well, at least that will keep their points sharp."

"Some consolation."

* * *

Their two long days paid off, as it was a short run down the hill into Kasnel. It did take a while to ford the Kasnel river, because the water was still high from the spring runoff, but the crew managed with professional skill. They hit the Dalmyn yard with plenty of time to offload some cargo and load the new goods destined for farther up the road. Then Aleria sent the men, working in pairs and threes, out to canvass the taverns and inns. Kasnel was a larger town because of the river junction and a small gold mining operation up the Kasnel river, so there were quite a few places to cover. Aleria doled out coin for the men's drinks, since they were on company business. "Only one in each place, mind you. If you do find these guys, I want your wits about you."

The only one who struck gold was Lavan. He returned to the yard early and came straight to Aleria's room. "They were here last night."

"Yes?"

"Stayed at the Barker Inn. Gone this morning, though."

"They were a full day ahead of us."

"Not hard. I told you about their horses."

She glanced at him, took in the rumpled shirt, the bare feet in unlaced boots. "How did you find out?"

He grinned. "I went into a bunch of places, told people I was lookin' for my brother. Made it sound like I was with him on the road, but I got in trouble back down the trail a ways, and he left me to catch up later. I made it sound like I screwed up, and everybody got a good laugh. It loosened their tongues, though. Only problem was the landlady at the Klenda Hotel wanted to take me in and give me some clothes, maybe lend me a horse. Took all my willpower to turn that down."

Aleria chuckled. "And you found them at the Barker."

"Pretty certain the same pair. I couldn't ask too many questions, of course, because I didn't know enough about them to fool anyone who knew them. The damn desk clerk was too quick. Asked me my name. I hemmed and hawed and made like I'd rather not say because of what happened back down the road, and got out of there. But that meant I didn't get their names, either. All I got was that they checked out this morning."

She nodded. "It's a result, anyway. Well done, Lavan. Let's see what the other lads find out."

He left, smiling and proud.

But no one else had any luck, and they were forced to conclude that their shadows had moved on ahead of them. Possibly trusting their friend in the convoy to keep tabs on her. She slapped her gloves on her leg. *Damn the man. What is he after?*

12. A Loyal Man

The following morning they paid for their easy day. They hit the first stiff pitch out of the river valley in the middle of a rainstorm. Slipping and cursing on the clay road surface, they nursed their straining teams up a twisting trail that at times looked more like a watercourse coming down. They harnessed Erlon's big pair in front of the quad team and the two spare horses to another heavily loaded wagon. Lavan stood by the worst mud-holes, tossing a rope to each successive teamster and pulling as much as his fine-boned runner could.

And at all times half the guards were on duty, watching the hillside above, the road ahead and behind. No worry about an attack up the steep, slippery bank to their left; the fatal part would be if someone went down it. The unlucky "off duty" guards wallowed in the mud with the teamsters, giving the wagons a lift from the worst mud-holes.

Aleria prowled the train like a sow bear with a wounded cub, attentive to the slightest hitch in their progress. She was painfully aware of their vulnerability and doubly watchful because of it. However, by noon they had reached the top with no damage visible.

She stood regarding the men as they ate lunch. "A sorrier-looking bunch of soaked spaniels I've never seen."

The crew glanced up at her, then went back to their meals.

"If my Lady will not take it amiss, I might note that her makeup has a certain earthy tone today as well."

She smeared a hand across her face and flicked the results at Erlon. "Here. Take care of it for me." She lifted her head to regard the group again. "A tough climb, but we've seen worse. Probably will again."

"Probably this trip."

"Exactly." She glanced at Maddoes. "How's Beauty's leg?"

"Beauty?" Maddoes directed his stare at one of the teamsters.

The man raised his head. "She slipped comin' outa that last mud-hole, almost went down."

"Serious?"

"We'll know if she stiffens up over noon."

Maddoes nodded. "Trade her out with the Roan in any case. She's earned a rest." He shot an accusing glance at Aleria, then back to the driver. "Next time tell me sooner."

The driver nodded and went back to his bread and cheese.

Aleria turned to the guards. "Any sign of our friends? Of anyone?"

There were glances back and forth, a general head shaking.

"Just another wet day on the road, then. We'll stay at Ten Mile Lake tonight if we make it. If we don't, we'll camp earlier. Take another ten minutes and we're back on the road. Her Ladyship needs to refresh her makeup."

She slogged ahead to the lead wagon, pulling a rag from under the seat to scrub at her muddy cheek. Then she used a wheel spoke to scrape as much of the sticky clay as she could off her damp boots and hunkered down under her slicker to rest.

"Ma'am?"

"Yes, Maddoes."

"Kin I talk?"

He was serious. Her mind skipped back to their last conversation. "Beauty?"

"Yeah. You shouldn't oughta done that."

"But I didn't realize…"

His hand motion cut her off. "I gathered that, Ma'am. But that kinda stuff is up to me. You ask me, and I ask them. Then this sorta problem don't come up."

"I get that clearly, Maddoes." She nodded. "I was outside my area of authority, and it made you look bad because you didn't know about it. We can't have that. I'm sorry."

"No problem, Ma'am. Glad you understand. You want the men loyal, they gotta know the chain o' command."

"A good point. I won't make the mistake again."

"I'm sure you won't."

She waited, but he seemed satisfied, nodding and turning away to check the harness of his horses. She huddled back into her slicker. *Maddoes isn't usually that touchy. Probably the rain.* She set it aside as a problem solved and sat, staring at the falling torrent.

But her mind was still turning. When Erlon came by she motioned him over. "Those two are following us, but there's not much we can do until they make some kind of move. On the other hand, if they have an accomplice in our camp, maybe we can smoke him out."

"You have an idea?"

"The beginning of one..."

As she laid it out, his eyes brightened, and he nodded several times.

By the time they were back on the road they had roughed it out. Over the cold, wet afternoon she sat on the wagon seat thinking, and he ranged the line as usual, dropping by to discuss details every once in a while, letting Maddoes in on the plan.

At least the first part of the plan. By the end of the afternoon, when they dragged themselves down to the campsite on Ten Mile Lake, they had it pretty well thrashed out.

After supper, with a warm meal inside and a hot fire in front, the crew was beginning to feel a bit more cheerful. Aleria stood by the fire and laid out her plan.

"This is the way it looks, men. Those two are following us, for sure. Our best guess it that they want something we're carrying. Our problem is that our guards are too good."

There was a general hum of amazement.

"That's right. As long as our picket line is secure, nobody is going to try anything."

Lavan frowned. "You mean you're going to weaken our line?"

She grinned. "You don't catch fish without bait."

"Pretty expensive bait."

"I'm not too worried." She lowered her voice. "The line will only seem weak. We're going to leave what seems to be a hole to the north of camp along the creek. Instead of patrolling all the way to the water, the guard will stop the other side of the big cottonwood, there. I've circled around, and from the outside it will look like simple laziness; the guard doesn't want to climb that brushpile. That leaves an open trail with plenty of cover leading to the centre of camp."

She pointed. "However, another guard can sit, safe and dry, under that wagon over there, and watch the hole. Anyone slips in and bang! We've got him."

There were general murmurs of assent.

"Anybody see any problems?"

Maddoes glanced up. "Are we sure they're gonna take the bait? What if they just stay out in the bush and laugh at us?"

"Nobody sitting out in the bush in this weather is laughing. But their general comfort is not our worry." She grinned. "We have another line on our two friends, and they are about to walk into a serious surprise in a couple or three days. Nobody messes with a Dalmyn train, and that isn't only because we're the toughest crews on the road, though it helps." She waved a hand at the forest around them. "We've got other resources out there as well. Don't you folks worry about that. You do your duty here, and the rest of the Dalmyn demesne will take care of the rest of the problem. Anything else anyone can think of?"

There was a general settling at this pronouncement, and no one offered further comment.

"Fine. That's how we do it. No change in the roster. Erlon and I will cover the inside position until after the midnight watch, then we'll close the line and shut it down. We all need our sleep, roads like this."

The camp settled into its evening routine, with guards posted in their usual rotation. It was well after dark when Aleria and Erlon started the second act of the plan. There was a scratch on the flap of her tent, and Erlon slipped inside. "This is the part I don't like, Aleria."

"Don't worry about not performing your assigned guard duty. Nobody will get through that hole without making a hell of a racket in those dead sticks, and I can see the break easily from here."

"I still don't like setting it up this way. Somebody is sure to see me sneak in here."

"Exactly. The whole idea is to make it seem that we're sloughing off on our duty. It's the only bait our prey inside the camp will take. Now get out there and do your real job."

He said nothing, only rolled out under the back wall of her tent and was gone in the darkness.

There was no reaction from their enemy that night, and it was a miserable day along a bench above the river to Dunaley. They camped that night under a grove of spruce trees that kept some of the rain off, but it was a cold, damp evening when they set up their trap, and colder and damper at midnight when they closed it down.

Aleria wiped rain off her forehead and shook her hand. "Are we wasting our time?"

"Safety is never a waste of time. We started a tale and we tell it to the end."

"Any sense the men are getting tired of the game?"

"Nobody's complaining yet. Of course, it's a good crew, and they trust us. They won't complain."

He didn't realize it, but that was the worst thing he could say. She lay in her cot for a long while, considering trust and all its varieties. Over and over again. Finally, the warmth of her body dried out the blankets and she slept.

* * *

She jerked from sleep, bolt upright on her cot, the image still burning through her brain. The wagon, spinning through space towards the river far below. Horses screaming in terror. The teamster, spread-eagled as he fell, his eyes pleading back up to her as she stood helpless on the road above...

She shook her head and scrunched up her eyes, her fists tight, and counted to a hundred. Calmer now, she listened. All was quiet in camp. *At least I didn't wake everyone up with my screaming. I must be making progress.*

She lay back down, but the image continued to run through her head. With a muttered curse, she got up and yanked on her camp sandals. She slipped through the tent flap and stepped onto the mud. Lousy footing for practice, but luck rarely gave you solid ground in a fight. Gritting her teeth and trying to relax her shoulders, she began the first practice pattern.

The next morning she woke to hazy sunlight and an equally vague mental state. Dressing and lacing up her boots, she strode to the edge of camp, clapping the sentry on the shoulder. "Quiet night?"

He nodded.

"Wish I felt the same. I'm going up the track a ways." She indicated the stretch of roadway where it ran straight across the benchland ahead. "I'll stay in sight."

He nodded, and she sprinted away. *Well, jogged would probably be a better word. Every muscle in my body seems to be on rest day today.* In spite of the aches she kept up her speed, running until her breath came in gasps. Then she slowed but refused to stop in spite of her body's demands. Finally – and it seemed to take much longer that usual – she could feel the aches diminish, the tendons stretch. Her stride became longer and smoother, and she began to feel alive.

She reached the corner much sooner than she liked and paced around it. Another stretch of flat road beckoned to her, but she stopped. *You don't make a promise and then break it, just because you're feeling better. Turn around and go back.*

She jogged into the camp, her breath even, her body working freely and, she hoped, her mind as well.

Erlon looked up from his coffee cup. "Bad night?"

"I guess. Don't really remember, but I woke up feeling like the worst of seven whiskeys."

"Better now?"

"If it is appropriate to come down to breakfast with your shirt already stuck to your back with sweat, I'm fine."

He gestured. "Pull up one of our delicate stone seats and join us. From the smell of it, the bacon is almost as hot as the beans."

Right on cue Maddoes stretched a plate towards her. The food was hot and pungent with spices, and she settled down to enjoy it immensely.

It occurred to her that the lead teamster did not usually serve her meals. She glanced up at him. "Thanks, Maddoes."

"No trouble, Aleria."

"Something on your mind?"

He thought a moment. "Is there supposed to be?"

"No, just wondering at the fancy service."

He grinned. "Just providin' the treatment a lady deserves from her loyal retainer."

"Huh. I believe that and you'll be asking to get out of guard duty next."

"I wouldn't never do that."

"Of course you wouldn't."

"Glad you knew it."

It occurred to her that their conversations always seemed to end up the same way. *Hmm. What's going on?*

As they continued their route over the next few days, the lead teamster seemed more talkative than usual. After he had mentioned the idea of loyalty three times, Aleria turned fully to look at him. "You wouldn't be trying to tell me something, would you, Maddoes? You know, without really saying it?"

"Oh, I'm not smart enough for that, Ma'am."

"Not smart enough?"

"Oh, no. I'm good with horses, but horses ain't that smart, right?" He spat and slapped the reins on the team's backs. "I'm not so good with people. And I'm real bad at ideas. My Pa told me. 'Maddoes,' he said, 'you ain't that smart. You got one talent, and that's horses. You work horses and you'll be fine. But you can do one other thing,' He told me. 'You can be loyal.

You don't gotta learn that, you just practice it.' That's what he said."

"I suppose that's true."

"So there ya got it, Ma'am. I'm good with horses, and I'm loyal." He gave the right rein the slightest twitch, and the off horse pulled harder. "That's me in a nutshell."

"That doesn't tell me anything I didn't already know, Maddoes, but thanks for all the other ideas."

"Oh, I'm no good at ideas, Ma'am."

"Yes, you did say that."

"But I am loyal."

"Yes."

They rolled along. The conversation seemed to be over. *Whatever it was all about.*

"A loyal man is very dangerous, you know."

"He is?"

"Oh, yes. Because nobody knows. Everybody just thinks he's only as loyal as anybody else. That he can be frightened off or bought off somehow. But only he knows that he's more loyal. So they can't figure what he's gonna do, ya see? They think he's like everybody else, but he ain't. So just when they expect him to duck out or sell out, then he does the right thing instead, and that messes their plans up."

"I can see how it might."

"Oh, yes, it's real simple."

"I'm not so sure it's always that simple. You're loyal to who? To me?"

"O'course. Well, I'm loyal to the Family, first, and that means Lord anDalmyn, o'course. But after that, it's you."

"And what about Erlon, here?"

The teamster looked over at the soldier, riding his horse alongside the wagon. "Well, he's a pretty loyal guy, right? So I'm loyal to him as well." He shrugged. "Long as he's loyal to you."

"You're only loyal to him as long as he's loyal to me."

"That's right, Ma'am."

"But what if he wasn't loyal to me?" She shot a quick frown to Erlon, whose face was twitching.

"Then I'd sell him 'cross the mountain, quick as anythin', Ma'am."

"Sell him 'cross the mountain?"

"Sure. Those slavers 'cross the mountain would like a big, strong slave like that."

"I don't know of any slavers across the mountains."

"Oh. Then I guess there ain't any." He lifted his whip and flipped it forward, lifting a horsefly off the shoulder of one of his team.

"That isn't necessarily so. But if there were, you would sell him, but only if he wasn't loyal to me."

"Of course, Ma'am. Long as he's loyal to you, I'm loyal to him."

"Well, I guess that means he'd better stay loyal."

"I s'pose that's up to him, Ma'am. I don't tell my betters what to do."

"That makes me happy, Maddoes." She glanced at Erlon, who seemed to have his grin under control. "So you're happy, are you? Being a loyal Dalmyn retainer? I'm sure loyal retainers are much better if they're happy."

"They are?"

"Of course. If I have to sell you 'cross the mountains, it makes it much easier if you're going to be happy about it."

"Now you're laughin' at me, Lady Aleria. You ain't supposed to do that."

"I'm not?" She regarded his stoic profile, emotionless as ever, staring out over the backs of his horses as he had done all his life. *What a strange man.*

"No, my Lady. If you laugh at loyal retainer, then he ain't so happy." He glanced at her. "And we already know what that leads to."

"Across the mountain I go. And I guess there's one thing more about loyal retainers."

"What's that, my Lady?"

"Well, if they're really, really loyal, sometimes they're allowed to tell their lady when she's done something she's not supposed to do. As long as they don't do it too often."

"Well, my Lady, I guess I musta knew that one already, ya think?"

"Hmm. I suppose you did."

He looked up at her, and a grin twitched the corner of his mouth. "And I only done it the once, my Lady."

Later that day, Erlon caught her alone, glancing around to see that they were not overheard.

"What's going on with Maddoes? He's been out on the road with me five trips now, sat on that wagon seat all day, sat round the fire every night, and I've never heard the like from him."

Aleria frowned. "I'll think on that. We already knew he's not as stupid as he lets on."

"I would agree."

"So why did he decide to let it slip now?"

"You're a very suspicious lady, Aleria."

"I am. What do you think?"

He shrugged. "Perhaps he thinks we need to know we can depend on his loyalty."

"Because something leads him to believe we're going to need it."

"A warning?"

"I'd say so."

"Is he smart enough for that?"

She shook her head and grinned. "Absolutely no idea." Then she thought a moment. "But considering our present problem, I'm afraid I won't like it when I find out."

13. Beyond Hungry Hill

The rain came on again later in the morning, and the wagon train continued to slog along slippery roads. That afternoon they had to scramble up another pass with the long, steep descent of Hungry Hill afterward, the stamina of the horses failing and the men's tempers flaring. They slid and stumbled down, with two wagons skidding off the road and three horses lame. When they reached the bottom, the grassy campsite beside Hungry Creek looked very inviting.

Aleria knew she had to make a decision.

"Erlon, that was the worst day I've ever had on the road."

"Didn't enjoy it much myself."

"I seen worse." Maddoes spat over the wagon wheel, hunched in his slicker.

"Should I be glad?"

He grinned. "Hungry Hill ain't a city street. I seen a wagon run away up there oncet. Killed both horses when it hit the bottom. Driver was lucky. Jumped off before it got goin' too fast."

"If he jumped before it was going too fast, he wasn't doing his best to stop it, was he?"

Once the wagons were circled, Aleria called everyone together. "Listen, now, men. There's one long pitch to climb, not too steep, before that stretch of benchland south of Oudonsford. Then the big hill down the riverbank, which is one of the more dangerous parts of the whole trip. I don't want a repeat of this afternoon, and we've got lame stock. Unless it's hot and dry tomorrow, we're taking a day off."

There was a concerted sigh of relief.

"However..." they groaned, "...because we aren't moving tomorrow, we can concentrate on our friends out in the bush." She lowered her voice. "That's the other reason we're staying here. Our extra forces want time to get into position. We'll run the same trick as the last three nights, with the opening over by the quad wagon along the creek bank," she pointed. "I don't know what's under that tarp, but it's my best guess as to what our friends are after. So we make the lure even easier for them, but this time we run it all night. Lavan, you take the first watch under the wagon. I'll take the second, Erlon the third, Maddoes the early morning. Everyone keep those eyes sharp! They're more likely to strike when we're wet and tired."

Later, when Erlon started to slip out the back of her tent, Aleria stopped him. "No rush tonight. They won't move until later."

"You think so?"

"I have an idea."

"You know more than you're telling me."

She winced. "I don't like playing it this close, Erlon, but the less people who know anything, the better chance I have of figuring out who is acting on the information."

He nodded in the dim lamplight. "I wouldn't trust me either if I were you."

She laughed but then spoke softer. "If there is an agent in our camp, he'll make his move tonight. He has to. He thinks my imaginary outside force of Dalmyn mercenaries is ready to swoop down on his buddies, and he has to warn them. If my guess is correct, he'll go out the back way, over here behind my tent. If I'm wrong, he'll go out the front."

Erlon nodded. "You're the lead in this flock, Aleria, and I have a lot of respect for that twisted mind of yours. Once this is over, can we tell the men what's been going on?"

"Why?"

"Because it's bad for morale. Young Lavan is getting snippy about catching me the other night."

"You can handle Lavan."

"But why should I have to? It isn't good, them thinking that their leaders are risking the safety of everyone so we can sneak together at night. If they got the idea that this whole plan of yours was to distract their attention, they'd stop watching as carefully."

She grinned. "But this whole plan is to distract their attention, only not from what they think. So we can't tell them unless we decide to unmask our traitor."

"You mean you won't unmask him?"

"That's why we don't want to catch him, just find out who he is. "

"I suppose. The best spy is the one you're aware of."

"That's right. But it's not that important. If he's getting away, grab him. Away you go. And feel free to detour past Lavan's post at any time you like."

"Now, that's an idea to think on."

Aleria had just turned off her lamp to get a short nap when Erlon's "Stand and be identified!" shout rang through the camp. She grabbed her sword, jammed her feet into her boots and rushed out.

Someone had already thrown sagebrush on the fire, and the flaring light showed the organized chaos of a camp under attack. She could see the backs of the sentries, protecting their night vision as they peered outward. Men in various stages of undress poured from the tents. Erlon was close by their second bolthole, staring into the darkness among the wagon wheels. The horses stirred restlessly in the centre of camp, their moving legs throwing shadows and odd shafts of light everywhere. Maddoes bustled around, adding more wood to the fire, laying out their store of torches.

Erlon turned to her in disgust. "He was coming in!"

"On this side?"

"I only got a glimpse of him. I was watching for someone going out and I happened to turn and caught the shadow of his head against the coals of the fire."

"So there is a stranger inside the camp."

"Or our man had already done his duty and was coming home."

"We search the camp."

He shook his head. "Doubt if we'll find anyone."

"Doubt if we will, but we do it anyway."

He raised his voice, calling the off-duty members of the crew to start the search.

Nothing showed up. After they had swept the camp twice, Erlon called everyone together and cancelled the trap . "Listen, now, men. I guess he got away. Don't worry. We've proved that we can catch him. He won't return tonight. Back to bed, back to the regular duty roster."

As they turned away, though, he spoke again. "Say, Lavan, what's that on your back? A target?"

The lad craned his neck to see, and the rest of the crew began to laugh. There was a white eagle feather stuck sideways under Lavan's suspenders at the back.

Erlon pulled it loose, held it out to him. "Wonder how this got there, and you being so good on watch."

Lavan glowered, turned to Erlon. "But you were..." his hand swung towards Aleria's tent, then dropped. "...but you weren't there, were you?"

"Now what gave you the idea you could figure out where I was?"

The lad grinned and took the feather. "Thanks. I'll stick it in my hat to remind myself."

Aleria stood forward, and her posture calmed the chuckle that arose. "And the lesson continues, my friends. It's good that you know what to expect from your leaders. It's also good to remember that your leaders have a better idea of what's going on than you do, and sometimes they may not do what you expect. For good reasons, not selfish ones." She ran her eye over the line of men, and few met her gaze.

She made a shooing motion. "Now, off you go to bed, my children. Sweet dreams." There was a general lightening of mood, and they trooped away. Once the crew had departed, Erlon and Aleria surveyed the quiet camp. "I'm sorry. I should have caught him."

"Don't worry. It worked out as well as could be expected."

"It did? Not much of a trap if it didn't catch the game."

"We were only supposed to find out who he was. Now I have a much better idea."

"You do?"

"Oh, yes." She slapped his shoulder. "And it isn't you. Go to bed."

As he turned away she chuckled. "Or if it is, I'm not letting on I know."

He merely grunted and walked away, shaking his head.

* * *

They stayed over in the same camp the following day, mending harness and drying equipment in the pale sun that finally came out in the afternoon. Aleria had given up on their little trap, and everyone got more sleep. The next morning was dry as well, and they rolled up the road in much better order.

"Bird bet, Aleria."

"Where?" Her eyes followed the teamster's pointing finger. Two eagles sat on a snag leaning over a nearby creek: a white-headed adult and a mottled yearling. "Eagles! Say, Maddoes, if it's eagles, it's got to be two pennies."

"I know it's eagles, and I called it. You wanta go three?"

"I hate to take your money. Two pennies it is. Your game, my choice. Let me see…"

"You don't call it and they fly, it's my win."

"I'll take the mamma. I figure she's teaching baby how to fish."

"Done. That one hatched last spring. He won't be learnin' anythin' from Mamma anymore. He'll be off about his own business any time."

They watched the eagles as the wagon creaked past, but neither flew. Aleria turned and raised her voice. "Bird bet. The white head is mine."

The teamster behind waved his hand. "White head is yours, Aleria."

She craned her neck as they moved on, hearing the word of the bet passed back along the line. Finally the road turned away from the creek, and she could see them no more.

A few minutes later, she heard shouts echoing from behind. Finally, the man in the next wagon called to her. "Sorry, Aleria. The young one went first. Maddoes the winner?"

"He is."

She turned to face the front. "Well, there you go, Maddoes. Your grasp of family life is better than mine."

He grinned. "Fifth time in a row."

"What? You've won five bird bets in a row? That's rare."

"Guess I'm just smart. Who'da thought?"

Lavan came trotting up from behind. "Hear you lost on an eagle, Aleria. Maddoes the lucky man?"

She poked a thumb towards the teamster. "Says it's not luck. He's won five in a row so far this trip."

Lavan slowed his horse. "Five in a row. That's wild chance operating. Say, Maddoes, let me in next time you're betting. I want a piece of that."

"Whaddaya mean?"

"Just tell me. You'll see." He touched a finger to his hat brim in salute to Aleria and trotted ahead up the trail.

By the time supper was over, everyone in the camp knew that Lavan was betting on Maddoes making six wins in a row, and he was only asking three-to-one odds. Needless to say, there were several takers. Aleria only shook her head.

* * *

The following day Maddoes bet one of the other drivers on a pair of robins, and the other man's bird flew first. There was a great deal of joshing about Lavan learning how betting worked, which he handled with good nature, and the incident passed.

They nooned on the bluff overlooking Oudonsford, and Aleria gave the teams a good rest, knowing that the steep, twisting downhill would take the rest of the day to negotiate. The trip wasn't over until the wagons were empty, and she wasn't going to lose a team this late in the journey. *I hope.* A wagon had gone off the bank here last year, rolling over the driver and breaking his back. The horse that wasn't killed by the fall had drowned in the river at the bottom.

While the others ate, she borrowed Lavan's spare horse and scouted the route. The condition of the road was probably no different from other times she had been through, but with the responsibility for the train on her shoulders every grade looked steeper, every mudhole deeper.

She pushed the sweating horse to the top and signaled them all back to their wagons.

14. Oudonsford Ale

The Dennal dockside at Oudonsford was a huge enterprise, extending along both banks of the Chanaan River and some distance up the Layon as well. Coal, brought in from the Northeast on Dalmyn wagons, was transshipped from the eastern shore into Dennal barges, to be swept downstream to Kingsport.

As she looked out over the valley, Erlon rode up beside her. "What's this betting going on? Lavan lost quite a bit. Doesn't sound like him."

She grinned. "Lavan's playing a deep game. You watch. The next time somebody gets a run on wins in bird bets, he'll be betting on them to win the next game."

"And…"

"Over the long run, he'll make money. The teamsters will take a while to figure out what he's doing, but he's getting three-to-one odds on a fifty-fifty bet. He bet a penny against four men today and lost four pennies. Chances are even he'll bet a penny against four the next time and win twelve."

"That sounds more like Lavan."

They watched a huge coal barge, all six sweeps pulling, heave its way out from the Dennal terminal into the main current. Once moving, single oars fore and aft were all that were needed to keep it pointed in the right direction.

Farther across, at the mouth of the Layon, she could make out a log raft in its final stage of construction, the trunks bundled with rope, then further tied by expensive steel cables strung around each section.

She was thankful they were staying on the east bank because at this time of the spring the ford was far too deep in swift-running water to think of crossing with heavily laden wagons.

She returned her attention to Erlon. "You don't bet?"

"You won't see many of the guards betting on something like that." He shrugged. "They play for more serious odds."

"Their lives."

"Aye. They'll play a game that requires skill or intelligence, but they don't like putting anything on the toss of a dice or flip of a coin. Too much like life."

"And on that cheerful note, shall we start on the most dangerous section of the road so far?"

He shrugged. "Hasn't rained here. Look at the dust."

"A dry road is a good idea. Hot is fine if we're going downhill."

As the first wagon wound down the steep riverbank it hit a hole and lurched, and she beckoned to Erlon. "Take a gander down the road and tell me what you think. We may want to space out more."

He nodded and reined his horse away.

She stood up in the stirrups and peered back. All the wagons seemed to be rolling straight and slow, but the dust curling up from the horses' feet showed the pressure on them.

"Look at that!"

The guard's shout stopped everyone, and they gazed out over the river to watch a rider who had been swept from the ford, his horse swimming desperately, rider clinging to the saddle and splashing himself ahead with his free arm, feet kicking as well.

"He's not turning back!" Lavan reined his horse left, then right, as if ready to take action but with no idea what to do.

Aleria scanned down along the valley and made a calming gesture. "The curve of the river will throw him towards our side. He doesn't look in any trouble." She grinned. "They'll be so far downstream by the time they get across, they'll have a nice long trot back up the bank to get them dry."

Horse and rider were soon swept along out of sight, still swimming strongly.

"Think they'll make it?"

114

"No reason to doubt it. Nothing we can do anyway." She raised her voice. "Show's over, lads. Let's roll. That bad pitch is just around the next corner. Check that your drags are working." She looked off to the west, where a dark cloud billowed low to the ground, its top white in the sunshine. "Let's move it. I don't want to show up wet."

By the time the wagon train had edged its way down the steepest grades and stretched out along the flats the rider overtook them, waving cheerfully as his horse trotted along. He was only a young, slim lad, and he seemed none the worse for his dunking.

A teamster cracked his whip over his horses, urging them aside to let the boy pass. "How's the water?"

The rider shook his head, spray flying from his shoulder-length dark hair. "A bit bracing, if you must ask. Not so bad once you get used to the chunks of ice floating by."

This sally was greeted with hoots of laughter, and the rider lifted his tired horse to a lope and left the wagons behind.

Aleria frowned. *There was something familiar about that voice...*but the boy passed them on the opposite side of the wagon, fiddling with his saddlecloth as he went by, so she didn't get a look at his face.

The teamsters snapped their whips and upped the pace to follow him. It had been a rough ten days from Kingsport, and their throats were dry.

While the Dennal deliveries were unloaded in their yard, Aleria strolled into the main office, a two-story log building with tubs of water braced on the ridgepole of the cedar-shake roof in case of chimney fires. Dennals took good care of their property and their people.

The office was in an uproar for some reason, and she stood aside to watch. There seemed to be a lot of people rushing around with loud voices but accomplishing little. However, the moment Arjan Dennal's office door opened there was silence. The yard manager stepped out, followed by the damp messenger, who Aleria could now see was not a boy, but a girl her own age or younger, and vaguely familiar.

"All is well, folks. Nothing to get upset about. The fire is under control."

A sigh of relief swept through the office.

"Nobody hurt, the fire lines held, the town is in no danger. Let's get back to work." He gestured toward Aleria. "We have guests bringing us presents. Let us greet them politely. As long as they come with a manifest." He held out his hand.

Aleria grinned back and passed the papers over. Arjan was the Twins' favourite uncle, much younger than his brother in the capital. He had always taken time to chat with his young nieces and their friends, teasing them gently in a flattering way. *And enjoying all that female attention, young as we were.* Aleria mentally slapped herself for being cynical.

"Good trip?"

"Not bad. The weather wasn't too cooperative. I gather that's not a thundercloud out to the west."

He shook his head. "The big thunderstorm was last week. That's the result. First forest fire of the season, and too close to Vandenhoven to be comfortable."

"I gather all is well?"

"It's under control, at least for now. Jameta brought in the message. You remember Jameta, don't you?"

"I thought she looked familiar when she rode past."

The young rider stepped forward. "I remember you, Aleria. Didn't you ride down on the log raft with us to Kingsport one summer?"

"You're the brat who kept pushing us into the river? You certainly have grown up!"

The girl glanced up at Arjan and made a show of covering her speech with one hand. "The boss wasn't supposed to hear about that. He thinks I'm a very mature young lady, and I never take part in that sort of silliness."

"I guess you got your own dunking today."

"Now, that was a bit silly. I never should have tried the ford on a tired horse, but I knew the people over here were worried, so I kept on. The pressure of the water edged him off the causeway, and away we went." She laughed. "Got rid of the sweat, anyway."

Arjan frowned. "If a big tree had chosen that moment to come floating down, it might not have been so much fun."

She winked at Aleria. "Uncle Arjan, I've told you a hundred times it doesn't work that way." She demonstrated with her hands. "If I'm on the ford and a log comes, it hits me at the speed of the water. Wham! Glub! But if I'm off the ford and floating, I'm moving at the same speed as the water, and nothing catches up to me. No danger."

"You take care."

"I do. You can see up the river for miles. There was nothing moving."

He shrugged. "We were glad of the news. Now run along and get your clothes changed. I assume someone is tending your horse?"

Jameta tossed Aleria a grin and turned out the door. "He's been telling me to 'run along' for so many years, he just can't break the habit."

The two of them watched her stride across the yard. Then they looked at each other, shaking their heads.

Aleria touched the manifest, a glow of satisfaction contained in the gesture. "All there in good order, Arjan. A heavy load, but well crated. The teamsters appreciate that."

"That Mechanical stuff better be well packed. It's a long way to the factory in Domaland, and spare parts are hard to come by."

"Mechanicals, is it? By the weight, it had to be."

"No trouble with the permits." He grinned. "Not for anything that brings the coal downriver to keep the rich folks at Kingsport warm in the winter."

She glanced at him. *A younger man of an allied family. Safe to talk.* "Not wishing to be indiscreet, but isn't that typical? These Mechanization taboos fade away when certain people have a need."

He laughed. "As long as we get to be the 'certain people' I'm not complaining." Then he frowned. "But it is frustrating to see smelter-grade coal passing through here, going down to the city to be used for heating fuel. All we need is a bit of iron ore and we could be machining those parts right here."

"Interesting idea. How do I tell iron ore when I stumble over it?"

"You're not likely to run into it with your wagon. If there had been any, they would have found it when they dug the roadbed."

She looked up at him. "Is anyone doing any prospecting in the mountains around here? I've heard that ore is often close to the surface where the land has fractured."

He shook his head. "Nobody that will admit it. Rumours say there were mines long ago, down in the Trench, but those are only folk tales, I'm afraid."

"Well, we're headed down the Trench on this run, so I'll keep my eyes and ears open, shall I?"

"I'm certain both our families could profit from an iron mine or two. We could get smaller barges up the river as far as Decker Canyon if we had anything to load." He clapped her on the shoulder. "You see to it."

"I will do that. Now, my men are at the bottom of ten rough days on the road, with our share of both rain and dust. Any local establishments that you recommend?"

"Since there are only two on this side of the river, and 'Edie's Eats' doesn't serve liquor, I suspect that the Angry Log will receive your patronage this evening as usual. You could toss your gear into a spare bedroom up at the house, or will you be staying at the Dalmyn yard?"

"I'd better check in there, coal dust or not. I don't suppose you've got any ongoing cargo for us?"

"We rarely send anything out into the Trench. When are you leaving?"

"Day after tomorrow. Give us time to forget our hangovers."

"If I scrounge anything up, I'll send a message."

"Great." She looked around at the busy teamsters. "Everything seems in order here. I'll stroll over to our yard."

"See you later then."

"Thanks, Arjan."

After a word to Maddoes to let him know her plans, Aleria grabbed her pack from the wagon and walked the shortcut through the trees to the Dalmyn yard. This was where the coal wagons were based, and it wasn't an alluring spot. Grime covered everything, blown up from the wagons and lodging in whatever cracks it found. The office was upwind of the wagonyard, however, and the inside was as clean as could be expected. She was greeted warmly by the staff and was soon elbow-deep in papers with the local manager. By the time they finished, the wagons that had carried the Dennal equipment rolled into the yard, and she went out to supervise their organization. Not that she was needed. Her teamsters knew their job, most had been here several times, and her guards were quick to lend a hand.

Once everything was tidied away, she called her men together. Sitting on a wagon seat, she looked out at them. *A good lot. All of them but one. Maybe.*

"Listen, now, men. Take a rest day tomorrow." There was a cheer at this. "We harness at sunup the day after. Be there. Be sober." There were chuckles and elbow jabs at that. "It's been a tough trip, and we held up well. But it's going to get worse, so don't get wasted. Once we head for the Trench, we're off the beaten track. Guards will be on double roster, horses hobbled at night. You know the drill." There were serious nods.

"But for now, relax. You've earned it. The office has pay advances ready." A cheer. "Small ones." A groan. "First round at the Angry Log is on me."

That brought a louder cheer, and they broke towards their bunkhouse.

Aleria glanced at Erlon, and he stayed. "Maddoes."

The lead teamster had been the last man leaving, and he stopped.

119

"You drinking with the boys tonight?"

"Am I?"

"Invitation's out from Erlon and me. We get tired of each other's company."

"Fair enough. You're the boss."

"Not when it comes to who you drink with. It's your choice."

He grinned and outlined an awkward bow. "Then I would be pleased to accept M'Lady's invite. I will attend yer Ladyship at supper."

Aleria sketched a courtesy with one hand, and he turned to follow the men.

"Any reason for that?"

She glanced up at Erlon. "We've discussed the dangers coming up. We could use a loyal man."

His mouth turned down, and he nodded once. "We could, at that."

* * *

Anyone unsure of the name of the Angry Log pub would be straightened out by the sign, which portrayed an uprooted tree about to sweep over a struggling bargeman. The Dalmyn crew swung in under this inauspicious sign in a mob, Aleria and Erlon in the lead. Playing her role to the hilt, Aleria sashayed up to the bar and slapped down a handful of crowns. "Feed 'em and give 'em each a drink. After that they're on their own."

The bartender grinned and swiped the coins away. "Good to see the Dalmyns in town."

"Aye. We're a high-paid, free-spending lot, we are."

"True, and you pay up after a fight. The boss likes that."

She dropped her head and looked up from under lowered brows. "Don't go looking for any extra cash tonight. We've got a long road ahead of us."

"I'll keep an eye open for trouble, then."

"I'd appreciate it." She slid another crown across the bar. "Pour 'em, and bring some of that whiskey your uncle makes to my table."

"Aye, Ma'am. That I will."

The food was good and plentiful and the ale, made locally, was reasonable and cool. The whiskey was as good as that served in the best taverns in Kingsport, but probably hadn't contributed its share to the realm's tax base. In no time, Aleria was more relaxed than she had been for weeks, as she and Erlon were enjoying one of their usual banters.

"...and that sword of yours! You swing it around like a farmer with a fencepost. That's not fighting. That's mowing."

Erlon took a shot of whiskey, chased by a slug of beer. "First I'm fencing, now I'm mowing. You know, Aleria, I've often found it more effective to get one good insult and keep it rolling. Scattering them around like seeds in springtime doesn't have the same effect as it does on a field."

She took an equal swig from her mug. "It 'doesn't have the same effect' doesn't it? Now he's even insulting my insults!" She leaned forward on her elbows. "Do you understand who you're talking to? You, my man, are not even in the same realm as I am, let alone the same class, when it comes to insults. I have taken courses in how to create and deliver insults."

That stopped him, his mug halfway to his mouth. "Really?" He put it down. "You had a class in that ladies' school that taught you how to insult people?"

"Well, not really." She laughed. "It was called Political Satire, but that's what it amounted to."

He shook his head. "Well, then, Lady Aleria, I must bow to your superior technique. I will resolve not to insult you in the future, for fear that I will be raked by your well-sharpened wit."

"A wise choice, my good man."

"But why do you keep calling me a farmer? I was never a farmer."

"Well, you look like a farmer. Who else is that big?"

He shrugged. "Maybe a mercenary?"

"Oh, certainly. I'm trading insults with a caravan guard and I call him a mercenary. Yep, that's sure gonna get his goat alrighty."

There was a change in the sound of the room. Aleria's head came up, her beer forgotten. Over by the bar, two men were facing each other in aggressive poses. She could see the group around them shifting their chairs back, watching each other. She glanced at Erlon, who nodded to her. She pitched her voice to carry, but not too loud. "Dalmyns take the north wall."

As the fight broke out there was a countermovement of her men, mugs in hands, slipping towards her. They lined up against the wall, grinning to each other and making bets on the battle.

Aleria watched the barman, his club in hand, hovering uncertainly. Too many of his patrons were involved, and furniture was beginning to break. She met Erlon's eye again, and he nodded. "He'd appreciate a bit of help."

She turned to her men. "Mugs down. Domin and Jatto, get the door open and keep it wide. Clear the room, boys."

The Dalmyn crew stepped forward in pairs and threes. They approached each fighter from behind, subdued him and hustled him at a run through the door. How he landed when he got outside was up to him. The two largest guards stood by the door discouraging any who tried to re-enter.

Soon the fight had dwindled to the original pair, now wrestling on the sawdust, clawing and clutching and not doing each other a whole lot of damage. The barman stepped over and tapped each one, not gently, on the head. They broke apart and lay moaning.

The barman regarded the empty room. "Thanks, Dalmyns. Sit yourselves down. There's a round or two coming your way."

Her crew cheered, and the barman signaled his servers from their hiding place in the kitchen. Then he went to the door and allowed his choice of the patrons to re-enter, collecting a toll from each one for his part in the fight.

After a short time the bar looked like nothing had happened. There were a few less patrons and a few more mugs on the Dalmyn tables, but the evening rolled on as it had before.

"That went well."

Erlon nodded. "Good for the lads to have some excitement. They don't care much which side they're on, as long as they get a hand in."

"They listened rather well, too."

Maddoes grinned. "Must be that note o' command in yer voice."

"I'll drink to that."

They clashed mugs, top and bottom, and did so.

Later, after the next round of fine whiskeys had turned into dregs, Erlon looked at her, then at Maddoes, sitting there nursing a mug of beer. "Which reminds me. Who's in charge of this lot of caravan hands right now?"

"Whadaya mean? I am, of course."

"Nope. You can't be in charge. You're too drunk."

"Well, you're one to talk. You've had twice as much to drink as I have."

"And I'm twice as big as you are."

"Hah! Which means you're precisely just as drunk." She wiped a hand across her mouth, which felt rather numb. "Gotcha there, didn't I?"

"Yep, I guess you did. Must be that mathematics trainin' ya got at that fancy school. But the question stands. Who's in charge?"

"I dunno." She turned to Maddoes, who was holding a smaller mug, she noticed. "Who's in charge, Maddoes?"

"I dunno either. I don't think anyone is."

She shook her head, which seemed very heavy. "Maddoes, Maddoes, Maddoes. You gonna be lead teamster, you gotta lotta learnin' to do. Somebody's in charge. There's always somebody res...sponsible."

"If you say so, my Lady." Maddoes shrugged. "Back down at the yard, I guess there's a foreman in charge. But we're sittin' in a tavern, off duty. Nobody's in charge of us."

She thought that over a moment, then turned to Erlon. "Whaddaya think, Erlon? He's got a point, doesn't he?"

He nodded as well. "You know, Aleria, I think he has. But in case something came up, you're too drunk, and I'm too drunk." His eyes turned left, then right. "And that leaves..." His big index finger swung to his left.

She pointed at the same time. "Him. That's it, Erlon. He's in charge. Maddoes, you're in charge, if anythin' happens You're the only one sober enough. The only one."

Maddoes regarded each of them in turn. "I guess you're right. I seem to be in charge."

"Good. That means you're sober enough to order another round." She fished out her purse somehow. "Go get it, man."

"I suppose if I'm in charge, that means I can tell you when you're too drunk for another round?"

She waved her hands in the air. She had meant to make some kind of firm gesture, but they refused to cooperate. "No, no, no. I said I was too drunk to be in charge. Not too drunk to drink some more." Her hands fell with a slap to the table, and she left them there. It seemed a good place for them. "So, if it pleases the boss, who is in charge, to order another round, will he please do it? Before I ask my large farmer friend over there..." she considered pointing, but her hand liked where it was. "...to hit you over the head with his fence post."

Erlon's eyes came up from where they had been fixed on the tabletop. "So it's a fence post again, is it? I thought we decided on a scythe."

"I was only speaking metapfff...meta...a...aphorically. If you want it to be a scythe, you just harvest away."

"Thank you. I think I prefer the scythe metawhatever. It seems to be more appropriate. Whaddaya say, Maddoes?"

The teamster raised his hands in surrender. "It's all right. I'll get another round. I hope ya don't mind if I join ya. I need ta fortify m'self for a long evenin'."

They returned to the wagon yard some time later; Aleria wasn't sure how long. She was too busy being miffed that they wouldn't let her sing. Even her assurance of her long and arduous training in the Art of Song had not swayed them. Maddoes, who seemed to have taken charge, insisted that, as guests in a strange town, it would be better if they did not stretch their hosts' hospitality past a certain point.

Other than that, there was a lot of swaying going on, and she kept one arm firmly around Erlon's muscular waist. It felt very comfortable there. When they neared their destination she stopped and hauled each man's arm to be certain she had his attention. "All right, you two. We are now approaching the wagon yard, where I am the boss, and you are men of resp...ps...onspible position. We are still off duty, but we maintain our pride. Please act accordingly."

They formed up on either side of her and made a creditable attempt to walk straight into the yard. Aleria, smart enough not to try speaking, slapped each man on the shoulder and stumbled up the stairs to the room that was provided for her. Where they went after that, she had no idea.

15. Jameta

The following afternoon while Aleria was trying to clear her head by running her guards through the most grueling weapons practice she could dream up, she notice a distinct falling off in concentration among the men. Looking around, she saw that Jameta was leaning with her folded arms over a fence rail, watching their practice.

Aleria clapped her hands for their attention. "Listen, now. Five more times through that drill and you can drop it for the day. I want you rested up for tomorrow."

A spate of good-natured jibes faded out into solid concentration, and she strolled over to the younger girl. "Want to join in?"

Jameta's face twisted. "Not allowed."

"You aren't?"

"Uncle Arjan is trying to make a lady out of me."

Aleria glanced over, trying to stifle her grin. "How's he doing?"

"Far better than I ever wanted."

"So you don't want to be a lady."

The girl scuffed her riding boot through the mud. "Why should I bother? I'm only Esteemed class. I live in country where you ride wherever you go. There's mud half-way up your legs part of the year and dust and snow for the rest. Nobody, and I mean nobody, pays you any mind you mince around and 'tut-tut' everything. I work with loggers, raftsmen and barge sweepers, and if I don't stand up to them they won't listen to me and what use am I then?"

"What do you do when you're being useful?"

"What I was doing yesterday. I ride messages. I have a string of the fastest horses in the North, and I'm lighter than any of the men. If Uncle Arjan wants a note or a package or even a small Mechanical part taken up to the coal mines or out to the logging, I'm the one he sends."

"I see. So I doubt if learning to ride sidesaddle would be high on your list."

The girl exploded in laughter. "Bloody right it wouldn't!"

"But he still won't let you use a sword."

"He says a fast horse is the best defensive weapon."

That jibed with something Master Ogima had told her. She nodded. "Once you start thinking like a swordsman, it changes you. Without one, you're better as a messenger, lady or no."

The girl glanced at her, probably unsure whether that comment was to her advantage. Then she grinned. "Anyway, I'm here doing my duty. Uncle Arjan says that if you have slaked your thirst sufficiently, would you care to join us for dinner tonight?

Aleria fingered her temples. "The headache is pretty well gone. Just enough there to remind me to take it easy tonight. Yes, I suppose I'll be an appropriate guest, won't sully the honour of the Dalmyn family."

Jameta nodded. "See you at seven." She started away but turned back. "Do you carry a dress with you?"

Aleria raised her eyebrows. "You'll have to wait and see, won't you?"

* * *

Dinner was a substantial affair in the Dennal mansion up on the ridge overlooking the river. If these were all family, there seemed to be a lot of them. Mostly of dark skin and rope-like black hair, and most with some level of hearing loss, it seemed. She grinned across the table at Jameta and filled her plate from the loaded platters passing around. If the girl was only a poor relative, she was placed in an interesting seat, across from the main guest and next to the head of the table where Arjan presided.

"Nice dress."

Aleria glanced down. "Thanks. Now you know. I do carry one. Divided skirt, though. Just in case."

127

"I could use one of those." She glanced at her uncle, but his attention was elsewhere. She glanced at Aleria, gave a loud sigh, and set her attention to her plate.

The food was hearty and full of spices, and Aleria turned to with a will. Tomorrow she would need her stamina.

After the meal was over, she swirled a snifter of suspiciously familiar liquor from an unmarked bottle. "Local?"

Arjan grinned. "Why serve anything but the best?"

"Want to move some of that around?"

"You might not want to do that. Word has it Dalmyns don't carry contraband."

"For our own use? Medicinal, for rubbing down the horses, that sort of thing."

"I could slip in a cask or two. They'd appreciate one up at the Army camp, but there would be a certain irony involved in bringing it to them since they're the ones supporting the tax collectors. Sorry, there's not much else for you to carry."

She shrugged. "We've split the other loads up among the empty wagons. We'll do better in the mountains that way. Glad it was you that needed those Mechanicals."

"Geared winch system for the coal. With that box of Mechanical magic, two oxen can pick up a loaded wagon and lift the whole thing out over the barge and dump it. No shoveling. If it works, we'll try one in the log yard next year." The Dennal manager looked around as if trying to find courage. He hitched his chair forward. "I do have one other load for you if you don't mind."

"Why should I mind?"

"You might. This whole political situation down the Trench concerns me. If hostilities break out it's bad for all of us. We've been lucky here in the north. Plenty of work for everyone, no upsets. It's a damn shame our own Ranking classes are starting the trouble."

"You'll get no argument from me."

"So I'd take it as a favour if you'd take a Dennal representative along."

She nodded. "Another sword wouldn't come amiss."

"Well, that's it. No sword involved."

She followed his glance across the table to Jameta, sitting with her hands knotted in her napkin, her eyes boring into Aleria's.

She regarded the girl. "This is shaping up to be a rough trip. Another woman doesn't concern me, but one without a sword...she may not be ready for a trek like this."

"But look what you did when you were my age!"

Aleria lowered her eyebrows. "What I did when I was too young and stupid to know better should have no effect on your choices. Look where it ended me."

Arjan held his hands out. "That's just it, Aleria. You know what it's like to be young and stupid in situations of that sort. You're one of the few people I would trust to take her."

"Aren't you afraid I'll bring her back in swordsman's leathers with several kills to her name?"

He threw up his hands. "It's too late to worry about that now. We have done our best. It is up to her to make her own way."

"Just like that. You've given up on her?"

"Not at all. We are confident that she has learned her lessons well. She has adapted to a rough life in a rough country, and we have every hope of success for her. We would not be sending her as a representative, otherwise. We value the Dalmyn connection too much."

Aleria took a deep breath. "And what do you say, Jameta?"

The girl's head came up. "I own three of the fastest horses you'll ever see. My Blackie outran a grizzly last year."

"A grizzly? Popular opinion has the odds going the other way."

"Well, it was a small grizzly, but we got away from him."

Aleria grinned. "With a grizzly it's hard to tell whether he really wants to catch you or not."

Jameta tilted her head. "The only way to find out is to stop running."

Gordon A. Long

Aleria made her decision and turned to Arjan. "If this is an official request from your family to mine I must respect your wishes. I will do my best to see that she comes to no harm." She fixed her eyes on the younger girl. "And you will continue to regard running away as the best move. It is a good technique at your age."

Jameta's smile beamed across the table. Aleria glanced at the girl's uncle, who wasn't quite so happy.

"Be at the yard at sunup. We can handle two horses. We don't herd a remuda with us. I assume they'll follow?"

"I never use a lead when I'm on the trail with a spare mount. They're sisters. They stick together."

Aleria nodded, then stood and bowed formally to her host. "Since I must be up at first light as well, I will take my leave."

He rose and saw her to the door. When he was sure his niece was out of earshot, he spoke quietly. "She is very intelligent, very headstrong and very well loved, but...no one in the family knows quite what to do with her. I hope she will be an asset to your party. If not, she is quite able to make her way home alone. She does it all the time."

She smiled. "Sorry, Arjan. Maybe I'm old-fashioned, but I won't be sending any girl her age unarmed and alone through those mountains. Don't worry. I'll keep her in line." She winked. "I've had inside experience of that sort of kid."

He smiled as well and turned back into the house, leaving her to ponder why she found herself a magnet for youngsters that no one else could understand. *Huh! I probably earned it.*

* * *

The next morning Aleria grabbed Lavan as soon as he appeared at the yard, earlier than the rest as he always was. "We have a problem, you and me."

"We do?"

She slapped his back. "Don't worry. It's nothing to do with the card games you've been having with the men. Their pay packets are their own concern. Oh, except Domin. He is not a good gambler."

"I noticed."

"But he is an excellent guard. And an all-round decent man with a family to support. Do you follow?"

"Sure. I can go light on him."

"Thank you. But there is a more serious problem than that, and I need your help."

"That's fine, Aleria. Anything."

"Do you remember that messenger girl who swam the river?"

"Jameta? Of course. I was talking to her yesterday. She's nice. Also pretty."

"You'll get a chance to find out how nice. She's coming with us."

"A girl like that on a trip like this? She doesn't even carry a sword."

"That's our problem. She's coming along as a messenger. As we know, she's a wonderful rider and her horses are fast. Yes, faster than yours. You'll have plenty of time to test that out along the road, as long as you're careful. I want you to keep an eye on her, remembering that..."

"Right. That she's Esteemed Rank and a member of an allied family."

"I was about to say that she's unarmed, and her first responsibility as a messenger is the safety of the messages she carries. That means her own life as well."

"Ah. I see how that might make a difference."

"Now that I think of it, women should make good messengers. They carry no burning desire to prove themselves brave." She tapped him on the chest with a forefinger. "Much less likely to get killed instead of doing their assigned task."

"Probably. How boring."

"Keep it that way."

"Yes, Ma'am."

"So you'll keep an eye on her," she clapped him on the back, "but don't forget the part about the Esteemed Rank and the family of an ally, either."

"Aye. You would remember that."

Jameta arrived soon after that, riding a dark brown mare similar to the one she had ridden before, a second, identical mare with a light packsaddle following loose behind.

Aleria stared at one horse, then the other. "They look so much alike."

"They're full sisters. Same dam and sire. Brownie is two years older than Doe."

"How do you tell them apart?"

The girl's response was a puzzled frown. "By their faces, of course."

"Right." She signaled to Erlon and Lavan, who strolled over. "Jameta will be on horseback with you. These roads are her back yard, especially for the next few days. She knows the ways of the country better than either of you. And her horses are faster than anything in our train. So assign the scouting duties as you see fit, Erlon. Jameta, if there's any trouble anywhere, your place is next to my wagon. Get there, no matter what. That's not only for your safety. A good messenger in the right place has won many a battle. You follow?"

The girl's dark face had paled at the word "battle," but she nodded grimly, her hands tight on the reins. The horse tossed its head in protest, and she calmed it expertly.

Aleria turned to her other tasks. The girl was in good hands, now. She'd learn a lot from Erlon. *The Gods know what she'll learn from Lavan. Hopefully not how to be brave.*

16. Troublesome Lords

They had little cargo for the Newsom demesne, but Aleria had no doubts about dropping in, even though she had a rather unpleasant chore there. She did not waste time, but pulled Lauf anNewsom and his intractable son, Ferrel, aside the moment she got off the wagon seat.

"I must talk to you, my Lord. We have strategy to discuss."

He raised his eyebrows. "So Geran tells me, my Lady."

He led the way into the Newsom fortress, too plain to be called a castle, but much too warlike for a manor house.

"A dusty day on the road?"

"I could use a drink."

He gave appropriate orders, and they made small talk until they were settled in his study with cool drinks.

"Now, what strategy does Dalmyn wish to discuss with me? I still have some unanswered questions."

She took a moment "Before the strategy comes the apology, my Lord."

"I knew it!"

She glanced at the lad. "Yes, you were right. We checked those crates as soon as we were safely out of sight. Twelve Lewis Sustained-Shot rifles. With ammunition."

"I told you!"

The elder Newsom's fingers clenched on the arms of his chair. "So what did you do?"

"I continued to Lexing."

"You what?" Now both of them were on their feet.

She grinned up at them. "And I unloaded his goods off the top of them and left them lying in the wagon bed in plain sight. I told him they were a delivery for the Royal Army Training Centre at Decker. Then I drove away."

"No." The father collapsed in his chair.

"You didn't!"

"Oh, but I did. His agent slipped them into the load unpapered, so they weren't on the manifest. He had nothing to say."

The younger man was still standing. "But what if he had just taken them from you?"

She narrowed her eyes and stared at him until his gaze dropped. "Nobody messes with Dalmyn wagons. Nobody. A lot of people need to understand that."

Lord anNewsom lay back in his chair, and the laughter escaped. When he finally could speak, he shook his head. "You dangled his own guns under his nose, and then drove off with them?" He burst into laughter again.

She grinned as well. "I had to tell you. It sort of makes up for the mistake."

"Oh, it does that. It does that very well, my Lady."

After some hesitation, his son joined in the laughter. When they had calmed, the lord's eyes narrowed. "So what now? You didn't come all the way here to make a joke with me, funny as it may be."

"That's right, my Lord. In the first place, I came to restore the Dalmyn name. Our trust was misplaced, it was our mistake, and you deserve the apology. However, it goes further than that. His Majesty is not amused when one of his liege lords takes it upon himself to flout a royal proclamation with the obvious purpose of causing dissent."

"I can't help but agree."

"So his Majesty's eyes are turned this way. He is anxious that affairs in his realm proceed in their normal, orderly fashion. He is prepared to support those with similar aims. He will be upset at those who attempt other objectives. Not an unrealistic expectation, would you agree?"

The lord took a moment before answering, and she could see his mind working. *Will he ask me?*

"And you have a way of learning his Majesty's wishes, do you?"

She didn't feel the need to answer. *Not in so many words.* "Up until now, I have only confirmed what your own logic already told you. Shall we leave it at that?"

He sat back. "Which gives me nothing."

"But if you combine the message with the messenger, you can draw your own conclusions."

The old man was nodding, but his son's head went back and forth between the two of them. "Whatever are you talking about? We have a neighbor who is..."

The sudden silence at his father's upraised hand gave Aleria hope. *The chain of command is in order in this demesne.*

"That's fine, son. We need no more." He returned his gaze to Aleria. "You can pass the word to any...concerned parties...that anNewsom can be counted upon to maintain affairs in their usual, orderly fashion. If my neighbors will act accordingly."

"Understood." She smiled. "And I should pass on to you that Dalmyn Cartage has been awarded the Royal Army contracts in this area. You will be seeing more of our wagons."

Newsom inclined his head. "And with the extra business, will prices drop accordingly?"

"Before this all deliveries were special one-way trips, and the costs were accordingly high. Now, any item added to a scheduled delivery to the Army post will go at regular cartage rates."

"Good. We shall be seeing more of you, then?"

"Once the bumps in the road have been smoothed out I will be handing this responsibility over to the regular managers. For the moment, though, I will be passing through frequently."

"In spite of the fact that it may result in fewer of these pleasant meetings, I still wish you well in smoothing out the rough spots we are experiencing. Anything Newsom can do to assist...?"

She rose. "Thank you for the offer. Should the need occur, we would be pleased of your support."

He stood as well. His son, a puzzled frown on his face, lagged behind. As she turned away, she noticed the son start to ask, and his father's calming gesture. She grinned to herself. Hopefully, the young man was smart enough to figure out what he had just been listening to. If not, his father needed to give him some more training in diplomacy.

Once they were on the road again, Erlon paced his big horse up beside the lead wagon. "So how did that go?"

"Very well. I have passed on a subtle assurance that his Majesty would appreciate the status quo maintained in this part of the realm, and received in return guarantees of assistance in that objective, should we require it."

He grinned. "And when do you go back to speaking like a normal person?"

"Sorry. Just got into the habit. How many men do you think he could spare us?"

"You didn't ask him?"

"We're not that close friends, yet."

"From the look of it, he's got thirty or forty. That little stone box only needs around fifteen to lock it up tight. Of course, that would mean leaving his whole demesne unprotected."

"So in an emergency he might spare us twenty men or so. Quality?"

He grinned. "We tested that already."

"Ah, yes. They did well enough."

"We'll keep them in mind."

Maddoes chuckled and snapped the whip above the backs of the plodding team. "Next stop might not be so much fun."

Aleria grinned up at Erlon. "Oh, it might be."

* * *

Achern AnLexing was not quite so hospitable as he had been for their last visit, but had the grace to offer her a cool drink in his workroom. *Or the intention of separating me from my men.* Aleria settled down to her task after the first sip.

"You have a new agent in the City, my Lord."

"Aye."

"A pleasant man. We like dealing with him."

"The last one was...deemed unworthy."

The fact that said agent had been arrested for dealing in Mechanical weapons and was soon headed for prison didn't seem to be worth mentioning.

However, Aleria had one more message to deliver. "I do have one point to make, my Lord."

"Yes?"

"His Majesty is upset with me."

"He is upset with you? And what is that to me?"

"He is upset because of the favour I did you."

"I recall no favour."

"He is upset with me because of what I did with the guns."

"What guns?"

"The shipment of guns I was carrying last time I came here. You see, his Majesty would much rather I had left them here and gone home and told him. He would then have sent a rather large number of soldiers to bring them back. I considered that option, but it is my opinion that by the time the soldiers got here, the guns would have been nowhere to be found. However, his Majesty has his methods. Some of them he would rather the general public was not aware of, but he will use them in emergencies. He would have found the guns. It takes too many people to move that much weight, and there would have been a weak link."

The lord sat back. "I understand the veiled threat. I don't think the other lords of this realm would like the idea of their sovereign torturing one of their fellows to find out the presence of contraband."

Aleria put on an air of relaxed confidence. "And I doubt if the other lords of this realm would take kindly to one of their fellows who broke the laws they all have sworn to uphold, for the purpose of relieving another of their fellows of his hereditary property. Lords tend to be touchy about that kind of ambition."

She leaned forward. "The message I was given was that you were exceptionally lucky that no contraband was allowed to remain in your demesne. His Majesty has a long memory, and should such an event or any similar one occur, this one will not be forgotten. Have I made myself clear?"

"You don't know what you are talking about. What assurances do I have that you are truly speaking for the king?"

"Do you dare risk that I am not?" She had endured his self-satisfied grin for too long. *Perhaps I shouldn't do this, but this man needs a slap of reality.* "Stop prevaricating. I must take back an answer."

The Lord stood, and his thick body swelled, his face reddening until his eyes bulged. "Young lady, you mistake the situation here. You are not in a position to be making demands." He smiled, an unpleasant grimace. "In fact, your perch is quite precarious at the moment. You have a small number of men, and at the moment you are separated from them by a door and several of my soldiers."

She slid to her feet as well, her body automatically going into the ready position. It wasn't necessary to move a hand towards her sword. "Oh, no, my Lord. It is you who misunderstand. If I were to break a fingernail here, you would find your little demesne overflowing with a hundred Dalmyn retainers, all better trained and armed than any of your men. They would lay your land and your castle to waste before the king has a chance to get his share of the fun."

She relaxed and smiled. "Don't waste your time threatening the messenger. If you have a problem, King Otta is the man to deal with. You need not answer. I have seen enough, heard enough. I bid you good day. When my wagons are unloaded I will take my leave. If you have other carting needs, I remind you that Dalmyn has the Royal contract for roads in this area."

She made her sword-swoop curtsey and turned her back on him.

Once again the Dalmyn train exited the Lexing castle in a mood of high tension, and once again the portcullis remained up.

Out on the road, however, she called her riders to her. They waited while she wrote a short message and sealed it. "Jameta. You're heading back to Oudonsford immediately." She flipped a hand in the air. "No, I'm not sending you home. This message must get to the Capital as soon as possible. And I'm sorry, but you don't get to ride like the wind as usual. I'm sending Lavan to slow you down. That may hamper your style, but this message is too important to risk. Lavan, she might need your protection. However, I'm putting her in charge. Do you know why?"

He glowered. "Because getting the message through is most important, and her attitude is more likely to achieve that."

"Excellent! We'll make a guard of you yet. Now, you two get your gear together for a long ride. Take your spare horses and switch off. When you get to familiar territory, Jameta, trade for fresh mounts if you think you must."

"There are fast horses along the way, but I won't need them unless one of mine comes up lame. It's not that far."

"Neither will I." Lavan's back straightened.

She frowned. "This isn't a race, you two. Pace yourselves. When do you think you'll be in Oudonsford?

Jameta glanced up at the sky. "By sunset if he can keep up...without racing."

"There are more ways to botch things up than getting in an unnecessary fight. This message must leave for the south tomorrow morning. Impress that upon your uncle. Can you do that?"

"My uncle values the messages I carry. That includes the instructions that come with them."

"Good enough. Erlon, you know what your job is."

"Clear their backtrail. Nobody leaves the Lexing demesne after them."

"Precisely. You two can catch us at your own speed somewhere south of Decker the day after tomorrow. I suggest the long route to the north." She smiled. "I don't think we'll be in very good odour in the Lexing demesne for the next little while."

Jameta smiled. "There's a cutoff trail that bypasses Lexing property and catches the South Road over by the river."

"I bow to your expertise. Away you go."

Before they left, she pulled Lavan aside. "Keep an eye open for those two riders that followed us before. You can outrun them if your horses aren't tired. If they are tired, you need another plan. You have plenty of time to think. Away you go."

"Don't worry, Aleria. The message will go through."

"Preferably it will arrive with both messengers."

They mounted, spun away and were gone, their hoofbeats echoing away into the afternoon as their dust cloud settled behind them. Aleria climbed back up on the wagon seat. "All right, Maddoes. Next stop is Decker."

* * *

They received a much more friendly reception at the Royal Army base. In fact, Captain Teille could be called effusive when he met them. The rattle of quick rifle fire from the direction of the range might have been the cause.

Aleria tipped her head in that direction. "I gather you kept them all."

He nodded. "My superiors consider that conditions in this area warrant extra firepower, but there are no troops available." He frowned. "You sound as if you already knew that."

She grinned. "If I wasn't told, my cargo might tip me off."

His smile widened. "Ammunition?"

"Several cases. But they come with a condition."

"What's that?"

She handed him the official mail pouch. "I assume you'll want to check that. I suspect it also tells you that Dalmyns are the assigned Royal Army Carriers at the moment."

"And more than that?"

"Perhaps we will find it convenient to work more closely together in the near future."

The officer hefted the pouch. "If you will excuse me, my Lady, I think I hear desk duty calling. Shall we speak again at dinner?"

"Officer's mess?"

"Full dress, my Lady."

"If I have to eat Army rations, at least I can eat them in style."

"I will put the cooks on their mettle." He matched her grin. "Until dinner, then."

She nodded in response to his salute and turned to oversee the unloading.

The rations were acceptable and the brandy served afterwards was far beyond that. Aleria took a moment to swirl the glass up against the light. Then she sipped, looking straight at Teille over the rim. "You have your orders?"

He nodded. "Quite simple, it seems. It is the style of the Army to give rather detailed instructions, especially to a lowly Captain such as myself. However, this time I am simply directed to assist Lady Aleria anDalmyn in any way required to maintain the King's peace in the region."

"That seems straightforward."

"It comes as close to making you my superior officer as that." He snapped his fingers. "Pardon my bluntness, but how does a lady of your tender age get that kind of power?"

"King Otta may have a different perspective." She shrugged. "He was younger than I am when he took the throne. He seems to have done a decent job so far."

"I'm sure he would be pleased at your approval."

"I'm sure he hardly knows who I am, except in a general way. This power that I have was not all of my own earning. It is out of respect for the bloc my family represents in court, and more important, the king's perception of our loyalties. It has come to my attention that loyalty trumps many more lofty abilities."

"You don't need to tell that to an Army man. Well, what do you want?"

"Nothing, at the moment. I'm on the giving end right now. I have sent a report to those who are making the decisions, telling them that the king's message was delivered to certain parties, whose response was to threaten the king's messenger."

The soldier's hand went to his sabre hilt. "He threatened you? How?"

"The threat in itself is unimportant. What is useful is that it combines with our other information to point the finger of accusation clearly in the direction of Lexing Manor."

"How shall we deal with him?"

"I'm not convinced." She swirled her brandy again. "He's guilty. There's no doubt of that, but of what is uncertain. He still might only be an obstreperous lord, touchy about his boundaries and afraid that his enemies have the ear of the king."

"That's true. He wouldn't be the first to take the law into his own hands and have the right of it. Especially out here, far from the king's reach."

"Exactly. But now the king is reaching closer, and I am one of his hands. There may be others I don't even know. Probably are, I should think. My task is to gather information, perhaps stir up action. We'll have to see." She grinned. "I'll keep you informed. Least I can do."

"If you expect me to show up with a dozen Double-S rifles, a bit of notice would be appropriate."

"Good enough." She finished off her brandy. "Now, a long day on the road and this wonderful nectar of yours has primed me for a good night's rest. May I be dismissed, sir?"

"Be at your ease, Soldier." He stood. "Come to think of it, I wouldn't like to have you as a soldier. No offense intended, of course."

She laughed. "Similar sentiments have been expressed by those of more exalted rank than yourself. I seem to bring out the worst in military people."

He opened the door for her. "And the reverse?"

"Quite possible, Captain. I thank you for your kind hospitality and bid you a good evening."

"And you, my Lady. Sleep well."

She walked towards her tent at the Dalmyn encampment outside the post gate, but her mind was still on the conversation.

Now, why did I say that? When I rode into this camp, I thought I had the problem solved, the guilty party all ready to tie up. Then, when I thought about asking Teille to arrest him, I just couldn't see enough evidence. Somehow, this isn't as simple as I thought. Typical.

She slipped into her tent, hung her sword in its usual spot close to hand and rolled into her cot. In spite of her fuddled head, sleep was a long time in coming.

17. Interrupted Bath

Erlon regarded the tumbled stones of the old bridge, barely visible in the driving rain. "This is the point where I'm glad you're wearing the wagonmaster's boots."

Aleria glowered up at him. "You keep your eyes on the hills. I'll do my job. Maddoes?"

"Allus here, Aleria."

"I don't need to be reminded. You haven't had a bath for a while, either. Let's get back to the train. We need to camp."

"I could use a nice, dry tent."

"Right. Pitch mine first, will you?"

"Of course my Lady." He grinned and trudged back up the road. Her tent would go up in the order it came out of the supply wagon. Not before, not after.

She pulled the collar of her slicker closer around her neck, well under the brim of her helmet. "Any danger you can see?"

Erlon wore no slicker. His shirt was plastered to his back, but it was a warm rain, and he seemed able to ignore it.

I wonder if he's aware what that does to his muscles. Damn, I am going to have to solve this problem.

"Visibility's tough." He swung an arm. "Jameta and Lavan are up there on either side of the valley. They'll let us know if there's any trouble. That spot we stopped is as good a campsite as we'll find. Circle up and hunker down, I say."

"That's your military opinion, is it?"

He shrugged. "The warmer and drier the camp, the sharper the men are when they get posted on watch."

"I like the warm and dry bit, but I've got to climb under a wagon in the mud to check that repaired axle first. Let's get moving."

It took a while to get herself clean enough to go inside her tent and haul out her chart box. She muttered imprecations at whom ever it was that kept the maps updated in this gods-discarded piece of soggy earth.

There was a scratch at the flap.

"What?"

"What are you moaning about in there? The rain has stopped and there's a great sunset over the mountains."

She swung the flap open. "You two look like the dog dragged you out of a pond. Your horses cleaned up?

The two young outriders slipped inside, Jameta shaking her head. "Not until we talked to you."

"Go ahead. I don't see any need to ride around, now that it's getting dark." She indicated the map. "Where are we?"

The two leaned over the paper, comparing their experiences. Jameta put her finger down. "Right here." Lavan, behind her, nodded.

Aleria studied it. "That's right on the road."

"It is. This is the road on the map, and that's the bridge that is out. We broke the axle when the wagon slipped off the ford here..." she pointed, "...and we were too busy dealing with the breakdown to see that there's a smaller road that leads off to the north here."

"That's not a road; it's only a trail."

"It was when the map was made. How long ago?"

Aleria snorted. "Around the time we chased the Old Ones out of this valley. When do you think that bridge went out?"

Lavan teetered a hand side-to-side "Spring freshet would be a good guess. It's recent, but there's grass growing between the rocks, and there's no mud left around."

She nodded. "At least that puts us on Llannon's demesne. His people will be out and about tomorrow, and one of you will run into one of them, if nothing else. Otherwise we'll assume the road is north of here and scout that way, come sunup. You two get yourselves and your horses cleaned up. It's been a bitch of a day, and I want all hands on watch but short turnovers tonight."

Jameta perked up. "You want me to take a turn at guard duty?"

Aleria shared a grin with Lavan. "Don't look so pleased. I usually put you bright young snappers on the dawn watch. You're used to being up till then."

"So I'd better get organized. An early sleep tonight."

Lavan shook his head and followed the girl out into the dusk.

* * *

By morning, the rain had moved on, leaving them to deal with a heavy fog. Aleria sat on a wagon tongue with her second cup of coffee, looking up at Erlon and Maddoes. "We aren't going anywhere in this."

Maddoes nodded. "Not in this rocky terrain."

Aleria considered. "We'll break camp late today. Maddoes, have the men check out the equipment more carefully than usual, in case our route goes cross-country. I didn't like that axle breaking, just out of nowhere."

"Right y'are. We'll check the axles better, Aleria. An' the rest as well."

"Is the off wheel horse on the quad still limping?"

"He's fine this morning but we should rest 'im anyway, if we can."

"The Roan didn't pull yesterday, did he?"

"He's as feisty as usual. We'll put him in beside old Mariory. He tries anything, she'll nip him good."

"Fine. Be ready to move in, say, two hours. Erlon, what do you think?"

"A real goat-killer, this."

She wrinkled her brow. "Goat-killer?"

"Aye. Fog so thick not even the mountain goats can see where they're going."

"Well, I'm not worried for the goats, but we need men patrolling the ridges until it burns off. Remind them that sound carries in this weather."

"And what is my Lady doing while we all work?"

"I'm going to take walk around, see what the terrain to the north is like."

Erlon nodded and turned away. Aleria walked over to where Jameta was tying down her saddlebags. The girl looked different, somehow. Then she had it.

"You've got wet hair!"

Jameta turned, hand to her head. "That fog was sure damp out on the moor this morning."

"And you smell…" Aleria stepped closer. "You don't smell! I know what that means."

"Do you, oh all-knowing caravan leader?"

"Yes. It means you've had a bath. Tell me!"

Jameta grinned and pointed. "Leave camp up the stream, and when you get above the fog head straight towards the mountain with the double avalanche path and go for…I'm not sure how long it will take, walking…and you'll come across a nice little pool below a boulder. Water's chilly, but it's deep enough you can get all the way under."

"Good enough. I was coming to give you an assignment for the morning."

"Doesn't my wonderful information get me a break?"

"We'll set that aside for a later favour. I want you to whip back to that ford where we made the wrong turn. Head down the other road far enough to be sure it's the right one, and come and tell us."

"How long do I have?"

"I've told the men we'll be pulling out in two hours."

"Which means I'll be back to tell you where to go in two hours." She swung up onto the tall horse. "Don't waste the soap. We'll take baths tonight in hot water anyway." She wheeled around and cantered off.

Aleria strolled over to where Erlon was giving orders. "New plan. I'm taking soap and a towel with me. Be sure the men stay in camp!"

He grinned and nodded.

"You, too."

He said nothing, just wiggled his eyebrows and grinned.

If he can joke, it means we got it straight. I hope.

She strapped on her sword, made sure she had a change of underclothes, a towel and some soap in her pack, and headed up the stream that tumbled down the hillside next to their camp. Lord Llannon was an important man in these parts, and if she could manage it she wasn't going to show up in his demesne smelling like horses and mud.

As she climbed higher the sun began to push the fog away, and soon she was walking over rolling moorland, heather purpling the hillsides, punctuated by splashes of yellow broom. The high mountains of the Eastern Wall towered close by, their western faces still dark in shadow.

Just when it began to get warm she came upon a tiny pool in the lee of a huge rounded boulder with only its top half sticking out of the moss. It was an idyllic spot, with birds chirping and rustling in the bushes. She jumped up on the rock and stared around. No one moved on the moor. Slipping out of her clothes, she washed her underthings, spreading them against the sunny side of the rock to dry.

Then she stepped into the pool, shivering as the cool water slid up her thighs. She steeled herself and ducked fully under, straightening up sputtering and shivering, scrubbing water from her eyes. It felt wonderful.

She was reaching for the soap when a stick cracked. She froze, her eyes shooting to her sword hilt, jutting out over the bank nearby.

"Um...hello."

Aleria spun. There was a man standing on the bank beside her clothes. A young man in homespun hunting gear but with no bow. Well-armed, both sword and dagger, but he made no move to draw either. Two sloshing steps and she had her sword in hand. "Hello."

There was a moment of silence. She could see redness creep up his cheeks.

"I...didn't know what to do. I didn't want to intrude, but it wouldn't be right to stand here and not warn you."

"The obvious solution would be to go away." She backed into deeper water, her sword still threatening. There was no point in covering her nakedness, and his attention was drawn to her sword point, anyway.

"I don't think that would be a good idea."

"Why not? When I chose this pool, I was seeking privacy. You're not helping."

"You're not getting it."

"Obviously not."

"I don't mean me."

She scanned their surroundings. "Who?"

"There is a troop of soldiers coming over that hill any moment. They aren't my men, they aren't supposed to be here, and I suspect their reaction to a naked woman might be...problematic."

"Crap." Aleria splashed her way to the bank, her sword point pushing him back. She started to drag on her clothes, but her shirt stuck to her wet body and refused to cooperate. She cursed again and tugged at her sleeve, forcing her arm into it.

"Could I help?"

"Keep your distance!"

"If you say so. But it will be difficult getting that shirt to fit, twisted at the back as it is."

She snarled at him and yanked the shirt off. Now it was soaked, and she straightened it with difficulty. She thrust it at him. "Here. Hold this up. Keep your eyes to yourself."

"You are making that very difficult."

"Listen, friend. If there really is a troop of soldiers coming, I'm willing to forgive all this. If there isn't, you will be very sorry."

"You put me in the strange position of hoping a troop of enemy soldiers appears." He held her shirt at arm's length, his head turned away.

"How do you know they are enemy?"

"I don't. Here, the collar is stuck."

"Thank you."

"Now these, I think." She turned. He was holding out her breeks. She grabbed them and stumbled back out of range so she could put her sword down while she tugged them on. When she was dressed, she shoved her feet into her boots, trying to keep her eyes on him and the top of the hill.

"Perhaps it would be a good idea to remove the rest of your clothing from sight."

She looked down. Her underclothes. With another curse, she grabbed them, stuffing them in her pack.

"I notice that this gods-bedamned problem only started when you showed up. I can't help but wonder how much you have to do with it."

"I can see that you might. However, everything is now under control. No need for blasphemy."

"Blasphemy! You should hear me when I'm upset." She jammed her helmet on. Her half-damp hair was going to be a real mess when she took it off again.

"And this is supposed to persuade me that you are worth saving from these ravening maurauders?"

"Speaking of ravening marauders, I have yet to see even one."

"True. I could have made this all up, just to enjoy your discomfiture."

She regarded him again. Homespun coat, but good quality. Fine linen shirt, leather-reinforced trousers. Good knee-length boots, and the sword slung on the worn baldric looked more than serviceable. And an educated vocabulary to top it off. "Who the hell are you, anyway?"

He glanced around. "There seems to be time for introductions. I am Kolwyn anLlannon. That's Llannon with two 'l's."

"Yannon with two 'l's?"

"Yes. The double 'l' makes a 'y' sound."

"That's in the Old Tongue."

"You know the Old Tongue?"

"I know it exists, and it's full of 'l's and 'y's and 'w's. That's all."

"More than most people."

"So you're Kolwyn anLlannon. Wonderful."

"I don't recall that as a correct response to an introduction, Miss...?"

"No, I suppose it's not." She settled her sword belt around her hips, feeling much better. "But for the moment, my Lord, my name is Aleria, and let's leave it at that. Once we've dealt with your approaching friends, maybe we can do the introductions properly and have our etymological discussion over tea. If we're both still alive."

He glanced over his shoulder. "Don't worry, Miss Aleria. I can probably handle this."

"Just exude confidence, don't you?" She was acutely aware of the way her wet shirt clung to her, and the fact that her breast-binding was in her pack. She angled herself behind him.

18. Standoff on the Moor

AnLlannon was preparing to handle a troop of seven well-armed soldiers who strode through the heather towards them. The leader, a large man in a hardened leather breastplate and leather helmet reinforced with metal strips, took an aggressive stance. "What're you doin' here?"

AnLlannon raised his eyebrows. "That is hardly a polite greeting, my man."

The soldier put his hands on his hips. "I see onea you and sevena us. Polite don't count for much, then, does it?"

The lord slanted his head. "Strange. I could have sworn there were two on my side. I suppose arithmetic wasn't a strong point where you went to school."

The big soldier scowled, unsure of the point, suspecting the joke.

"And since you're on Llannon land, perhaps you might prefer to rethink the idea of manners."

"I ain't on Llannon land. This here belongs to Lord Lexing, 'n' you know it."

"If you were to check that stone over there, you would find that you have crossed a boundary you might wish you had not. Assuming that reading was on the curriculum at the school from which you played hooky."

The soldier looked in the direction that Lord Llannon pointed. "That ain't a boundary stone..."

He started to turn back, but the point of Kolwyn's sword against his throat froze him. Aleria thought it wise to draw her own weapon and stood at the lord's back, menacing the three soldiers who had circled behind, their grins fading. The young man's voice came from behind her.

"I don't recall giving it a name, but it is a stone, and you have definitely crossed a boundary. The one between life and possible death. Whether you return over it in one piece will be up to your soldiers. Ask them to move away."

There was no audible response, but the soldiers she could see took their hands away from their weapons and stepped back.

"Good. I like well-disciplined men. What I want them to do is form up and demonstrate how well-drilled they are by marching up to that ridge and over the top. What they do after that is up to them, but I suggest they wait for your orders."

There was an inarticulate growl, followed by a yelp of pain. "Do it now! That is not a suggestion."

"All right, all right. You heard what he said. Form up and march out."

There was muttering and hesitation, but finally the soldiers she was watching moved. She turned as they marched away, glancing back over their shoulders but marching nonetheless. Her new friend was still holding his sword to the officer's throat. When the men had retreated a good distance, he lowered it.

"Here is what is going to happen. Once your men are out of sight, you may go. My friend and I will head in the opposite direction. Once you reach your troop, you are quite welcome to turn around and chase us. That is, if you think you can catch us and are certain of the outcome if you should be so unlucky.

"Your other option is to go straight back to Lord anLexing and tell him that you made the mistake of straying into Llannon territory and thus have created an incident that will make relations more difficult between us. Do you have that?"

"Yeah, I got it."

The young man shook his head. "Don't they require manners, over there? At least you could allow me the privilege of my Rank."

"What's yer rank?"

"Not my rank. My Rank. You know, in the Lists of..." The lord sighed and ran his free hand down the side of his face, shaking his head. "Just go away, you horrible man. Go back where you came from, and don't return to my land." His head came up and his shoulders firmed. "Because the next time, you may not be lucky enough to leave alive."

The soldier glowered but seemed to have no heart for more. He turned and strode away through the heather, making no move to draw his sword.

"Why didn't you take his weapon?"

The lord shrugged. "I didn't want to embarrass him further."

"Embarrass! You stood him down in front of his men and sent him running home."

"A lord is allowed to do things like that. Rather expected to, don't you know?" He glanced at the soldier, halfway to the ridge, now. "Time we left?"

"I'm with you, my Lord." She shouldered her pack and they strode away at a good pace. As they walked, she glanced at him. Tall and rangy, wind-tanned face, broad in the shoulder, but he walked with a freedom she was not used to seeing. Not a military man.

"I'm curious, my Lord. Where did you come from?"

"Me? Oh, there's a little glen over there." He tossed a hand to the west. "I go there sometimes when I need a think. Your splashing distracted me."

"I do apologize, my Lord. I had no intention of disturbing anyone. I was only looking for a private spot for a bath."

"You didn't pick a very good one."

She felt her cheeks warm. "I didn't realize the heather would be boiling with males the moment I took my clothes off."

To her surprise, he blushed as well. "I'm sorry, Miss Aleria. I wanted to call out, but they might have heard me."

"Where are we going?"

"The nearest safe spot, I suggest." He glanced around. "We surprised those men and out-played them, but they're only soldiers. Given the time to think, there's really no guarantee they won't do something stupid."

She nodded. "My camp is just over that ridge."

His eyebrows rose. "Your camp?"

"Yes. The Dalmyn wagons."

"Of course. You're with the Dalmyns. But our reports had you coming in yesterday. What are you doing over on Clynecoom?"

"We took a wrong turn right after the ford, so we stopped for the night. This morning I ordered the men to strike camp while I surveyed the area. Actually, I was also hunting an excuse to get away from them, you know what I mean? No, I suppose you don't."

"I suppose I do." He grinned. "I was on a similar mission. You just get so tired of them after a while, don't you? Always asking you questions and looking to you for all the answers and generally expecting you to be their father and their mother as well as their lord."

She grinned back. "Well, there may have been some of that, too, but I was also looking for a place to bathe in private before we got to your manor. We've been on the road for weeks."

"When we get to Tyn Terfyn, you can have all the hot water you want. And a considerably more private place to use it."

"I'll hold you to that promise." She remembered her duty. "Now tell me about those soldiers. What were they doing on your land? Surely they know the boundaries."

He shook his head. "Not really. The boundaries aren't established in that valley. Father has petitioned the king, but...well, you don't want to hear that sort of..."

"I most certainly do. It's the argument with anLexing about King Buhl's Treaty, isn't it?"

"Where did you hear about Buhl's Treaty?"

"I suppose I should introduce myself properly. Aleria anDalmyn. I'm in charge."

"Of the wagons."

"And other things." She shrugged. "I'll have to wait and see before I tell you more. In any case, something must be done about these boundary disputes. We can't send our wagons into a position where they might be attacked by one or the other of you warring lords at any moment."

"We're not warring!"

She grinned at him. "That soldier who had your sword at his throat might think otherwise."

"I didn't have another plan."

"Oh, I'm not complaining. It's too early in the morning to have to kill a bunch of innocent soldiers."

"You were thinking of killing?"

"Lord Llannon, you were the one who bared his sword. If you draw a weapon, the assumption is that you're of a mind to use it. The man at the sharp end will think so." She pinned him with a glare. "Were you?"

He shrugged. "I suppose."

"Thank you so much." She shook her head and walked on. "You're ready to get me into a fight, but you're not sure you would have actually fought in it yourself. Remind me not to hire you on as a guard." She paced a bit farther. "Or sign a treaty with you."

He had lagged a step but now he hurried to catch up. "Say, now, that's a bit unfair, don't you think? I thought I handled that pretty well."

"Oh, you did fine. It's the hemming and hawing afterwards that bothers me. I like people who say what they'll do, and then do what they said. It makes life much simpler."

"Well, don't worry. If I draw my sword, I'm ready to use it."

"And can you?"

He shrugged. "I'm considered competent."

"Competent. You were about to get us into a seven-on-two, and you're only competent?"

"They were common soldiers. I doubt if they were competent."

"So, mister 'shucks-I'm-just-a-country-boy,' how good are you with that sword?"

"I'm good enough. How can I tell you without bragging?"

She dropped her hand to her hilt. "We could have a little test right now."

His head came up and looked around. "With seven hostile soldiers in the vicinity? I think we're better to keep walking."

She nodded. "Good choice."

"What do you mean, choice? Was that some kind of a test?"

"Always."

"You mean, you never really wanted to try me out?"

"You're catching on."

"Hmm." He did not speak until they topped the rise and saw the Dalmyn camp, now packed into the wagons, still circled up but harnessed and ready to go. The fog had risen, the guards had moved to farther hilltops and Erlon was already striding towards them.

The young lord nodded slowly. "Not surprising you ended here. The road used to go this way until early this spring. It's a far better surface than the other route, but there's a bridge out up ahead."

"We noticed. Hence the camp."

"It crosses a rather steep ravine. We can't afford to fix it. So now we go the long way round."

"We'll consider that as well. What's the best way to get to your manor?"

"Depends."

His shrugs were beginning to annoy her. "On what?"

"If your wagons are light and your teams are strong it's not far. If you need good road, we go all the way back."

"My teams are the best, my teamsters without peer and my wagons are mostly empty. Lead the way."

He looked at her, apparently decided she was serious. He pointed. "That way."

"Let's wait for my guard Captain."

Instead of stopping below them, Erlon continued until he was at an equal level on the hillside, forcing Aleria to turn away from Kolwyn to look up at him. The soldier did not speak but subjected the lord to a head-to-toe examination.

Kolwyn returned the inspection, but from a height disadvantage.

"Kolwyn, this is my guard Captain, Erlon. Erlon, this is Kolwyn, Lord an Llannon."

Erlon waited long enough to complete his perusal. Then he dropped his head, but not his eyes. "An honour, my Lord." He turned to Aleria. "Orders?"

"Lord Llannon says that if we can climb this hill, we'll reach the other road easily."

Erlon nodded but did not move. *What's wrong with him?*

"So, let's go."

"As you wish." Erlon turned back down the hill and signalled the wagons to follow.

It was only after he had gone a fair distance away that Kolwyn spoke. "That's a formidable sword he carries."

"He's very good with it."

"That must give you confidence."

"I have a good outfit. We've run into one bit of serious trouble recently, and they handled it well."

"Not on this trip, I hope."

"No, things have been going smoothly. Until today."

"Good." He turned, scanning the ground nearby. "Let's see if we can keep them that way. Perhaps over there would be the best place to start the ascent."

Aleria glanced over the area he indicated, then waved to Maddoes, who reined his team in the correct direction.

The route was rough and steep but passable. The horses were blowing and sweaty by the time they reached level ground, but there were no injuries and no equipment had broken. She surveyed the road ahead. "This looks better."

"It suffices. I do wish we could fix that bridge, though."

"Give me a reason for Dalmyns to run a regular route out here, and maybe we can make a deal."

"Are you serious?"

"Why would I joke?"

"I have found, in my short and uneventful life, that people joke about all sorts of inappropriate things."

She sized him up. "And you've had your share of being the subject?"

His usual shrug. "It has happened."

"But not since you learned to use that sword."

He glanced down at her and a smile formed. "It does seem to make a difference."

"I think that once we get settled at your manor, you and I just have to cross swords."

"Another test?"

She imitated his shrug. "Yes, but this one might be all sorts of fun."

He rattled his sword, grinned, and stepped up to the lead wagon. "Let's go. My mother is waiting. She's looking forward to meeting you."

Just as they headed out there was a patter of gravel, and Jameta pushed her blowing horse over the bank. She cantered alongside Aleria's wagon, her shirt soaked with sweat.

"Spoiled the effects of your bath."

"I'll get another. In case you're wondering, you're on the right road."

"Are we? And how would you know that?"

Erlon grinned from his saddle on the other side of the wagon. "Because she rode up here and back," he pointed to the road, "around an hour ago."

The girl frowned. "How do you figure that?"

"Unless somebody else around here has a long-legged horse with those light, rounded shoes that your family's farrier makes, that was you."

"But the time? How can you tell the time on a hard road like this?"

Aleria chuckled. "By arithmetic."

"Arithmetic?"

"He saw when you left camp and divided the time in half."

The girl made a sound of disgust, then glanced at the third passenger on the wagon and inclined her head. "Good morning, Lord Llannon."

"Good morning, my Lady. You're one of the beauteous Dennals, are you not?"

"No, I'm only one of the regular Dennals, my Lord. Jameta. I brought you a letter last year."

"Ah, yes. I should have recognized the horse. That was a timely delivery, as I recall. Very fast."

"Thank you, my Lord. You are too kind. Except for the part about the horse."

"What? Oh...I didn't mean..." He began to redden. "I meant..."

Aleria burst out laughing. "Don't bother, Kolwyn. Whatever you say, she'll take it wrong, and you'll be no further ahead."

He smiled sheepishly and said no more.

"And now that you have proved your worth and insulted our host, young lady, you trot on up the road to cool your horse down and check that there are no ambushes, washouts or errant flocks of sheep in the way."

"You just want to keep him for yourself."

Aleria put on her best scowl. "Precisely. Scoot!"

Jameta lifted her reins and floated away at an easy lope.

"Where did you find that one?"

"She has been foisted upon me as penance for my multitude of sins."

He glanced down at her. "Must keep the trip interesting, anyway."

"Interesting, I don't need right now."

"No, I can understand that."

The serious tone broke the laughter of the moment, and they sat on the wagon seat in silence for a long while.

19.   Tyn Terfyn

Lady Favia anLlannon stood at the top of the steps leading up to the main hall of Tyn Terfyn, two smartly turned-out soldiers flanking her, a major-domo in somber black at her shoulder. Aleria and Kolwyn were forced to stop two steps below and look up at her.

"Lady Aleria, I may I present to you Lady Favia anLlannon. Mother, Lady Aleria anDalmyn."

Aleria, as the higher-Ranking, nodded her acceptance. It was proper form for the lower Ranked to speak first.

"So this is Aleria anDalmyn. Not quite what one might expect from the Elite class."

Aleria stood straighter, regarding the tall, gaunt woman in front of her. Lady Llannon looked a well-preserved fifty, her carriage unyielding, her face too long to be called anything but handsome. Her dress was quite up to the styles of Kingsport, however, and if her jewelry was real, she was dressed for an occasion.

Since this family was a potential ally, Aleria decided to smile. "Perhaps I am what one might expect from the wagonmaster of a long-range wagon train, just off the road." She removed her helmet. "The problem with my hair is a longer story, involving an unintentional but embarassing interruption."

"I am all agog to hear it."

Kolwyn grinned weakly and shifted from one foot to the other. "I promised her a bath, Mother."

The woman gave a short sniff, which hopefully had more to do with elevating her nose than with Aleria's state of hygene. "At least you found enough manners to demonstrate appropriate hospitality."

"Where's Dad?"

His mother demonstrated where her son learned his shrug. "Your father is out getting his hands dirty, I suppose."

"That means around the farm somewhere. I must get the Dalmyns settled, mother. We can talk at supper."

Lady Llannon nodded. "We dine early out here in the country, Lady anDalmyn. Would seven suit? Do you require a maid?"

Aleria had no need for a maid, but someone to pump about local conditions was always useful. "That would be delightful, my Lady. Until dinner, then."

They exchanged proper curtseys, which Aleria carried off despite the lack of a dress. She had developed her own adaptation, which involved running the side of her hand gracefully down her scabbard instead of along the sweep of a full skirt. Kolwyn said nothing, but bowed to his mother and led the way into the manor.

"So that's your mother."

"Yep. That's her."

"Dresses well."

"I suppose she does. You impressed her."

"I did?"

He grinned. "Yes. It's the only way. Stand up to her."

"I didn't notice you following my lead."

The shrug again. "She's my mother. I show due respect."

Aleria thought it best to keep her opinion on that to herself.

"That was an interesting curtsey."

"We adapt as we must. I think the sweep of the hand is meant to indicate the form of the lady's dress. Either to show it off or to beg approval, depending on her attitude."

"So your sweep shows off your sword. Is that a threat?"

"It might indicate that my sword is at your service. Take your pick."

"You certainly are entertaining. I do hope we aren't enemies."

"Hmm. A real flatterer."

For some reason he reddened, and they paced a moment in silence.

"Should we see to your men?"

"Thank you. I am sure anLlannon provides appropriate quarters."

He grinned, "I'll have to remember that one."

She shrugged. "It suits a lot of occasions." She glanced up at him. "And who would dare give Erlon sub-standard accommodation?"

As he pushed the outside door open the sound of clashing steel brought a meeting of their eyes, but a cheerful shout relaxed them, and they went out the main gate to investigate. On a stretch of grass beside the castle wall, Erlon had his guards working on some basic exercises. A few Llannon soldiers lounged nearby, probably hoping to be invited in.

Kolwyn raised his eyebrows. "You don't stand down for long, do you?"

"We've had a few surprises lately. Puts us on our mettle."

Her host ran his sword half out of the scabbard, then back in. "Seems I remember a certain invitation."

She tugged her helmet down tight. "Yes. I promised you some fun."

They stepped into an open space and squared off.

It wasn't fun. The moment Aleria stepped onto the training field with Kolwyn something changed. His deferential mood evaporated, and there was no hint of a shrug. He attacked strong and fast, and she was hard put to keep him at bay. In the first five passes he made three touches, the third a hard blow to her helmet with the flat of his sword that made her ears ring.

In desperation, she picked up the speed of her attack, using quick chops and lunges to probe for those small holes that his larger sword was too slow to cover. In this way she managed a touch on his outer thigh, but then she was back on defence again. She was sweating heavily and her breath was coming in gasps when he stepped back and grounded his sword, his free hand waving. "Good enough. I can't take too much more. Where did you learn to fight like that?"

"Me? Where did *you* learn to fight like that? I thought we were having a friendly match."

"Oh," a slow grin. "I just wanted to show you that once I had drawn my sword I was willing to use it."

"You rogue! You set me up for that!"

He held up a hand defensively. "Not on purpose. I didn't expect you to be able to match me. I thought I'd demonstrate my level, and you'd quit." His head slanted to one side. "You don't quit, do you?"

"Not as a rule." She studied her blade for nicks. "Maybe you'd prefer a go with Erlon, there. He might give you a better run."

Kolwyn regarded the big soldier, leaning on his hand-and-a-half sword near the castle wall. "Now who's being set up? You wear me down and then turn your biggest ape loose on me." He tipped his head to Erlon. "Not meaning any offense to apes, sir."

Erlon strolled over. "No offense taken, my Lord. Surprised you a bit, did she? I always have trouble when she starts nipping away like that. Just can't get my sword around in time."

"Like fighting a pack of terriers."

"So, shall we stand here discussing my merits as if I'm a prize mare, or are we going to practise?"

The two men's eyes met, and it was Erlon who shrugged. "You're tired, my Lord. You want to spar a bit, slow-time, just for fun?"

Kolwyn nodded. "You learn things when you're tired."

Aleria stepped between them. "Just remember. This is not a competition. We are trying to forge ties here, not break them. My Lord Kolwyn, you are on your honor. Erlon, you are under orders. Keep it light!"

Erlon winked at Kolwyn as they strode to the centre of the training ground, the soldiers giving way before them. "Note that I don't seem to have any honour to appeal to. But I do follow orders."

"We should be all right, then. Have at you, sir."

"Have at you, my Lord. May the best man survive to work with Aleria next."

It was an entertaining bout, and the importance of the lesson was emphasized by the fact that the audience of soldiers and guards soon stopped cheering and began to watch both fighters carefully. The two were mismatched: Erlon with his powerful, slow weapon, and Kolwyn with his shorter but faster horseman's sabre. As they fenced, their speed increased; soon they were both sweating freely and the clang of the swords came quick and loud. Aleria watched their faces, not their weapons, and was satisfied that there was no emotion taking over. In fact, if she was any judge, they were enjoying themselves immensely.

Finally they parted by unspoken agreement, each wiping a hand across his brow. The audience set up a cheer. The two fighters turned and bowed, then gave each other a formal salute.

"Well, that was instructive." She glanced at each one. "Learn anything?"

Kolwyn snorted. "Aye. Don't come anywhere near him in a fight."

"Don't worry, my Lord. I'd be avoiding you as well."

Aleria shook her head. "That was fine, but it doesn't help us much. Give me a moment."

Puzzled, they both nodded, and she turned to set her guards to one of their standard exercises, helping them to include those of the castle soldiers who wanted to try. When all was going well, she returned to the two, sizing them up.

"What do you mean, 'It doesn't help,' Lady Aleria?"

"A fight against a friend is all very well for developing respect, but in a battle you'll be on the same side, and that's a completely different matter. If we were to be attacked some day, I can see two scenarios. First, you, Lord Llannon, will need to blend in with our forces."

Kolwyn nodded. "And second, you will be supporting me, and I'll be finding a place for him with my men."

"That's right. And the most difficult adaptation you might require is fighting side-by-side. The spearhead is one of the most effective attacks, especially if the strongest men are at the point. If the two of you led a charge together you'd be wellnigh invincible. If you didn't get in each other's way."

"That's easy." Kolwyn grinned. "Send him in front, and I'll fill in on his left side. I just stay away from is backhand."

"Right. And if there are three of us, I get the sweet spot under his sword. He fights the high line, and I stay low. Got it?"

Erlon frowned. "Why do I get the feeling that there are clouds gathering?"

She grinned and walked over to the bin of practice wands. "Better use wooden ones for this. We wouldn't want you hurting anyone."

She called her guards to attention and explained the situation. "I want you to attack these two and see how you fare."

Domin hoisted a wand and flexed it. "How many of us, Aleria?"

She surveyed the grounds and pointed. "We'll put their backs to that wall, and you get as many as can get a reach in."

The guards began to grin, but she shook her head. "Don't expect it to be easy."

They became serious and lined up.

The practice was more like a melee, with little progress made by anyone. However, a few of the castle guard soon joined in, and Aleria took her turn as well, both on the attack and as part of a defending trio. Everyone was having so much fun that they got very enthusiastic. It was a good thing the swords were made of wood.

Once it was all over and Aleria, Erlon, and Kolwyn were sitting in his workroom with pints of ale in front of them, they looked at each other. Kolwyn raised his mug. "That wasn't only fighting practice, was it?"

She grinned and they touched rims. "Every practice has several objectives. The main intent for this exercise is still going on. In here and out there." As they drank, laughter echoed through from the main hall.

Kolwyn nodded, his smile disappearing. "What are you preparing us for?"

She leaned her elbows on the table. "I did not come here intending to take sides, but things have worked out differently from what we expected. Don't they always?"

"In what way?"

"I am not at liberty to give you all the details, but I will say that those who are interfering with you have also broken the king's law in a serious way. So I can predict that, should this come to hostilities, your people will probably be on the same side as mine."

He glanced at Erlon. "I think I'd enjoy that."

The big mercenary raised his tankard in thanks.

"So any training our men can get together is to our advantage."

"Anything else I can do?"

She sighed. "This is a bit delicate. I can't give you too much information..."

"...because you don't trust me yet."

"Glad you understand. Just because you were a gentleman this morning doesn't mean you're an all-round hero and loyal subject of the King."

"Oh, but I am. Well, a loyal subject, anyway. I have yet to prove the first part."

"If you'll take my advice, that's your best plan. Stay loyal and you'll be supported. I can't guarantee how much, but it's got to be obvious that King Otta is turning his eyes this way. Your little out-of-the-way valley is attracting attention."

"And not all the good kind."

"Not all of it."

Talk ran on a while, but there was nothing important to decide.

Then a smartly dressed page knocked at the door and in the most correct terms required Kolwyn to attend his mother. The young lord gave a proper response, sent a crooked grin to Aleria and started to leave. Then he turned back. "You haven't seen your rooms yet."

"I haven't."

He turned to the page. "Letham, see Lady Aleria to her rooms. You know where she's quartered?"

"Aye, my Lord."

"Good. Then you can inform Casseya that she is wanted."

"Aye, my Lord."

"Then check on the hot water for the lady's bath. Got that?"

"The lady to her rooms, the maid to the lady, bath water."

Kolwyn reached out and ruffled the boy's hair. "Good lad." He grinned at Aleria and strode away, leaving the page to straighten himself, busily hiding his pleasure at the attention.

Erlon and Aleria strolled back to where the Dalmyns were quartered, the lad trailing by a respectful distance.

"Like him a bit, do you?"

She started to frown, then relaxed. "I like him. And you?"

"He's some fighter. Plays fair in practice. Plays too fair in politics."

"What do you mean?"

"I'm not sure I follow that shrug and the, 'Don't mind me, I'm not important' line. It doesn't suit a swordsman of his abilities."

She considered. "I know what you mean. He does seem a mix, doesn't he? Of course, if the demeanour was developed young, and then he learned swordplay..."

"Could be. What are the parents like?"

She glanced around to be sure the page was out of earshot. "The mother's a character, no question. Had me pegged and told me so in no uncertain terms. Haven't met the father yet."

He nodded. "Any orders for the men?"

She shook her head. "Couple of days rest: check the stock, maintain the equipment, take it easy, no fights with the locals, no pregnant girls left behind. Have a good time."

Erlon grinned. "A couple of those may be mutually exclusive."

She slapped his shoulder. "Where would a hill boy from Shaeldit learn an expression like that?"

"I dunno, Ma'am. Maybe he learned ta lissen when 'is betters was talkin'."

"Well, keep lissenin', boy. There's lots around here ta learn."

He nodded and stepped out into the courtyard where the teamsters were cleaning harness.

She turned to wave the page ahead of her. "To my chambers, young fellow."

"Right away, my Lady." He strode away down the hall, and she had to skip to keep up because her mind was elsewhere. *I ask a question, and he ducks back into his 'dumb merc' role. And manages not to answer me. Hmm.*

20. The Lore of the Old Ones

Tyn Terfyn was the biggest of the manors they had visited, a proper fortress with a crenellated curtain wall supported by sturdy turrets at each corner. The huge main hall looked rather empty that evening. Aleria, fresh from a bath and with her hair braided by a well-trained maid, took special care with her dress and wore all the jewelry she carried. Which wasn't much, but she had chosen it carefully, and she thought it did the trick. Anyone with her blue eyes and those sapphire earrings didn't need much else, anyway.

Lady Llannon knew the proper Ranking of everyone, and Jameta was placed to Aleria's left at the head table. The food was excellent, and the harpist who entertained them was well beyond competent.

She smiled to herself, thinking of Fauvé and his pretenses.

"My Lady is amused?"

She glanced over at Kolwyn, sitting to her right. He was dressed in a deep blue crushed velvet doublet now, his blond hair swept back and held with a band at his collar, revealing the sculptured line of his cheek. Not exactly the rough country lord she had crossed swords with this afternoon.

"I was comparing your hall to several other places I visited recently. This is very pleasant."

"We do our simple best."

"And import your spices from Samnia." She turned to Lady Favia. "Am I right?"

Her hostess allowed her a smile. "The cinnamon on the apples came from Samnia, yes."

"It is difficult to keep it fresh when it comes so far."

"Not if it comes overland."

Aleria could not hold back a frown. "Overland? That's a long journey as well."

Lord Llannon, who had not spoken much, coughed gently. "We have...contacts to the east."

"Down the Trench and through Monteglina Pass?"

"There are perhaps more ways through the mountains than is generally known in the Capital. This is the territory of the Old Ones, you see."

"And the Llannon's keep the lore of the Old Ones?"

"Much of it handed down through the old ways, less of it in written form."

Aleria leaned forward. "You mean that you have writings here that survived from the time of the Old Ones? Writings that they do not have in the University Library in Kingsport?"

"The material has been made available to the Library." Llannon smiled. "A few scholars have seen my store, and fewer still consider that any of it has value."

"You think otherwise."

The elder lord's eyes twinkled. "The scholars who came were interested in poetry, history and philosophy. As one who must live in this valley, I am more concerned with the lore of those who farmed and hunted here for the past two thousand years."

"That long?"

"I believe so."

"How did you learn to read the Old Tongue?"

"We are not completely devoid of education, far as we are from the centres of learning."

She felt her face warm. "Of course not, my Lord. I did not mean..."

He waved a calming hand. "You meant that the Old Tongue is difficult and the sources of learning are few. However, my family has passed that lore down through the centuries as well."

She turned raised eyebrows to Kolwyn.

He nodded. "Oh, yes. Winters are long and snowy here in the mountains. What better way to spend my time than in poring over moldy documents?"

She thought about that for a moment. "Do any of your moldy documents make reference to the boundaries of the land in those days?"

Father and son exchanged glances, then both shook their heads. "What use could we make of that?"

"There is a gap in the records, and ancient boundaries of any sort might indicate how more recent borders were drawn."

Lord Llannon nodded. "Perhaps it would be worth another perusal although our papers are poorly organized, and we have more pressing events to keep us occupied."

"Please, Lord Llannon. I am interested in all aspects of this area. My family business is considering expansion here. Anything useful...."

The older man smiled without humour. "If the Old Ones left us something useful it might make up for the other things they have cursed us with."

"What curse is that?"

"They seem to have left us with one of their legends. It killed three sheep in the upper pasture last night. Carried one away and slashed two more."

"A powerful legend."

"Dad, I still think it was a bear."

"The tracks show no claw marks, so it isn't a grizzly. I have never heard of a black bear with feet that big. Or that shape. If I wasn't an educated man, I would be certain that the Ghost Beast is back among us."

"The Ghost Beast?"

He turned to her. "Yes. It is an old legend, passed down to us through the tales of our families, probably from the Old Ones themselves. There is supposed to be a huge monster that lives up in the mountains around here. Bigger than a boar grizzly, but with needle-sharp claws. According to the legends, it moves on its hind legs much more easily than a bear. Vicious and smart. Rarely seen. Moves at night. Tears its victims apart, gobbles them down or carries them away. Apparently it can haul off a full-grown steer. It certainly managed a large sheep last night."

"Does it attack people?"

He shrugged. "According to the lore, yes. No evidence of it in my memory."

Kolwyn leaned closer, and she couldn't help but notice the clean, slightly sweaty smell of him. "Don't worry about your stock, Aleria. The Beast lives in the mountains, only attacks the sheep on the upper pastures."

She turned her grin to him, refusing to lean away. "I'll take your word for it."

He reddened and sat back.

His father was regarding Jameta. "And what of the Dennal family, my Lady? What does your uncle have to say to us?"

The girl frowned as if in thought, but Aleria knew it was for show. "I call him Uncle Arjan, but he is my full cousin in the second generation. My father's cousin would be my first cousin once removed, wouldn't he?" She appealed to Lady Llannon.

"She has the right of it, Grayton. Well done, my Lady. Your family keeps the traditions, I see."

The girl twinkled at Lord Llannon. "When your family is as large as ours, it's hard to keep everyone straight, otherwise."

The older lord nodded. "It is also a tradition of Samnia, is it not, to be careful of family lists?"

"Oh, yes, my Lord. It isn't that many generations ago that our people worshipped their ancestors. Of course we left that sort of thing behind when we came here."

Lord Grayton shook his head. "Isn't it wonderful how the people of our realm come from so many places? Their stories must be fantastic."

"And are you gathering them?"

"Alas, no." He shook his head. "I read what I can, but I can spare no time for the travel involved."

His wife patted his arm. "And you'd much rather be at home taking care of your acres and sleeping in your own bed."

"And there you have it." He smiled across at Aleria. "A scholarly career mired in wheat chaff and sheep dung."

"If you cannot go looking for the people with stories, it follows that they must come to you."

"And you, young lady, wave the magic wand and presto! They come?"

"I do, my Lord. It's called Dalmyn Cartage. Once our wagons start rolling through here on a regular basis, the world will be passing your doorstep. You have but to hold out your hand."

"I'm afraid this is still the back side of the mountain. Why would anyone come here?"

She shrugged. "Eventually, there could be a circular route from Kingsport around the northern loop to here, then down the Trench and out the southern end and back to the capital."

"And what would persuade the wagons to make that long a trip?"

"Time will tell. Perhaps iron?"

The Lord burst into laughter. "And you listen to the lore as well. Iron mines in the mountains." He calmed. "Can you imagine how many men come through here with maps and stories, claiming they own the secret to the lost iron mines of the Old Ones? And most of them either don't come back, or we find them weeks later, lost and raving. No, the mountains around here are steep and unforgiving. It doesn't take a Ghost Beast to make them dangerous. If there is iron, it will not be found in my lifetime."

She took a sip from her goblet. "Well, there must be something. The scenery is beautiful. Perhaps we can bring parties of Ranked folks from the capital for visits. They enjoy going rough for a change."

Lady Llannon's eyes opened wider, but after a moment's thought she shook her head. "I had not thought to spend my declining days as an innkeeper."

Aleria laughed. "My Lady, much though I'm sure most of the Ranked in Kingsport would love to stay here in Tyn Terfyn, I was thinking of more rustic surroundings. Duke anCanah has a wonderful mansion on a lake up in the

Northwest, built completely of huge logs. It is a renown structure, and to be invited to visit is a great honour."

"And you have seen this building?"

"Raif Canah is married to my best friend." She shrugged. "I could hardly avoid it."

The older lady's eyes flicked to Aleria, then away. "And that name was dropped with consumate grace."

So we are playing this game, are we? Aleria put on her 'polite' face. "I do apologize, my Lady. I must assure you that my own relationship with the Canah family is purely social. My father's company carries the lumber from the Duke's mills. That is all." *Let her take that as she wishes.*

"I see." The lady glanced at her husband, and their eyes met for longer than was necessary.

Aleria held her grin back. *Now they have something to chat about at bedtime.*

Kolwyn slipped a comment to Jameta into the pause, and the conversation rolled in other directions. The evening soon wore down, as several of the participants had been up early, and all had put in a full day. Soon Aleria and Jameta were strolling back to their quarters. The younger girl glanced across a couple of times, and Aleria finally took pity on her.

"Go ahead and ask."

"Well, I didn't want to pry, but..."

"But you're curious as hell and you want to know what was going on."

Jameta shrugged and grinned. "Will it help my family?"

"Of course it will. That was me besting Lady Llannon at the name dropping game."

"I saw that part of it. What happened after?"

"When she challenged me, she was playing the 'tough but straightforward old lady' game. So I responded with the 'naïve young girl who has overstepped,' but she knew I didn't mean a word of it."

"I caught that part. But it sounded like there was a whole lot more to it."

"There is much more to the connection than I let on, but she couldn't ask me, could she?"

They walked in silence. "You left her with a lot of unanswered questions."

"And a lot of information to think over. When she decides what she really wants to know she'll ask me straight out. Or her husband will. My bet is her."

Jameta grinned. "Bird bet?"

"You're on for a penny."

"A penny it is."

Aleria frowned to herself as she made ready for bed. *And I must think very carefully how much I answer. Too quick a judgement could be fatal, but if it comes to a choice...*

* * *

Aleria lost the bet.

The following morning, Lord anLlannon returned to the dining hall just as she was coming in for breakfast. From the way he was dressed and the dirt on his shoes he had already been out and around his demesne, but he took a cup of coffee and sat down beside her. "Do you have time for a chat, today?"

"I am at your disposal, my Lord." She made a move to pick up her plate, but he laid a hand on hers, smiling.

"No hurry. I'm not rushing off anywhere. No Ghost Beasts to chase today."

"Oh. Good. Say, Erlon is a bit of a hunter. Want to make a try for it?"

He shook his head. "Maybe some day when the trail is fresh. I've tried it before. Got tired of losing dogs."

"That bad, is it?"

"Yes, it's too smart to come to bay. It circles around, kills a few, disappears again. Must be very fast."

They sat thinking about that until she had finished her breakfast. Then he signaled a servant to refill their cups, and they strolled to his office. The lord flicked a finger to his son, who followed them.

Once she and Kolwyn were seated, he threw himself into a big, soft armchair and steepled his fingers in front of his face. "Lady Aleria, I do not follow my wife's diplomatic style. I think it is time for us to sit down in a friendly way and lay out our plans, see where they mesh, find solutions if they collide."

She nodded. "We can do that."

"And since I have no plans with regard to you, it behooves you to start."

"And I can do that."

"But before you do, it is usual to present some credentials. You represent Dalmyn Cartage, and I can deal with you happily on that basis. However…"

"…there is more to it than that. Correct. I have thought long and hard about this, and I consider that recent developments require an open approach." She reached into her belt pouch and pulled out the waxcloth-wrapped package that had not left her possession the whole trip. She took her time opening it and handed him the parchment folded inside. "You are the first to see this."

"Should I be pleased?"

"Considering the circumstances, yes. The only other way I envision needing it would involve you leaving with me. In chains."

"I see." He scanned the document. "It's rather simple, isn't it?" He raised his eyebrows; she nodded, and he passed it on to his son.

She shrugged. "It seems useless to try to predict the whys, wherefores and howsomevers in a situation like this. It is better if his Majesty trusts his agent to act in an appropriate way."

"He obviously trusts you." Kolwyn put the letter back on the table with a certain reverence. "This gives you a degree of latitude."

"If you had seen the orders given to Captain Teille you would understand how large a degree."

Lord Llannon pushed the letter towards her. "Then aren't I glad this is a friendly meeting?"

"I assume we both are." She packaged the letter again, put it away and tied the strings. "So, now that you have the ear of the king, do you have anything to say?"

He gave that question the time it deserved. Finally he lowered his hands to the table. "Yes, I do. It is most important to have the issue of the boundaries solved. Most of the lords around here are strong men, used to fighting for what they can get. They wouldn't survive otherwise. Given a fair and firm set of rules, they will all play the game. However, given a weakness in the rules, each will assume – quite rightly in many cases – that his neighbor will take advantage of that weakness at the first opportunity. So he feels quite justified in starting his own play."

"A fair assessment in any situation, so I see no reason to question it in this case. And the boundaries are the weakness. Everyone is agreed on that. But what can I do to help you with them? King Otta understands that there is no sense in forcing a boundary. That's why the arguments are here now, because of poor diplomacy in the past."

Grayton threw up his hands. "And if Old Forbach hadn't burned himself up with the contents of his office, there might not be any problem. But having no deeds or descriptions means that all our information is lore and hearsay, which is notoriously open to interpretation."

"But you have a collection of papers from the Old Ones? I hadn't heard of them, and I'm sure nobody back in Kingsport even knows they exist."

"Oh, they exist, all right. I have scouted through all of them at one time or another. There are no maps, and nothing I remember that looks like a deed or land description."

"Any records of legal cases, assizes?"

"Nothing. I will go through it all again, of course. If I thought it would help, we could package a bunch up and send them to the University, where they read a lot faster than I do."

"We'll do that, at least."

"But there is one more source...I suppose."

She had no response, only looked at him expectantly.

"The Old Ones."

She saw the twinkle in his eye and refused to respond.

Finally he gave in. "All right. There is no secret tribe of Old Ones living in the hills. But we have the next best thing. Tyn Dyfnant."

"Which sounds like a fortress."

"Yes. Reputed to be the last redoubt of the Old Ones, when the modern people of Galesia drove them out."

"And in what sense do you have it?"

"The road starts in my demesne. The citadel is in the mountains to the east. Not far, on the eagle's path."

"But on the human path, I assume it is a bit farther."

"A trifle. And rather up and down in places."

"But you're not the one going up there."

"Of course not. You young ones go and play your games. Kolwyn has been there before. Several times that I am aware of."

She glanced at Kolwyn, "That you are aware of?"

The elder Llannon grinned. "My son has been known to go wandering in the mountains. Good for the soul, apparently."

Kolwyn gave his noncommittal shrug. "Any opportunity for peace is not to be made light of."

"What are we likely to find there that will help us with the boundaries?"

Grayton sat back and sighed. "Not necessarily anything. The place has been open to the weather for centuries. But it delves far back into the mountain, to depths the forest animals never go. Once there were libraries there: parchments, scrolls, maps. That is where our collection comes from." He smiled. "It is an unofficial rite of passage for our young people to go up there the summer they turn sixteen and search through the ruins for what they can find.

We try to stress books, but they often come back with tools and weapons. Some even useful. Kolwyn's sword came from there. But he has also brought back many parchments over the years."

"But what is left, after a thousand years?"

"Now, that is your Galesian education speaking. Your people first came here a thousand years ago, granted. But the takeover wasn't as sudden as that."

"Of course not. We are taught all those eras. There was the Emigration, the Great Migration, then...I think the Warring Kingdoms, the Pact, the Rebellion...I get those mixed up..."

"And you just burned through six hundred years of history, while the Old Ones were all along living happily up here in the mountains, barely recognized by anyone on the plateau below. It wasn't until around four hundred years ago that the Kingdom of Galesia was formed, uniting all the small warring principalities and expanding its boundaries to their present extent.

"Over the following hundred years the Old Ones closed their doors and disappeared over or into the mountains, never to be seen again. The soldiers of the Kingdom made a show of ransacking the final fortresses when they found them, but there was no one left to fight and nothing of value left to steal, so they came home."

"Leaving the hidden hoards for future explorers."

"That's the picture. And speaking of hoards, there is another legend."

"Let me guess. 'The Hidden Treasure of the Old Ones,' or something like that."

"Where did you hear...?"

"I read Romance novels, but I didn't realize that we had the setting for one in our back pasture. What is this tale specifically?"

He smiled. "Rather nonspecific, as you might expect. With Tyn Dyfnant, it happens to be jewels. The Dowry of the Last Princess."

"And so four or five waves of invaders have ransacked the place searching for them. Too bad. They probably destroyed anything valuable, like books and maps."

"Considering that the last few waves were Llannon youngsters, it's not that bad. And now you will become the next wave."

"I suppose we must."

"And maybe..."

"...maybe we'll run your rogue black bear to ground while we're at it."

"It could happen." He raised a finger. "But please remember. This is only a slim chance of a solution. If it comes to risking even one of your party, you must stop."

She sighed. "That's a decision I make on a daily basis. Don't worry. I take good care of my people."

"That, my dear, is not the same thing."

"No, I suppose it isn't. But you don't get far in my business with any other attitude. I hope you realize that is whom you're sending your son and heir out with."

"My son and heir is capable of making his own decisions. I'm sure he'll do just fine."

Aleria turned a firm eye on Kolwyn, and his growing smile faded. "Just remember that there may come a time when he doesn't get to make his own decisions." She pointed to her belt pouch. "And that letter says I'm in charge."

Kolwyn nodded. "If it comes to battle, only one leader. Stands to reason."

She glanced at him again, but his easy acquiescence seemed genuine.

"Right. When do we leave?"

The elder lord laughed. "Why the hurry all of a sudden?"

"You might not have noticed yet, but I have a wagon train of animals and employees at the moment making inroads into your larder. I can't rationalize having them sit here for long while I take a camping trip in the mountains."

"Don't worry about the fodder. If anything you do solves any of these problems, it will be worth it. And having extra

181

armed men sitting around my castle gives me a sense of security I haven't had for a while."

"Even so, we should leave soon." She raised her eyebrows at Kolwyn.

"Tomorrow is fine. Choose your companions. I'll take a couple of local hunters. They're good trackers and they use bows. For hunting only, of course."

"I won't complain. Erlon's bow is meant for convenience, not power. I wouldn't want to match it up to a grizzly."

"Or anything tougher."

"That would be certain."

She began to rise, but Lord Llannon's gesture stopped her. "There is one other matter."

She sat back.

"Did you bring any other men with you?"

It didn't take her long to figure that one out. "You mean any others that did not come into Tyn Terfyn when our train did? You mean two competent-looking men riding dark brown horses? You didn't happen to find their bodies in a ditch, did you?"

"As it happens we didn't. Two such riders have been seen recently. Once before you came, once last night. The consensus is that they are good at their trade, assuming we can guess their trade."

"Too bad. I thought perhaps your Ghost Beast might come in handy for once."

"So they are no friends of yours?"

"No idea. They have been shadowing us since our first day on the road and not bothering to be subtle."

"And if we run across them?"

"You might give them my compliments, remind them that the Samnians are holding their Solstice Celebrations on the other side of the continent next month, and suggest that it might contribute to their good health should they attend."

He grinned. "I'll keep that in mind. Do you think they'll be any problem for this expedition?"

She glanced at Kolwyn. "We'll be alert enough already, and they haven't caused us any trouble so far." She rose. "Kolwyn...?"

He preceded her to the door, swept it open.

She dropped a quick curtsey. "Until later, my Lord."

Grayton rose and nodded them out.

21. The Ghost Beast

Aleria took Lavan, Jatto, and Domin. Jameta insisted on representing her family despite the lack of horses. That left Maddoes in charge of the train. He seemed unhappy with the arrangement, but couldn't argue, considering his position. There seemed no good reason for his desire to go, and she filed that away for further thought.

The pack she was carrying as they left Tyn Terfyn was heavier than she liked, considering the mountains of the Eastern Wall that reared their heads over the upward-winding path. However, it was two day's hike to Tyn Dyfnant, and they needed food for a couple of days of searching at least. Plus three or four days of emergency rations. Kolwyn said they could hunt for meat, but you never knew...

Still, it was good to get out and moving under her own power instead of sitting on a hard wagon seat. They followed the road upwards, heading due east. Soon they turned a corner, and Tyn Terfyn was out of sight. Now the valley narrowed to a canyon, and rock walls closed in. Open scars down the mountainsides showed the paths of slides, some of them reaching all the way down to the stream, which meandered across the valley floor, avoiding the piles of rock in the easy way of running water.

Just after lunch they came to the place where the road ended. Steeper canyon walls had forced them farther and farther up the mountainside, and the road clung to the side of a rocky face. Considerable energy had been required to hack a path across the steep spots and fill in the chasms. Finally, they reached a corner where all the forces of nature came together. The road ran a narrow ledge beneath a tall avalanche path, and a larger-than-average spill had wiped it off the face of the mountain. The piles of broken rock ran all the way down to the stream, damming it into a small lake at that point. The double track of the road simply ran into the rubble and disappeared.

Now they were on an animal trail that wound among the rocks of the slide. Huge boulders piled into caves and canyons, dark shadows on the bright mountainside.

"Grizzly."

All eyes sprang to one of Kolwyn's guides, who pulled a tuft of hair from a sharp corner of rock along the trail.

"How recent?"

The little man smelled the wad of fur. "Bin rained on."

They nodded, filing that technique away for the future, and trekked on. They were more watchful, though, and it wasn't long before Jatto called quietly for attention, pointing across the valley. Sure enough, a large, dark-brown bear with light tips on his outer hair was lumbering along, turning over logs, breaking stumps and generally enjoying himself in the sunshine. Erlon strung his bow and slung it across his shoulders, switching his sword to his belt. The two guides already had their longer bows canted the same way.

Soon the road reappeared and walking was easier. All afternoon they climbed. The track widened and narrowed, but always succumbed to the might of the mountains.

At one point Aleria admired a drystone causeway, partly destroyed by a huge boulder that had smashed down the mountain and stopped, unable to penetrate the man-made obstacle, but blocking the road anyway. "Must be expensive, keeping a road this rough open all year."

Kolwyn nodded. "I gather the Old Ones let it fall to ruin long before they left the area."

"Stands to reason. Make it difficult for an attacking army."

Aleria wiped her sweaty forehead. "How much farther?"

"We usually stop overnight at an old way station. Aldwyn?"

"I'd say 'nother coupla hours, M'Lord."

Kolwyn had introduced her to the two shepherds he had brought as guides and hunters, Aldwyn and Blodwel, but she was having trouble telling them apart. Small, dour men in similar sheepskin vests and knitted hats, they did their work with efficiency but, it seemed to her, little joy.

But the eyes of the one that trotted up to her later that afternoon– Aldwyn she thought – were positively snapping.

"My Lord, Lady Aleria. Come see this. You gotta come!"

She glanced at Erlon, and they shucked their packs. The little man led them up a steep canyon, then across a ridge where the ground fell away on both sides into nothingness. Aleria clutched her sword hilt for security and strode ahead.

On the other side of the ridge their path swooped down behind a pile of boulders. A small spring made its way to the surface, creating a swale where flowers peeped through reeds and grass. And where huge feet had pressed their imprints deeply into the soil. Feet as wide as both of hers together and over twice as long. A curved row of pinpricks showed the span of the claws.

It might have been comical the way they all looked down, took a moment to register what they saw. Then, as one, their hands crept to their sword hilts, and every eye swept the surrounding mountainside.

"It's fine, M'Lady. He's long gone."

She snorted. "As long as it doesn't decide to come back. What is it?"

"Dunno, M'Lady. Big."

"It is that. Bear, I suppose. Claws barely showing, and sharp points. That means a black."

"Yes, but it ain't no bear."

"Why not?"

"Cause the back foot is same to the front, M'Lady."

"And a bear's?"

"Back foot's long, same's ours, front foot's short 'n' wide."

"What makes prints like this?"

"Dog 'r cat, I guess."

"A dog or cat this big?"

"Can't be a dog, M'Lady."

"Not enough claws showing."

"Aye. 'N' th' shape's not right."

"So it's a cat."

The tracker held out his hand. "Shot a mountain lion oncet. Cat was as long as Lord Llannon, standin' up. Paw was big as m'hand, not countin' th' claws. That's all. Cat that makes a track this big? He held his hand out, raised it above his shoulder until he could stretch no higher. Then he regarded his hand and hid it behind himself, shaking his head. He scanned the ridges around them. "Hope he don't come back."

"Any more tracks?"

He glanced at her. "You wanted me to look for more?"

She shrugged. "Well, he's long gone…"

"Aye. That he is." The tracker began to move ahead, his eyes down. Then he looked back. "Yous might as well go on back down t' th' trail. No sense everyone getting' et up at oncet."

Aleria shot him a grin and turned back down the ridge. "Be a fine thing to come back and he's stolen our packs."

The sharp ridge seemed much easier on the way back, and she navigated it swiftly. Blodwel was lounging near their packs. He looked up. "Didn't git et, then?"

"No, he decided to save us for tomorrow." Kolwyn leaned down to stare into the little man's eyes. "He's eating the ones that taste like sheep first. Get out on the other side of the trail and keep your eyes open. If you find him, do lots of yelling while he eats you. Give the rest of us a chance to run."

"Aye, M'Lord. Glad to be of use, M'Lord." The man picked up his bow and strode into the rocks.

They shouldered their packs and continued.

They were up in the alpine, now, a light breeze cooling them. Stunted trees only survived in sheltered ravines, and bare rock and flower-strewn moss bordered the trail.

"This is a decent path, considering it's never used."

Kolwyn kicked at the moss. "The wagon track is still here, underneath. It's in much better shape at this altitude. Still viable, except for the small slides and windfallen trees in the gullies. Once you get through the slides down below, it's not too bad. Take ten men a summer to put it back in use."

"You think so?"

187

"I know it. Came up with an engineer from Kingsport last summer."

"Why would you do that?"

He shrugged. "You never can tell when you'll need information, the way the politics are working out. The man was down the Trench working for another lord, and I hired him for a day. Didn't cost much, and now I know."

Aleria hung back a bit so she could talk privately to Erlon, who had heard the exchange. "I wonder what he has planned up here that he's not telling us."

"Anything to do with iron?"

"My first bet."

"No takers." His head came up, and he indicated the trail in front of them.

She turned to the front, where Kolwyn was standing still looking down. "Watch your step. Bear sign."

He was regarding a large heap of something bright red, scattered with what looked like small seeds.

"Whatever causes that?"

"Raspberry season. They're always the first ones to ripen. Bear's been down on the lower slopes. No berries this high. Grizzlies come up here for the grass roots along the streams."

"And to get away from the flies, as the other animals do." Erlon mopped his brow and shook his hair in the breeze. "Sure blows the webs out."

Everyone nodded and put their shoulders into their packs again.

* * *

The way station was in reasonable shape: four good walls and half a roof. Perfect for letting out the smoke from the fire. It also only had one doorway and backed into an overhanging cliff, which made it defendable. Once they burned up the packrat nest they found in the corner it was almost cosy.

When supper was over and the sun was down, they sat around letting the fire die with the fading light, allowing their night vision to develop naturally.

Erlon turned to Kolwyn. "What do you think the chances are of trouble tonight?"

"Bears? Not a party this size with somebody on guard."

"I wasn't thinking of bears."

"Ah. Our bigfooted friend from this morning. Again, no evidence of any attacks in my lifetime. And there's hunters and herders up here all the time. Any humans you're worried about?"

Erlon glanced to Aleria, raised his eyebrows.

She considered. "There's always our usual shadows, but they haven't made a move in two weeks. Anyone else? None of us is particularly special. Well, maybe Kolwyn."

"Me?"

"You want to start trouble, you kill off somebody's heir."

"Or a representative of a certain important somebody."

"There you go. Worth posting guards, not much else."

Talk rose and fell among the men, and Aleria caught Levan's voice and the word, "courage." She began to listen.

"It's very difficult to show true courage."

Jatto's voice contained a hint of laughter, although his face was clear. "And why is that? Because you got none?"

"No, because the only way to handle a dangerous situation is to prepare yourself for it. If you go in shaking in fear, you can't function. But if you prepare yourself emotionally, then you're not afraid any more, are you? So by your definition of courage as going ahead even when you're afraid, you aren't showing courage."

"That wasn't exactly what I meant. I was sayin' that if you went into a situation that was dangerous, but you didn't know it was dangerous, then that wasn't really courage."

"I agree with that, but I think that people who are seen as courageous are often just prepared and competent. The danger is less to them because of it."

"So how do you show true courage?"

189

The lad shrugged. "Exactly what I'm saying. It's difficult."

"Guard the outside of a door."

Their heads turned to where Erlon leaned on his elbow a short distance away.

"What?"

""If you want to imagine how you'd react in a dangerous situation, think of this one. It happens. Your client is trying to escape from pursuers. You come to a door and go through. If you lock and barricade that door, it's going to slow the enemy down for long enough for your client to escape. Where do you set yourself up to make your stand?"

The other guard scoffed. "That's easy. Behind the door. It takes them a while to break it in. Then they come storming through, off balance, with bits of the door in the way. You make a stand there as long as you can, then retreat if you can." He shrugged. "If you can't, well, you've done your duty, and you can die proud."

There were nods around the campfire, but Erlon shook his head. "Of course that's the safest way, Domin, but you're giving the enemy free access to the door. If you stand on the outside of the door, maybe that gives your client a chance to do a better job of the barricade inside, and more time to get away. If you're good, the enemy never gets to the door."

Lavan's waved a hand. "But your odds for survival go way down. What good is that?"

"But we're talking about bravery at the moment, not practicality. Too many people consider bravery to be making some grand gesture. For the soldier, bravery means putting your duty above your personal safety. What we do on the average day isn't worth the wages we get. Many days we sit around and do nothing. What we're getting paid for is the possibility that we might be forced to put our personal safety aside.

"If you stand on the outside of a locked door, you're saying, 'This is my stand. I have no retreat. I win or die.' That's courage."

Lavan nodded slowly. "I see what you mean. That makes it rather difficult, doesn't it?"

They all nodded, and silence fell: the silence of the mountains that spreads its vast presence over the puny human soul. Aleria couldn't help but feel closer to her little band, allied against such might, such beauty.

Except, maybe, for one of them. She hoped she had left that problem back at Tyn Terfyn. *No way to know until it's too late. Nothing to be done for the moment.* She nodded to the duty guard and strolled away from the camp, allowing the star-washed night to enfold her.

"Company?"

She didn't turn. Kolwyn's smooth baritone was unmistakable. "Only if you don't break the spell."

"Now you see why I live here. I'm glad I brought you."

She turned. "I thought I brought you."

"Now who's breaking the spell?"

"Hmm." She turned her gaze outward. "I do that."

"Keep me in my place?"

"You're as sure of your place as anyone, and nothing I could do or say would shake that conviction."

"Have I just been flattered?"

"If I may quote a barmaid of my acquaintance, 'It's only flattery if it ain't true.' And only you know if it's true."

"A barmaid of your acquaintance?"

"If you only came out here to quote me to myself, I'm going to find it very boring, very soon."

"Sorry." He was winding a kerchief around his hand, all his attention on the job. "I'm just trying to get a handle on who you are."

"Hundreds have tried. Including me."

"Any luck so far?"

"A work in progress. Best I can do at the moment."

"Aren't we all?" He rested his elbows on the battlement, regarding the kerchief, wound around his fingers.

"You? I thought you had it all settled."

"Hardly. Knowing my place is a start, but it makes my plans for the rest of it more difficult."

"It does? I'd have thought it would help."

"No. Restricts all the other choices." He pulled on the ends of the kerchief, and it seemed to slide through his hand, leaving the fingers free. "But I can live with that."

"I see."

"What about you? Free to choose?" He began winding again. Back and forth, crossing over and over.

"Huh. Everything that has ever happened to me has restricted my choices. If you'd come to me three years ago and told me that right now I'd be up in the mountains watching the stars with you, I'd have laid fifty-to-one against it. Just goes to show."

"And if you'd made the same prediction about where I'd be, I wouldn't have considered it worth a bet. But who I'd be with? No idea. Turns out its you."

"You comfortable with that?"

"A challenging quest with a competent crew. Not much chance of success, but worth a try. I'm fine with that." Again he tugged the ends, and the cloth came free as if it had not been wound around his fingers at all. "You?"

"Couldn't be happier."

"You mean that, don't you?"

"Why would I lie?"

"Yes. Why spoil a beautiful evening?"

They stood for a while longer, gazing out at the star-lit mountains, rolling away out into the dark. After just the right time, without a word, they turned and strolled back into camp.

After her duty watch Aleria tucked herself into her bedroll and slept the sleep of the weary who have earned it.

22. Tyn Dyfnant

To wake in the morning with several well-earned aches. From the moans of the rest of the party, she wasn't alone.

"Not used to this sort of torture?" Kolwyn was grinning. "You should spend a month or two overseeing a demesne like mine. You'd soon harden up."

"Don't be unsufferable. If I took you to sit on a wagon seat all day, you'd have your own reason to groan."

"I'm sure I would, but until that time, I'm happy to feel superior."

He was interrupted by a discreet snuffle from one of his hunters. "Yes, Blodwel?"

The man indicated a direction with his head and turned away. Intrigued, Aleria followed the two. Off in a grove of trees beside the waypoint a patch of earth had been recently turned over. Aleria leaned closer but was driven back.

"What is that smell?"

Kolwyn, too, turned away. "That would be a latrine, is my guess."

"Oh." She frowned. "Whose latrine?"

Kolwyn beckoned the little guide over. "What do you say, Blodwel?"

"Bin used by a lota men, M'Lord. Two, three days ago. Rained up here since then, so we ain't seen no signs on the trail."

"So there's been a group of, what, eight or ten men, either up or down this trail a couple of days ago?"

"Somethin' like that, M'Lord."

"Any way of telling if it's up or down?"

The little man grinned. "Nope. People tend to crap the same way, goin' uphill or down. Begin' M'Lady's pardon, Ma'am."

She smiled. "That's fine, Blodwel. Keep your eyes open from now on. I don't want to meet a dozen men by mistake up here."

"You got that right, M'Lady."

They returned to the fire and sent the whole group to scour the surroundings. Sure enough, they found a buried garbage tip. The men were more willing to investigate this find, and they came to the conclusion that the meal had been for ten or twelve men. They covered it over again and returned to their camp.

Aleria looked around the circle of faces. "Well, there it is. There might be twelve men up here ahead of us. There might be two behind. We've got a Ghost Beast prowling around. Maybe we'll be lucky, and they'll all run into each other first."

That brought a few smiles.

Kolwyn frowned. "A thought occurs to me. They're using the way station, but they left the rat's nest intact. Why?"

"And why hide their garbage? Only reason I can think of is that they don't want anyone to know they've been here."

Kolwyn nodded. Erlon met her eyes with no disagreement.

"So, eyes open and swords loose in the scabbard. There's no reason to believe anyone is hostile, but no reason to trust any of them."

Kolwyn stepped forward. "Another thought, Aleria. We haven't been acting as if anything's wrong before this. I don't see any reason to advertise our presence any more than necessary. Let's stay on the trail today. Don't leave any evidence of our presence unless necessary."

"Good thought. Aldwyn, you can bury our garbage right on top of the other pile. That'll mix them up if they come looking. Now, breakfast is probably cold, but the coffee ought to be strong enough to make up for it."

They ate well, stocking up their reserves for the day ahead. And lightening their packs. Then they pushed their protesting arms into the shoulder straps and threw their aching backs against the load.

So they slogged on up the trail, over two separate passes, following the watercourses that roared down from the glaciers that hung above them. Aleria didn't like the noise of the streams because it made ambush more likely, but they passed the day unmolested, as the trails divided and narrowed. Soon only the local knowledge of their guides kept them oriented.

The uncertainty disappeared as they approached their goal. Tyn Dyfnant had been a massive structure, choking a side pass that led out of a broad, meadow-scattered valley. Both gate towers had tumbled outward, and their stumps sat like broken fangs on either side of the pass, the fallen stones stretched like welcoming arms across the valley floor. Behind the ruined wall, tier upon tier of empty windows climbed upward and faded into the rock face on either side. The roofless trunk of a huge round keep speared the skyline of the pass.

Kolwyn pointed to the keep. "That's where we camp. The old royal chambers a couple of floors up have bigger windows and a balcony. The spring in the inner courtyard still flows, and one inside the fortress as well."

"Nice to be treated with appropriate accommodation for my Rank, anyway."

Kolwyn laughed. "If it didn't leak in the rain it would be perfect."

Up the valley they trod, watching the fortress loom over them, higher and higher as they neared.

"There's so much stone lying around."

Kolwyn looked at Jameta. "What did you expect?"

"I have been to several of the ruins of the Old Ones, and usually there's no loose stone. It's all gone somewhere."

He grinned. "You mean the local people stole the dressed stone for their own buildings. No locals were left here, and it was too difficult to get this stone down to the Trench once the road washed out. If you're thinking of rebuilding, it's just a big puzzle, all the pieces here for you to put back together."

They all laughed, but later Aleria noticed the girl walking around looking at different stones, then up at the broken walls, as if trying to find their homes.

They entered the fortress, skirting fallen blocks as high as Aleria's waist, treading on equally-large flagstones, cracked and heaved by the frosts and erosion of centuries. The entry court was a good hundred yards wide and almost as long. A series of wide steps led up to the main entrance of the keep, its doors long disappeared, nothing but rusted pins indicating where they had hung.

"They had iron."

"So it seems. Perhaps the doors were still in place when they left."

They proceeded into the building, the grass and weeds thinning as they went from the direct sunlight into the cavernous space of the main hall. Curved staircases marched up opposite walls, meeting in a presentation platform high above the floor. From there, straight staircases led to the floors above. Aleria paused for breath on the platform, looking out over the hall. "Can you imagine giving a speech from here? This place could seat a thousand people."

She clapped her hands and listened to the sound echo around the chamber. "If they were so powerful that they could build all this, why did they give way for us? From what I can gather, the Galesians never could agree on anything for long enough to mount a serious army."

"From the lore of my family, I gather that the population had dwindled by that time. The upkeep on a place this large takes a thriving economy to support it. Perhaps they were defeated before you came."

"By who?"

He shrugged. "Time, ennui, disease, political upheaval."

She turned and looked around. "Well, we're here to find out more. Where are my chambers?"

"Right this way, my Lady." He led the way up the stairs to the left, and they climbed up to a set of rooms with a crenellated balcony overlooking the weedy main square and the fallen towers. Everything seemed solid here, although black streaks showed where water regularly ran down the walls and across the floor. It seemed strange to be rigging canvas inside, but they soon had a fine camp set up against one wall, the smoke from their fire suctioning up the huge chimney.

Kolwyn stood out on the balcony watching the smoke rise from the chimney top, far up the mountain above them. "Hate to advertise our presence, but we're here legitimately."

"We have a right to be here," Aleria loosened her sword. "And the strength to defend ourselves."

Erlon grinned. "Let'em come."

Dusk was creeping into the old fortress. Since the valley ran south, the sun went down early behind the high mountain on their right shoulder, and shadows stretched across their view. The air was crisp, and they were happy to gather close to the fireplace. The necessity of hauling firewood from a copse in a sheltered canyon several chains away kept the fire small.

"Maybe they ran out of fuel."

"There is coal all over these mountains, some of it right out on the surface."

"Then why are we hauling wood?"

"Because we haven't had time to look for coal. Tomorrow, while those of us that can read search for documents, we'll send the others out with Aldwyn and Blodwel to hunt for fuel and meat and scout the area for large bodies of men. A nice juicy yearling mountain goat or sheep would look very homey, roasting in this fireplace."

"It would. Which rooms contained the libraries?"

"The real libraries were closer to the light and easier to destroy, by either man or nature. Any scrolls out in the open would be stolen or burnt for fuel. What we're looking for are cupboards, chests, high shelves that might have been missed. Maybe some sort of secret panel. The farther back into the mountain we go, the better chance we have."

Aleria nodded. "Because the darker it is, the smaller number of people show the nerve to go there."

"That's it. Keen to try?"

"Shouldn't we wait till morning?"

"Daylight doesn't make much difference back there. I brought paraffin lanterns." He hauled them out and set them on the stone bench. They were basically brass cylinders with handles on the top. Attached to one side was a rough wheel.

"Those look rather...Mechanical, don't they?"

He grinned. "I suppose you could say that." He picked one up and twisted it. Part of the cylinder slid around, revealing a glass tube inside. He rolled the wheel with his thumb and a spark flew. Then a soft glow appeared, and Aleria was looking at a standard lamp. In a very non-standard cage.

"Very clever. How does it work?"

"The body is simple. It's one tube inside another. You can close it right down to a fine slit," he demonstrated, "or twist it open wide to light a room."

Erlon picked up one of the other lamps. "And the lighting part must have a piece of flint in there somewhere, like a flintlock gun."

"Exactly. The wheel is rough tool steel, and it rubs against the flint and throws a spark onto the wick. Presto! Light."

He passed one lamp to each person, and they all experimented.

"If it won't light you adjust the flint and the wick. I suggest you figure that out right now because it's darn difficult in the pitch dark."

After a few minutes of experimentation, everyone felt confident.

"Ready to go?"

The first few rooms were disappointing: dust, water stains, packrat nests. The group pushed farther in, losing the signs of animals and running water but stirring up more dust. When they had walked for several minutes and made several turns that seemed random, Kolwyn halted them.

"Right, now, children. Time for fun."

"Fun?" Aleria flashed her lamp around. "Yes, this certainly looks like fun."

"We call this area the Nursery. It is a maze of small, interconnected rooms. We always stop here to get newcomers acclimatized. We divide into two teams, and the first team tries to catch the second team. Half way through, we switch roles."

Erlon nodded. "Good practice. In case we do it for real."

"Right. So everyone pair up with an opponent the same size and speed. Now everyone step back two steps. Those facing me are the prey. You run on my count. The hunters flash a light on you and call your name to catch you. Prey, your job is to sneak around and get back to me. Ready? Go."

The prey spun and disappeared, the flash of their lanterns on the walls showing where they went. Aleria had been watching Jameta and was primed to catch her.

Kolwyn raised his voice. "Hunters? Three...two...one...go get them!"

Aleria sprinted towards the room where Jameta had disappeared, her lantern on full beam. The moment she entered she realized her mistake. The lantern lit the whole room – a mess of broken boards and dust – and obliterated any other light. Immediately she twisted her lantern shut except for a thin beam and pressed forward. She assumed that the girl would take the opposite doorway, at least of the first room or so. She checked the dust on the floor, and sure enough, a set of small, clear tracks skirted the junk and went out that door. She followed, flashing her light suspiciously into every shadow. The best technique for the prey would be to circle back or to hide out and let an unwary hunter stomp right on by.

After five rooms she had lost sight of any tracks and wasn't completely sure which way was home. *Let me see. I came straight through the first two rooms, then left out the next, then sort of angled right. I think. Time to change tactics, Aleria.*

She stopped and closed her light. Immediately she could feel the weight of the darkness close in. She slipped the light open again, relieved that it lit the room. Then she realized that she couldn't remember which door she had come in. *I think it was that one...* She went to that door, but there were no fresh footprints in the dust.

I've learned my lesson. I'm getting nowhere, wandering around in the dark. Time to go back and set up an ambush.

With painstaking tracking and wracking her faulty memory, she worked her way back to where she could see the glow from Kolwyn's light. Then she retreated into the third room, relaxed behind a pile of broken boards and, after a momentary gathering of her courage, closed her lantern. As her eyes became accustomed, she could pick out the glow of Kolwyn's lamp touching the far doorjamb. This gave her something to focus on, and she felt better. Soon quiet descended.

She listened, starting to distinguish individual noises. Over the next few minutes she heard fragmentary shouts, laughter and running feet, but everything echoed and bounced, so it was impossible to tell which direction it was coming from.

After a while, a light passed outside her room, and she got up and crept up behind the bearer. When she flashed her lantern open, it was Domin, the caravan guard who was a hunter in the game.

"Caught anyone?"

"Not a chance. I was lucky to find my way back. This place is impossible."

"I'm in that room. You take the one over there. Hide out, and we'll catch one of them coming in."

"Good idea." He faded into the darkness.

But no one passed near them. Conversation from the direction of Kolwyn's light showed that some had found their way home, but it was too quiet to tell whether it was hunter or prey.

Then three sharp whistles cut through the murk, followed by Kolwyn's voice. "Game over. Everyone in."

She widened her lamp beam and stepped into Domin's room. They shrugged at each other and walked out.

It didn't take long for most of them to return. From the conversation, everyone had experienced the same difficulties and hadn't gone far.

"It's completely impossible in there. The moment I turn the light off I can't see, and it scares the hell out of me. If there was someone waiting for me with a sword..."

Kolwyn laughed, but there was sympathy in his voice. "That's the reason for the game, Domin. How did the prey find it?"

Levan spat on the floor in disgust. "Same problem. If you turn off your light you can't go anywhere. Then you turn it on, and anyone can see you. Plus the the footprints on the floor. The best way is to find places to walk where there isn't any dust."

"Did you find any of those?"

"No."

"Didn't think so. Anyone missing?"

Aleria glanced around. "Erlon and Jameta."

Kolwyn whistled again, and was answered by a return whistle a few rooms away. Soon Erlon strode in, holding a frowning Jameta by the scruff of the neck. "Look what I found wandering around the corridors."

She twisted away and slapped his hand. "You never would have caught me if that pile of junk hadn't slid."

"No, I wouldn't. But it did. And I did."

She shrugged. "I suppose you did." She looked around. "Anyone else get caught? What, no one?"

Aleria laughed. "No one else had Erlon after them. What took you so long?"

Erlon dusted his hands together. "It was luck. I wasn't after her at the start, but I caught a glimmer of light and followed. She was really moving, and in a straight line. I had to hoof it to catch her."

"I heard him coming and ducked into a hole, but the wood I hid behind fell apart. I almost covered him with it! " She gave an evil grin. "I should have pushed harder."

Kolwyn looked around at them. "We've made a good start. Let's switch positions and try again."

The next half of the game went in a similar fashion, although Erlon and one of the shepherds made it back. Everyone agreed that they were getting more comfortable in the dark.

Kolwyn nodded. "Which is why we had the practice. Let's head back to camp, eat supper and make plans. By the way, how many people were worried about finding their way back? I thought so. There are only two ways in and out of this maze, so you can't really get lost. That's why we play the game here."

"Then Jameta put her finger on the other way out. There were only her tracks in the latest dust, and we were in a long hallway, leading...west, I think." Erlon pointed.

Kolwyn frowned. "You can tell which way west is?"

The big man raised his eyebrows. "Sure. It's that way." His finger wavered. "Or thereabouts."

"Is he right?" Aleria looked around the chamber. Every wall seemed the same.

Kolwyn shrugged. "Probably. Most people get turned around pretty quickly in here."

They straggled back to camp, discussing their experiences in the dark. Aleria walked beside Kolwyn.

"Is there any kind of navigating technique you can teach us?"

"There are ways, none of them reliable, but they do help. In the morning, I'll train the search teams, and we can start looking. People tend to get better at it as they get used to it."

She shuddered. "I don't think I'll ever get used to the pitch dark. It feels as if the whole weight of the mountain is going to crush me."

He glanced down. "Do you want to go out with the hunters instead, tomorrow?"

"Don't concern yourself." She gritted her teeth. "I said I didn't like it, not that it would scare me off. I'll be fine."

"There's no dishonour. If closed spaces bother you, they bother you. It's not your fault."

"I'm not the type to panic. As I said, don't worry about me."

"I worry about everyone. That's my duty."

"Thank you for that. I'll tell you if there's any problem."

"Fine."

They entered camp and everyone dusted off. Blodwyn stoked up the fire and began to prepare the meal.

Aleria got a damp cloth and wiped the dust off her face and neck. "Ah, that feels better!"

Jameta passed her a small vial. "Try some of this. Gets that awful musty stench out of your nose."

She pulled the stopper. The smell was beautiful, a combination of light floral scents with a deeper musky accent. She shut the vial and handed it back. "I don't think so. I might need my nose if my eyes don't work, and it wouldn't be too useful with that surrounding me."

"You mean I can't use it?"

"Maybe that's how Erlon found you."

The girl's mouth turned down, and her brow wrinkled. "I never thought of that. I guess I'll go smelly from now on."

Kolwyn leaned over. "Couldn't help but overhear. You ladies want to come for a little walk with me."

He led them deeper into the citadel on a corridor that was well cleared of dust by many feet. Up a narrow staircase and a right hand turn, Aleria heard the sound of running water.

She glanced at Kolwyn. "Functionaries?"

"That's right. The Old Ones invented a very effective type of plumbing." He rounded a corner and pointed with pride as if he had created this wonder himself. A stream spurted out of the wall and dashed along a series of basins at waist height, disappearing into the floor.

"The water's cold but perfectly drinkable here." They followed him along to the next room.

"You ladies are down this corridor." A large "L" was scratched in the stone of the wall. "Gentlemen on the other side. No need to flush. The stream runs underneath."

They inspected the facilities, which were very impressive, especially considering their age.

"So. Anyone staying, or shall we return together?"

The two women made eye contact, one of those quick glances that conveys an instant message, and followed him back down the corridor.

"I've always wondered how you do that."

"Do what?"

"You know. Women always want to straighten their hair at exactly the same time. And they never say so out loud, they just suddenly get up and walk out. Quite disconcerting, when you're sitting right there and miss the whole thing."

Aleria reached forward and slapped his shoulder. "Don't worry, I've seen soldiers do that kind of thing when they're fighting. They don't say anything, but suddenly they both move exactly the same direction."

"I suppose."

They reached the bottom of the stairs, and Kolwyn slowed. "Listen." He froze, the lantern held high.

They stopped, waited for the sound of their own heartbeats to settle.

"Hear that?"

"Voices."

"We're not that close to our camp yet, are we?"

Kolwyn lowered the lamp again. "Sound echoes strangely in all this rock."

Aleria elbowed him. "Say, let's take the chance to pay Lavan back."

"For what?"

"For being Lavan. Shroud the lamp and we'll sneak back and see if we can catch them off guard."

"But they aren't guarding this side of the camp."

"Maybe they should be."

He nodded, and they crept forward in near-darkness, the single ray of light from the lamp focused on the stone directly in front of them.

Twice the voices faded, then returned again. It was difficult to tell, but now they seemed to be getting louder. Not only louder, but more urgent. She touched Kolwyn's shoulder, and he stopped. They both listened.

"I don't recognize that voice."

"Nor do I."

A deeper voice seemed to be dominating the conversation, rising and falling as if the speaker were telling a story. The responses of the familiar voices were sharp and louder.

"They're trying to warn us."

"Let's take it quietly." Now they moved even slower, and as soon as the light from the fireplace began to filter into the hallway, Kolwyn blew out the lamp and they stood, letting their eyes get accustomed to the darkness. Then they peered around the arch of the doorway.

Lounging on an ancient stone bench by the fire, his back against the mantel, was Achern anLexing, a chicken bone in one hand and a goblet in the other.

Kolwyn's voice hissed in her ear. "That's my cup."

"And the chicken is our supper."

"Glad our people are providing proper hospitality."

AnLexing waved the chicken leg to make his point. "...this whole area is part of his domain. At least that's what the legends say. I wouldn't camp in these ruins for any pay. Not even for any...fabled treasure you may have heard about. This is where his masters lived, and he comes back to look for them. Especially at the full moon. Which is coming soon."

Kolwyn put a hand on her shoulder. "Full moon isn't for about ten days. Stay here. There's a way around."

"Fine. You go in first. I'll follow when I think it's time."

He disappeared down the corridor, and she turned her attention back to the camp.

Lavan was doing his best. "If you're so afraid of this beast, why are you here?"

Gordon A. Long

"I saw your fire and thought to be neighbourly. You never know who might be wandering around up here in the mountains, ignorant of the dangers they faced."

"That was kind of you, but I meant, what are you doing up here in these dangerous mountains at all?"

The lord tossed the chicken bone into the fire. "Oh, a little hunting, a little fact-finding." He grinned. "I might even be searching for lost treasure. Perhaps you have heard the lore? Ah, I see you haven't. Good. No use wasting your time." The smile faded. "But I'm not playing that kind of game. You lowlanders can't be expected to know what's important up here. And how important it is not to get involved." He sat a bit straighter, lanced Lavan with his glare. "You, for example. I wouldn't cast you as the leader of this group. Who is really in charge, and where is he...? Or she, as the case may be."

"Like you, our leader goes where he...or she chooses, allowing no one the right to enquire or the knowledge to comprehend her...or his movements."

AnLexing was on his feet, attempting to tower over Lavan, but hardly succeeding. "I asked you a polite question, young man, and you will find it safer to return me a polite answer. Where is she?"

Lavan stood his ground, eye-to-eye with the lord. "I was given no instructions by the leader of my expedition as to how I should treat guests. I was merely trying to be polite on my own. Now perhaps I should be clearer. I have no instructions to tell any outsider anything. So I politely decline to answer your question." He sketched a bow.

The Lord's snarl was bestial in the deep red shadows cast by the fire. "You had best count your supporters, boy, and consider the number of my men that surround your camp."

There was a clatter, and all eyes shot towards where Kolwyn stood in the outer doorway, a pile of swords at his feet. "Five would be the number to consider, Lavan. Good evening, Lord anLexing. Perhaps you should have a word with your men about approaching a peaceful camp with their swords drawn. They may take them when you leave."

206

He strolled forward, lifted his cup from the other lord's hand and tossed the dregs toward the corner. "I hope you enjoyed the wine. It took a certain amount of effort to carry it up here, and I wouldn't want it to be wasted. Is there anything else you would like to discuss?"

The stocky lord's fists clenched, and his eyes bored into his opponent's. "You! I might have expected it. What are you doing, bringing lowlanders up here? They have no right to what is in these ruins. You tell them about things you shouldn't, and they'll be swarming all over. There are many riches in these mountains and the lowlanders have no right to any of them."

"I don't see that there's anything here to attract swarms of anyone. We're looking for maps that might give an idea of the old boundaries."

"So that's the tale you're telling, is it? Make sure you stick to that story. And if you do find any maps, you make sure I see them. When it comes to boundaries, I trust you Llannons about as much as I trust that lowland king."

Lord anLlannon drew himself up. This was not the diffident young man Aleria had come camping with. This was a textbook example of how to dominate an opponent. "Well, since he's the king, I suppose I can't take exception to what you just said. Perhaps I should let your insinuation slide and we'll leave it at that."

The stocky lord thought about standing up to his peer, but the difference in their heights came home to him. His eyes tried to stare into Kolwyn's. Then they slid away, glancing around the room. There was no support.

"Good. Then your men may come for their swords." Kolwyn raised his voice. "One at a time would be polite, don't you think?"

There was a moment's hesitation, and a man in a helmet and a leather breastplate slipped through the door and picked up a sword, his eyes fixed on his lord. Then he disappeared into the darkness, to be followed by four others as instructed. When they were gone, Kolwyn strolled over to

Blodwel's kitchen area and made a show of rinsing and drying his cup. Then he held it out, and the cook poured some wine in. "I bid you good even, my Lord." He raised his cup in salute, took a drink and went and sat on the stone bench by the fire, exactly mimicking the other lord's position of a moment before.

There was silence in the big room, except for the crackle of the flames and the whoosh of the wind up the chimney. Then Lord anLexing turned on his heel and strode out.

Immediately Kolwyn was on his feet, his hand on his sword. Everyone in the room followed his example and stood listening. Finally a soft whistle sounded up the staircase, and Kolwyn relaxed and resumed his seat.

"The rest of you can come in. They're gone."

Aleria and Jameta came out of the inner doorway, and the two guards slipped in from the front. Of Erlon and Aldwyn, there was no sign. They would be escorting their guests back to their camp for a little fact-finding of their own.

Kolwyn looked up at Aleria and raised his cup again. "Well, that's our friendly neighbour."

She sat on the bench opposite. "Do you think that was well done, Kolwyn? Of course we had to put him at a disadvantage. I'm not sure it was wise to make such a fool of him, though. It won't help us solve any problems."

His smile faded. "I can't see any other approach working, Aleria. He has made no secret of his enmity, and I don't know of any way to deal with him besides slapping him down at any opportunity."

She ran a hand over her face. "You might well be right. At least he never saw Jameta and me. Or Erlon."

"Some of his men might have caught a glimpse of Erlon when we took their swords. It was dark, though. We can hope that he thinks this is only an expedition of mine."

"But he is specifically looking for me. Well, the less he finds out, the better." She mused a moment. "What else does he know?"

"He might know how many there are in our party. I doubt if his scouts got close, but anyone could have counted us coming up the valley. You could see that he thought you were here but he wasn't sure."

"That's to our advantage. As long as he isn't sure, he has to be very careful."

"Why is that?"

"Because I threatened him with the might of anDalmyn if he crossed me. I suspect he finds that more of a deterrent than the king's good opinion. He's the kind to do his dirty work himself and isn't surprised that someone else might."

"And would he? Your father, I mean."

"My father is cool and calculating in business and judicious in court."

"But where his daughter is concerned?"

She shrugged. "My parents and I enjoy a close relationship."

"I'll keep that under consideration in my own dealings."

She allowed him a full smile. "You are such a diplomat."

"There's something else he might know."

"What's that?"

"You heard what he said about the lore. He sounds very comfortable with it. Perhaps he has ancient knowledge of the Dowry of the Princess."

"Do you believe it really exists?"

He shrugged. "Mostly not. There's a song that mentions "winding ways" and "the darkness of smothering stone," and that sort of generic stuff. We all believe when we're young, but a trip up here to search soon brings home the reality of it. You're beginning to get the picture already. It's a huge place. It's dark and dusty, and anything that is left is rotten and broken."

"So we're not too optimistic about running across a sackful of jewelry?"

He grinned. "Each to his own dream. Or hers."

"It sounded like he was interested in them, but trying not to show it."

Lavan nodded. "He was certainly on about that treasure. Before you showed up he accused us of being lowland tomb robbers. That's when he started talking about the Ghost Beast. I'm sure he was trying to scare us off."

Aleria smiled. "You certainly didn't scare. We were watching."

"You were?" His face became redder in the firelight.

"Yes. You handled him well. His Rank requires good manners, but there's no need to knuckle under."

"Oh...Thanks." He turned and sat down, trying to look casual. Aleria kept from smiling.

* * *

Erlon and Aldwyn returned later and everyone, with the exception of the man on guard, sat around the fireplace to hear their report.

"He only has five men back at his camp. It's farther up the trail into the mountains." Erlon tossed a hand to the east, glanced at Aldwyn.

"That little lake under Hangman's Peak, M'Lord. Nice camp."

"It is. Too bad. We usually to go up there for a swim when the weather gets hot. This is a dusty place to be stomping around."

Aleria handed Erlon a drink. "Learn anything else?"

He grinned. "If I hadn't already heard it from the teamsters, I'd have a lot of new vocabulary. He was some peeved."

"That doesn't tell us anything new."

"No. The campsite is pretty much in the open, and it isn't dark yet. Couldn't get close enough to hear anything."

"And no sign of another five men?"

Erlon shook his head. "We'll do a better survey in the morning."

Aleria looked to Kolwyn, who had nothing to add. "So in the morning we go back inside to find what we came for, we keep a couple of guards at the entrance, and the rest of you are out and about."

"I'll do breakfast."

She turned to Jameta. "You will?"

"I'm already tired of that mush you people enjoy so much."

"He who complains cooks the next meal."

"Exactly. I'm a great hand with pancakes. Cultural specialty. I even got the kitchen to toss in a twist of cinnamon."

"Our gain. Take first watch tonight so you get a good sleep."

"Thanks."

There was a general settling of duties and watches, and then everyone sat around on benches or blankets. No one was in a hurry to go to bed; the stones of the floor had little give in them.

Aleria looked over at Kolwyn. "What do you think of this place?"

He shrugged. "I think more about the people who built it. Can you imagine how much work it was?"

"Centuries."

"Exactly. And what's left?"

"A pretty darned impressive hunk of architecture." She shuddered. "Much though I dislike being in it."

"Don't like the dark?"

"It's more the distance to the light. I'm not really afraid of closed spaces. It's the thought of all those long, dark tunnels I'd be forced to travel if I had to get out in a hurry." She shrugged. "I know it sounds crazy when I say it out loud."

"It affects everyone differently."

She glanced around. "What about you, Lavan? How does it affect you?"

He shrugged. "I don't let it bother me."

"You don't let it?"

"That's right. You must keep that kind of emotion under control. Otherwise you can't function."

"So it doesn't scare you? Don't you worry what it would be like if your lantern broke and you were all alone in the dark?"

"Only to figure out what I would do if that happened. Make plans, prepare my mind for it."

Aleria sat for a moment, then rose and looked around. "Jameta, I've been considering your talent for running away."

The girl looked up, her brow furrowing. "And what do you think of it?"

"I doubt if it goes far enough."

"Why not?"

"Consider a scenario. Some big bruiser comes after you on his horse. What do you do?"

"My horses can outrun anything in the realm."

"Your horse comes up lame, and he catches you. What then?"

"I can outrun anyone who ever tried to catch me on foot."

"You come around a corner and run smack into his buddy, who grabs your wrist. What do you do? Close your eyes and pray?"

The girl started to shrug, but Aleria shook her head. "Certainly, fatalism is the best approach when there's really nothing you can do. I've had that experience too. But when he grabs you, why can't you still keep running?"

Jameta frowned again. "Because he's three times as strong as I am and he has hold of me?"

"Here. Grab my wrist."

With a doubtful grin, the girl did so. Aleria twisted free.

"Come on, try harder."

The same result.

"But you're stronger than me. Of course you can get away."

"Grab my thumb."

Again she slipped free.

"But your thumb is hard to hold onto."

Aleria looked around the circle of faces watching. "Kolwyn, you're no weakling. You grab my wrist."

Grinning, he reached out and grabbed. In a flash her hand was free. Without comment, she held out her wrist again, and this time he really bore down. Giving him a moment to be sure, she again slipped her hand out.

"Wait a moment, now. Let me try this…" This time he came from underneath, forcing her hand upward. She levered down, and his hand was forced open.

She turned to Jameta. "You see what I'm doing?"

"No. You pull loose, no matter what. I can't believe you're that strong."

"It's not strength; it's technique. Hold up your arm. Now look at my thumb. Which is stronger?"

Jameta grinned. "My arm, I hope."

"Right. So if I grab your arm, you only need break the hold of my thumb. So if you lever down against my thumb…" she demonstrated slowly.

"I see. Let me try. Hold on."

This time, the girl was successful. "You weren't trying very hard."

"I was, but this time I'll try harder. Go ahead."

Jameta wrenched downward, and Aleria was barely able to hold on.

"So it didn't work that time. Try this. Instead of pulling away, push upwards and toward me. When I start to push against you, pull back in the same direction I'm pushing…see? I threw your arm out of my own grip."

Lavan stood up. "There's a disarm that works like that. You get the opponent pushing against your sword, then you hook it in the same direction."

"Exactly. If you've taken any weaponless combat, you know how to use the same trick against the opponent's balance."

Jameta's face was glowing. "So even if they grab me, I can keep running."

"They might catch you, but they still have to hold on to you. Here's another one. The strongest grip is where the fingers overlap. Like a big hand around a small wrist. But if, instead of pulling away, you push down, you force the larger part of your arm into his hand, and you're using much better leverage against his fingers." She demonstrated.

Soon the group around the fire was practicing all sorts of holds and trying to find ways to break them. Aleria stood back and watched with a satisfied feeling.

"Now, that was an impressive little lesson."

She glanced up at Kolwyn. "A lesson with only one objective is a waste of time."

They both grinned at the general cheer when Jameta was able to trip Lavan and pull herself from his clutches, leaving him on the ground at her feet.

"You certainly know how to forge a troop."

"My life might depend on it. Some of their lives will depend on it."

"Not sure I'd like to lead that life."

"No discredit. I don't think many would like it. But I do. It suits me." She looked up at him again. "And so far I've been good enough at it."

"How good? Without bragging, of course."

"I haven't lost a man yet."

"Another joy to look forward to."

She suddenly didn't feel so cheerful. "I suppose. But I can't let that affect the decisions I make. Killing an enemy is easy. Killing a friend is more difficult." Then she realized that there had been a long silence between them. "I'm sorry. I rather spoiled the mood, didn't I?"

His smile came slowly. "No, no, I'm the one who spoiled it. I just had to try to go one up on you. It wasn't fair, and it wasn't polite."

"You're right; it wasn't. But it would have been much more fun to let me say so first."

"A general spoilsport all around tonight. Do you want me to pin you to the ground to make up for it?"

She glanced up at him from the corner of her eye. "You try me, big fella."

Suddenly the import of what he had said came through, and his face went scarlet. "I'm...I'm...I meant..."

214

She laid a hand on his arm. "Sorry, Kolwyn. I know exactly what you meant to say. That was mean of me. I only play those games with my friends for fun. Please don't take it amiss."

Again the silence stretched between them. Finally, he patted her hand. "It's good to hear that, Aleria. Many people play those games and say it's in fun, but they somehow end up winning every one."

She cuffed his arm with the back of her hand. "Don't worry, I'll let you win the next three to make up for it."

23. A Dusty Search

It was an uneventful night, and everyone was up early in the morning, tucking into Jameta's pancakes with gusto. Aleria and Kolwyn prepared the document search party, leaving Erlon to handle the outside group. Lavan insisted on coming inside with them.

"I'm not so great at hunting and hiding in the wilderness. I'd probably mess up and leave tracks all over the place or get seen. I'm better off inside. Besides, who says there are no dangers in here as well?"

Kolwyn nodded, and Aleria handed him a lantern. "Jameta needs a partner."

As the four made their way back through the passages they had covered the night before, Kolwyn coached his team. "These lanterns will last you a full day, but check the reservoir regularly in case. You'll soon be able to tell how full it is by shaking it. We'll try to stay together, but we always work in pairs. If you get lost, follow your footprints. No one has been here for a few years, so our tracks are clear in the dust."

Aleria flashed her lantern around at the rough-hewn walls, stained dark by runnels of water. Arched black entrances gave into bare rooms. "Or the mud."

"The water's only out near the front because the roofs fell in. Back inside it's drier."

"Any other way to tell where you are?"

"Most corridors don't go that deep into the mountain. If you walk more than, say two hundred paces in one direction, you must be walking sideways along the citadel. Turn ninety degrees and you'll soon either hit a blank wall or daylight.

"There is a tendency for the air to move into the castle and up the staircases. It might help. Don't worry. We won't get far in half a day. Every room has to be searched, and the whole area is riddled with rooms."

"Is there any specific pattern that will help us?"

"It isn't a perfectly square grid, but close enough to get by. There are places way back in and out to the west end where the pattern breaks down bcause they used old watercourses. Navigation gets tricky. Best technique is not to get lost. I suggest we stay on this level, at least for today."

It took them a few more minutes of walking down a wide corridor before the old footprints in the dust began to peter out. Finally Kolwyn indicated a larger side corridor. "Let's try this one. I've been in a ways, and it looked interesting. See? Those are my tracks from three years ago, the only ones. Why don't you and Jameta take the left hand side, Lavan? Aleria and I will take the right. Until we get comfortable, let's keep in touch."

The first few rooms they entered were mostly empty. Odd bits of plank and scraps of cloth were scattered around, sometimes attached to the walls. "These are storage rooms. I see no evidence that anyone actually lived this far from the light."

"So why would they leave their books here?"

"Safety, I suppose. Any place that's safe is by definition hard to get to."

They left that room, and when they turned into the hallway, Aleria shone her light down. The floor lay in deep, untrodden dust from side to side.

Kolwyn shone his light around as well. "Just think. Nobody has been down this corridor for three hundred years."

"I hope the last one out left us a map and shut the door behind him."

The next set of rooms had been fitted with doors, broken now and lying in pieces. Lavan touched one with his toe, and it disintegrated in the dust.

"A lesson to us about these maps. If they are exposed to the damp on the floor like that wood, they will fall apart."

Aleria frowned. "This project is becoming more and more chancy as we go along."

"But aren't we having fun?"

She turned to Kolwyn. "We have to take this seriously."

217

Gordon A. Long

"I am taking it quite seriously. There's no reason why I can't enjoy myself as well. I find being this close to history to be fascinating."

She did not answer, merely turning through the doorway that gaped before her. Wooden shelves lined the walls, many broken but some still intact. She wiggled one and it felt firm. "Must be a different kind of wood."

He flashed his lamp at the floor. "Deeper dust. No water in here."

There was nothing useful, and they moved down the corridor. The slightest movement stirred up the thickening dust, and soon there was a haze that dimmed their lamps.

"Go faster and try not to stir up dust. Otherwise we'll start choking."

Jameta turned her lamp back at the mist behind them. "Does this count in the 'having fun' part of the journey?"

Aleria could see his grin in the reflected light. "Depends how quickly you learn to walk softly. Don't worry. By the time we come back it will be settled. I hope."

They continued down the corridor, finding nothing of value, although Lavan picked up a tiny white ceramic lamp, empty and wickless, from a pile of junk in one corner. He stuck it in his pocket. "I'd like to see that in sunlight."

Soon they came to the end of the corridor, a blank wall that was partially tumbled in. Kolwyn picked up a stone and tossed it away again. "I've found this before. They stopped when they came to fragmented rock. Too unstable for tunneling, I suppose."

They turned around and made their way back to the main corridor. The dust had mostly settled or blown away, but they were sneezing and covering their noses with their sleeves by the time they got out of the smaller tunnel. Except Jameta, who simply brought her neck scarf up over her nose.

Lavan looked at her in envy. "I always thought that was for decoration."

"It is. Until I get out on the road with a herd of cattle or a wagon train and the wind is blowing the wrong way."

Now that they had the pattern they split up, with the younger two taking the first cross-tunnel and the older ones taking the next one. Aleria and Kolwyn moved more rapidly now, one on each side, scanning the walls quickly and sorting through the rubbish with less enthusiasm. In one room the floor was covered with pieces of broken crockery, and in another a huge rat's nest, long dried and abandoned, filled one corner. Kolwyn shrugged when she called his attention to it. "Water source probably dried up. It might be worth going through. Pack rats pick up shiny things. At least the modern ones do. Maybe pack rat styles have changed in a few hundred years."

She did a quick search before the dust she roused drove her out, and got several coins and a small iron knife as her reward. "They certainly aren't shiny anymore."

They rendezvoused at the junction and returned to the camp for lunch. By tacit consent, the moment they reached daylight they all went straight out into the open sunlight. There they stopped, looked at each other and burst out laughing.

"Well, aren't we just tarted up for the spring ball?"

Kolwyn looked to the left up the valley. "I sure hope Lexing moves on today. By this afternoon a swim is going to feel really good."

Lavan stretched his arms. "Just the wind blowing through my hair is all I need right now."

"Gets oppressive in there after a while, doesn't it?"

Lavan looked out over the valley. "Makes me wonder whether I should be learning bushcraft this afternoon."

Aleria regarded him. "Giving up on us?"

He shook his head. "No, what I said this morning still holds. I'm of more use in here." He glanced sideways at her. "If you would have let me quit, anyway."

"I wouldn't, but it's nice you made the decision yourself."

He stuck his hands in his jacket pockets and brought one out with a cry of dismay. He reached in more carefully and brought out a handful of shards. He twisted one, and it snapped easily. "I guess the years affect other than wood and cloth."

Aleria looked at Kolwyn, but said nothing. Their chances of finding a legible map were getting slimmer.

They scrounged together a lunch and ate on the balcony in the sun. Soon Aleria's sense of duty prodded her, and they trudged back along the dark gallery to begin the afternoon's work. They made quick progress because the area they moved into had once contained stables, with decaying stalls and tack rooms scattered with rotten harness. There was even a skiff of hay in the mangers, dry as the dust it crumbled into when touched.

Aleria turned her head from the cloud she had roused. "I suppose if we really cared we would search through all this, in case someone hid a case of maps."

"If we searched that well with this small group, we'd be here all summer. This is a big fortress."

They separated a few iron rings from the desiccated harness and tried to move on, but the stables were another dead end, and they had to reverse their path back towards the outside.

Aleria had been thinking. "If we don't have time to do it all, can we figure out a way to maximize our work? For example, there were stables here. Do we know anything about the social classes of the Old Ones? Nowadays, nobody with the kind of education to be dealing with maps would work anywhere close to the smell of the stables."

"Maybe they had good ventilation." He swept his lantern beam upwards to show a dark opening in the ceiling. The dust was lazily swirling up to it. "Remember, I said the wind tended to go upwards in here."

"But there would still be a smell."

"A good point. Let's do a quick sweep of the next few corridors and try to figure out what they were used for."

By the end of the afternoon they had pretty much given up on that floor. It all seemed to be rough storage, animal housing and fodder.

Aleria turned in the last doorway, regarding a roomful of piles of lumber. "Well, if we run out of firewood we know where to come."

"I doubt there's much good left in it. Burn up like paper: fast and furious, little heat."

"And it's probably quicker to look outside."

"So, are we done for the day?"

"I think so. It's difficult to figure out the time, isn't it?"

Aleria flashed her lamp around. The walls seemed closer, and the distance they had to walk through the dark and the dust seemed very long. "Let's go."

They strode out to the main corridor, picked up their two companions and trekked back to the central keep. From their balcony, Aleria looked out over the valley in the westering sun. "Out there. Somebody coming our way."

They peered to the east, where a small party showed intermittently through the tall brush along the trail. As they got closer, it was possible to pick out the large form and blond head of Erlon in the lead.

Aleria directed Kolwyn's attention. "What's that they're carrying?"

"Looks like game on a pole."

Lavan grinned. "Either that or they caught a prisoner."

Aleria frowned. "That better be game. The situation isn't bad enough to be treating anyone like that."

Sure enough, when the party got closer, they could see it was a mountain goat slung between two men. Erlon looked up and waved, and they waved back.

"Fresh meat for supper tonight."

They trooped downstairs to meet in the entry court, and Lavan and Kolwyn took their turn at carrying the game.

Once Aldwyn was busy cutting up supper, they retreated from the smell out onto the balcony again, where they celebrated with a sack of wine.

Aleria leaned back against the warm stone, enjoying the bright sunshine and the open space around her. "Well, boys, what did you find?"

Erlon grinned. "Even more good news. AnLexing and his crew headed for home and left us with a beautiful swimming hole." He glanced around. "Which some of us need. Mentioning no one in particular for reasons of good manners."

That brought them to their feet. Aleria glanced at Erlon. "You're sure they're gone?"

"They went down this morning. We were hunting along the valley side and we watched them go down the trail. Six of them. Aldwyn followed them down to the mouth of the valley, and they were moving right along. The rest of us went east to the lake."

"Well, it stands to reason. He went up there somewhere," she tossed a hand eastward, "and left five men, then he's going home. All we have to do is keep an eye out in case that five have mischief in mind."

Kolwyn shook his head. "Or else he was taking ten men up and bringing ten others back, but only brought five back because we are here."

"Which means he has fifteen men up in the mountains? Guarding what?"

Erlon picked up his helmet. "If you're going up for a bath, I'll tag along. The men who were with me today had a swim already, so they can stay and guard the supper."

She looked into the kitchen area. "What about Aldwyn?"

Erlon glanced at Kolwyn. "I gather he...uh well, he doesn't bathe that much, so he's fine."

"And this is the man who is cutting up our food?"

Kolwyn shrugged. "It gets cooked afterwards."

24. The Secret of the Mountains

They spent the whole of the next day going through the area of the next floor above the keep and found nothing of interest. This floor went deeper into the mountain, but most of the rooms were cleaned out. While the larger crew made the job go faster, the excitement began to wear off.

At noon they sat around in the sunshine, nobody saying much. Finally Aleria stood up. "We're not contributing much to the cause by sitting around, pleasant though it might be."

Lavan grinned up at her. "Bored in there, bored out here."

She frowned. "Is that a feeble attempt to get me into an argument so you don't have to go back to work?"

"Not at all. It's a feeble attempt to start an argument, so it won't be boring when we go back to work."

"Well, it didn't work. Let's get going."

"We haven't found that out yet." He stood. "The argument is barely started."

Aleria grinned, but only to herself. "What's wrong, Lavan? Afraid to go back into the dark where the boogyman will jump out and grab you?"

He sniffed and pushed into the lead. "You know me better than that."

"So what are you afraid of?"

He paced along for a moment. "I guess what everyone's afraid of. That something will come up that I can't cope with, and I'll be afraid of it. That's why I try to prepare myself. In my imagination, I put myself in situations where I might be afraid, and figure out how I'll feel, and how I'll deal with the fear, and how I'll get out of the situation."

Kolwyn chuckled. "All right. Here. See this doorway?"

They all stopped. It was a simple arch where a smaller corridor joined the main tunnel.

"Jameta is on the run with an important message. She just ducked down that corridor. There are twenty soldiers about to come around that corner. What do you do?"

The young swordsman glanced up and down the hall. Then he placed his lantern on the ground just outside the door: beam set on wide, lighting the bigger tunnel. He drew his sword and stood in *guarde* position in the doorway, only partially lit. His point flicked out of the darkness at them.

Aleria nodded. "That's pretty good. Aren't you afraid?"

"Of course, but I use my fear to heighten my senses, look for anything around me, hear all the sounds. I think, 'Attack, attack, attack,' until the enemy is on me, and then it's too late. I just fight."

Kolwyn shook his head. "Sounds like it might work. Just outside a doorway would be a good place to be, as long as you were careful not to get drawn forward. If one got behind you, you'd soon be dead."

"Yes, and if they start pressing me, I move back into the doorway, which restricts their movements, and fewer of them can get at me at one time." The lad's eyes shone in the lamplight. "I bet Erlon could hold off all of Lexing's men right here, with no problem."

Aleria snorted. "Until one of them came around behind him. Come on. You've used up a good chunk of time. Now we go back to work."

Lavan sheathed his sword and narrowed his lamp beam. "Can't get one past Aleria, can we? Oh, well. I tried." He turned and marched off down the hallway.

She glanced at Kolwyn, but he shrugged. "You never know how brave you are until it happens."

"No argument there."

* * *

Several dusty and fruitless hours later the group stopped at the functionaries before returning to camp. They had worked with a will and covered several main corridors, but their only finds were clouds of dust and collections of junk.

Aleria plunged her hands into the basin and scooped water onto her face. "I'm getting very tired of this little project."

Kolwyn grinned. "Want to take a day off, maybe more?"

"I wouldn't mind, if I had an excuse. I don't have forever, though. My freight wagons are calling me."

"But we have an excuse."

"Exactly. Five enemy soldiers somewhere up the mountain from here. Surely whatever they are guarding is worth a look."

"So, tomorrow let's head up the valley as far as we can make it in one day." He drew their course on the counter with his finger. "We'll set up camp there, scout farther for half the next day and return to the same camp. An easy walk back down the third day, and we'll cover a lot of ground."

"Then one more day in the tunnels, and I have to get back to my duties in the real world."

"Fine with me."

"If we leave most of our food and equipment at the overnight camp we can move faster."

"Let's dry off and go back and give everyone the good news."

As they walked down the stairs, Aleria jingled the bag she was carrying. "The Old Ones must have been very rich."

"Why do you say that?"

"Because they left all this iron behind."

"Maybe iron wasn't as valuable to them."

"Why not?" She held up a hand. "Don't answer that. Because they had lots of it. They had iron mines!"

"It's one theory."

"It's not a theory. It's a legend."

"Many legends are based on fact."

"Kolwyn, if we find an iron mine up here, all this searching for maps is small change."

"I suppose. What does an iron mine look like?"

"A lot of rusty red stone around, I suppose. An old mine of any sort would make it worthwhile bringing in a geologist."

"A geologist that specializes in iron? Where do you find one of those?"

"Domaland has huge iron deposits, and their geologists are always looking for more."

"Fair enough. Let's bring in a Domalian geologist."

"Not on the basis of a few hunks of iron left behind four hundred years ago. Wait and see what we find up the trail."

* * *

The crew's enthusiasm to move on up the mountain received a great boost the next morning. Aldwyn went out to the room where they had hung the meat and came back to Kolwyn with his face pale. "M'Lord, you should see this."

Curious, Aleria followed them. Their cache had been hung by tossing a rope over an outcropping, then pulling the meat up and tying the end of the rope around a large stone. Now all that was left was a short length of rope around the stone. A dark stain showed where the meat had dripped its juices on the floor.

Kolwyn shone his light around. "Grizzly?"

"I bin hangin' meat like that all my life, M'Lord. If the grizzly can't reach it, he leaves it alone. No grizzly ever bin smart enough to chew through the rope at the other end."

"Humans?"

"Doubt it. The ropes' bin chewed, not cut."

"Well, no meat for breakfast. I guess we go hunting again."

The little man smiled. "Mebbe Jameta'll make pancakes."

"Or maybe we'll eat mush and get out of here."

Back in their camp, they discussed their intruder while Jameta worked.

Erlon scratched his head. "You mean to say that animal figured out how to cut down the meat?"

"That's right."

"In the pitch dark?"

226

Kolwyn's eyes opened further. "I never thought of that. Grizzlies see as well as us, I think, but no one can see in the pitch dark."

"Anybody hear anything?"

Aleria had been only half listening to this conversation. Something was bothering her. She went back to the room where the meat had hung, then made her way more carefully to their camp. When she came back, everyone was looking at her.

Erlon stood up. "I see that look, Aleria. You've just found sand in the flour."

"Maybe. It just occurred to me. How do you get to the meat room?"

He frowned, pointed. "Through that door, of course."

"Right. Which means that our silent friend either came right in through our camp, which I doubt..."

"...or he came in through the back. Through the fortress."

"Stands to reason."

They all looked at the inner doorway.

Aleria strode to her pack. "Which means I, for one, will be quite happy to move out into the open for my next night's sleep."

Kolwyn nodded. "And we'll make sure that nothing we leave cached here is of any interest to a carnivore."

Everyone turned to their packing, and by the time break-fast was ready they were all set. They rolled the pancakes, ate them with their fingers and were on the trail not long after.

Aleria called Erlon and Kolwyn to walk with her. "We're going into enemy territory, Kolwyn. Do you know what that means?"

"Not really, but my men are careful."

"I'm sure they are. Erlon, order of march?"

"To start off, one advance scout and one behind, like right now. Once we leave the lake we're in new territory, and we scout both sides. Your men are best for that, Kolwyn, leaving mine to take care of the line of march, point and rear. Us three will stay in the centre with Jameta."

He looked at each of them, received nods and strode ahead to give orders.

Through the morning they climbed along the valley floor. With their reduced packs they made good time. Once past the lake the trail zigzagged up and over a ridge, coming out in a higher valley. Now they proceeded at a more careful pace to allow the scouts to keep ahead. Everyone was at a high stage of alert, but as the day wore on they saw nothing, heard nothing. In the middle of the afternoon Aleria called a halt. They rested while Kolwyn whistled the scouts in and everyone sat, looking at each other.

"Well, nothing so far. Any thoughts?"

Kolwyn looked back down the valley, then ahead. "If Lexing camped at the lake and he was only three days ahead of us, he would get to his goal some time the second day. So we aren't really expecting to find anything today, are we?"

Erlon nodded. "And we're not pacing up like he was."

Aleria looked at the two guides. "Anything interesting out there?"

They exchanged glances. "Plenty of bear sign, but nothing human, M'Lady."

"And on the trail?"

"Lots of traffic. Both directions."

She nodded. "So we go ahead. No change."

The two guides got up and left without a word. Everyone else rose at a more leisurely pace and away they went again. Twice during the day the trail petered out to nothing, and they waited while the guides searched for the reason. Each time their quarry had crossed an open rock face, leaving no tracks, to join a new trail that cut over to another valley.

"Difficult place to find."

Kolwyn wiped sweat from his brow and nodded. "I didn't know there was a trail, here. Well, there isn't really a trail, here, is there?"

"Which makes me wonder even more where it leads."

"Quite."

In the process of watching her surroundings, Aleria couldn't help but notice how beautiful they were: sheer faces of rock with massive jumbles of stone at their feet, glaciers sweeping around cloud-shrouded mountain peaks, avalanche paths that plunged down out of sight.

A soft whistle brought her out of her reverie. Aldwyn was beckoning from a nearby ridge, ravens swirling above him. They trudged up and found him regarding a battle scene. Moss was torn from the rocks, small bushes uprooted, rotten logs splintered. And in the middle, a torn mass of blood and fur.

"Grizzly."

Aldwyn nodded. "Big one, M'Lady."

"What can do that to a grizzly?"

Kolwyn shrugged. "The males get into some pretty fearsome battles in mating season, sometimes to the death."

"It ain't matin' season M'Lord."

"It is not."

Erlon was bending over the corpse. "Look at this."

They moved in, their breathing shallow because of the stench. Where he was pointing the story was easy to read. The hide and flesh of the bear had been scored deeply by sharp talons.

"Our little friend again?"

"I think so. Those claws were too sharp for a grizzly, and there isn't a black that big anywhere. The Ghost Beast has now proved that he's no ghost."

Aleria wrinkled her nose. "But this was several days ago."

"Probably six or eight. Doesn't matter, does it?"

"It doesn't. He's here, and he's one more thing to look out for."

Lavan gave a snort of laughter. "No wonder Lexing's got five or ten guards up here."

She nodded. "I'm beginning to wish we had."

They stared at the dethroned monarch of the mountains. Kolwyn gave his usual shrug. "Not sure ten or even twenty would be enough for this one."

They made their way back to the trail and continued. If there had ever been a concern about the alertness of their watch, it no longer existed.

They camped that night far off the main route in a little canyon hidden from the larger valley, with an animal trail that escaped at the far end out onto the scree above. They used little wood and killed their fire as soon as supper was cooked. Aleria curled up in her blankets on top of a juniper bush, hoping for relief from the hard rock. It wasn't too bad a bed, and she got a bit of sleep at least, although she was awake for several hours in the night after a dream of huge claws tearing through her crew.

In the morning she regarded her group. "Any reason to change our plans?"

No one spoke.

"So we stash our bedrolls here, make as good time as we can up the trail until just past noon. If we don't find anything, we turn back."

"A suggestion?"

"Of course, Kolwyn."

"There's always the chance someone will find this camp. Let's make a smaller number of bigger blanket rolls so it looks like there are less people."

"Whatever we can do to confuse our trail. Same order as yesterday. We must be getting close. Keep very sharp. Those guards are there to guard something, and they might be good at their task."

Once again they moved ahead, and Aleria was aware of the difference between the beauty of the scenery and the death that lurked within it. She took solace in the fact that Aldwyn and Blodwel had lived in these mountains all their lives, and that her guards were the best. *If only I could be sure that every man is loyal. All our precautions might be completely useless.* She found herself watching her men instead of her surroundings, then stopped because that felt disloyal to them. That was what really hurt. *I'm loyal to my men, but one of them could bring it all tumbling down around us...*

She turned her thoughts to more positive use. *What would we do if...*

"Everybody off the trail!"

She dove under a stunted tree before she even registered that it was Erlon who spoke. He wasn't whispering. That meant that the danger wasn't near. She waited. There was a rustling beside her, and he eeled under her tree. "We've found it. Just over the ridge ahead. We're very close, but it's too late now." He raised his voice. "We sneak over to that little copse of dwarf balsams to the north of the trail. Don't all move at once. Blodwel and I will deal with our tracks. There's no rush. No sign anyone has spotted us yet."

Slowly, one person moving at a time, they made their way towards the thick mat of trees. As they reached it and moved inside, they found that the tops started at shoulder height but the branches spread sideways, leaving an empty, covered area around the lower trunks. Lying in a group with their heads together, they held a conference.

Erlon stabbed a thumb over his shoulder to the east. "Blodwel says there's a camp over that ridge. Most of you can unbend here, and Aleria and I will go on. I can't think of anywhere safer. Aleria, push your head up through the branches. Do you see that ridge to the northeast? They'll have someone watching the trail, but if we come out along that ridge we'll be above them, hidden by the rim. From the far end, we should be able to see the whole story. We'll take Blodwel. Comments?"

Aleria's nod confirmed his plan so they squirmed away, using the balsams as far as they could, their little guide leading them from cover to cover until they topped the ridge and slipped down the other side, hidden from the trail.

It was a long, hot and prickly crawl along the ridge, and Aleria was glad of the padded knees in her swordsman's breeks. However, soon they were squirming out behind a pinnacle of rock at the end.

Erlon leaned close to her ear. "Our only problem comes if they've got a guard post up there."

She reached out and grabbed the heel of Blodwel's boot, making a 'stop' gesture. The guide obeyed, and Erlon moved ahead. She worked up beside the shepherd. "If there's anybody to be killed, that's his job."

"Good enough for me, M'Lady. I kills animals all the time, but never done any people."

"Let's try to keep it that way."

It wasn't long before Erlon returned, beckoning her forward. Leaving the shepherd to guard their backs, she followed Erlon into the rocks and they raised their heads cautiously.

Aleria heard the big man's gasp and released her own breath. Spread out across the rust-tinged rock of the eastern slope in front of them was a huge camp. It was well organized, with a row of bunkhouses for workers, low barns that would house a large number of animals, and the workshops, cookshacks, and other paraphernalia of a working operation. And in the centre of it all, a mineshaft running horizontally into the hill. As she watched, a group of straining workers heaved a cart along a track out of the tunnel mouth and dumped it onto a large wooden table. There, men with hammers attacked the reddish ore, tossing most of the rock behind them over the edge of a ridge and sliding the rest to the end of the table, where other men were pouring it into sacks. A line of mules, patiently waiting, completed the picture.

"How many men?"

Erlon pointed. "If there's triple decker bunks that would be twelve to a cabin. Six cabins, seventy men or so. Ten guards; ten bosses, cooks, and that lot; five smiths and farriers; maybe five teamsters. That means forty miners. That's a big mine."

"They're working two shifts. Look at all the men sitting around."

"So, twenty men belowground at a time. Still, a sizeable working."

"Anything more we can see?" He did not respond. "We must get out of here."

"That we must. Let's go."

They retraced their painful steps, even more cautious now, aware what their knowledge was worth.

When they reached the rest of the group they held a hurried conversation in which Aleria described the mine. "The whole game has changed. Now that we know about the mine, Lexing can't afford to let us out of this valley alive. For our part, it's important that this information gets back to Tyn Terfyn and eventually to the king, so I want everyone to know. No matter what happens to the rest of us, if any of you end up taking the message alone, do so. Everyone got that?

"Listen, now. We need to sneak out of here as quickly as we can and get moving back down the trail. Ideas?"

Kolwyn pointed. "Aldwyn was working on that. We scoot over to that gully over there where we can stand up and still be out of sight."

"Let's get it over with. I'm tired of this crawling."

Once again the group spread out and moved in parts, and soon they were stretching their aching backs and legs.

"We can talk normally, now. Let's skedaddle back to last night's camp and pick up our packs. It's downhill, so we should be able to get much farther down the trail by nightfall. Once we camp for the night we can make further plans."

They went faster now, striding with purpose down the trail, but stepping on the hard spots, leaving no tracks if they could avoid it. They had point and rear guides out, but they did not wait for anyone to make his way along the sides. That would slow them down too much, so they had to risk a chance hunter or scout spotting them.

Soon they reached their camp in the canyon and repacked their belongings. Or started to.

Erlon froze, his hands in his pack. "We've had company."

"What?"

"I tie my pack with a special hitch. It's got a normal bow on it now. Someone has scouted through this camp."

Aleria pointed. "Aldwyn and Jatto, out to the main trail, one up one down. Blodwel and Domin, check the back trail out of this canyon. The rest of you, eyes in all directions. It was probably only one scout, but they might have left someone to wait for us. Pack up as quick as you can, but keep it light. If we don't need it, leave it. When Blodwel and Domin get back, we get out of here."

They packed efficiently, stowing everything as tightly as possible, leaving anything they could to lighten their packs. They carried all the food, though. As Aleria noted, "It doesn't look like we'll have much time for hunting."

Then they were out on the trail, once again with eyes keen to note every movement in the brush around them. It was evidence of their anxiety that they took the sighting of grizzly tracks that covered their upward trail as a positive. Soon they saw the bear across the valley, his nose up as he scented them.

"Nobody's been by recently." Kolwyn grinned as they watched the big animal lumber away.

"And no Ghost Beast either."

They strode on through the afternoon, the sun slanting into their sweating faces, the lengthening shadows making footing difficult.

As they crested a ridge they met Aldwyn jogging back up towards them. The moment he saw them he made frantic halting signals.

When he reached them, he was gasping for breath. "Lexing. More men. Up the trail."

Aleria frowned. "He's back again? What does that mean?"

Erlon looked left, then right along the ridge. "That way. Aldwyn, you lead. Hide in those bushes. Blodwel with me to brush out tracks. Once they're gone, Aldwyn can scout the trail again, and the rest of you keep going. We'll catch up to you later. The rendezvous point is the old camp in the keep at Tyn Dyfnant."

Kolwyn shook his head. "We won't make Dyfnant before nightfall, and that Beast sees far too well in the dark. There's a good campsite off the trail at Burringer creek, just below the lake. We can get that far. Blodwel knows where it is."

"Good enough." Erlon and the shepherd started back up the trail, scuffing out any marks they could see. Aleria went last of her group and turned to lie under a low bush with a good view of the trail.

It took a while for Lexing and his men, red-faced and puffing, to make it to the top of the ridge and disappear up the trail. Aleria counted as they went past. Five soldiers again. He had gone home and turned back immediately with more men. The only reason could be her presence.

She turned to Kolwyn. "They will have to go back to the mine before they find out what was happening."

"Won't they meet the guards coming out with the scout who had found our camp?"

"Right, but that won't be the full complement. If I were him, I'd stop for a breather and send a runner back to get the rest of the guards. They'll need supplies from the mine as well. Look at the light packs those men are carrying. Let's say he leaves two to guard the mine. That will leave him thirteen men. I wonder how far behind they will be?"

"No way to tell for sure. Five of them are already tired, and Lexing isn't a runner."

"So there will be at least thirteen men on our trail, and they won't be coming fast. Of course, our people have been walking all day as well."

She motioned Aldwyn forward, and they all slipped silently out.

Aleria stopped them at the top of the ridge. "We're in a hurry, but don't run downhill. A broken ankle is pretty useless to us right now. Let's go."

They hurried down the path, their knees aching with the strain.

25. A Long Night

It was stumbling dark by the time Aldwyn pulled them off the trail. He walked them along a ridge of rock, then doubled back by balancing on a fallen tree. The tired troop found it difficult going, but he used several tricks to hide their tracks and their numbers before leading them to a cosy den under an overhang of rock. A creek babbled at the bottom of the slope, not close enough to mask the sound of an approaching enemy. They ate cold food, drank creek water and rested. Everyone was too tired to talk, and there was nothing to say. They kept a small fire burning, well sheltered from view and the night vision of the guards.

Aleria sat down beside Kolwyn to eat. "We have a decision to make."

"Do we?"

"Yes. The easy thing to do would be to scram down the trail to safety at full speed and get this information out to the king."

"But you don't think that's the best thing to do."

"I don't know how much you follow the politics in the capital, but I can imagine how that would work out. We go down and report this ilicit mine. We accuse Lexing of being part of it. He says, 'Oh, no, I was up there hunting. I was as surprised as everyone else to find it.' Then the negotiations start, and there are 'other considerations' and 'mitigating circumstances' and that sort of thing, and in the end he walks free to continue his campaign for power."

Llannon frowned. "I don't like that picture very much at all."

"Unless we can catch him in the lady's chamber with his pants down, he's going to find a way out of this."

"You have such a way with words." His grin faded. "I couldn't agree more."

"I hoped you would feel that way. The other possibility is that we send out a message with a small, fast party."

He nodded. "And we stay and stall Lexing until the reinforcements show up, catching him in the act."

"No, it has to be worse than that. He has to be caught in an aggressive attack against someone important."

"Meaning you."

"I've been his target all along."

"True."

"So we send our messengers and hole up in Tyn Dyfnant and wait for your father to send help."

He shrugged. "The Old Ones held it for four hundred years. We ought to be able to manage a few days."

"We'll only have six or seven people."

He took a moment. "I think we should...no, I know it. We have to do this."

"We are agreed? I have to do this, but you don't. You're the heir to your demesne. You have other considerations. You and I are the only ones responsible, here. Our people are loyal. At least, most of them. If we mess up, it's on our consciences. On mine, actually."

"Remember you told me that there might come a time when you had to make a decision and I had to follow it?"

"I did say that."

"Well, this is it. As it happens, I concur completely. We stay."

Soon Erlon and Blodwel showed up with nothing to report. They had swept the trail until they heard the soldiers catching up, hidden until the enemy passed, and then come back.

Aleria got out her writing implements and began her reports. When she had finished, she gathered Aldwyn, Blodwel, Jameta and Lavan, and sat them down with her.

First she regarded at the guides. "All right, you two. Who's the better poacher?"

The two men looked at each other.

"Well, who's the most likely to get away when the gamekeeper comes?"

They grinned, and both pointed at Aldwyn.

"I have a task for you, Aldwyn. Jameta and her messages must get to Tyn Terfyn. Must. Do you understand?"

"Yes, M'Lady."

"I'm sending Lavan with you because he's good with a sword if you need one. But he's not that good in the bush. Come to think of it, Jameta probably isn't, either, but I imagine she's better than him." She glanced at the two, and they both shrugged. "That's fine, because she's the one that has to get through."

"I get it, M'Lady. If anyone stands and fights, he will."

"Exactly."

She regarded the three of them. "And I'm putting Jameta in charge."

There was a brief pause while the other two took this in. Lavan broke the silence. "I understand."

"Good." She left it at that. They would work it out among themselves, and nothing she could say would change that.

"Aldwyn, there will be an ambush along the trail. If I was lord Lexing, I'd leave one when I came through. I'm guessing maybe five men." She raised her eyebrows at Erlon, who nodded. "You're the one familiar with the trail. You know where to look."

"Aye, M'Lady. We'll duck 'em."

"Jameta, there are two messages here. You are to take the first to Maddoes at Tyn Terfyn. It tells him to bring our crew to Tyn Dyfnant as quickly as possible, leaving two teamsters to take care of the stock. Once he has his message you can tell Lord Llannon what's happening here. He will do what he thinks is best.

"Then you take this second message to Decker. By yourself. I have no doubt that anyone who might cause you trouble is otherwise employed right now, so you'll only face the usual dangers of the road. The other two will guide the reinforcements back up to Tyn Defnant."

"What do you want me to do after that?"

"Once Captain Teille has his orders, you're on your own. It's up to you whether you come back or go on to Oudonsford to tell your family. Don't decide now. Circumstances may change."

She turned to the two men. "Your job is to bring my crew back. Keep it subtle, but anyone who tries to stop you is the enemy. My guards will know what that means. Oh, yes, and will you please remember this verbal message for Maddoes. He is to bring all his loyal men with him. All of them. He'll know what that means, I hope."

Levan frowned. "But he's leaving two to take care of the stock."

"That's different. Give him my words exactly, 'All his loyal men.' Any other questions?"

Jameta gave them three seconds. "Can we leave right away?"

"Will you travel at night? It's your call."

She turned to her two companions. "Lord Lexing and his men will be after us as soon as it's light enough to see the trail. Grab your gear. Put on your best walking shoes, because we've got a long way to go between now and full dark."

In a very short time they were slipping out into the night, following Aldwyn back to the trail.

"Did anybody notice that it's full dark already?"

"She's a messenger, Kolwyn. If the message has to go, she'll take it."

She turned to Erlon. "Where do we sit?"

He winced. "Well, we have, what? Twelve to fourteen men coming down the trail behind us in the morning. They might send someone ahead during the night. We are six swords. We can assume that Lexing has hired good men. We have to make our stand at Tyn Dyfnant. If we don't get there, how will our reinforcements find us?"

Kolwyn pondered. "If we leave at first light, we can be in Dyfnant by noon."

"Let's leave the moment you can see your hand in front of your face. If we get a moon, we leave immediately. Rest is a luxury."

"No moon left tonight, Aleria. Already set."

"Thanks, Blodwel. First light it is. I'll take first watch; everybody else get to sleep."

This was an optimistic wish. Aleria had finished her watch, and just as she was dozing off there was an exclamation and the campfire flared. She started up, hand on sword.

Jatto was standing, his back to the fire, pointing out into the darkness. She was on the wrong side of the fire, and could see nothing.

"What is it?" She kept her voice low.

"Out there. Eyes."

"Eyes. That's all?"

"Big ones. Far apart. Glowing in the light of the fire."

"Oh. That kind of eyes." She motioned the others back into their blankets and joined the guard. As her sight became accustomed to the dark again, she started to see the shapes of trees and rocks, dimly reflecting the firelight. Then, as if just coming into focus, she became aware of two unwinking eyes, low to the ground, staring at her. "There it is. Beside that tree."

"Glad I wasn't imagining it."

She slid forward, her sword ready. The eyes disappeared.

"I wouldn't go any farther."

She stepped back. "No, I don't think I would either." She raised her voice. "The rest of you, back to sleep. We just went onto double watches. I wouldn't ask anyone to stand alone with that thing out there."

By tacit agreement, they divided the area in front of the campsite in two, and they stood shoulder to shoulder, peering into the darkness to either side until their eyes began to play tricks on them, and everything seemed to be moving.

She stood on watch until her legs were beginning to give out, then roused Domin and Erlon, sending Jatto to bed. She may have slept a bit during the rest of the night, but she certainly didn't feel like it.

At one point, she rolled over and held out her hand. There was a dim shadow in front of her face. She sat up.

Erlon was rising. "Time to go?"

"Let's have a bite, first."

"Food's dry. We could eat on the trail."

"A good plan. "

The others were stirring, and soon they were moving again. She paced herself at Erlon's shoulder. "Any thoughts?"

"They could send a few ahead to ambush us."

"In the darkness?"

"Our messengers went."

"But they're special." *And I sent them.* She set that thought aside.

"I hope they're alive. With that Beast out there..."

"Don't think I didn't spend several hours going around that in my head last night. I'm taking the optimistic approach. If it was circling our camp, it wasn't out eating our friends."

"I like that thought."

"We'll just have to keep our eyes open." She stumbled over a root in the trail.

He steadied her arm. "Once we can see anything."

It turned out they didn't see much. Aleria was leading at the time. There was a dark blotch on the trail in front of her, and she stepped over it...

...and slipped on something squishy. She fell, her hands squelching into a foul-smelling mess. She scrambled to her feet, leaning down to feel around. What she came up with felt like a leg with a greave on it. It moved easily under her hand, and she dropped it. "Oh, shit. Oh, shit, shit, shit. Make a light, someone."

"What? We don't want a light, Aleria."

"Make a light! MAKE A LIGHT DAMMIT!"

There was a scratch of flint, and a piece of paper flared for a few seconds. It was all she needed. She took a deep breath and clamped down on her terror.

"Fine. Do we have any lanterns in our packs?"

"I always carry one. I'll light it right away. Is that what I think it is?"

"If you think I just slipped and fell on a dead body, I think you're right."

Erlon cursed and struck the flint again. The lantern steadied, and in its glow they could make out the pieces of a man lying in the trail. Light gleamed off metal strips of armour.

"I guess Lexing did send someone ahead. I wonder how many?"

"At least two." Erlon was doing a strange dance up the trail, avoiding the dark blobs that lay there.

"There's nothing we can do. Bring the light back. I'm already covered in blood. I'd prefer not to fall in any more."

He lighted a path through the carnage, and they moved on, trying not to think about what they had just passed. Aleria stopped at the first creek they crossed to wash her hands, at least. She had no idea what her clothes looked like.

They pushed on in the growing light, their eyes probing the darkness, their ears tuned to any sound. They doused the lamp when it stopped being of use or comfort and pushed on in the growing light.

They rested when they reached the lake because the dawn showed that Aleria needed more cleaning. She hastily changed her shirt and directed Erlon to use the clean parts of the bloody one to dab at her neck and face. Then she tossed it into the bushes.

"I feel a bit better now. I might even be able to eat something in three days or so. Let's keep going."

"How far do you think Lexing is behind us?"

She considered. "I'm hoping he'll slow down because he thinks he has an ambush to stop us."

Erlon slowed, then stopped. "Aleria, I spent some thought on Lexing and what he's doing. Why is he back up here so quickly, and with only five men?"

"I wondered about that." She strode on, and he followed. "He must have got back down and found out something."

"Or he made a plan on the way down."

"And the only way he would come back up would be to bring more men."

"And where are they?"

She stopped and looked at him. "He left them down the valley ahead of us."

"So there must be an ambush. How can we know for sure?"

She called a halt to discuss the problem with the others.

Kolwyn dropped a hand on the remaining shepherd's shoulder. "Why don't we send Blodwel ahead to check it out while we go to Tyr Dyfnant and set up our defences? If he finds an ambush, that's a good piece of information. If he finds evidence that our messengers didn't make it, he comes back and tells us, and we forget the evidence-gathering and make a run for it."

"A sound plan, depending on Blodwel's ability to run twice as fast as Lexing's men can march. Are you up to it?"

In answer the shepherd dropped his gear, pulled a package of dried meat from his pack and shoved it into his shirtfront. "I'm off, then, M'Lady."

"If we get caught inside the fortress, and you get caught outside, you head down the valley to make sure the new information gets home. Got it?"

"Aye." He turned and jogged off.

Erlon picked up the extra pack and slung it over his shoulder. Kolwyn picked up the bow, and they strode on.

At a spot where the trail widened, Kolwyn paced up beside her. "There is one small hole in our plan."

"Yes. What if it's a really good ambush, and no one gets through?"

"Do you think they did?"

She shook her head. "There's no way to tell. They were our best chance, and it's up to them. The rest is up to us. We play delaying tactics for three days. If no reinforcements come, we assume the worst and change our tactics."

"What do you have in mind?"

"We go on the attack. We get that bastard Lexing if it kills all of us."

"That plan appeals to me."

She motioned Erlon to close up behind them. "So how far is he behind us?"

"The only difficulty is in figuring where he met his outbound party."

"Well, the scout didn't get to the mine before we left, or we would have seen them forming up. So they must be some distance behind us, but they could be close." She frowned. "If the scout pulled into camp the moment we started back, it would take them about half an hour to get organized."

"On the other hand, he must have ducked us on the road. Might have seen us, even counted us."

"So they didn't start more than two hours behind us."

"I expect they didn't go much past that ridge where they passed us, two hours back up the trail from Burringer. They didn't catch up to us very fast when Blodwel and I were cleaning the trail, and Lexing looked pretty tired when he went by. And I guarantee he didn't get his men out as early as we did this morning. He and the soldiers with him had been on a forced march for two days."

Kolwyn nodded. "The ones he sent ahead last night would be fresh men from the mine party. Poor sods."

"So we're somewhere between two and four hours ahead?"

"Good estimate."

Erlon pondered that. "Then we'll have time to set up our defences."

"Yes, We've got plenty of water up on the next floor above our old camp in the keep. We'll need firewood. Any chance of barricades?"

"That's a problem. Any stone big enough to be of use is too big to move. Any wood inside is so old it has no strength. That keep isn't built for defence by an army of six. The doorway is too big."

"Any sign of bows in his group?" She glanced at him. "We have two."

"His Majesty takes a dim view of anyone who uses a bow to shoot another person."

"This is done in his Majesty's service. His soldiers carry guns. Besides, I'd sooner be alive to argue afterwards."

Erlon shrugged. "You're the emissary. Your game, your rules."

"That's right. We're playing by my rules, now. That means you can use any little tricks you picked up in your diverse and eclectic experience."

"I'll keep that in mind."

"Could we be spotted coming down the valley to the fortress? They could ambush us there."

"We don't have time to sneak up. We walk straight in and hope for the best. AnLexing must have a pretty good idea of our numbers by now."

"Fine. We walk in, settle down and get ready for a running battle back through the corridors. Kolwyn, Does Tyn Dyfnant have a back door?"

"Not that I know of. We plug the main door of the keep and we're safe as a house."

"Not a house with that many windows."

"The windows are pretty high." Erlon frowned. "We'll have to check them."

"You'll find the Old Ones built well. The only entrance is the main door of the keep."

"And then up the stairs? I doubt it."

"Why not? Oh. The stock."

"That's right. There has to be an entrance at ground level for the animals."

Aleria slipped ahead as the trail narrowed. She raised her voice to speak over her shoulder. "When we get there, Erlon, your task is the front door. See if there's any way to plug it or the staircases inside. Kolwyn, you search for the stock entrance, see if it can be stopped up somehow. The rest of us will get wood."

"Not just firewood. Anything that we can use to barricade the doorways as well."

"Not much time for chopping, but we'll do what we can."

26. The Final Defense of Tyn Dyfnant

When they reached the fortress, Aleria's lungs were aching, and her legs were columns of pain. She knew the others felt the same, but they turned to their work without complaint. After using her outstretched arms to measure the width of the keep door opening, she went out to the stand of trees where they had gathered their firewood, in a protected fold of the mountain about a hundred yards east of the keep.

There were fallen logs all over, and she found three that looked strong enough to be of use but small enough to chop through with swords in the time available. Setting the other men to work, she grabbed up an armload of dry limbs and hurried back to where Erlon was straining to move a huge stone.

"I'll get three logs for you, longer than the door opening. If there's time, three more."

"Good enough. Keep an ear cocked for visitors." He returned to his task.

She went back to the copse and drew her sword. "I can chop as fast as you can, Domin, but you're a lot stronger. Take another load of firewood in, then help Erlon move stones."

"Right you are, Aleria."

She took his place and hacked away as the sweat stung in her eyes and her hand, hardened to the sword over the years, still felt as if it would drop her weapon any moment. She switched to her left hand. No sense wasting her sword arm on wood. The day might yet hold a battle.

When their logs were cut the two men carried them back to the fortress. Aleria finished hers and went to look up the valley and report back. "Nobody coming. Time for three more logs. Will that help?"

"With three more logs and six more of these stones I could hold off an army here. At least an army that wasn't strong enough to move the stones."

They went back to their chopping, and just as they finished, they were startled by a shout.

"They're coming!" Kolwyn was leaning out of a window, pointing.

"Is there time to bring the logs?"

"Certainly."

"Tell Erlon we're on our way and give him a hand."

The two men hefted a log. She carried firewood.

When they got to the door, three logs were piled on top of each other, spaced a hand's breadth apart. Erlon's shirt was soaked with sweat, but he still moved swiftly, helping them to put the log in place, directing Domin and Kolwyn to drop a smaller rock to wedge it firmly.

"Anything else you need?"

"Besides a derrick to lift these rocks? No."

"Well, you'll get the full crew in a moment. There's only two more logs, and Lexing is coming."

"I gathered. You'd better come in before the wall gets too high."

She regarded the barricade critically. "It's easy to climb."

"It's meant to be defended. If they are left to it, they'll climb over or chop through in the same time as you took to cut the logs."

"But not if someone is there," she pointed, "and there. With bows."

"Those clever Old Ones. You'd think they put those windows there for a reason. Give me a hand with this big stone. It needs to be tighter in."

All of them heaved, and the huge square stone slid tight against the logs.

"That looks better."

"Nice of them to leave this loose stone lying around."

She glanced at Kolwyn. "Find the other door?"

"No."

"That's too bad."

"No, that's good. I found an old path that leads straight towards the wall, but it has been covered by a heavy fall of rock. I doubt if they'll ever find the door, let alone dig it out."

"Any sign of Blodwel?"

He shook his head. "Any time now would be good. When do we expect our reinforcements?"

"It will take our messengers all of today to get down. It will take them a day and a half to get back up if they hurry. So noon, day after tomorrow at the earliest. More likely late afternoon."

"Two days." Erlon frowned. "If wasn't for our ghostly friend wandering around out there, I'd stay outside and whittle them down."

"Yes, I would agree. That scattering of human pieces up on the trail is a strong argument, though. I got an idea of its size from how far apart the eyes are, and I don't think even your big sword is enough."

"Fine. I prefer the real enemies to the metaphysical ones. I'll come inside and fight men instead."

By this time, the loggers had brought in their final offering. Everyone climbed inside, and they jammed the last trunk in place, spending the rest of the time they had piling every rock they could move against the barrier. Aleria went up the stairs to the balcony, from which she could see their enemy striding down the trail. Except they weren't striding. She took heart in the fact that they were definitely straggling, and Achern anLexing was far in the rear. There were thirteen men in front of him.

"The birds are in sight, boys. Time to set up the shooting blind."

Her little army joined her on the wall. She regarded them. "We're in pretty good shape. We brought food for nine and there's only six of us. That barricade is much stronger than I had hoped. We have a limited number of arrows, but a limited number of enemy. They are wearing nothing near full armour, and all you have to do is disable them. One bowman in one of those arrow ports above the door should be able to keep them from chopping the barricade down."

She turned inside. "I've been looking at the design of the main hall. There is a choke point at the entrance to the presentation platform and one at the top of each stair, where two men can hold off a large number because only two can approach at once. If they have archers that's a problem, but we can put bows there and there," she pointed, "to cover the defence points. If they win up the stairs, then we're back in the dark corridors, and things will get interesting."

"I assume we defend the barricade with swords."

"Erlon?"

"That depends on whether they have bows. It's not hard to shoot through those spaces, but it's too easy to climb over the barricade if there's no one there to stop you. The answer is, yes. If we can, we defend it. If not, we put the two bowmen in the windows, and they do their best. I'm sure the steps in front of the door were put there to slow down any attack."

Domin looked down. "I suppose they could pile brushwood against the barricade and burn through it."

Erlon nodded. "If they had unlimited men they might manage. They're lightly armed and too exposed to our bowmen if they try."

Aleria tossed up her hands. "The accepted ratio for holding a good defensive position is one man to five in the attacking army. This isn't a good defensive position, but the numbers are still with us. If we were to whittle down five or six of their men, they'd only outnumber us two to one. That's great odds for a siege. And we only have to hold out for two days.

"Other things to keep in mind. I don't think Lexing has a good grasp of our numbers. I doubt if he knows about our reinforcements coming. He doesn't know what a hurry he's in. So this is a stalling game. We don't have to beat them, only slow them up and whittle them down."

"But we don't know how many men they left down in the pass."

Gordon A. Long

"We don't. Any sign of Blodwel?"

Kolwyn shook his head.

"Damn. I hope he's all right. I'm still guessing near five. He now has about fifteen up here, and he has to leave some men to guard his manor. Best part is that however many are at the ambush, he seems to be leaving them there."

"Of course, if he caught one of our messengers, he might know about the reinforcements."

"And if they caught all of them, our reinforcements aren't coming. If we are overrun, we split up and head across country, every man for himself. We must get someone through." She grasped her sword hilt, the anger boiling inside her. "But first we kill as many of them as we can get our hands on."

She looked out at the mountains. *Not very good country to try to head across. Well, at least Kolwyn might make it. And Erlon's a mountain man.* She began to feel better.

Lexing's soldiers had drawn up in the main courtyard a prudent bowshot from the barricaded door and were lolling around waiting for their lord to come up. Aleria took heart from his speed.

"He's not hurrying. Good sign. They'll rest before they attack."

"We could use a rest as well. I never wanted to be a stonemason." Erlon wiped his forehead. "I'm threshed with a flail."

"Fine. Take food and water to your positions. We hope to be here for a while."

He hefted his water skin. "Aleria, would you stay up here for the first part of the battle? A good set of eyes..."

"Fine. I'll come down if I'm needed."

They filed out, and she went onto the balcony. *I should have said something. A speech to make them brave. That's what leaders do.*

She slid her head around one of the crenellations, looking down into the courtyard. Lexing was standing with his men, staring at the barricade. She counted them. It didn't add up.

She pattered back down the stairs. "Erlon, there are some of his men missing."

"If I was him, I'd send someone out to scout around."

"Of course." She slapped his shoulder. "Thanks."

As she returned to the top of the stairway, she berated herself. *Why couldn't I figure that out for myself?* She stood where everyone could hear her. "There are ten men in front. The others will be scouting for another entrance. They probably won't attack for a while. Keep an eye open for Blodwel."

Various murmurs of assent drifted up to her, and she went back to the wall to wait.

Down in the courtyard, Lexing sat for a while on a block of stone in the shade of one of the tower stumps, eating something. Then he prowled the courtyard, staring up at their defences, his eyes probing. Then back to his perch in the shade.

Then he started up, shouting to his men and pointing towards the base of the keep on the eastern side. They all began to run forward, but then stopped, turned around and went back about their duties. Lexing cursed and sat down again.

There was a scrabbling sound down at the barrier, then silence.

"What's going on?"

Erlon's voice rose up the stairs, chuckling. "It seems the lost is found. He's coming up."

Aleria's heart settled as she stood at the top of the stairs watching a panting Blodwel drag himself up each flight. "What's wrong, soldier? Not up to the pace?"

The little shepherd grinned. "Bit of a sprint at the last, there, M'Lady."

"How did you get close enough to even try?"

He shrugged. "Snuck 'round to the east while Lord Lexing was speechifyin'. Kind of him to keep everyone lookin' his way."

"Well done, in any case. What's happening down the valley?"

"Five men in an ambush exactly where I'd expect 'em to be, M'Lady. Aldwyn woulda spotted 'em for sure."

"Perfect. Take a rest. You deserve it. There's a wineskin on the bench over there."

"Don't mind if I do, M'Lady. Hot day."

Aleria slapped him on the back, and he strolled away. "Everybody heard that? Settle in, folks. All is as it should be." *Considering the alternatives, anyway.* Aleria made herself as comfortable as the stone would allow, and waited.

They waited several hours, during which three men trickled in and reported to Lexing. He did not look pleased at their results.

Finally, with a gesture of disgust, he got to his feet and stepped forward, stopping below the main steps with his hands on his hips.

"AnLlannon."

Kolwyn did not answer.

"Llannon, I know you're listening. I can see your puny barricade. I have twice the men you have. I can sit here until you starve." He waved a hand back down to the west. "I blocked off the pass into this valley . Any search party will fall into my hands as well."

He turned and paced as if he was thinking, hands behind his back. "I'll tell you what, Llannon. There is a lot of business to be done in this valley. There is a lot of iron to be mined. I have the contacts in Aesmark to smelt it and sell it. Think of it, Llannon. Iron! Enough iron to buy guns and weapons and Mechanical tools. We don't have to listen to those backward-looking lowlanders in Kingsport. The power to rule ourselves, Llannon. Think of it! A realm all our own, up here in the mountains where they can't touch us."

Keep talking, Lexing. The more you say, the more you tell us. And the more time we waste.

"It's too much bother to fight you for it. Why don't we make a partnership? Come on out and let's talk."

There was no response.

"All you have to do is hand over that king's representative. She's poison, Llannon. She'll spin your head with her talk of loyalty and advantage. Turn her over to me. I'll deal with her, and you won't know anything about it."

Still he got no answer. Finally, he nodded. "That's fine. These are big ideas, new thoughts. You take a bit of time with them. I'm in no hurry."

He began to turn away, but stopped in a studied move, as if he had just thought of something. "I'll tell you what. If you come in with us, I'll give you this place. You can search all you want, take anything you find. Anything."

He strolled back to his place on the rock, his hands still clasped behind his back.

Aleria slipped down to the barricade.

Kolwyn was sitting on the main stairs, out of sight in the shadow from those in the bright courtyard. He grinned up at her. "What do you think? Turn you over to him, and my troubles will be solved?"

"Certainly." She nodded. "Make it purely business and you can have an independent realm all your own. And you get your own castle, with any lost treasure you can find. The princess is a little too old to be needing her dowry any more. Isn't that generous?"

"I wonder who gets to be king?"

"Oh, I'm sure it would be very modern. Everyone would get a vote."

"Everyone, as in all the businessmen who supported him?"

"Those that survived, at least." She thought about Lexing's speech. "He gave us a lot of information, there."

"Yes. He doesn't know we sent the messengers out."

"But he does have the valley bottled in. Our men coming up will be ambushed."

"They know all they need to. They will be watching for opposition." He glanced south. "Aldwyn is guiding them."

"That's assuming Aldwyn and his party got through the ambush on the way down."

"Blodwyn's comment about how easy it was to spot makes me feel a lot better. Otherwise we are in deep trouble."

She grinned. "That was the best gift Lexing gave us in that little speech. If he had them he'd be parading them in front of us. Or their bodies. That's his style."

"So he will continue to keep his forces divided, thinking he has all the time in the world."

"I hope so. Do you think he'll attack today?"

"I don't see him as a patient man."

"I'll chat with Erlon. Be ready."

She made the circle and had a quick word with everyone. Erlon agreed with their analysis. "He will attack soon. I'm trying to think what he'll do as a diversion, first."

"As long as we can tell what's the diversion and what's the attack."

He smiled. "That's always been the trick."

"I'm depending on you to tell the difference, Erlon."

"Let's stay within reach, Aleria. The two of us together make the smartest general I ever ran across."

A warm glow suffused her, and she laid a hand on his shoulder. "Thank you, Erlon."

"Just careful analysis, Ma'am. That's what I'm here for."

"Keep it up, Soldier. It seems to be helpful."

She stood, looking out over the enemy's encampment. "It occurs to me that I may not be dealing with this problem the right way."

"No?"

"I have been acting the same way I always do. The role of caravan leader runs along certain paths, and you deal with problems in a very specific way."

"Which works well, in my experience."

"For a caravan. This is not a caravan, and I am not only a caravan leader. I am also the king's representative, trying to solve a problem and prevent possible political upheavals."

"And you discovered the source of serious trouble to come. Seems to me that removing him would solve most of it."

"Perhaps, but I don't have that much latitude. No, it seems to me that I should be acting like a diplomat, not a general."

"You mean go out and talk him to death?"

"But don't you think I should try? We escalated this conflict to a level where people could be killed, and I didn't once try to deal with Achern anLexing. All I did was walk into his castle and slap his face. That wasn't very responsible of me, now that I consider it. If I go back to his Majesty and report my actions, I doubt if he will judge that I did my best."

"So what are you going to do?"

"He knows I'm here. Why don't I offer to talk to him? It can't do any harm. I won't invite him inside. We can stand at the barricade. He'll be in more danger than I am."

"I can't see anything wrong with that. As you keep telling us you learned from Master Ogima, the best war is the one you don't fight. How do we arrange it?"

"Formally, would be best. Lord anLlannon can be my ambassador."

Lord anLlannon was not quite so enthused with the idea. "Aleria, I know you think you have to try, but you're wasting your time and putting yourself in danger as well."

"I don't mind wasting time. How in danger?"

"Anything he agrees on will mean some kind of advantage to him. Count on it."

"Then I expect you to make arrangements that are as safe for me as possible."

"Wonderful. So if you get killed it's my fault."

She smiled. "I don't want to take credit for everything. I'm not that sort of woman."

He stepped out on the balcony and shouted across to the enemy camp. A garbled call returned. It didn't take long before he came back.

"I don't like this at all."

"Why not?"

"He agreed to everything."

"Why is that a problem...?" She remembered the man's sly look. "Ah. Let's be extra careful. So he wants you all out where he can see you, and all his men will be visible as well? Fine. He and I meet at the barricade. He stands in the clear. What can go wrong? You'll all be there watching."

"We're on top of the wall. We can't see the barricade underneath."

"Well, he's hardly going to charge at me all by himself, Kolwyn. Do you have any evidence that he's any kind of super swordsman?"

"No."

"Thank you for your service and your concern. You have done your duty admirably, and now I will do mine."

"You just be very careful."

"Why, Kolwyn, I didn't know you cared."

"Aleria, you joke too much sometimes. Be careful."

"I'm not joking. Keep your eyes open."

It was Erlon who answered. "We will."

Her men stepped out onto the balcony, and she descended the stairs. When she showed herself at the barricade, Lexing started out from the line of his men. He strode across the courtyard and stopped two steps below the barricade, looking up at her.

"Well, well. The king's ambassador is not so chipper now, is she?"

"Lord anLexing, I did not ask a parlay in order to continue old arguments. I am trying to find a solution to the problem we have."

"Yes, I imagine that would be rather important to you now."

She gestured to the fortress, to his soldiers. "I don't mean this problem. I mean the larger one."

"I don't see any problem."

"Do you honestly think you will get away with making an alliance with Aesmark and creating your own kingdom in the Trench? Do you think King Otta will sit back and let you? I'm trying to understand how that could work."

He sneered. "The reason you don't understand is the reason that it will work. Otta sits in his city with his nobles gathered around him, none with the slightest idea what's going on in his realm. This archaic idea of not using Mechanicals has nothing to do with religion or tradition. It's a ruse for keeping the king and his cronies in power and the rest of the population in servitude."

"Much though I agree that the rules on Mechanicals need to be relaxed, I don't think that the rest of it follows. You cannot imagine that he will allow you to do this."

"And who is going to stop me?" He pointed at her. "Not you. I can guarantee that." He raised his arm, and there was something about the gesture that wasn't natural.

Her muscles tensed.

"Aleria! Down!"

Her reaction was instant. At the first sound of Erlon's voice she was moving, and by the time he had finished the two words she had dived to safety – from what, she had no idea, but it made a loud bang and whirr – behind one of the larger rocks that held up the barricade. Sword in hand, she peered out to see anLexing scampering as fast as his short legs could carry him towards his men.

He reached them and turned back, staring at the keep. He said nothing for a while, then spat on the ground and turned away.

She heard footsteps on the stairs and turned her head. Erlon beckoned to her, motioning "low and fast." She scooted towards him and stood when she was in the protection of the wall.

"What was that?"

"We're in more trouble than we thought. They have a rifle."

"Damn it!" She rammed her sword back into its scabbard with more-than-necessary force.

"Yes. The idea was to get you out into the open far enough that the gunner could get a clear shot at you. He was hidden, but I saw the barrel move when he took aim."

"Well, once again my life is in your debt." She started up the stairs. "You must let me pay you back one of these days. It's only fair."

"I'd much rather keep the moral credit."

"Check your contract when we get back. If it doesn't contain a bonus clause for saving the boss's life, we'll write one in."

"But in the meantime, let's deal with that gun. It probably has twice the accurate range of an arrow."

"And it's twice as illegal. Add one more to our pile of charges against lord Lexing."

27. No Promises

The three of them leaned on the battlements surveying the courtyard as darkness fell. The fire in the enemy camp – she felt justified in calling them enemies, now – was bright enough to reveal a soldier sitting on a stone block cleaning a long-barrelled rifle. Brass fittings winked in the light of the flames.

"We must deal with that gun." Erlon slapped the stone with his hand.

Aleria gestured down towards the gate. "I'm in agreement, but there's one little problem."

"Yes. Our great advantage has one small drawback. One way out; one way in."

Kolwyn smiled. "Not using our eyes, are we?"

Erlon straightened slowly. "By which you mean…?"

"We're standing in front of a way out."

"Very good. Straight out and straight down. Splat."

"There are other windows, some not so high."

Erlon raised his eyebrows.

"And a coil of rope in my pack."

"Ah. Long enough?"

"Easily."

Erlon started to turn, but Kolwyn's hand on his shoulder stopped him. "And I'm going."

"Not a good idea. You don't have the manhunting skills."

"But I do have the other skills. Do you know how to climb a rope?"

"I can get up a rope."

"That's not what I asked. Do you know how to rappel down? How to climb up quickly, not haul yourself up hand over hand? How well do you know the layout of that courtyard?"

Aleria stepped forward. "You just talked yourself into a mission, Soldier. Do you need a diversion?"

Erlon was on the problem, regarding the length of the crenellated wall. "A small one, perhaps. We don't want the camp upset, just enough to attract the attention of everyone who is up and about."

"That will help." Kolwyn thought a moment. "Let's watch what he does with the gun. Then I'll go out one of the windows along the western wall and come in behind that line of stones over there, see?"

"Right. If you're coming in that way, I'll show myself on the battlements, over there, to the east. If I flash the lantern around as if I'm working it will keep them watching until you're finished. If I create too much disturbance and they start milling around, I'll stop."

Aleria tried to think of what could go wrong. "We have a good view from here. What if there's a problem, and we can see it, but you can't? How do we call you back?"

Erlon grinned. "I've been wanting to drop a flaming arrow into Lexing's tent but didn't want to waste the arrow."

"But it's out of bowshot."

"Bowshot depends on the bow. Mine's got more snap than you might think. Give it to Blodwel. Even if he misses, it's a pretty noticeable signal."

"Fair enough. Let's watch that rifleman."

The gunner took his time, polishing his weapon with a rag to finish off. Then he leaned it against his shoulder and sat back, staring into the fire.

"Idiot. What good is a gun that's not loaded and a gunner with fire in his eyes?"

"Much less good if he doesn't have the gun at all." Kolwyn slipped away into the night, and Erlon departed for the far battlement.

Aleria watched the enemy camp, alert for any change, but nothing happened. And then nothing happened for a long time. And longer. Finally, when she thought she just had to jump up and move, one of the soldiers around the fire looked up. He nudged his partner and pointed. Aleria followed the signal and saw, faintly, a light playing along the battlements out on the east wall. Then it was gone. The soldiers were more alert, now, watching intently. One of them started, and again she saw the light flicker.

Aware that Kolwyn must see the same light, she watched for him to move, but outside the enemy's firelight she could see only blackness. The soldier with the gun noticed the light, too, and soon all five men visible were watching the far battlements.

What if the rifleman decides to load his gun? Well, what if he does. Kolwyn can wait. ...unless that dratted Beast comes back. Damn. Why didn't we think of that when we started this fool stunt? Of course, Kolwyn thought of it. We have to get that gun. She thought of his muscular torso shredded by huge, sharp claws, and a shudder ran through her. *Settle down, girl. He'll make it.*

After a while Aleria looked back at the gunner. He had lost interest and gone to sleep, slumped over. Then she saw the gun was gone. She headed out to the north battlements, arriving as Erlon was starting another session.

"He's got it."

"Great. I'll make this a short one. I've been moving away. I'll start back towards the keep, now. Make it look like I've finished whatever I was doing. That will lay them back but still keep them looking."

They made their way back along the wall, flashing the lantern around once in a while. By the time they got back, Kolwyn was there, showing off a rifle, gleaming with steel and brass. He looked up as the two entered.

"Stupid gunner. If he'd loaded it, we'd have one shot at least. I tried, but I couldn't get to his powder pouch or his shot."

"Intelligent help is hard to find. He looks rather relaxed out there."

"As relaxed as he'll ever be, I'm afraid."

He didn't offer any more details, and she didn't ask. "I'll hide this up by the functionaries. No sense destroying it. We might get our hands on the ammunition somehow."

There was a sudden uproar in the camp below. Lexing's voice rose above the ado. "You murdering swine! You sneaking, nasty, repulsive, Galesian bitch!" His voice rose as he ranted, describing her habits, her looks, and her morals.

"He really doesn't like you, Aleria."

"I got that impression."

The lord kept on and on, and suddenly Erlon's head came up. "To your posts. He's roiling them up to attack!"

Erlon drew his weapon and headed down the stairs.

Aleria turned to Kolwyn. "Better Dalmyns handle this together. Blodwel has the bowman's window. You and Jatto hold the choke point at the top of the stairs if anyone gets by us." He nodded, and she followed Erlon. "No sense staying up there in the dark."

"Fair enough. We can use the extra sword down here."

When they reached the barricade, Domin was still on guard, peering out. "What's going on?"

Erlon slapped his shoulder. "Lord Kolwyn just grabbed Lord anLexing by the tender parts. He stole the rifle and slit the rifleman's throat. Now Lexing is mad enough to attack at night when they can't see anything. Big mistake."

Aleria drew her sword. "Not that we can see much, either."

"Stand to the side." Erlon pointed. "They'll slow as they scramble over the barricade. There's room for three of them to come over at a time, and they can only come straight ahead. Once the first three are over, you two take them from each side. I'm counting on you to get the first two right away, then both concentrate on the middle one. I'll slide behind them and throw the next three back."

"You think you can do that?"

"I can hold them up long enough for you to finish off the first wave. Then you stand back to the side, I'll retreat, and we'll do it over again with the ones that follow me. If everything goes according to plan, I'll take the middle one, and there will be three of us to push the next three back. If six men disappear into the darkness, I figure they'll pull...here they come." The campfire flared bright, and the silhouetted shadows of a mass of men surged up the steps towards them.

The first two men over the barricade were easy prey, stumbling around in the dark, swinging their swords wildly. Aleria dispatched hers and turned. The third attacker was about to hit Erlon from behind. She lunged desperately and managed to deflect his sword. He rounded on her, and from that moment she knew nothing but the flash of treacherous steel in the firelight.

Whoever faced away from the light had the advantage, and she spun her back towards Erlon, counting on him to hold his place. Her opponent made a wild swipe at her, and she ducked his blade and ran her sword through the darkness where she thought his body was. There was a reassuring resistance, and he screamed and staggered back. She followed, striking once more to be sure, then spun around.

It seemed the battle was over. Erlon was shouldering a limp form back over the logs. He turned and saw her. "Light?"

"We don't have one."

"Didn't think of that. Throw them back over."

It was nerve-wracking work, searching for bodies and wounded in the dark, never sure when one of them might stab out with a dagger, but eventually they found five figures, at least two still moaning in pain, and dumped them onto the steps outside.

She took two deep breaths, then raised her voice. "That was a stupid move, Lexing. I didn't notice you at the front of the attack. I wonder why? You have wounded, here. I'll give you time to haul them back."

Again his voice rose, this time attacking her family and her descendants.

When he stopped for breath, she called again. "You're wasting time, and they're still bleeding. I'll count to a hundred, and then I'll tell my archers to start shooting anyone who moves. Look. One of your men is trying to crawl back to you. Show some heart, man, if you want your soldiers to be here when you wake up in the morning."

He hissed a few more curses, then several figures separated from the bulk of the men, sliding forward hesitantly.

When they got near, she spoke to them softly enough that their lord could not hear. "Don't worry, men. You're only soldiers doing your duty, and this is a truce. Nobody will attack you. There's one still alive over here on the left as well. Better you take the dead ones, too. Tomorrow you won't get the chance."

They muttered among themselves, sorting out the still forms on the flagstones and dragging them away. One of the wounded cursed and demanded that his rescuer help him up. Soon the two were lurching back towards the fire.

"Anyone hurt?"

There was no answer. "I'll stay here, you head up to the fire and check yourselves over. Somebody relieve Blodwel from the bowman's position. Send him down to cover here, and I'll come up."

"Are you hurt?"

"Not so that I've noticed. Away you go."

They trudged away without further comment, and she tucked herself behind the archway where she could see the enemy camp. There was a great deal of action around the fire, and one man was still lying down. The one who had walked back was sitting up, so he probably had been wounded the least. It had been a bad enough blow to knock him down at first, though, so perhaps it would disable him. She watched as they tended him and decided that it was both an arm and a head wound. Probably knocked him out temporarily. Too bad. *Oh, well, at least four down, maybe five.*

There was the slightest scuff on the stair above her, and she turned to see Blodwel descending. She moved into the light so he wouldn't be startled, and he slid down beside her.

"Keep an eye on the one lying down. I want to figure out how badly he's hurt."

He said nothing, only nodding his head, a motion she could barely see in the shadows.

She turned up the stairs. As she climbed, a feeling of elation began to churn in her. *We won the first skirmish! The odds are better, now, and the enemy will be disheartened. How can I take advantage of this?*

The mood in their camp was likewise jubilant. Jatto was passing a wineskin around and Kolwyn, a bandage around his left forearm, was cleaning is sword.

"What happened to you?"

He shrugged. "No idea. I discovered it when I got up here in the light. I washed it out with wine, and Erlon bound it up. Not deep enough to need stitches. Sort of ragged."

Erlon chuckled. "I think it was someone's teeth."

"I don't think so, Sir." Domin grinned. "I bet he caught his arm on a sharp branch, tossing the bodies over afterwards."

"Thanks a great deal, Domin. I'll remember you when it's time to give out the Solstice Bestowals."

The soldier guffawed. "I'm sorry M'Lord. I made a mistake. I saw it happen. You took a sword on your bare arm to protect Lady Aleria from a lateral attack. You saved her. You're a hero, M'Lord."

Kolwyn grinned at Aleria. "There you are, my Lady. I have saved you from certain death, in an heroic deed witnessed by your loyal man. How shall you thank me?"

"Ask me that question in a week, after your arm drops off. Once you've died of blood poisoning in my defence, I'll feel much more charitable towards you."

She turned to Erlon. "What do you expect now?"

"I doubt if they'll attack tonight. Hard to get the men up for a second go after that kind of a whipping."

"We've proved that the barricade works and that we have enough men to cover it. Blodwel had bad luck shooting in the dark. Wounded one in the arm, he thinks, but in daylight he'd get a couple more. Lexing has to deal with that barricade."

"How?"

"That's why I brought you along, with your vaunted experience at violence and mayhem. How would you deal with it?"

Gordon A. Long

He shrugged. "The usual way."

"There is a usual way?"

"A battering ram. If he can figure a way to shield his men, he can bring a big ram in here and knock the first two logs off the top at one blast. Then the rest of the soldiers rush in. It could work."

"And how do we stop it from working?"

"Big rocks."

Aleria turned at this new voice. "What rocks, Jatto?"

"I seen it happen. We was tryin' to break into a place, and we got a log to bust the door. We had dried cowhides over the guys carryin' the log 'cause of the arrows. But they had big stones up above the door, and they dropped them on the guys. Cowhides ain't much good against boulders. They shot anyone tryin' to take the log back. We never did get through that door. Had to burn the place down."

She slapped him on the shoulder. "Well, I don't think anyone is going to burn us down, but I can see plenty of stones big enough to drop. Let's keep an eye on them, and if they bring a log, we'll find the stones."

She looked around. "Any other ideas?"

"Set a watch, get some kip?"

"Fine idea, Erlon. I could use a rest."

It remained an idea. She was still keyed up from the battle, and the other ideas spinning in her head left no room for the thought of sleep. After a long time squirming on the cold, hard stone, she got up and walked out onto the balcony.

It was a clear, starry night, and the moon was just setting behind the mountains. It struck her to the core that such beauty could exist, ignoring and ignored by the evil that confronted her. She leaned her forehead on the parapet, taking comfort from the cool solidity of the stone.

"Nice night."

She started upright. Kolwyn stood some distance away, as if needing permission to intrude.

She glanced up at the stars. "Part of it, I suppose."

"Still." Kolwyn leaned back against the parapet and gazed up at the inky sky. He was twisting the kerchief in his fingers again. "Beautiful, aren't they?"

"Especially when you've just been crawling through the deepest passages of human evil."

He turned to look at her. "You do have a talent for the utter destruction of a romantic mood, don't you?"

"Is that what you were doing? Creating a romantic mood? Silly of me not to notice, in the circumstances."

He finished his twisting and gave the two ends of the kerchief a tug. Nothing moved. He extended his hand to her, the ends of cloth hanging down.

She pulled on them, and the silk slid through his fingers like smoke. Or as if his fingers were smoke. "Cute." She passed the kerchief back to him.

He looked away. "Your mother is of Exalted Rank."

"One of the Founding Families of the realm."

"Yes. My mother told me."

"And my mother told me about your mother."

He turned quickly. "Your mother knows my mother?"

"They are acquainted."

"Hmm."

"Are you leading up to something, here?" She turned to stroll away along the balcony.

"Not really." He followed. "I like to keep things straight."

"The romantic approach didn't work, so you're trying the Ranked Match approach. Do you know what happened to the last person that tried to arrange a marriage for me?"

"Who would that be?"

She stopped and turned to face him. "Have you ever heard of the Duke of anCannah?"

"Everyone has heard of Duke anCannah. What was he doing, trying to arrange a marriage for you? More to the point, what happened to him?"

"He was trying to arrange a marriage for me with his son, of course."

"Which obviously didn't work." His face was raised to the sky, but his head slanted towards her. "What happened?"

"I arranged a marriage for his son with my best friend. I thought it appropriate, since they were in love."

"I see." He gazed at the stars a while longer. "No, I don't see. What has that got to do with me? Will I end up married to Jameta or someone?"

She chuckled. "No, I'm keeping up my end of the conversation, waiting for you to get to the point."

He shrugged. "There is no point. I'm just getting things straight."

"Well, I hope you've got something straight, because as far as I'm concerned, this conversation has been going around in circles and getting nowhere."

"So all my approaches haven't worked," he turned to face her. "I'll try one more."

"I'm all ears."

"If we get out of this..."

"Bad start. You mean, 'When we get out of this,' I assume."

"I stand corrected, my Lady. I do not deem this the appropriate place or time for this discussion. Therefore, when this altercation is over, is there a chance you might be interested in...I mean..."

She smiled gently as she watched him wind down like a dying clock. "Let's assume that I understand what you are talking about. Otherwise we could be here all night."

"Well?"

"Well, what?"

"You're not trying to make this easy for me, are you?"

"Not really. It's rather fun, actually."

"Fun?" His brow furrowed. "You think this is fun?"

A wiggle of memory sent a warning flash through her mind. "No, no, not that kind of fun. I'm just thinking how happy you'd be if I said, 'Yes,' that's all."

He peered at her a moment. "Are you serious?"

She grinned. "It's difficult to keep track of where we are, but I am trying to be serious." She took his arm and led him further along the parapet. "Look, Kolwyn, I have made some mistakes in my life, and I swore I would make none of them on this journey. There are too many important things at stake. So my personal feelings cannot be allowed to interfere in any way with the execution of my duty to the king. Do you understand?"

"Of course. I've seen the letter. It's a lot of responsibility to carry."

"Well, then. If I come to a point where my decision is between your life and the good of the realm, I don't want to have any personal entanglements causing me to act in a way that would make me feel sorry at a later date. Especially when I am in front of his Majesty, reporting my progress. Do you follow?"

"I follow." His face screwed up. "It makes my pathetic attempts at romance look rather selfish, doesn't it?"

She laid a hand against his cheek. "No, it makes you look rather human, and it makes me seem heartless and driven." She removed her hand. "But there comes a time when the good of the kingdom must take precedence over my personal desires. This is that time. I'm sorry, but that's how it is."

"I, too, have sworn my allegiance. I believed every word I spoke, so I have no choice but to agree with you. But at a later date, when these weighty matters are disposed of..."

"...and around we go again." Her heart sank. *This has to be done.*

"I'm sorry. You're right. Even a promise to make a promise is too much to ask."

She looked up at his face, stark in the moonlight. "Do you understand that?"

"I am a Ranked peer of this realm." He shrugged. "How can I expect you to act any other way?"

"You didn't say you understood."

He smiled. "Right. I will give you that much, disappointed though I am. I understand. The matter is closed. Perhaps we will discuss this at a later date." He moved a step away.

She resisted the urge to follow, to move closer, to touch his arm, his face...

"At a later date, then." The flash of teeth in the moonlight left no doubt as to his feelings. He turned back into the fortress.

She shook her head. *After all that, did we really change anything?* She returned to their camp and opened her bedroll. The stone floor was still cold and hard, but there was warmth at the core of her being. She left all her clothes on and kept her blankets folded under her hip and shoulder. Somehow, she slept.

28. Outside the Door

"Aleria! Aleria, you've got to wake up!"

She roused with difficulty, bleary with sleep, grabbing her sword by instinct, jerking upright. "Wha…What is it, Jatto?"

"It's Domin. He's not here!"

Her heart gave a lurch as she realized that light was coming in through the windows. "It's dawn. You were supposed to wake me! Why didn't someone wake me?"

"That's it. I was supposed to be on watch after Domin. But he didn't wake me. He's gone!"

"Gone? What do you mean, gone? He couldn't just disappear."

"I dunno, Aleria, but he ain't there."

She jammed on her boots. "And we've had no one on watch for how long?"

"An hour, maybe? Lord Llannon woke me. He told me to get you and went back out to the archer's window."

"You go relieve Lord Llannon, and I'll look for Domin in here. Erlon!"

The guard Captain was already tying his boots. "I've got a lamp."

"If he's our traitor, why didn't they attack?"

They stepped into the corridor where they had set the watch post. Erlon shone the lamp around. The hall was empty. They moved deeper into the fortress, searching for tracks in the dust.

"It's too well trodden here." Aleria peered around. "I can't read anything."

"Nor I. No, wait…"

Down the hallway, something gleamed in the light of his lamp. They hurried forward.

"His sword." Erlon picked it up. "No blood. Couldn't be a fight. We'd have heard something."

"There's a lamp. Squashed flat."

"I don't like the look of this." Aleria hurried ahead to see where his lantern was pointing. There was a long scuffmark in the dust as if someone had slid on his back. At the end were several small dark spots. Aleria touched one, brought it up.

"He wasn't the traitor."

The skid mark continued, a growing trail of blood in the middle, and they followed it. Then Erlon stopped, switched the lamp to his left hand and drew his sword. "Look at that."

There, in a clear patch where the dust was undisturbed, was a large footprint.

"That damn Beast is inside!"

She turned, her eyes searching the darkness of the corridor in the other direction. Nothing.

"Back to the fire."

Out in their camp, the others were waiting. Aleria regarded them, and her throat went dry. She glanced at Erlon, but he was looking to her.

This is where you earn your authority, girl. She took a deep breath.

"Kolwyn, any idea what happened?"

The young lord shook his head. "Domin usually passed by me regularly. He didn't make the usual contact, so I waited a while, then got worried and came in looking. When he wasn't there, I grabbed Jatto and headed back out to be on guard."

"We found his sword and lamp, some blood and a track from the Ghost Beast in the inner corridor. It took him."

"Any chance he's still alive?"

She looked at Jatto and shook her head. "After what it did to those soldiers on the trail, I doubt it."

"So it's inside."

"We were already suspicious of that when it took the meat, but I didn't think it would attack right in camp like that. It has far less fear of humans than other wild animals. The question is, what do we do, now? Kolwyn, what's Lexing doing?"

He shook his head. "Nothing. As far as I could tell, they all got a good night's sleep."

"Are we sure they're all there?"

"I counted them as soon as it got light enough. I assume Lord Lexing is in his tent, the rest of them are all out in the courtyard, plain to see. Most are still in their bedrolls."

"One bit of luck. Any more anyone can think of?"

"Well, the animal seems to be around only in the night. No one has ever seen or heard it in daylight." Erlon turned to Kolwyn. "That so, my Lord?"

"As far as the people in my demesne report, yes."

Aleria nodded. "So we're fine as long as we're out here in the daylight. But we can't retreat into the corridors as we planned if they break through out there."

"Yes, we can."

"Sorry. Of course we can. It's just more dangerous."

"And it's as dangerous for them." Erlon bared his teeth with little humour. "The Beast's tally as it stands is one of us and two of them. Two to one sounds like good odds, but there aren't enough of us to absorb that kind of loss for long."

"I think the solution to the Beast is to stay together. We had two watchers at opposite ends of our redoubt. It picked off one of us. Two men watching each other's backs should be able to spot it. Especially if they have lights. Domin was supposed to be depending on the light from the fire, but it doesn't extend down the corridor. We thought a human coming down the corridor wouldn't be able to see him in the shadow." A thought popped up. "Unless the Beast hates light."

She sat on a stone bench. "I was hoping for a chance to go back into the fortress today, find a place for us to make our next stand. Now I don't dare, because I can't go alone, and we can't leave this spot undefended."

Erlon shrugged. "Let's not bet on birds that haven't landed yet. We've got to get through the day, first. If we're still here tonight, we'll set ourselves up in a more secure spot. For the moment, let's concern ourselves with our friends outside."

"One battle at a time. Let us observe the daytime enemy."

They filed out onto the balcony and stood between the crenellations, staring down into the sleeping camp. The sentry spotted them and gave a low cry. Another man raised his head, looked at them, and laid it back down again. The sentry resumed his pacing, his head turning continually to keep them in view.

Aleria slapped the stone. "That's one day gone, and we've killed five of them. A day and a half to go. Let's go eat breakfast."

As they walked inside, she found herself beside Jatto. "He was a friend of yours, wasn't he?"

"A good friend. Always a laugh, always a good word. He had a wife and a young son, you know. Great kid."

She laid a hand on his shoulder for a moment. *What can I say? Maybe nothing is best.* She slapped his shoulder once, and they continued into the fortress.

The mood was not cheerful around the fire as they spooned their porridge, but it was at least businesslike. Jatto and Blodwel were discussing ways to fight a large animal with a small knife. It seemed the consensus was to attack the roof of the mouth, which sounded rather last-gasp to Aleria. *But I suppose if you are facing a large animal with a small knife, you're happy if you can still gasp.*

An hour later, they were back on the main balcony again, regarding the enemy camp. "Any count on their wounded?"

Kolwyn shrugged. "Some of them are still in their bedrolls. Can't tell if they're wounded or not."

Aleria frowned. "Not like Lord Lexing to let his men sleep in."

Erlon was staring into the enemy camp. "Wait a moment. The guy with the head bandage is sitting over there. The guy with his arm in a sling is by the fire."

Aleria rushed over to the wall. "Has anyone seen Lexing, himself, this morning?"

No one responded.

"Look at those sleepers. Do you see anything strange?"

"They sure aren't moving."

"That's right. Because they aren't soldiers. They're stuffed bedrolls. Lexing and four of his men are gone somewhere."

She turned to Kolwyn. "Are you sure there isn't any other way into the citadel?"

"We never found one," He shrugged. "But that doesn't say there isn't one."

"Where would it be?"

"I would guess out at the west end. The tunnels get sketchy in the farthest section, with natural watercourses and long corridors with no rooms. It also goes deeper into the mountain, so we never went back there very much."

She glanced at Erlon. "So it's possible that Lexing knows another entrance and he's gone around with four of his men to find it and take us from the rear."

Erlon frowned. "We can't hold this camp against attacks from two directions."

"But that might not be what is happening. Maybe they went to change personnel, or for ten other reasons."

"But none of those reasons means much to us unless they're inside, behind us. We have to send someone to find out."

"I know the corridors the best." Kolwyn fingered his sword hilt. "It will have to be me."

"Take Blodwel. The three of us can hold against five of them. One in the archer's balcony and two at the barricade. As long as the others don't get in behind us."

"They won't attack without Lexing." Kolwyn mused a moment. "There are a couple of points they will have to pass to get here from the west end. We'll check those and come running if we see anyone." He looked at Aleria as if for permission.

"Sounds good to me."

Erlon held up a restraining hand. "Any way of passing by that stock entrance to make sure it's still covered with rocks?"

"Good idea. We'll do that on the way." He slung his pack on his back and nodded to the shepherd. Then he turned back.

"If we get separated we'll meet at the stables. Does everyone know where that is?"

"Erlon and Jatto don't, but I'll give them instructions. We've got nothing to do but wait."

"We'll hurry."

The two flicked their lamps to flame and strode into the dark corridors. Aleria, Erlon and Jatto sat down to wait, their eyes on the enemy camp while she explained the route to the stables.

She didn't stay there for long. With nothing to do, her thoughts strayed to the lost guard. Domin with the honest face, trying so hard to win at cards. Domin throwing his big shoulder to the wheel of a stuck wagon. Domin with huge jaws clamping...a lump began to grow in her throat. She jumped up. "This isn't going to last."

"Probably not."

"So this is the point we planned on. Where we fade back into the passages to play hide-and-seek."

Erlon nodded. "And we can't take all our supplies with us."

"Exactly. Let's pack up camp and hide whatever we can. We'll take a day's food on our backs and leave the rest. Where can we make a cache?"

Jatto tossed his head in the direction of the functionaries. "Those rooms on the next floor up, with all that stone shelving. They're full of junk. We could stow stuff in there, and they won't have time to search it out."

"Right. They won't even realize it's there. Jatto, you stay on watch here. Erlon, let's move."

They hurried into their camp, sorting and piling, and soon they had a decent stash of supplies and equipment moved to the upper floor.

"It's the third door past the men's functionary on the left-hand side. We can describe that to Kolwyn easily."

"Right. Let's get back to check on Jatto."

They hurried down the stairs, out through the abandoned camp and onto the balcony. All was quiet.

Aleria looked more carefully at the enemy camp. "Where is everybody?"

The faked bedrolls had been removed, and a faint tendril of smoke rising from the fire was the only sign that anyone had been there.

Erlon's eyes slid to their surroundings, his hand to his sword hilt. "I don't like this."

She started down the stairs. There was a cry and a rushing of footsteps outside the barricade. Five men vaulted the logs, swords drawn. Lexing clambered over close behind them.

Jatto faced them from the second step of the main staircase. They spread wide, circling like wolves to the kill.

Aleria pointed. "The viewing platform. Top of the main staircase. We can hold them there. Jatto. Retreat up here!"

Seeing them, the men stopped. The shouting died. Lexing strode forward, grinning. "I seem to have caught you off guard, my Lady." He flung a hand towards Jatto. "Move, and we attack!"

The Dalmyn guard stopped his downward prowl, glancing back at Aleria, his sword at the ready. "It looks like I'm on the outside of the door, Aleria."

"Don't worry, Jatto. We'll be down soon."

"I'm not worried. I can hold them here long enough for you to get away. Might even take a few of them with me."

Lexing sneered. "These heroic sentiments are so touching. How has the treasure hunting been, my Lady?"

"Treasure? We were looking for maps."

"You already tried that. Paper? After a thousand years? I somehow doubt it."

"We are looking for any maps that might help settle the boundaries to everyone's satisfaction."

"Nothing to do with jewels?"

"Myth and nonsense created by people who wanted to dream."

"I think not, and I have very good information. AnLlannon isn't the only one to keep the lore of the Old Ones. The first part of my prediction has come true, as at least one of your men has discovered."

How did he know about Domin? There's hardly anyone left to be a spy. He must have found the...remains. "Been in the tunnels this morning, have you? I thought so."

"But you didn't expect me back so soon, did you?"

"If you want to search for treasure, I'm sure you have my permission. Go ahead."

"Oh, no. You poked your Elite little nose into things you had no need to know. I can't allow you to leave, now. You and the Llannon pup. Your lives are forfeit. If the Ghost Beast doesn't finish you, I will."

"Then you'll have to come into the fortress and take equal risks. Let's go, Jatto."

"He moves, he dies."

"I move and a bunch of your men die, Lord Lexing." His sword threatened one of the soldiers below him, and the man started back. Jatto glanced up at Aleria. "My fault. I knew somethin' was up, but I shoulda called you insteada' comin' down to see." He checked Lexing's men. "This is the time, my Lady. I can whittle them down, and you get away to fight again."

"Jatto..." *What can I say? We'll never get to him in time.*

Jatto grinned at her, saluted with his sword and turned to the enemy. "Six to one. Lot of sissies, it seems to me."

Lexing's face reddened. "Take him!"

Instead of retreating, Jatto dove down the stairs, his sword slashing flesh left, right, then diving into the breast of a third man. Before he could withdraw, the others were on him, driving him to the floor in a welter of blood. Aleria was halfway down the stairs when he fell.

She charged anyway, Erlon beside her. Lexing's men, seeing the attack from above, turned from Jatto and sprinted for the barricade.

Aleria knelt beside her stricken man, pain flooding her breast. Blood flowed from too many wounds, but he still breathed, his eyelids fluttering. She looked up. Lexing had been too slow to vault the barricade, but two of his men stood beside him. The other two were frozen on the outside, uncertain whether to come back or stay. One of these had no sword, and blood flowed down his arm. One body lay on the floor with Jatto.

The lord tossed his head in triumph. "I will allow you to take your wounded. But I will be after you as soon as you are out of sight." He sneered. "He'll only slow you down."

She assessed her chances. *Only four men against us, now.* Anger began to seethe. But Erlon's hand on her shoulder stopped her rise.

"No, Aleria! We'll choose our own time to avenge him. Let's go."

She had no choice. Erlon hoisted the wounded man over his shoulder, prompting a fresh flow of blood, and they mounted the stairs, Aleria facing sideways, her sword menacing the enemy. At the top, Erlon turned into the darkness of the fortress, and she followed.

She heard Lexing urging his men on, but the quick battle and the charge up the stairs winded them, and she and Erlon escaped easily into the well-known passages near their camp. She paused to light her lantern, and they forged on, ducking up a staircase and catching a cross-corridor that took them above the stable area. Soon the sounds of pursuit faded, and they slowed to a walk.

"Jatto, can you hear me?"

Erlon slung the wounded man off his shoulder, carrying him in his arms like a baby. "I don't think he's going to make it, Aleria. Lost too much blood."

"Damn. Damn, damn, damn!"

Erlon did not answer.

"Why did he do that? Why didn't he retreat when he saw them coming?"

"He doesn't think like that. He knew you were in danger if he didn't stop them. If you get killed there will be a war. He knew his duty."

A great knot of pain formed in her throat. "But why did he attack? Why couldn't he find another way?"

"He's a soldier, Aleria. He doesn't think any other way."

"Well, I should have thought of another way. That's what leadership is for."

"We'll cut down this corridor. I think it leads to the stairs down to the stable level, and you can find our way from there."

"You didn't answer me."

"I didn't hear a question."

"You know what I mean."

"Of course I do. This is the first time you have put one of your men in harm's way and he hasn't been able to get out of it. That's a tough time. You are bound to blame yourself."

"There. It was my fault, and you agree."

"No, I don't. I'm talking about what you're going through. Sooner or later every leader has the same experience, and it hurts every one of us. We always blame ourselves. You're lucky. You didn't do anything wrong."

"But I didn't do anything right, either. I shouldn't have broken up my forces. I should have..."

"If you mean you didn't predict the future properly, that's true. Whether such a thing was possible is something you can figure out for yourself. The more you think on it, the greater the chance you'll do a better job the next time the situation arises. Because it will. Given the way things are going, it could happen today. The next one could be me."

He turned to her and took both her upper arms in his hands, the soldier's body between them. "The one thing you can do wrong is lock up and not decide. You are the leader, and you must continue to make the decisions. If you don't, the whole crew will fall apart and then you *will* have our blood on your conscience."

She did not answer, but turned from his grip and walked on in silence, stifling the sobs that threatened to burst out.

"At the moment, you have only Jatto's blood, and I don't mind speaking for him when I say he wouldn't see it that way."

"What do you mean?"

"I'm not saying it was his destiny or anything like that. I'm saying that death is always a condition of the mercenary's life, and I think he was glad to finish that way. One of the only consolations is to know that, when the time comes, you will die well for a good cause and be remembered for it."

"Well, I'm certainly going to remember him."

"You do that." His head came up as the clang of metal on stone sounded through the corridors "But right now, we have other problems to think about. I don't want to let him down if there's a chance he'll make it, but Lexing's men are looking for us, and they're moving fast. We should split up."

"That's stupid. It's always better to stay together."

"This is the time for 'always' to be wrong. I am in no real danger, with only four men after me. If I'm crowded I'll put him down and run, count on it. You must get free. Don't make his sacrifice in vain, Aleria. Go."

"I..." She had no answer. He was right.

Erlon pushed her shoulder. "Take that hallway. There are all sorts of tracks leading in and out. They won't find you. Wait until they stop hunting, then meet at the stables as we planned." He pointed to the dark spots on the floor where blood still dripped from Jatto's dangling fingers. "Don't worry, I'm the one they'll be following."

She did not argue but walked away, gazing back over her shoulder for a last look at her friend and his sad burden. Then she turned and trudged on.

29. Alone in the Dark

She pointed her lantern at the floor and found many tracks in both directions. Someone must have checked this area on another trip. *After all, they've been coming here for generations. Lexing's family too, it seems.* She slowed, trying to follow the best-used paths, on the theory that they must lead farther in, and that her tracks would be hidden better.

This section did not follow the usual tunnel-with-cross-corridors pattern of the rest of the fortress, but was more like a maze, with corridors branching randomly at strange angles. She was lost but had a vague idea of where she had come in, so she kept pushing in the opposite direction, her legs beginning to feel the strain.

In fact, her whole being was exhausted. Aleria felt numb. She couldn't drag up sorrow for Jatto, or even for herself. *Here I am, alone. There were so many other ways to handle this. But no, I had to bull ahead in my usual stupid fashion and now look at me. On my own with a bunch of soldiers on my trail. Lost in these dank, dark, smothering tunnels.* She searched for somewhere to sit down. *I'm just so tired...*

A dislodged stone clattered somewhere in the dark behind her. She froze, listening. Men's voices. More than one of them. *Lexing split his forces, and I'm doing exactly what they expect.* Her fear overcame her fatigue, and she began to jog as quietly as she could along the hall. *Time to do something different.* She kept a close watch, pointing her lantern into each room that she passed and along each corridor that she rejected.

She heard the ring of steel and glanced back. Was that a gleam of light? Shielding her lantern, she saw the faint, wavering glint of an approaching torch touching the wall at the last corner. Somehow, they were catching up. They must have taken a shorter route.

There! A smaller hall that turned backward the moment it left the main tunnel. They might ignore that. She dove in and sprinted along. There were no rooms leading off this tunnel, and it twisted back and forth through the rock. As she went along, she could sense the floor rising and getting rougher, and see that the walls were not so straight. *Must be a watercourse. Have I put myself in a trap?* She pressed forward, and the walls closed in. Panic began to bubble under her breastbone, but she fought it back with movement and forged on.

And then she came to the end. She turned a corner, and her lantern beam hit solid rock. She waved it left and right, but there was no opening. She stood in a small, uneven room with only one entrance. Her heart sank. *If one of them comes down that tunnel after me, I'll have to fight him, and that will bring the rest.* There was no chance she could stand up to a series of experienced soldiers.

She sagged against the wall, breathing heavily. *Is this it? Caught like a badger in his den, all alone, my men killed and scattered. Well, Erlon and Kolwyn will get out. At least the king will know.*

She turned and drew her sword. *This tunnel is too narrow for a real fight. That suits my style. They won't be long, now.* She lowered her sword and waited. And only then did her mind begin to work again.

*Wait a minute. I've been walking up a watercourse. It can't just end. The water has to come from somewhere...*her lantern beam wavered upward. On the left-hand side of the passage there was a ledge, just above head height. All was darkness above it. She reached up and felt around for a handhold. Sure enough, there was a groove in the rock of the ledge at exactly the right place for a climber to get a grip. Flashing her light down, she found a small bump, perfectly placed for her foot. *This is no accident.*

She swung up and scrambled onto the ledge. Beyond it, there was an indentation in the wall barely large enough for a small person to fit. She craned her neck and pointed her light back down the tunnel.

Shit.

A single line of footprints in the dust led straight to her like a tattletale arrow. She jumped down, sprinted back along the tunnel until a glimmer of light showed. She scuffled her feet around in the dust, then walked back, stepping in her old tracks. As she reached the end, a scrape echoed from the tunnel behind her. Without further thought, she vaulted onto the ledge and wedged her back into the nook, her face outward and her sword in her hand, down along the ledge where it wouldn't shine. She shut her lantern, hoping the smell of hot metal wouldn't give her away. The darkness covered her, smothering her breath. It felt as if the rock was closing in on her, but she held her position, held her fear in check. *If you move, you die. That ought to help you stay still, you idiot!* She clamped a firm hold on her terror and forced herself to sit. Time stretched out, and she could feel the pressure to move building in her muscles. Her breath began to come quicker, and she longed for light. She tried to focus on something else, but her mind was blank. All she could feel was rock and blackness and…

Another scrape of metal on rock. She pictured a soldier with his scabbard bumping against the narrow walls of the passage. Then footsteps. Soon a glimmer of light began to grow in front of her. Her hood over her hair and her arm bent across her face, she waited.

Then light spilled into the tunnel, and the crackling of a torch filled the space. She ducked her head, but she couldn't bear not to look. The soldier held his torch high, and its light reached her, but his head was below the ledge.

The man below her cursed and swung his torch around. "Dead end. Dammit!" He stood there a moment, breathing hard. *Don't look up. Please, don't look up!* She wanted to cringe further back into the shadows, but she didn't dare move. *And don't look down, either.*

After a long, terrible moment, he turned back down the tunnel, his footsteps getting faster as he went. *So I'm not the only one who doesn't like this tight tunnel.* Soon his light and the sound of his bootheels faded, and the darkness descended again. Aleria breathed easier, but she stayed where she was. *I'm safe for the moment. Silly to get caught by a simple slip. If any of my men are still alive, they will be harder to catch than me. Of course some of them are still alive. I dearly hope they are. I'll wait for a while. Sooner or later, Lexing will stop hunting, and then I can start.*

As she sat there in the blackness, a strange feeling came over her. Without her eyes, everything changed. In the stillness of the dark, she could hear her own heart beat, feel the blood rushing through her head. She could feel the rock at her back, the air moving against her cheek...

...the air moving! Kolwyn said the air moves up and back. I wonder...

Listening once again for movement nearby, she cautiously raised a hand above her head and behind her. Instead of bumping rock as she expected, it met nothing. She held it still and could feel a soft flow of air against her skin. Cautiously, she opened the lamp a slit, pointing the beam upward. A rough, round tunnel slanted up and away as far as the ray of light could reach. It was big enough to take her bulk easily. Big enough for a large man, even. Chisel marks patterned the walls.

A tunnel that was smoothed out must go somewhere!

Clamping a fierce hold on her fear, she wormed her way in. The passage grew until it was large enough for her to crawl on hands and knees, and she forged upward. As she twisted and turned through the rock, the idea of the long, narrow passage behind her began to grow in her mind, and the need to crawl down it towards armed men. Again she forced the fear down. *Better than dying. I can do this.* She pictured a small tunnel opening onto fresh air and sunshine, and held it firmly in her mind.

Fortunately, the passage was not much longer. Soon it opened out, the ceiling lifted away and then she was standing in a room. A real room. She opened her lantern and swung the light around. Blocky chairs, a heavy table. She thumped a chair. A cloud of dust rose, but the wood felt solid. The legs of the furniture were stained and partly rotted, but only half way up. *So the water still comes down here, but not much and not often. Hope there isn't a storm.*

Brushing off the seat of a chair she sat gingerly, but the legs held. The dust, instead of swirling around her, drifted towards one side of the room. Her light showed an opening large enough to walk through. She rose and stepped in. A short tunnel led to a larger room, this one bare, but a trickle of water ran down the far wall into a shallow basin, slid across the floor and disappeared through a crevice.

So that's why they built this. A secret refuge as a final retreat. I wonder if there's any way out? She flashed her lantern around. The walls were solid. She lifted the beam to the ceiling, then turned it away. *What's that light spot up in the corner?* She strolled over and looked up. And up.

She stood at the bottom of a narrow vertical shaft. Far above a light glimmered. Blue light. The sky. There was no way she could ever squeeze up that slim vent.

With that thought her fear rose in her throat from the knowledge that she had to crawl back down that narrowing tunnel into the darkness and the danger below. Somehow having the blue sky up there above her made it worse. Like looking up out of a grave. She imagined herself trapped here, standing under the sky so far above, screaming and screaming for help that never came.

So what are you going to do, Aleria? Fall to pieces when nothing is threatening you? Some bravery, girl. You're fine. You're unhurt and you've found a safe place.

She turned her back to the alluring light and returned to the furnished room. There were shelves along one wall. Full shelves. Scrolls, supplies, stone lamps, folded clothing: everything someone would need for a prolonged stay. In one corner, a wider shelf with the crumbled remains of what might once have been food.

I need a plan. There was enough oil in her lamp and in her pack for two days of light. She should wait until night before she moved, because she was sure Lexing's men would retreat to the outside then. So here she sat. She grinned to herself. *At least I'll know when night falls.*

The thought of staring up that shaft chilled her, and she searched for a distraction. *Well, we came looking for books.*

There were only a few scrolls, and she handled them carefully, opening a few by sliding her dagger between the rolls and prying. They opened with crackling noises, but none fell apart. All words, all in the script of the Old Ones. Nothing that looked like maps. She set them aside and began to explore.

There was little else to see, and too many unpleasant things to think of. She sat, but soon rose to prowl the room again. Finally the pressure became too strong. Against her better judgement, she started down the tunnel.

She felt better once she got moving. She was going somewhere, doing something. Soon she was jogging along the winding corridor back to the centre of the fortress.

When she reached the main passageways, they seemed broad and open. She moved more cautiously, keeping her lamp slitted and stopping to listen often, but it seemed that Lexing and his men were elsewhere. Trying to keep her footsteps soft, she crept on.

30. An Old Song

They met in the stables, each one slipping in silently, nodding to the others. Kolwyn was last, and the dust and cobwebs in his hair showed that he had been exploring.

"Anything?"

He shrugged. "I've begun to recognize Lexing's bootprints. He's been through here more than we thought. Mostly in the western end."

"Which is where we think he got in."

"Exactly, but I can't figure out where."

Erlon had been sitting on an old bench, saying nothing. He raised his head. "What about the eastern end of the citadel? We've only seen from the keep west."

Kolwyn shook his head. "We call that the 'Old Town.' A complete ruin inside. It must have been built first, then abandonned when they moved over here. Much less organized, smaller rooms, more rockfalls, and absolutely nothing of value. I wouldn't want to get caught over there. Too much chance of getting stuck in a dead end."

"Just an idea."

"This leaves us rather exposed." Kolwyn looked around. "Anyone else find anything?"

Aleria grinned. "I found a winding way with smothering stone."

"Huh. Everyone found plenty of that."

"Yes, but this is a secret one. It takes off from the end of a stream tunnel and leads to a couple of hidden rooms, far back and higher up in the mountain. Believe me, the stone feels smothering when you look up an air shaft and see a spot of blue sky, completely unattainable."

"It's got a ventilation shaft?"

"As I said. Fifty yards straight up."

"And you can see the sky? Like a coin, far above?"

"Why is that important?"

"That dratted song, is why. The next line after 'smothering stone' has 'a coin of blue' in it."

"Well, princess or not, it's the ideal spot for us to hide. It'll be a tight squeeze for you big fellows, but Blodwel and I will have no difficulty."

"Any exits?"

"I didn't see any. If Lexing finds us, he could trap us in there. Maybe build a fire and smoke us out." She shuddered at the thought.

"Any evidence he knows?"

"There were no tracks showing when I entered that tunnel. Stupid of me not to think of it. If the soldier who was following me had had any brains, he could have figured out that I was still there. Now there's two sets going in and two coming out, so no one would think to look."

Erlon rubbed his hand on his sword pommel. "We need a safe spot."

Aleria raised her eyebrows. "Want to see it?"

"Better now, with no one around to bother us."

"Except our Beastly friend."

"We'll stick together. Shall we go?"

Kolwyn nodded, and she led off. When they reached the entrance to the tunnel, she stopped. "See what I mean? This main passage has a lot of tracks, but the little one..." she pointed to the two sets of prints, large and small, going and coming. "But if we start going in and out of there..."

Erlon paced up the main passage, his lantern flashing back and forth. "Lexing and his men have been through here at least twice. You can see the hobnail boot pattern. If we go straight past and keep going, then come all the way back to the cross corridor over there, we can make enough tracks that no one will ever notice. If we only had a plank..."

"...long enough to bridge the distance to the first corner..."

Erlon snapped his fingers. "The lumber rooms are on the next floor down. There's got to be a few planks strong enough."

Aleria's hand on his shoulder stopped him. "We go together."

He grinned in the light of her lamp. "That way we can carry more planks."

It was a slow job, rigging the planks up on rocks to keep them out of the dust, but finally they had a safe path. They walked in, lifted the planks and hid them around the corner out of sight of the main tunnel. Then Aleria led the way deeper into the mountain, Erlon right behind.

"This tunnel is rising. Quite steeply."

"It is a watercourse."

"Typical at the west end of the citadel." Kolwyn's voice echoed from behind. "I've never been in this one, though."

"I wish you had. There'd be more tracks." She shone her lamp ahead. "The floor gets rougher the farther we go. Harder to read."

"That helps."

Erlon grunted. "But the damned ceiling is getting lower."

"Smothering, isn't it?" She tossed a grin back over her shoulder.

"Huh!"

By the time they got to the dead end, she realized why the soldier had been so quick to turn and leave. Erlon's bulk pretty well filled the passageway, and she began to wonder if he could get through the upper opening. She glanced at him, shrugged and stepped up. There was no use stopping, so she wormed her way up the smaller tunnel until she could turn easily, then called back. "How does it look?"

"Damned tight. I'll take off my gear. Just a moment."

"I'll come down and get it."

"Please do."

She moved down to take his sword, bow and pack, then shuffled backwards up the tunnel dragging them.

There were grunts and scraping sounds down the tunnel, and finally Erlon's blond head showed in her beam. She turned and ascended the shaft to give him space. She could imagine how it felt to look ahead and see the way blocked above you. Soon he was standing, dust-covered and sweat-streaked, in the first room. He stretched his arms. "Don't want to do that too many times."

She grinned and widened her lamp beam. "I doubt if anything big enough to kill a grizzly can get through there, anyway."

He grimaced. "I never did see myself as a rabbit, but I do understand the benefits." He looked around. "A real den."

Kolwyn appeared behind him, equally dirty. "Say, this is something. Completely untouched since the day the Old Ones left." He shone his lamp around. "If there's anything worth finding in the whole citadel, it's here."

She indicated the scrolls on the table. "I couldn't read them, but if they weren't important, why hide them here? No maps that I could find." Her sweeping hand included the shelves. "Plenty of equipment and supplies, most of it rotted and rusted to some degree. The higher up, the drier. The rot on the table and chair legs tells how deep the water came."

Kolwyn grinned. "A regular little anthropologist, aren't you?"

"I'll have you know we had a class in Ancient Studies at school."

"Ah, the benefits of a Ranked education. I took that class, too. I'm not sure how those old 'explorers' distinguished themselves from the tomb robbers that preceded them."

"So let's not destroy anything we don't absolutely need."

Erlon prowled along the shelves. "Anything that looks like royal jewels?"

"Nothing like that. Can you sing the song for us, Kolwyn?"

"You don't want to hear me sing. I told you the lines that count. They led us to these rooms. We only have to look."

"Well, don't let your treasure-lust carry you away. We are in the middle of a battle of sorts."

"Yes, Ma'am."

Apart from a few jars of rancid but perhaps burnable lamp oil, the supplies were destroyed by time and insects. There were scrolls and tools and a number of weapons, their scabbards and hilt leathers cracked and rotted, but the steel solid under a patina of rust. Erlon fingered a metal-hafted mace with points as sharp as the day it came from the forge. "I thought the Old Ones were small people."

Aleria used both arms and managed to get it halfway over her head. "Obviously some of them were rather strong."

He took it from her and twirled it with one hand. "If we get to keep souvenirs, I want that one."

Kolwyn laughed. "If I get to give them away, it's yours."

"What are you going to do, keep it under the seat of the lead wagon?"

"No, I'm going to hang it on my wall and make up stories of how I used it." Then his face sobered and he slid the weapon back into the rack. "But I doubt if it would be much good out in these narrow corridors."

That returned them to a serious mood, and they explored both rooms as fully as they could. Finally Aleria called a halt.

"I don't think we can expect anything in here that will help us survive another day. What time is it?"

Blodwel scooted into the other room. "Still bright, M'Lady."

"Time to search more if you like. I don't see anything, though."

Kolwyn was strolling along the wall of shelves, beaming his lantern up at the top. "That's what comes of being small, Aleria."

"May I assume the insult preludes an explanation?"

Kolwyn grinned at Erlon. "You want to show her, or shall I?"

The big soldier shook his head. "Don't get me involved. Have your fun and let's see what we've found."

Kolwyn made a show of disappointment but turned to Aleria. "If you look up at the top of the shelves, there..."

"I see a dark line. There's a niche in the rock!"

"And I think there's an object in it. If we pull that table over..." He and Erlon suited actions to his words.

The moment they set it down, she jumped on top. "...and the advantage to being small is that I won't break the table. Let's see. What have we here...aha!" With careful fingers, she eased the container out of the hole. It was a long leather tube six inches in diameter. She handed it carefully to Kolwyn and jumped down.

One end of the tube had a cap, held in place by a thong. He plucked, and it came free, broken into three pieces. "That gives us an idea of how delicate this leather is. I hope the contents are in better condition."

Gently, he tugged at the cap. It resisted, and when he pulled harder, it came off with a crackling sound. He winced.

Aleria leaned forward. "Let's see what's inside. Looks like parchment."

Kolwyn held the tube steady, and she eased the roll out. When she laid it on the table it retained its shape.

"Now what? If we try flattening it the parchment will probably crack, it's so dry."

"Why don't we dampen it a bit?"

"What if the water washes the ink off?"

"We only dampen the back. Assuming that there is a back. There doesn't seem to be anything on this side."

Erlon reached across with one of the old lamps that he had filled at the spring, and she dampened the outside of the roll with her fingertips. It was a long, painstaking job, but after she had allowed the water to soak in, she was able to peel back one turn of the first layer. They craned forward.

"Definitely a map. Beautifully drawn, and look; the colours are still there. Only a bit faded."

Aleria stretched her aching back. "We've got what we came for. Let's go home."

Erlon glanced at her. "Wish it was that simple."

"So do I, but we don't need to spend any more time playing archaeologist. Someone with a whole lot more experience than me should be opening these."

Kolwyn nodded, reaching for the maps and rolling them carefully up again. "And we need a plan to deal with our friends outside."

"I'll check our little hidey hole." She jumped back on the table. "Maybe there's something else inside...yes, there is. Only this little bag. I guaranteed there's no maps in it."

It was a leather bag, fitting into the palms of her two hands. Unlike the map cases, this leather was still soft. She peeled it open and looked in, the others leaning close to observe. The gleam of jewels winked back at her. She poured them onto the table while the men stood in silence.

There were thirty or more, of all colours. They weren't cut into facets like modern jewels, but were polished to a high sheen like creek agates. Kolwyn reached out and picked up a deep green egg the size of the end of his thumb. "That might be an emerald."

"In which case it's worth as much as my whole wagon train, complete with cargo."

Erlon put his hands behind his back. "So, who do they belong to?"

Their eyes slid to each others' faces.

Aleria shrugged. "I guess the maps will tell us. If it's in the Llannon demesne, they're yours, Kolwyn. If not, they belong to the king."

Erlon frowned. "And the people who discover them?"

"There's a law about found treasure. Dad was telling me." Kolwyn rocked his hand sideways. "It's something like half to the finders, half to the Crown."

Aleria nodded. "Fine. In that case, one of us should take care of them until ownership is assigned."

Kolwyn grinned. "I nominate you."

"Why? Don't want to carry the extra weight?"

"No, I'd rather take the maps. They won't fit in your pack, and they're more important to me. You can carry the less valuable stuff."

"Erlon, you happy with that?"

"Not for me to say, Lady Aleria."

She met his eyes. "That's how you see it, do you?"

"Is there any other way?"

She scooped the gems back into the bag, bounced the weight on her palm. "We can discuss that later, too. But for the moment, be assured that every man who survives this escapade will benefit from the profits. Even those who stayed back at Tyn Terfyn tending the stock."

Erlon grinned. "Great diplomacy, Aleria. That will certainly keep us from bonking you on the head and disappearing into the night with the loot."

"That and the fear of the rest coming after you for their share." She dropped the bag into her pack and buckled it. Then she looked up at the others. "Listen, now. Play time is over. Back to work."

Kolwyn dragged a chair up to the table, tested it and sat. "Right. What do we do with Lexing and friends?"

Erlon sat as well. "Assuming they're coming in for us..."

"If they don't, we win. He has to come. He's that sort of man."

"Then we should decoy them. They're safer in one group. The moment they divide, we'll outman them.

"And likewise, we can't separate."

Erlon frowned. "It may be necessary."

Kolwyn nodded. "Any way we can get them apart?"

"Bait."

They looked at her.

"We need to distract him with someone."

"You? I won't allow it."

She smiled. "Why Kolwyn, I didn't know you cared. No, I wasn't offering my lilywhite body as a sacrifice. Maybe we can think of something else."

Kolwyn shrugged. "This isn't my forte. Got any ideas?"

"We could always attack them."

"And that will split them up?"

Erlon nodded. "If we attack from two different directions, then make it look like they're winning, they'll chase us."

"And still outnumber us when they catch up."

"But we know this place better than they do. At least, you know the east end, Kolwyn." Aleria drew with her finger on the dusty table. "We'll find them, see where they're going. You and Blodwel hide and let them pass. Erlon and I lure them from ahead, then attack from the front, You attack from the back, then run and hide somewhere. You don't need to fight them. Erlon and I will draw the front group along, then ambush them in the dark."

The young lord shook his head. "You'll still be outnumbered."

"Don't worry. You just stay safe."

"Don't you worry about us. Now. How can we find them?"

Erlon shook his head. "They don't want to stay split up any more than we do. They'll have a rendezvous point somewhere, probably their camp in the courtyard. Let's assume they're coming in from the east and making a quick search of each passageway. How far are they by now?"

Kolwyn grinned. "I wouldn't like to be them, trying to find us. There are still areas of the citadel I haven't shown you, parts I've never seen either. But all they have to do is sweep through the areas with lots of tracks, so that helps them. Let's start at the stables and work west. If we don't find them, we'll move up to the next floor and sweep back."

Aleria glanced at Erlon and nodded. "It shouldn't be too hard to find them if we get close. They won't be quiet."

Erlon grinned. "They don't realize that they're the ones being hunted."

31. Inferno

They slipped down their safety hole one at a time, Blodwel bringing up the rear. Trailing two large men who had difficulty squeezing through the narrow exit, Aleria didn't have the nerve to be frightened, and soon she was cheerfully following them out into the fortress.

They moved quickly, using as little light as possible. For once, they were lucky. It wasn't long before Kolwyn, in the lead, stopped.

"Listen."

At first it was only disconnected sounds echoing around from all over, but as they crept forward the noises took on meaning and direction. The tromp of steel-shod boots, the calls, the banging of metal on rock, coming from the eastern end of the fortress.

Aleria held up a hand and they circled in the middle of the hallway. "This is backwards from what we planned. Erlon and I want to lure them back towards the stables, so we'll hide and let them by, then attack from behind. Kolwyn, once you and Blodwel make contact, disengage and run away. Don't try to be heroes. That's not the idea."

The two men nodded.

Erlon held up a hand. "Wait a minute. We need a signal. How do we know the other troop is in position?"

"How about that whistle you use to get the soldiers' attention?"

"You mean this one?" He pursed his lips, and a short, piercing "chirp" sounded.

"That's it. It should carry, but it will echo around and no one will be able to tell where it's coming from. Kolwyn, attack any time after you hear that whistle. I want you to start the fight. Lexing will send his soldiers ahead, so when we hit them from behind, we'll be closer to him. He'll be sure to see me and send the bulk of his men after me. I hope he'll pull the ones chasing you back to protect himself."

"Sounds like a good plan. I agree with your assessment of Lexing."

"If you pull a small enough number of them, ambush them. Otherwise disappear, and we'll see you back at the hideout."

The young lord grinned. "We ought to be able to get at least one if we choose our own time."

"We should. But no heroics. Remember, the idea is to survive and get the news of that mine out."

He saluted. "Yes, Ma'am. I know my orders."

She put on a frown, then slapped his shoulder. "Fine. Do you know of a good place for us to hide?"

Kolwyn looked around. "Yes, I think...follow me."

He led them along the hallway then inward, away from the sunlight. A pile of loose rock blocked the end of the cross tunnel he had chosen. He pointed his lantern beam up to the left. "There's a partial tunnel up above. They probably quit digging when this fell in. You could hold off an army up there if they found you, but I don't think they will. Go up around the back so you don't leave tracks."

They clambered up the rocks and were soon in a narrow tunnel that ended abruptly. It was easy enough to stand back out of sight. Kolwyn shone his light up from the bottom. "See you back at our bolt hole."

"Stay safe."

Then they were gone. Aleria turned off her lamp and they sat in the reflected beam of Erlon's, their ears alert, watching the dust settle.

Aleria started when Erlon grabbed her arm. The sound of two pairs of boots became distinct from the rest, coming closer. Then growing light. Soon the reflected flicker of a torch reached into their tunnel.

"Anythin' there?"

"Nope. A rockfall."

"Good enough. Let's git outa here afore any more comes down."

The soldiers tromped off, and Aleria grinned at Erlon. By the layers of dust, the last rocks to fall had been several hundred years ago.

They waited until the sounds faded, then crept downward. Using only one lamp, they began their stalk.

Which turned out to be easy, as the soldiers were noisy, light-blinded, and too concerned with what was in front of them. Aleria's only mistake could come from getting ahead of a searcher who had gone down one of the side tunnels.

Erlon looked at Aleria, and she shrugged. There seemed no good time to start. He shrugged as well and sent out his chirping whistle.

There was a shout down the tunnel ahead of them, the clang of blade on blade and a man's despairing yell. Aleria could pick out Lexing's deeper voice calling his men in. Soldiers sprinted from the tunnels in front of them and headed away.

She and Erlon began to run as well. Fifty yards down the tunnel they came upon the backs of the enemy, well lit with their torches held high, all crowding forward. Aleria was just considering whether she could stab an unaware man in the back when someone turned and shouted. Then she had no time for qualms. The man swung at her, and she ducked, then ran him through. The next man tripped over him, and she was able to slash his arm, but the rest were turning, and she had to retreat.

Erlon held them long enough for her to get moving, then disengaged, felling one more opponent as he did. They both sprinted back along the corridor into the welcoming darkness.

Lexing called out, and there was silence. Then his voice came, softer. "You two, you, you and you. I want them dead! The rest of you stay with me." Then boots started to clump down the corridor after them. Erlon slapped her shoulder and turned her ahead of him. She ran.

"No rush. They'll take enough time to check every room. We don't want to lose them."

She slowed. In truth, they were losing their pursuers already. Erlon flashed his lamp back down the corridor. There were shouts, and the running feet picked up their pace. He grinned at her and they trotted off again.

"Same hiding place?"

He shook his head. "We need them in the stables. I have an idea."

She nodded and followed him along the main hallway.

When they got close to the cross-corridor leading to the stables, they made sure they were spotted again. Then they tore up the smaller hallway. Aleria began to glance into the rooms they passed, looking for a hideout. She found one with a deep, narrow doorway and stuck her torch inside. The floor was littered with junk.

"In here."

They slid into the shadows as the troop of soldiers hurried by, each one with a torch sputtering in one hand, several unlit ones thrust crosswise through his belt. They were doing a poor job of the search, thrusting a torch into each room, taking a quick look and moving on. Light flamed briefly in their room as they flattened themselves on either side of the doorway, swords ready. The torch was withdrawn. The soldiers continued down the corridor towards the stables, and Aleria and Erlon followed, slipping from one room entrance to the next.

As they entered the stables, one was lagging behind his companions, staring around. Erlon allowed them to get well into the huge room, then slipped forward silently, slapped his hand across the last soldier's mouth and drove a dagger into his back. As the body fell he grabbed the torch and ran back, dragging fire across the hay in the mangers. A line of flames shot up behind him as the tinder-dry fuel caught. There was a whoosh of air, and smoke began to funnel toward the hole at the far end of the ceiling.

Since the fire was behind and the smoke was boiling at them, the soldiers in front made the mistake of running forward. By the time they discovered that they were caught in a dead end, Erlon had lighted the other mangers, and the wood of the stalls was beginning to catch. A wind began to build, rushing in from the corridor, and a conflagration raged through the stables.

"Watch behind." Erlon stood with his bow half-drawn.

Aleria needed no prompting. She trotted back to the junction with the main corridor to stand watch. She did not see what was happening behind her, but the screams and the swish of arrows gave her a good idea.

It did not take long, and Erlon strode out behind her. "That will bring attention. Best we leave."

"Tally?"

"Got three. The other stayed out of sight. He might live if the smoke keeps going up."

They jogged back down the corridor to the stairs and mounted swiftly. Back at the entrance to their hideout, the others waited. Aleria opened her mouth to question why, then realized that Blodwel was leaning heavily on his master.

"What happened?"

The little man ducked his head, and Kolwyn snorted. "He discovered that a bow isn't much good for parrying a sword slash. Got his leg. I bandaged it, but we thought we'd wait for you before we tried to get him up that shaft."

"Any luck?"

"He shot at least one, and I downed another, maybe wounded one more. You?"

"Four plus various wounds. He's down to four or five."

"And we're down to three in fighting trim."

Erlon grinned. "I like those odds."

Aleria turned to the shepherd. "How are you feeling, Blodwel?"

"I've felt better, M'Lady, but I c'n walk. Lord Kolwyn bandaged me up."

"Can you climb up to the tunnel?"

"If someone gimme a lift, I'll make it."

"Let's go."

It was a scrabble getting the little man up into the tunnel. He couldn't crawl properly, dragging his wounded leg straight behind him, but he made it, and there was no new blood seeping through the crude bandage Kolwyn had wound around his leg.

Once they were back in their rooms, they cleared the table and their patient clambered up on it. Erlon took the bandage off while Aleria washed an ancient bowl and brought water from the stream. The leg didn't look good. It was a deep gash the full length of his thigh, but the bleeding had mostly stopped.

Erlon nodded. "Lucky in one way. Didn't hit any major blood vessels. Either of you know how to stitch a wound?"

They shook their heads.

"I guess it's my trick, then." He looked at his patient. "Not your lucky day. I've been told I have a terrible bedside manner."

The shepherd shrugged and accepted the small flask his lord passed him. "Not often I get to taste the fine folks likker. Guess I'll put up with it."

"Don't just taste it. Knock it back. Can't think of a better use for it."

"Thanks, M'Lord." He took a long slug, then a deep breath. "Good stuff, M'Lord." He offered it to Erlon. "You want some?"

"You don't want me drinking before I do this."

Aleria provided a sliver of soap from her pack, and Erlon washed his hands well. "No chance of sterilization, but we'll wash my hands and the wound with wine. My sewing kit has been boiled and sealed. Not much else we can do."

Aleria and Kolwyn watched, unable to help, as Erlon plied his trade. Blodwel bit his lip and stared off into space, his face stolid. It took twenty-three stitches, and by the time he was finished Erlon was almost out of thread.

Then he bound up the wound. "Don't repeat this mistake, any of you. I'd have to use thread out of your blankets."

"We'll be more careful, now that we know the penalty."

32. Meeting the Monster

They ate and drank and settled in for the night. At least, they tried. After tossing and turning for an age, her mind roiling in similar motion, Aleria got up and lit her lantern.

"Erlon?"

"Yes?" His response was instant. He was awake, too.

"I've been thinking."

"I could tell."

"There's something else going on, here."

"With Lexing?"

"Yes. Besides the iron. Him, this fortress, the Beast and probably the jewels."

"You might be right."

"Yes, and I might be wrong. But whatever it is, it might be the solution to this whole problem."

"And you are going to do something about it."

She regarded Erlon. "I'm not asking your opinion on this. I don't know if I'm doing it for the right reasons or the wrong ones, but I will make this decision on my own. And you will follow me because that's your duty."

He grinned. "What if I'm your secret spy?"

She brushed that away with a sweep of her hand. "I figured that out a long time ago. You're loyal, and you'll do your duty. I will take responsibility. That's my duty.

"Here's how I see the situation. He has about five men left, some of them wounded. He knows what kind of fighters he's up against. He's not going to mount any kind of attack. I'm betting he comes into the citadel tonight. Alone, looking for the jewels."

He stretched and rose from his blankets. "And we will be there to…what?"

"I'm not sure. I think just follow him and see where he goes, what he does."

"Whatever you say. Kolwyn?

"He will stay with Blodwel. He's not fit to move."

There was a stirring across the room. "You are not going out there. I forbid it."

She widened her lamp beam to include Kolwyn. "That's the second time I've heard you say that. You have to learn one small thing about me..."

He stood, shedding his blankets, and raised placating hands. "I know. That wasn't the best way to put it. But don't you think it's a bad idea, splitting up our forces when we've got our enemy whittled down to even numbers?"

"He's not going to bring his men back in here. Every time he does, he loses more. He's not stupid. He has to adapt his tactics." She leaned her elbows on the table. "The game has changed. He no longer has the upper hand. He can't expect to wipe us out and go on with his mining unhindered. The only way he could still come out ahead is if he finds the fabled jewels. Another reason not to bring his men with him."

She tossed out her hands. "Or else he has something completely different planned that we don't even know about. In that case, we still need to know what's going on. I have no choice. If he comes into the fortress, I have to be there."

"And what are you going to do?" He strode to the table and sat beside her.

"Improvise. Erlon's coming with me, and we'll figure it out as we go along. You'll be safe, here, I guarantee it."

She could see his face redden in the lamplight. *Oops.*

"I'm sorry. I said that wrong. Blodwel will be safe here. I'm not worried about you." She grinned and ran a hand over his shoulder. "At least, not as worried."

He looked away, but then his eyes slid back to her. "I suppose."

She met his glance. "Actually, probably more worried than I should be. But we'll discuss that when we get out of here."

"I'd like that."

"Because if we don't get out of here, there won't be anything to discuss."

"That's what I find so attractive about you. Your romantic streak."

She stood, dusting off her breeks, then her hands, in a businesslike way. "Besides, this is one of those times when I get to make the decisions."

He waved his hand in front of his face. "Well, it will be nice not to have you here, always moving around and stirring up dust."

"Fine. If we don't show up, wait until noon and then sneak out. If it comes to it, I suggest leaving Blodwel here with most of the supplies and heading out on your own. You've got a better chance than most to make it. He'll have enough food for a week or so, and maybe by that time he'll be healed enough to make his own way back. But he's your man, and if I don't come back..." She shrugged. "You'll be making your own decisions."

She turned to Erlon. "If I don't make it for some reason, then the next most important person is Kolwyn. We already talked about what will happen if Lexing isn't caught with his hand in the jewel jar. Nobody will listen if you're not Ranked. Kolwyn is the best one to tell this story and be heard."

Erlon merely nodded. She glanced at Kolwyn, her eyebrows raised.

He frowned for a moment, then shrugged as well. "Face that when we come to it. I'm for sleep. Good hunting. And take care of yourself. I mean that." He put an arm around her shoulder and gave her a squeeze, but just as she raised her face to his he turned away.

Right. No time for this. Concentrate on living through the next day. Then there will be time for...all sorts of things. She wished she had said it out loud, but somehow...

Her heart warm, she shouldered her pack and prodded Erlon towards the mouth of the tunnel. "Let's go. Please don't get stuck in the hole."

He shuddered. "I'll do my best, believe me."

They made their way out along the corridors, keeping to one slit lamp beam to guide them, but they met no one. Once out on their usual balcony they spied on Lexing's camp. It was late, and the glow of old coals lit the area. From the look of it, there wasn't anyone on sentry duty, but perhaps he was hidden.

She motioned Erlon away, and they went back into the fortress to talk.

"He will come in through here because he can't wander around on the mountainside with the Beast out there. Unless, of course, he's controlling the Beast. We can sleep in the room where we hung the meat and keep an eye on the corridor from there."

"And if the Beast comes?"

"We stand against the wall and think cheerful thoughts. We don't show fear and we don't show aggression. We don't point our lanterns in his face. If we're lucky, he leaves us alone. And if we're not lucky, we fight."

"And if Lexing comes? How do we handle him? We could capture him, and that would be it."

"There's more to it than that. I want to know what's going on with this Beast. If he has control over it, I want to know. I've been thinking as we walked. If he's alone, I'll follow him. You and Kolwyn can go out and round up his soldiers. They won't give you two any trouble if you rouse them from sleep."

"Haven't you got the plan backwards?"

"No. He's my problem. I can't send my hired sword to kill him. You two can handle his troops. Without his brains to order them, they'll be easy to overwhelm."

"That leaves you back in the fortress with Lexing. I don't like it.""

"I'll keep track of him, that's all. I want to know what he's doing. Don't worry, I don't need to fight him any more. He's finished. He just hasn't discovered it yet."

Erlon shook his head. "You're the boss."

"Good man. We'll make a soldier of you, yet."

"I hope not."

"An expression of my father's."

"I'll take it as a compliment, in that case."

"It shouldn't be hard to keep track of him. He has no lamps, and those torches spread light around."

"And if he really is in control of the Beast?"

"I'll bet on that bird after it lands."

He shook his head. "The boss speaks. If we were out on the trade routes I'd find all sorts of objections. But we aren't, and you know as much as I do about this style of warfare."

"Thank you for that vote of confidence. Let's try for a rest. I'll take the first watch."

He spread his blankets and lay down. Then his head came up. "Don't you dare creep off without telling me."

"So much for the confidence. Go to sleep."

He lay back, and she settled in. Every once in a while she would lose patience with the waiting and creep out to monitor Lexing's camp. Nothing changed for what seemed like hours.

She had no idea how to read the time by the stars, but she could see that they had moved quite a bit, and she was just considering going back in and waking Erlon when, out of the corner of her eye, she caught a movement down below. She searched the spot, but there was nothing. Staring at things in the dark made them look like they moved, so she let her eyes roam across the area.

There! Another movement in the shadows. *Got him.*

Now that she had his direction she could follow his route as he made his way towards the barricaded entry. She heard the slither of cloth over tree bark, and then he was stumbling up the staircase.

She slipped back inside, laid a hand on Erlon's forehead. He stirred under her touch, then sat up.

"He's coming. Alone, I think."

They stood and waited on either side of the doorway.

After a while, there was a scraping sound in their old camp and the flash of flint on steel. A torch flared. She looked around in the dim light that spread into the hallway outside, but their hiding place stayed dark. *The only route is down the corridor. If he comes in here for any reason...well, I'm glad Erlon is with me.*

But Lexing was on a mission; he did not pause. He strode, sword in hand, away down the corridor to the west. The two slipped out and followed at the very edge of his torchlight, confident that his flame-seared vision would not detect them in the darkness. When they got to the turn towards their bolthole, Erlon reached out and grasped her shoulder. She touched the back of his hand, and he faded into the darkness, leaving her alone with her enemy.

Feeling vulnerable, she held back farther, keeping her eyes off the tempting beacon of his torch.

As she expected, he made the correct turn to take him to the west end of the fortress. *He must think we were looking for the jewels out at this end. He's had almost two days in here to get his bearings and read the footprints in the dust. Now things get interesting.*

She hurried ahead and caught the glow of his torch as he turned again on the proper route. Soon they were in unfamiliar territory, but he strode with confidence through a lower archway. As his torch lit the entrance, she could see that this tunnel was different. More rounded and natural. *Could be the original watercourse. If I was looking, I'd choose that one, too.*

Sure enough, when she entered this tunnel it soon deviated, twisting and doubling back, widening then becoming narrow. She moved faster, confident that his torch would warn her.

Then she flashed her lantern beam on the floor and stopped dead. *Most of the tracks here are the Beast's.*

She pointed her lantern back down the tunnel. Nothing but the blank wall of the last turn. She flashed it ahead. Same view. *Well, I guess if I go forward there's the chance it'll eat him first. He must know it's up here. He must be headed for its den! There's only one way he would dare do that.* She followed, deeper and deeper into the mountain, the rock looming heavier above her as she went. She held her fear firmly in check and paced on.

Then she heard a light "clack" behind her, like a nail on stone. She straightened, every sense alert. A faint, fetid smell brushed her nose. *The wind blows up this corridor. The Beast is behind me!*

She pointed her lantern back, but there was nothing there. Turning, she hurried forward. The light of Lexing's torch splashed the wall at the next corner. She waited, her heart beating wildly, until it faded. Then she moved ahead again. When she turned the next corner, she saw a dark hole in the tunnel wall. She poked her lantern in. It was a small room, hollowed out like an eddy in the banks of a stream. She glanced ahead. Lexing's torch. She sent her lamp beam behind her.

Two eyes, spaced far apart, flashed in the darkness.

She slipped into the room, put her back to the wall and drew her sword, but kept it down by her side. Lantern in one hand, sword in the other she waited, calming her breathing, relaxing her muscles, preparing herself for battle. A stillness came over her, and she breathed a silent thanks to Master Ogima. *Whatever happens, I'm ready.*

The light sliding of talons on the uneven rocks became louder. Click. Clack. Silence as he traversed flat floor. Click. She did not shine her lamp on the door, but on the wall of the room beside her. If it didn't like light, it didn't want a beam shining in its eyes. She would save that for a desperation move. *As if anything could be more desperate.*

There was a thickening of the darkness in the doorway, and a huge shadow paused outside. The gleaming eyes turned on her. She stayed dead still. There was a snuffle of breath as the animal drank in her odour. She couldn't stand it. She had to do something.

"Hello there, boy. Nice kitty. Um…happy hunting." *Well, that was sufficiently stupid. I hope he isn't intelligent enough to notice.*

The head cocked to one side. Then the eyes swung away, and the shadow was gone. The clicking faded. She breathed again.

She stood there a moment, but then her knees had no strength and she folded down against the wall. Suddenly she needed all the light she could get. She twisted the lamp fully open, disregarding what it did to her vision.

She kept the light open until her breathing slowed and she realized that there was nothing to see, anyway. She closed the lamp down to a slit again and sat, thinking.

What do I do now?

There was a shout from up the tunnel: a wordless blast of sound. It was answered by a roar the like of which she had never heard. The man's voice sounded again, rising and rising into a scream of agony, sharply cut off. Then there was silence.

I guess I know what happened there. The Beast has done the kingdom a favour, I suppose. Now I can go home.

She rose and sheathed her sword, shouldered her pack.

...but I haven't seen his body. How can I say that I finished my mission when I don't know for sure? I have to go up there.

Now, that is really stupid. There is a monster up ahead that killed at least four men in the past three days. And I'm going in to look for its latest victim? Not a chance.

She started down the corridor, but her pace lagged.

But what if I could?

She stopped, half-turned.

Aleria, think this through. There has to be a logic, here. Why didn't the Beast attack me? Because I was calm and dimly lit. No challenge, no pain, no fear. When I talked to him, he listened. Then he left. He recognizes a calm human voice. Lexing shouted. He was afraid. He had a bright torch and a sword. I can do it. I must.

She shrugged to herself and started up the tunnel, trying not to think about what was ahead. *I remember this feeling. I thought it was anger last time. I'm not angry now. Maybe this is what courage feels like. I still have to go, no matter what. My duty demands it.*

Too much thinking. Eyes open, head up, Aleria.

She took keen interest in her surroundings. The tunnel was even rougher now, losing its shape in many places, widening and narrowing at random. The evidence of man's improvements faded, and her way became merely a path cleared through the rocks that littered the floor. There was less dust, but there seemed to be even more tracks. Large, hobnailed boots.

This must be Lexing's way in. So maybe the Beast has gone out. I'll whip in, find the body, pick up some evidence, and leave again. With any luck, I won't even see the Beast. If I do, I'll keep my lantern on a tight beam, down and to the side, and talk quietly. If he comes toward me, I'll turn my lantern wide open. If he attacks, I'll stick my sword into the roof of his mouth when it opens up to bite me.

This is the stupidest stunt I ever tried. Holding her lantern high, she strode forward. *But for the best reason.*

Just ahead, there was an uneven, broken opening in the stone of the left-hand wall. The pungent odour and scattering of bones in the tunnel told her what she would find there. She turned her light away. Yes, there was a faint, uneven glimmer coming from the hole. And silence. She crept forward and peeked through. It was a low, tight room with a jagged ceiling. A dying torch lay in the corner, sputtering and glowing. In the uneven light, she could see all that she needed: Lexing's body, torn and mangled.

Why did he go into its den? Oh. He thought it was guarding the jewels. She almost giggled. *He fell prey to his own stories.* She shrugged. *A fitting end for a predator. Came across a more powerful killer.*

Lexing's sword lay against the wall. She stretched in and picked it up. There was dark blood on the blade. Gingerly choosing a dry piece of cloth from the rags strewn around the corpse, she wiped it clean, slipped it through her belt on her right side and started back down the tunnel.

At her first step, a movement in the shadows froze her. She lifted the lantern and turned. Back up the passage, yellow eyes gleamed.

Her hand jumped to her sword. The animal did not move. She did not draw, but slanted her lantern away. For a moment, they stood there, immobile. All she could discern was a huge, hunched figure, the eyes glowing in the lantern light. Against such a beast, her sword seemed puny. *What to do now?* If she moved back, the creature might see it as a sign of weakness and attack. She certainly had no plans to attack. *Should I get away from its den, or should I move towards it?*

Dredging up her courage, she turned back up the tunnel, trying to see through the gloom. As she swung the lantern closer, the animal seemed to flinch. Well, that solved the problem of whether to turn and run. She forced her breathing slower and stepped forward. The animal cringed back. Now she could see, faint beneath the gleaming eyes, the sheen of white fangs, bared in a snarl. A growl rumbled from the deep chest.

"What the hell are you?"

She strained her eyes, trying to see without pointing the lantern directly on the beast. The hunched shoulders stood higher than her waist, and she could see rippling muscles on the limbs, heard the clack and scratch of talons as the hairy paws shifted uneasily on the stone.

"Well, you aren't exactly a beauty, are you?"

She turned the lantern forward. The creature cowered away, its head turned from the light. She pointed the beam away and took a risk, stepping forward again. "Why haven't you attacked me?"

The Beast crouched, its front elbows resting on the stone, its head in a submissive position, ears back.

She lowered the lantern, pointed it at the wall beside her. "Does the light bother you?"

The head came around, low; the growl faded, but the snarl remained.

She turned the light on her own face from the side, so that she could still see the beast's eyes. The flattened ears began to rise. She leaned forward. "Do you see my face?"

The ears lowered.

"Are you going to remember it?"

The chin sank to the paws. As far as she could make out, that would be a difficult position to attack from. "So, you know people, do you?" She sat on a boulder, placing the lantern enough to the side that they could each see the other. "It's time we had a talk."

Now the ears came back up.

"Yes, you do know about people. I thought so. You aren't a wild throwback to something the Old Ones bred. You're somebody's idea of a pet. Or more likely a guardian. Am I right?"

The tension began to leave the animal's body, so she kept on. "That's a bit of a cut, there on your shoulder. I don't suppose you'd…"

The moment she raised her hand, the ears went back.

"I didn't think so. I suppose you've survived worse. You aren't really a murderer, are you? It's just that people keep attacking you."

"What are we going to do with you? I can't sit here chatting all day." She eased to her feet, and the animal stayed down. "You don't look much like you're going to attack, and I'm not stupid enough for that either. But I don't somehow think that turning my back is a good idea. Maybe if I could get you to go ahead…"

She edged the lantern to the right, and the creature turned away from the bright flame. As she moved ahead, the animal rose and slunk to the side, turning away from her. She gestured with the lamp, and it padded back up the tunnel, glancing back, first one side and then the other. She crept along behind. "Take your time, friend. I'm not in a rush."

As they paced up the passage away from the creature's den, a faint grey light diffused in from ahead, and she allowed the lantern to drop lower. The Beast did not seem to notice, but it began to move with more confidence as the faint light from in front diluted the brightness of her lamp. She didn't want to douse her lantern, but neither did she want to push the animal, so she dropped back. The Beast did not slow but quickened its pace until it disappeared ahead.

"Uh-oh. Where are you?" *Now I'm in trouble. If he decides to circle around on me...*she opened the lantern wider and continued, her eyes prying into the semi-darkness. Now she was in a cavern rather than a tunnel: jagged and uneven, with wide spots and narrow places and ragged areas where it faded off to one side or the other out of the reach of her lantern beam.

Eventually she reached a turning where far ahead a bright glare interrupted the gloom. There was enough light to see that here the wall to her left was dressed stone, and up ahead an arrow-slit let light in. Lowering the lantern, she looked behind her one last time. Nothing. She blew out the flame and slipped the device into its loop on her belt. She glanced out the arrow slit. A surge of joy ran through her at the sight of a valley and mountaintops tinged with the first rays of the morning sun.

With illumination behind her she walked faster. Soon more light beckoned ahead, and the wall broke away until she could step out onto the mountainside. Her view was to the north where the peaks, majestic and snowcapped, piled row upon row up into the sky.

She turned back to face the rough opening. "Well, Ghost or Beast or whatever you are, I'm going to leave you to your lair. The legends ought to be enough to keep people away, and those who are stupid enough to ignore them will get what they deserve. Whatever else is in there is better off kept safe. Guard it."

33. Double-S Assistance

There was an animal trail along the mountainside to the east towards the keep. It brought her to a postern door at the base of the tower, broken down and covered with bracken, so she lit her lantern again and slid inside. To her amazement, a short passageway led straight into an alcove in the main hall. She poked her head out to find her view obscured by a fall of large blocks. A squeeze and a quick, quiet scramble and she was out.

There were voices above, but she could not identify them.

Then, faint and far away, she heard a rapid, uneven series of popping noises. The voices above rose, and she recognized Kolwyn.

"What the hell was that?

"Gunfire." That was Erlon. "A lot of shots in a hurry."

Her heart rose.

"Which means someone has a lot of guns."

"Or someone is using Double-S guns. And I doubt if it's Lexing's lot. If he had them, he would have used them."

"Should we go find out?"

By the time they had finished these observations, Aleria was at the top of the stairs.

"We will do nothing of the sort. Where are Lexing's men?"

The two turned, their faces comic in surprise.

"Where did you come from?"

"Back there. You missed a door, O trusty local guide."

"From where?"

"From the back of the mountain. You come out the Ghost Beast's bolthole, follow the path along the foot of the rock, and here you are. No wonder he got in and out so easily. Now, do I get an answer to my question? Lexing has been taken care of. What about his men?"

Erlon gestured with his head, and she went over to the doorway of their camp. Four soldiers, their hands bound, sat against the wall, three of them sporting bandages. Another man lay bound in blankets and bandages on the floor.

"That's all?"

"That's all we could find."

"I hope any others still alive are smart enough to come in. They're only soldiers, most of them hired from the look of it, and they were under orders. The man who gave the orders has met an appropriate end. That finishes it."

Erlon raised his eyebrows and gestured a sword lunge. She shook her head. "Nothing to do with me. He brought in the Beast. He thought he could control it. He couldn't."

"Where is his body?"

"In there. I'm not going back for it."

"I gather the Beast is hale and hearty?"

"I'll give anLexing points for bravery. He got one cut to its shoulder. Heavy pelt mostly turned the blade, so no serious damage."

"Except to anLexing?"

"I didn't stop long. It was a bird bet, and I was certain I was gonna take off first."

Kolwyn shook his head, a worried frown marring his handsome brow. "That might be a problem. When it comes to legalities, a body is always a good idea."

"I'm the king's envoy on this expedition, and I saw the body. At least, enough parts of it to know that the rest isn't going to function. I brought out his sword. That good enough for you?"

"Oh, I imagine it has to be."

"There is an alternative..." she gestured towards the inner fortress.

"You know, the more I consider it, the stronger your word sounds."

Erlon frowned. "Did you run across the Beast yourself? Of course you did. You saw the wound."

"As near as from me to you." She stepped forward. "Twice."

"How did you get away?"

"Diplomacy. The Beast doesn't like light, and he doesn't like fear. He really doesn't like people pointing swords at him."

Erlon nodded. "I see. So if Domin shone his light in its eyes, smelling of fear with his sword out…"

"I suppose."

"And you walked up to it barehanded and shone your lamp…elsewhere?"

"He walked up to me, as it happened. I had no time to be afraid, and he didn't seem to be attacking. I was polite, and he went by. I guess he had other business on his mind. Lexing made the mistake of going into the Beast's den. I suppose he thought the jewels must be there. Stupid, really, because he'd been past there many times. I think he was getting desperate and started to believe in his own myth too much.

"The Beast objected, and quite rightly. It was his den, after all. Once he had finished displaying his objection he left. Then he got curious and came back. We sat down and had a little chat, and then he led me out."

"A little chat."

"He likes the sound of a calm human voice."

"I bet it doesn't hear that very often."

"The only reason I can find for how he responded." She held up her hands. "Unless I'm missing a finger or two that I didn't notice."

"They all seem to be there."

"Then all's well. Let's eat breakfast and wait to see who comes up the valley."

It was a large party straggling up the trail. The tightest group resolved itself, when they got close enough to see, into five soldiers with their hands tied, Dalmyn guards marching in front. Behind them strolled two dark-haired men with shiny guns slung across their shoulders.

The first ones into the courtyard were their three messengers. Jameta stumbled over and sat on a stone, dark circles under her eyes.

"How did you get back so soon?"

317

The girl gave a ghost of a smile. "Fast horses. I had to be here."

Lavan's big grin decried the bandage around his arm, and little Aldwyn was hanging back as usual, although he was smiling as well.

"Any trouble?"

Lavan showed his arm. "Met a soldier on the trail by mistake. Don't know what he was doing, but they never should have let him out without his nanny."

"I see. So, Jameta. Did you learn anything about courage from Lavan?"

"I don't think so. He was very brave when that soldier attacked, though."

"Lavan? Learn anything about bravery?"

He shrugged and grinned. "Not a thing." He raised his wounded arm. "That soldier stumbled into us so quickly I had no time to think. I went at him and the best man won."

"And there's the lesson for both of you." She smiled at their puzzled faces. "Think about it. Where's Maddoes?"

"Back there with his new pals. He's not so great at hiking. Too much time on a wagon seat, I guess."

"I gather you had no problem with the ambush?"

He shook his head. "Some kind of an ambush that was. They were all gathered together on one side of the trail. Their sentries were less than twenty feet from the main force."

"We probably have the Beast to thank for that."

"On the way down Aldwyn led us around them. On the way back we had superior firepower, and they gave up after the first volley."

"Ah, yes. The superior firepower. Maddoes!"

"Yes, M'Lady." The teamster came hobbling up, followed by the two strangers.

"I gather you have someone to introduce to me. At last."

"Yes, M'Lady." His head dropped and he looked up at her through his shaggy hair. "I'm sorry, M'Lady."

"If they collapsed that ambush without injury to our side, I'm not sorry." She turned to them. "And I'm sure their

318

credentials are impeccable." She ran a finger down the barrel of the weapon held by the larger of the two men. "I recall having seen some like this before. Any trouble getting Tielle to part with these beauties?"

"No, my Lady. As you say. Good credentials."

"And you are?"

"Solovey, my Lady. Lieutenant of His Majesty's Fusileers. Very pleased to be at your service. This is my sidekick Muir: Sergeant."

"Charmed, my Lady. Your reputation doesn't do you justice."

She regarded him a moment, "It's easy to be a diplomat when you carry a Double-S."

"It helps."

"But it won't help your boss when I catch him. What in the name of all the spirits in the trees did he think he was doing?"

"Well, my Lady, I don't really know. He told us to tag along, to be there just in case."

"Right. But you weren't here, were you? Do you know what a difference those two rifles would have made in the last three days?"

The Lieutenant shuffled his feet. "It didn't work out quite as we expected, no. Until your messengers came through, we thought you were on an archeological expedition of some sort."

She sighed. "Well, that was the case at the beginning. And everything has turned out pretty well in the end, except for a certain number of good men killed. And eaten."

"Eaten?"

"Yes. The tales of the Ghost Beast of the Old Ones came distressingly close to fulfillment."

"And Lord anLexing?"

"He's filling his share at the moment."

The man made a face. "Really?"

"Yes. He was the victim of his own little trick. Along with several others."

"That makes things easier. Lord Raif will only have to deal with the mine when he gets here."

"Oh, so Lord Come-Lately is finally showing up?"

"Yes. He was on the road from Kingsport the moment he heard about the mine. He sent a rider ahead to the Royal Army camp. He'll be behind us by a couple of days with the rest of these." He slapped the breech of his rifle. "Our orders are to meet him at Tyn Terfyn. As long as you don't need us for one of your hare-brained schemes. His words exactly, my Lady."

"I'm sure they were. Captain Teille will be happy to get out in the field with his men. I imagine he's tired of serving as armourer for a bunch of random agents passing through."

Muir grinned. "He may have expressed feelings of that sort."

"There seem be a lot of unhappy feelings around. Maddoes. Your face is rather long. Your reputation suffering?"

"I'm afraid so, M'Lady."

"Don't worry, man. Your loyalty has never been in question. You gave me enough information weeks ago to figure it out."

"I hoped you would."

"It was quite obvious in all your talk about loyalty that you missed the part that goes above the head of our family. How could you be loyal to Father and still be working for someone else? Only if it was the king. If my father ever gets on the outs with the king you'll be faced with a moral dilemma, my friend."

"I don't know what that is, M'Lady, but it don't sound good."

"Oh, it isn't. But relax. For the moment, the chain of command stretches in its wonted direction, and your loyalty has always been rock-solid. Get your men bunked down wherever," she waved a hand around, "Blodwel can tell you where. And then rest your aching legs."

"I could do with a little of that, M'Lady. A tough march. Not used ta walkin' that far."

"And stop calling me names. It wouldn't work if I was really mad at you."

Maddoes sighed. "Aye, Aleria. Whatever you say." He turned and limped away.

"And now time for a little conference." She beckoned to Erlon and Kolwyn. "Lieutenant Solovey, please join us."

She strolled over and took Lexing's favourite stone, and the others sat nearby. "First: thanks for getting here so fast. We didn't expect you till noon at the earliest."

Solovey grinned. "Motivated, Ma'am. You ahead and Lord Raif behind." He made a pushing gesture.

"I'll take that as a compliment. Second: chain of command. Lieutenant Solovey and Sergeant Muir are Royal Army, from Raif's old regiment. They will obey me because I have no doubt their senior officer has impressed upon them the disadvantages of not doing so. Erlon is Dalmyn, in charge of our guards. Lord anLlannon, you and your two men are a separate group with no allegience to anyone. Once we meet with Lord anCannah he outranks everyone, so that will all disappear. Until that moment, we will cope. Unless we come under attack, it shouldn't be a problem."

Kolwyn grinned. "Once the swords come out, Aleria is in charge, and the rest of us do what we're told."

"That would be helpful."

"It kept us alive."

"Let's all keep believing that. The truth can wait for later." She rubbed her hands. "Now, what about food?"

Kolwyn shrugged. "Plenty for our reduced numbers. Lexing's men will have lots. There's only a third of them left." He raised an eyebrow at Muir.

"We brought plenty because we didn't know how long this would take."

"Then I suggest you send your cook and whoever was in charge of Lexing's food up to our camp in the keep. That fireplace makes the best kitchen."

She regarded their expectant faces. "That's all. Your men are probably starved. If we have two days before Raif gets to Tyn Terfyn, we have to start down tomorrow. Lots of time after lunch to discuss whatever." She thought a moment. "Mainly, how to find the bodies to bury. Without disturbing anything that might create more."

"And what to do with those miners. Lord Cannah was very interested in them. Any ideas, my Lady?"

"Yes, they're bound to get antsy when Lexing's guards don't come back. Maybe we could find a small rockslide to cover their escape route out to Aesmark. Lieutenant, perhaps you and your sergeant could be of use there?"

He nodded. "I'd be pleased."

"But don't make too much mess. Until we know exactly who we're dealing with on the Aesmark side of the operation, we don't want to destroy any possible trade routes."

"I understand completely, Ma'am."

"Take the Dalmyn guards if you like. I'm sure they'll be happy to do their share, once they rest their tired feet."

She looked around at the others. "But I don't see anyone cooking."

They grinned and rose to their feet. Soon the camp was bustling.

34. An Arm to Swing On

When they broke out of the Eastern Wall in the pass overlooking the Trench, a number of flags flew over Tyn Terfyn. "Some kind of party going on?"

Kolwyn shrugged. "No idea. That's our family banner, but I don't recognize the one flying over it. Who can fly his flag over ours in our own castle?"

"The king, of course. Not likely he'll be here. I never paid much attention to that heraldry business. It could be his Majesty's official envoy."

"More official than you? And who would that be?"

She shook her head. "I'm afraid to find out."

"That sounds like you know something."

"Only deep, dark, suspicions, my friend. And long years of experience with this particular person."

"That doesn't sound good."

"Oh, it's not bad. Except for him."

He frowned, then tried to smile.

She took his arm. "I'm not saying any more until we find out more. Don't worry. All will be well, no matter what."

"Glad to hear you say it."

"It's been a tough trip, Kolwyn. I couldn't have got through it without your support."

"Well, I couldn't have got out of it without yours, so there we are. Of course, it took your help to get into it. Hey! That hurt!" He pivoted his wrist out of her tightening grasp.

She grinned at him. "A little warning. And my pet has bigger claws than these."

"I stand corrected." Then he turned to her. "Do you think anLexing was controlling the Beast?"

"No one was controlling it. I don't think you can."

"Like certain people we know."

"Keep that little memory in the back of your head. No, he brought it here and turned it loose. He probably lured it down to your pastures by leaving carcasses around. Then when he stopped providing food, it went for the next closest prey – your flocks."

"Risky, with all his men travelling the valley."

"I don't think he cared. As long as they travelled by day and kept a fire up at night they were fine. If they didn't follow orders, a dead body or two was exactly what he wanted."

Now the trail widened into a double track and Jameta strode alongside. "Aleria, before we get down there, can I talk to you?"

Aleria glanced at Kolwyn, who made a courtesy appropriate to the drawing room and quickened his pace.

"What's on your mind? Need time off for good behaviour?"

"No. I'm considering the opposite."

"You want my approval for bad behaviour? I'm not crossing Uncle Arjan. He's important to business."

"I was afraid of that. Now I don't know what to do."

"Go home, receive the adulation you deserve and go back to being a good girl."

"That sounds horrible."

"Since I have no idea what you're talking about, I can hardly help. Have you decided to run away with Lavan to become a messenger for the caravans in foreign lands?"

To her surprise, the girl's dusky skin went darker. "Oh, not Lavan. He's just a kid, you know?"

"He's probably two years older than you, but yes, I know. If not him, then who...?" She looked to where Jameta's eyes rested on the broad shoulders of Erlon, striding down the trail beside Kolwyn, his head thrown back in laughter at something the lord had said.

"Oh, no. No, no, no. Not him!"

Jameta frowned. "Why not? Is there something wrong with him?"

"Well...well, no, not that I know of. But that's the problem. Besides the fact that he has the most dangerous assignment on the most dangerous caravans that cross the mountains.

Do you realize that we're heading through Tantamo pass into Ferboden next?"

"Yes, he told me. It sounds fascinating."

"Fascinating. Yes, it would sound fascinating, the way he tells it. But that's not the real problem. It's him. Do you realize that I don't know anything about him?"

"You don't? But he works for you. You've known him for over two years, he says."

"That's what makes it even more suspicious. Any time I ask him about himself, he ducks. Oh, he'll give you bare details, of course. Where he was born, that sort of thing. But there are huge holes in his life story that he won't fill in. What was he doing? Maybe he was in prison, for all I know."

"I don't think he was in prison."

"I don't either. Can you believe he knows about sterilizing medical equipment and stitching wounds? That's the latest advancement in the hospitals. Where did he learn it?

Jameta shrugged. "Maybe he's been wounded a lot."

"But that's the point. We don't know, and he won't tell us."

"He tells me a lot."

"Obviously. I'm going to tell him something as well."

The girl's hand on her arm reminded Aleria of Mito's grasp once, years ago. *This really matters to her.* She refrained from breaking free, looking into the serious face. "Fine. I won't say anything. You asked for my opinion, and I gave it." She shook her arm slightly. Jameta glanced down, gave a guilty start and released her.

"Come to think of it, I didn't give you my opinion of him, only of his suitability as a suitor. You know what I think of him. He's a wonderful guard Captain, solid as a rock, and a good friend when you need one. He's also loyal, handsome if you like that sort..."

"...I love that sort...!"

"...then why am I even trying? What do you want me to do?"

"I don't want you to do anything. I only wanted to hear what you would say."

"And has it been useful?"

"Oh, yes. Very."

"In what way?"

"I was checking to see if you were in love with him."

"Me?"

"Well, that would make things rather difficult, you admit."

"I suppose it would. And you conclude that I am not?"

"Oh, yes, of course. You just gave me all your reasons. You weren't talking about me. You were talking about your decision and why you made it."

"I see. And when you aren't running messages around for your uncle, do you provide a shoulder for the lost, the bereft and the lovelorn to cry on?"

The girl shrugged. "I'm a well-known stranger with a sympathetic face. People do tend to talk to me."

"Wonderful. I'm thinking what your uncle is going to say to me."

"He said I was on my own to make my own choices!"

"He said he wouldn't mind if I brought you back swinging a sword. He didn't say anything about swinging on the arm of a caravan guard."

"He's not just a caravan guard. Have you listened to the way he talks?"

"Aha! You've been down that road, too."

"You do like him, don't you?"

"Yes, we even discussed at one time whether we should...you know. But we decided it wouldn't be a good idea."

"That's fine, then. If you'll excuse me, I have an arm to go swing on."

She trotted ahead and did just that. Erlon glanced back and caught Aleria looking at him. He gave a helpless smile, and she merely tilted her head and went back to looking out over the valley.

When they reached Tyn Terfyn the castle was crowded. A squad of soldiers was drilling outside the gates: a well-armed and well-trained drill with rifles glittering. They broke off and formed ranks to salute briskly as Aleria's party strode by. Inside the walls all was abustle, and several supply wagons with Royal Army insignia were lined against the curtain wall.

The approach of Aleria's troop was heralded and a welcoming party waited at the top of the stairs. Kolwyn put his foot on the first step, but Aleria stopped at the bottom.

"Oh, no. We're not playing those games." She pointed at the blond-haired figure in the dress coat. "You come down here to me!"

Laughing, Raif obediently trotted down to engulf her in a hug. "Phew! You've been out in the hot sun for too long."

She grabbed him around the neck for a fierce moment, relief coursing through her at his presence. Then she released him. "And you've been wearing that high collar for too long, and it's cut off the blood to your brain. What were you up to?"

He tucked her hand under his arm and led her up the steps to where Kolwyn was greeting his parents. "It's more a matter of what you've been up to. I played a very small role, it seems."

"Not small enough, in my opinion, but we'll let that ride for a while. Good afternoon, Lady anLlannon. That gown has a particularly fine cut, if I may say so."

"Thank you, Lady anDalmyn. I have a seamstress visiting from Kingsport at the moment. Would you like something turned out for the celebrations?"

"It would help to know what kind of celebrations I am attending, my Lady."

"Then you must talk to those with more information." Her graceful courtesy ended with a hand sweeping towards her husband.

"Thank you, my Lady." Aleria smiled and made her usual curtsey, turning it towards the gentlemen.

"So, Lady Aleria. You have been dragging my son through Tyn Dyfnant."

"Yes, my Lord, and through several other situations as well."

"Good for you. Good for him, I say."

"And you might be interested in this." She gestured, and Kolwyn handed over the old leather case. "I don't need to tell you how to handle them."

"Have they been flattened yet?"

"Only enough to see how important they might be."

"I will give them the respect they are due." With a show of gentleness, he tucked the case under his arm and regarded the company. "Please come in, everyone. Your men can go back to their old quarters, Erlon. Would you join us for dinner? Much of the story we will be hearing involves you, I suspect." He lifted his regard to the rest. "There has been water heating since morning, so any who wish may bathe."

He presented his arm, and he and Lady Favia turned through the main entrance like a royal couple approaching their coronation.

Aleria noted a quick finger-wave from Jameta to Erlon. She took the girl's arm and turned towards Raif.

"Jameta, I don't believe you know Lord Raif anCanah. Raif, my favourite messenger, Jameta anDennal."

Jameta looked less certain than Aleria had ever seen her. She dipped her head. "Lady Aleria has mentioned you, my Lord."

He held out his arm. She took it, and they turned towards the main door together. "And none of it flattering, I'm sure. If you are one of the indomitable Dennals, you will have me quaking in my shoes before the evening is over."

"You know my cousins, my Lord?"

"Oh, yes, my Lady. To my great chagrin. They team up with my wife for the express purpose of polishing my manners to the point where I can be accepted in polite company. That's why I greet Aleria with such relief. All she does is threaten to chop various pieces off me if I mess up. I find that much more straightforward."

"I can understand that, my Lord. I have been observing her technique for the past weeks. Her leadership skills are a sight to behold are they not?"

Aleria gave Raif's shoulder a shove. "Some of us are anticipating a bath. Can you two continue this drivel at a more appropriate time and place? You're blocking the door. And considering the size of the door, that takes talent."

He grinned back at her. "All right. Shall we get your report over with before supper?"

"Whatever you say."

"Half an hour, then. Lord Lexing's workroom."

"I am at my Lord's command."

"For a change." He winked at Kolwyn and turned back to his conversation with Jameta.

She glanced at Kolwyn. "We have our orders. I assume Raif will inform your father that the king has commandeered his castle. If he's lucky, the poor man might even get invited to his own workroom."

"Am I invited?"

She threaded an arm through his. "It's your report, too. Half the blame goes where it's deserved."

"As long as I get my small share of the glory."

"Oh, you wouldn't want that. Think where it might lead you."

He looked thoughtful as they followed the rest of the party into the castle.

35. A Promise at Last

She and Kolwyn spent an hour giving their report, and while that caused dinner to be rather late, it made the meal a relaxed affair. Aleria tucked into the feast, which was so much more appetizing than camp fare. *But I must remember to thank Aldwyn. He hunted, butchered the animal and cooked it, while doing all his other work as well. Tough little men, those shepherds. Loyal as well. I suppose one gets used to the smell of sheep after a while.*

Happy to be clean again, she sat between Raif and Kolwyn and thoroughly enjoyed herself. She noted with interest that Erlon was rather adept with the silverware and kept up his end of the conversation as well as any. Jameta, who had somehow found a flowing gown of embroidered silk, positively glowed in his regard.

After dinner, during a pause before the evening's entertainment, she and Raif took a stroll on the roof of the keep, looking out over the green fields of the Trench to the snow-capped mountains reaching deep shadows towards them.

Raif glanced down at the formal position of her hand on his arm. "So here we are again."

"As usual." She turned to face him. "Why the interference?"

"It was considered that you might find my men useful."

"It was considered by whom? Whose men were they?"

"All right." He held his hands up helplessly. "They were my men, but it wasn't my idea."

"I hoped not. Higher up?"

He nodded. "And I had to let your father in on it because we needed a completely loyal man to carry it off. He said it had to be Maddoes. I don't know why. It didn't work so well. Your Maddoes plays too stupid. My men didn't give him any credence when he told them that you were onto their games."

He turned and regarded her. "How stupid is he?"

She looked innocent.

He slapped the parapet in front of him. "He was playing a double game, wasn't he? He was following my orders to the letter and working for your side the whole time."

"There are different levels of loyalty, Raif, and they don't always follow the Lists of Ranking. My father and his people are completely loyal to the king, but in the end, Maddoes did what was best for Dalmyn. As far as his orders permitted, anyway." She grinned up at him. "Perhaps that's why nobody messes with the Dalmyns."

"I'll remind his Majesty of that."

"You do what your loyalty requires. Just like Maddoes."

"Maddoes." He shook his head. "From what I gather, the moment your message came through about the mine, he hauled my men out of hiding, tore a strip off them for playing games and put them to work under his orders." He frowned as if at a sudden thought and looked into her eyes. "They were useful, weren't they?"

"Once they stopped playing hide and seek I put them to work on the 'harebrained scheme' I told you about. They'll be reporting in a couple of days. But why did you decide to show up?"

"Because you had completed your mission."

"You'll have to explain that."

"You were sent with a task. From the sound of it, you had accomplished all that we expected and more. So it was time for the next stage, which required my presence."

"Oh. Considering how things stood when I sent the message, I fail to see how you considered my task finished at that point."

"We never expected you to solve anything. The reason you were sent out was to stir things up. Get people to make mistakes. You're good at that."

"A lifetime of practice."

"And you didn't let us down. We already knew that something was going on. You confirmed our suspicions of whom. Then you discovered the mine. That solved the problem of why. It was time for someone with more political clout to come out here and make the king's will known." He stared across the valley, a frown forming.

Then he turned to glare at her. "I do have one complaint."

"Only one?"

"Why ever did you go into that animal's den when it had just killed Lexing? That was completely foolhardy."

"Don't think I didn't consider that. At first it was an emotional reaction. I knew I had to go. But I stopped myself and thought about it, and I realized that it was the right decision, no matter how dangerous it was."

"That took a whole lot of courage." Raif turned and paced away, then spun to face her. "It doesn't surprise me, but I still don't see why it was so important. Everyone would believe that he is dead."

"I'm not sure if it's courage when you're forced to do it." She stepped towards him, ticking points off on her fingers. "I wasn't happy with the way I handled the whole situation. I came out here with the king's letter, and I threw my weight around. I pushed Lexing into a corner, but I pushed myself into a corner as well." She looked up at him earnestly. "Now, I'm not saying I owed it to him, or anything like that, but I had to earn the power I took on. I tried to picture me facing you and the king, and telling you I had wielded the power I was given but did not have the courage to complete my task. I needed proof, not just a scream in the dark. I weighed the chances, and the odds were good." She looked at her splayed fingers and made a flicking motion. "So I went."

He shook his head. "I'm trying to picture me facing Mito and telling her that I sent her friend out, and she got...eaten. I'm not sure I'd survive that one."

"You're the father of her child. Safest man in the kingdom."

He shrugged. "Well, you did it, and that's that. We never expected you to get this far. At least, most of us didn't. I can't say I'm surprised. You have a habit of finding unlikely allies of the right sort."

She thought of large yellow eyes in the lantern light and sharp claws grating on stone. "You don't know the half of that."

He waved a hand. "And now I get here, and you have, as usual, exceeded your mandate and solved most of the problems. Now all I do is put you on a very obvious leash and sit back and perform my diplomatic skills."

"Which you aren't accomplishing too well, right now." She put on her best scowl. "What do you mean, put me on a leash?"

"Every lord in the Trench is sitting in his castle shivering for fear that you'll show up at his door next. Every one of them has ambitions, has made mistakes, has corners he doesn't want the light of the king's regard to fall into. As long as I demonstrate that I have you firmly under control they'll be crawling all over themselves to be cooperative."

She thought that over a moment and decided to let him have his fun. "Fair enough. Just rattle my chain when you want a growl. How is Mito faring?"

"Oh, getting fat and grouchy."

Her hand curled in the lace on the front of his shirt, tightening ever so gently. "Mito does not get grouchy."

He shrugged her off. "Of course not. Not grouchy. Just...particular. Particular about what she eats. Particular about where she sits. Particular about where I sit. Particular about what I'm doing about a friend of hers who is in danger."

"So that's the real reason you came."

"Well, his Majesty did mention settling the region."

She surveyed the valley. "It seems rather settled."

"Yes, definitely peaceful."

"This is a pleasant area. I like it here."

"I suppose he'll do."

"What?" She turned slowly to him. "Did you just say what I thought you said? Of course you did." She took in his smile. "And you did it on purpose."

"It is still possible to make a touch on Lady Competence. How nice."

"If I pull my sword on you, it won't be touches at stake."

"Ah, but that's it." He raised his hands, open and helpless. "The husband of your best friend. Safest man in the kingdom."

"And you think that will protect you?"

"From mortal injury, yes. Anything less than fatal, I'll take my chances."

"And you realize you're riding hell-bent into the almost-fatal part."

"I must make a token protest on behalf of the poor victim."

"Victim?"

"Yes. The least-safe man in the kingdom right now."

"And he and I will work it out, won't we? By ourselves." She tapped his chest, not lightly, once for each point. "Without any outside help. From you."

"Is there a message in there somewhere?"

"Perhaps there is, O great spymaster. Decode it for yourself."

He laughed and clapped her on the shoulder hard enough to make her stumble. "I have no intention of intruding on your romantic arrangements in any way. The only one who ever tried that was my father, and he had absolutely no luck."

"Which was lucky for you."

"I suppose, considering the result."

"How is she doing? Tell the truth."

He grinned. "She's doing fine. She has enough of the best medical attention in the realm to drive her batty, but that's my father's doing and she can't refuse him."

"Oh? I had the distinct feeling it was the other way around."

"It is. Watching them have an argument, each trying hard to give away the very best to the other, is a real laugh at times."

He regarded the valley again. "In any case, she's as healthy as can be expected, and all my worries are simply the fears every expectant father has and I keep telling myself that."

"And when you wake in the night with a start, and the thought of some terrible tragedy occurring to them slips into your mind like cold steel, that lets you get back to sleep, does it?"

He looked down at her. "Of course not."

She reached an arm up around his shoulders. "Get used to it, Raif. It's a condition of your life, now. For the rest of your life."

"How would you know that?"

She shrugged. "I worry about my crew that way. I can only assume worrying about your child will be worse."

"You still have dreams, then."

"Doesn't everyone?"

"Are yours ever happy ones?"

"I'm not sure I need any." She indicated the beautiful valley, the snug keep. " My reality is doing pretty well at the moment."

"Hmm. My cue to disappear, I think."

She turned.

Kolwyn was standing in the doorway. "Am I interrupting?"

She nudged Raif, and he slid away. Taking Kolwyn's arm, she led him along the battlement. "If I don't want your interruption, you'll know."

"I suppose I will."

"And right now no one is going to interrupt me."

"No?"

"No, because I am talking to you."

"I see."

"Because I have something to say to you."

"I quiver in anticipation."

"Nothing like that, I'm afraid. When this to-do is over you're going to be very busy, here."

"I am." He leaned on the stone and looked out over the valley, the kerchief twisting in his fingers. "If that mine turns out to be a working proposition there will be a lot of business in this area. No matter what the Old Ones' maps say, the mine road starts in our demesne. Our position here will become more important."

"As will your loyalty to his Majesty. About which I will be certain to remind him." She caught one end of the cloth and whipped a hitch around his finger, pulling it snug.

"Thank you." He tugged the other end. The kerchief stayed where it was.

"I, on the other hand, will be heading back down the road to Kingsport." She tossed a hand to the west.

"I was afraid of that."

"And after that I have a caravan heading for parts unknown." They continued to walk the battlements.

"And that pretty well eats up the summer."

"It does. But in the future there is going to be a lot of cartage moving through this area. A lot of new Mechanicals to deliver, I suspect. There will be good reason for me to return."

"At times. And more reasons for me to visit Kingsport."

"At times. You understand." She stopped walking, turned and looked up at him. "Will that be enough? Because if it isn't…"

He took her upper arms in his hands and pulled her closer. "It will never be enough, Aleria. But if that's how it is, it will have to do."

She grinned and broke his hold in a way that left her arms around his neck. "I'm here for a few days. We'll take advantage of what time we have."

"Taking advantage. That sounds like fun."

"We'll work on it." She lifted her lips to meet his.

About the Author

Brought up in a logging camp with no electricity, Gordon Long learned his storytelling in the traditional way: at his father's knee. He now spends his time editing, publishing, travelling, blogging and writing fantasy and social commentary, although sometimes the boundaries blur.

Gordon lives in Tsawwassen, British Columbia, with his wife, Linda, and their Nova Scotia Duck Tolling Retriever, Josh. When not writing and publishing, he works on projects with the Surrey Seniors' Planning Table and is a staff writer for <indiesunlimited.com>.

More from Gordon A. Long

Other Titles by Gordon A. Long available at
<smashwords.com> and <amazon.com>:

"Out of Mischief" World of Change Book 1
"Into Trouble " World of Change Book 2
"Storm Over Savournon," a Novel of the French Revolution
"A Sword Called...Kitten?" Romantic Comedy with an Edge
"The Cat with Many Claws" Sword Called Kitten Book 2
"Why Are People So Stupid?" Social Humour with a Point

Look for Gordon's books, selected reviews, poetry and short stories at <airbornpress.ca>

Gordon's opinions on humanity are at the
"Are People Really That Stupid?" blog:
<http://airbornpress.ca/arepeoplestupid/>

Find his weekly reviews and his ideas on writing at
"Renaissance Writer:" <http://airbornpress.ca/newdir/>

"Sword Called Kitten Serial" Free online:
<airbornpress.ca/kittenserial>